Medillia's Lament

A novel by Jody Clark

DEDICATION

To all my family and friends.
Especially Erica and Owen for their endless support and encouragement.

ACKNOWLEDGMENTS

A special thanks to Don Gargano for the beautiful book cover photo.
You can check out more of his amazing work at
www.dongarganophotography.smugmug.com
or at his Facebook Page - Don Gargano Photography

A note from the author

Medillia's Lament was the third screenplay I ever wrote. I came up with the idea back in 2003, and by early 2004, I had a solid first draft written. I knew at the time, if I could properly convey my ideas into the perfect words then this story had a chance to be something very creative and special.

I spent the next eight years or so trying my best to get it onto the big screen. After endless amounts of roadblocks and dead ends, I decided to start turning my nine screenplays into novels. Out of everyone who has read my screenplays, hands down, "Medillia's Lament" has been their favorite – especially my wife. So, without a doubt, I knew "Medillia's Lament" would be novel #1!

From the first time I told my wife about wanting to turn my screenplays into novels, she always told me, "These are your stories, so you should be the only one turning them into a novel." Unfortunately, I had very little confidence in myself as a *novel* writer. I didn't believe I was talented or a good enough wordsmith to pull it off. I decided to bring a co-writer on board to help me transform my "Medillia's Lament" screenplay into a book.

Nearly four long years later, due to many creative differences, the project stalled, and ultimately, I was forced to pull the plug on it. Even more than devastated, I was depressed. So much so, that for a brief time, I lost all desire to ever write again. I even contemplated burning all nine of my screenplays! And if it wasn't for the endless encouragement and support from my wife and son, I would have done just that.

Fast-forward almost five years: I have not only turned five of my screenplays into novels, but I've semi-successfully branded Vacationland Books as my own personal publishing company. The trilogy, in particular, gave me tremendous confidence in my writing ability. After finishing the final book of the Soundtrack to My Life trilogy last summer, I knew it was time for me to once again attempt to tackle "Medillia's Lament" ~ this time, completely on my own.

So, from conception ~ to the screenplay ~ to now, the completed novel, it has been 17 long years. Like most people, it would be easy to say it took so long because sometimes *life just gets in the way*. But I truly think in this case, life didn't get in the way, but rather *living* life allowed me to *find* the *way*… the *way* to fine-tune this story where it needed to be… and the *way* to have more confidence in my writing and storytelling ability. I very much appreciate everyone's support over the years, especially my amazing wife and son! So now, without further ado, I give you "Medillia's Lament."

Jody Clark

When I was younger, I was told that sometimes people pass away with so much regret or pain in their hearts, their soul gets trapped between this world and the next. When this happens, they sadly wander around in limbo, searching for something to make them whole again... something which will allow them to find happiness and to finally move on.

I used to think this was the most depressing thing I'd ever heard. But the truth is, there are so many *living* people who walk through life in that same way - lost, lonely, empty - desperately searching for happiness, forgiveness, or simply, to just find their way.

I think both cases are equally sad. But sometimes, just sometimes, the universe takes pity on them, and with the use of a little creative magic, the universe helps them find the answers, the happiness, and the forgiveness they so desperately search for.

They say that *beauty* is in the eye of the beholder. Personally, I think *truth* is in the eye of the beholder as well. Although the following story may seem unbelievable, unrealistic, and at times, fantastical... I assure you, it's 100% the truth... at least in my eyes.

* * *

Long before the English settlers came to America, the Native Americans inhabited much of the country. Just off the coast of Maine was a small island which was occupied by the peaceful Abenaki tribe. The island was named Applewood.

To the Abenakis, their ultimate Creator was known as the Great Spirit, but they also found solace in praying to multiple spirits. Animals were at the top of that list, as were the ocean, the sun, the moon, and the stars. There was one star in particular that hung high above their land. This was no ordinary star, but the brightest one in the sky. The Abenakis named the star Medillia, and they believed she gave direction to the lost.

Unlike the North Star, which was used as a compass to those who were physically lost, Medillia was used to give direction to those who were emotionally lost. To the small Abenaki tribe, the radiance and glow of Medillia not only provided hope to the downhearted, but she provided the light needed for them to find their way again.

As the years passed, however, Medillia slowly started to lose her shine. The same brilliant shine that had guided so many lost souls was slowly fading out. Ironically, Medillia herself was losing hope. And as legend has it, on one fateful night, with all hope lost, Medillia plunged from the night sky and crashed just off of the coast of Applewood. As Medillia crashed into the rocks, an explosion of the brightest and most beautiful stardust was emitted. The entire sky was lit up for a second… then went black.

As the legend goes, for the next nineteen sunrises, remnants of her stardust continued to fall onto the small Maine island. And it is said, during that brief moment in time, Applewood was turned into a magical place; a place where old wounds are healed, and a place where regrets find second chances. During this occurrence, time becomes irrelevant. The past, present, and future all get blurred together

somehow, and within those nineteen sunrises, anything is possible...
anything.

This occurrence became known as Medillia's Lament, and
supposedly, throughout the years, there have been other occasions
where stars have lost their shine and have not only fallen into the same
rocks of Applewood, but have emitted the same magical stardust.

1

Chicago - 2003

What's the best thing about living in Chicago in the summer? Drinking a cold beer on a hot day while sitting in the friendly confines of Wrigley Field. Well, that's what John and Kevin Mathews would tell you. They rooted for all of Chicago's major sports teams, but it was the Cubs that held a special place in their hearts. Baseball was their first and deepest passion. It was also one of the few things the brothers had in common.

John was strictly a classic rock guy with Led Zeppelin leading the way as his favorite band. Kevin, on the other hand, was more of an 80s and 90s pop music kind of guy. Zeppelin versus the Police was a common argument amongst the two brothers. Comedies and documentaries were Kevin's film preferences, while horror and action movies were John's. Sports were the one thing they almost always agreed on, and baseball and the Cubs were at the top of that list.

Despite never having a real role model growing up, another common thread with the brothers was their work ethic. Kevin's first job was as a dishwasher at a small Italian restaurant owned by the Rosetti family. Due to his upbeat personality and how hard Kevin worked, Mr. Rosetti quickly took him under his wing.

By the time he turned twenty-one, Kevin had moved up the ladder from dishwasher, to prep, to Mr. Rosetti's right hand man on the line.

His cooking days didn't last long, however, for Mr. and Mrs. Rosetti both agreed that Kevin's personality was going to waste in the kitchen.

Mrs. Rosetti's exact words were, "A people-person belongs out with the people."

It was at that point, Mrs. Rosetti took him under *her* wing and showed him the ropes of the dining room. She also paid for him to take a bartending course. It was behind the bar where Kevin truly shined.

John's hard work was more of the physical nature. Unlike Kevin, it took John much longer to find his true calling. For the longest time, he did odd jobs, such as construction, landscaping, and even snowplowing in the winter. Kevin's wit and personality were his strong suits, but for John, it was his imagination and working with his hands.

When John turned twenty-three, he caught a huge break and landed a job he absolutely loved. It wasn't the typical construction he was used to, but more like finely detailed woodworking. John's boss was an old Polish man named Mr. Kowalski, who had turned his garage and basement into the perfect woodworking studio. Mostly, he did custom-made furniture.

Just like Mr. Rosetti did for Kevin, Mr. Kowalski took John under his wing. He was immediately amazed at John's raw talent and creativity. In the three years he worked for him, John's passion and woodworking skills improved greatly. Sadly, just after John's twenty-sixth birthday, Mr. Kowalski suffered a fatal heart attack.

Too sad, and not wanting to live alone, Mrs. Kowalski eventually sold the house and moved in with her daughter across town. Upon leaving, she told John he was welcome to take as many tools and equipment as he'd like. At the time, John had just gotten married and lived in a tiny one bedroom apartment with his wife. He knew how much the equipment was worth, so he ended up renting a storage unit with hopes that one day he'd have a place to put it all to good use.

With barely a penny to his name, John was forced back into doing odd jobs, and he eventually landed a job for S & J Construction. They did roofs, decks, siding, and everything in between. He hated it. Not the job itself, but who he worked for. In John's words, his boss was an "unappreciative prick."

Fortunately, he was an unappreciative prick who paid really well. When you have a pregnant wife to support, you do what you have to do to pay the bills. Eventually, they had saved enough to buy a small house of their own, but it still didn't have enough space for all of Mr. Kowalski's tools and equipment. John's woodworking dream would have to wait a bit longer.

On that particular summer's day, John's asshole boss was the furthest from his mind. It was a Sunday, and not only was the sun was shining brightly, but the universally hated New York Yankees were in town for a little interleague play. Most people thought this would be a preview of the World Series.

The most common phrase among die-hard Cubs fans is *"This will be our year."* It was usually a hopeful sentiment, but in 2003, it was spoken with more conviction than normal. Cubs fans honestly believed this was indeed their year. This fervor, combined with the Yankees as their opponent, made scoring a ticket nearly impossible. You either needed deep pockets or to know someone with influential connections. John and Kevin had neither, which is why they were forced to watch the game at the well-known Cubs bar – Murphy's Bleachers. They might not have had ticket connections, but Kevin did have bartender connections, hence the two saved seats front and center at Murphy's.

With cold beers in hand, the brothers were in heaven as they watched Kerry Wood outduel Roger Clemens for a 5-2 victory. There was no doubt how much John loved his wife and daughter, but there was also no doubt that he was at his happiest yelling and cheering his Cubs on with his brother by his side.

Long after the game was over, the large crowd continued celebrating at Murphy's and all throughout Addison and Clark streets. When the brothers finally had their fill of beers and cheers, they began the seven block trek to Kevin's place.

At one of the intersections, Kevin motioned for them to take a right. John shot him a curious look and laughed.

"Are you too drunk to remember your way home? We still have a couple blocks to go before we turn right."

"I know where I live, ya idiot. I just wanna show you something, that's all."

John followed his brother down the dimly lit street. It wasn't the worst part of town, but it had definitely seen better days. Most of the business fronts on either side of the street had *For Lease* signs hung all over them.

"Dude, where the hell are…"

Before John could finish his sentence, Kevin stopped in front of one of the vacant buildings.

"What do ya think?" asked Kevin.

"What do I think about what?" said John, staring at the *For Lease* sign hanging in the large picture window.

Kevin cupped his hands around his eyes and peered into the window. He motioned for John to join him. There was a small light on which allowed them to get a general idea of the interior.

After a few moments, Kevin pulled away from the window and gave his brother a huge smile and said, "So, what do ya think? Pretty cool, huh?"

"I think you really *are* drunk," John laughed. "What the hell is so cool about a run-down building in the shitty part of town?"

"This *used* to be the shitty part of town. It's in the beginning stages of a major revitalization."

Kevin looked around and pointed out a handful of new businesses: A coffee shop, an upscale bistro, and a couple of boutique shops.

"Umm, ok. And your point is?" asked John blankly.

"My point is this would be the perfect location for a neighborhood bar... *our* bar."

"Our bar?" laughed John.

"I'm being serious. Think how cool it'll be for us to have our own business... be our own bosses."

John knew his brother's looks all too well. He knew when Kevin was bullshitting him, and he knew when he was being serious. And at that very moment, he could see that Kevin was indeed being serious.

"You do know I'm in the construction business, right?" John knowingly asked.

"What I know is you complain about it every chance you get," Kevin pointed out. "And besides, you've worked at a bar before. Remember?"

"Like ten years ago," laughed John. "And I was just a lowly barback, that's all."

"But I remember you had a blast working there, right?"

John thought back a moment then said, "Until I got fired."

"Well, you were caught banging the owner's daughter."

John's smirk turned into a full-on smile. "It kinda was a pretty fun summer job."

"That's what I'm talking about!" Kevin excitedly said, smacking John on the back.

Kevin went on to paint a vivid picture of their future bar. He did such a good job, even John found himself being swept up in the dream. John took another long look into the vacant old building, and it was then that reality set in.

"It all sounds great, but where does the start-up money come from?"

Kevin smiled and said, "I'm thirty-one, never been married, consistently work fifty plus hours a week… so, needless to say, I have a pretty good nest egg saved."

John laughed and responded with, "Well, good for you, but I'm married… with a kid… and a mortgage. So, needless to say, I have no nest egg. Probably a negative nest egg, actually. Sorry, bro, but I think you need to find another partner. As much as I would actually consider it, right now it's just not feasible."

Kevin responded with a look. It was another look that John knew all too well.

"Oh no, no, no," John quickly spoke. "I am totally not hitting up Kristen's parents for money!"

"Oh come on, John. They have more money than they know what to do with. Lest you forget, I've been to their mansion up in Highland Park."

John did his best to underplay Kevin's comment. "It's not really a mansion… more like a stately manor."

"Uh huh," smiled Kevin. "And what about their summer cottage on the lake? Their five bedroom, three-bath cottage?"

"Two and a half baths," smirked John, leaning against the old brick building.

"Come on, John. It doesn't hurt to ask."

"Actually, it does hurt. It would hurt my pride a lot."

"Fuck your pride!" shot Kevin.

This caused John to laugh. Kevin very rarely used the F word, and when he did, it was as if he expected his point to be taken more seriously. Of course, it had the opposite effect on John, who always cracked up laughing.

"I'm being serious, John. It's not like you'd be borrowing a ton of money. Just think how much money we'll save by having you do the build out."

"Me?"

"Well, yeah. I figure you could hand-make some of the tables and booths. Not to mention, you'd be in charge of the centerpiece of the place."

"The centerpiece?"

"Yeah, the custom-made bar top and stools that you're gonna build."

John's attention was caught, and Kevin didn't even have to drop an F bomb to get it. Kevin knew the exact buttons to press, and he saved the best button for last. He motioned to the smaller store front directly to the left of the first.

"And the realtor said if we take both these buildings, he'd give us an extra special deal."

John looked at Kevin as if he was nuts.

"Now you want to open two bars?"

"No, you idiot. The one on the left is much too small for a bar… but it's the perfect little size for a woodworking studio."

By the look on John's face, Kevin knew he had him hook, line, and sinker. John hesitated a moment then cupped his hands around his eyes and peered in through the dirty window. As he gazed around the small, vacant interior, his mind began to race.

Kevin didn't say another word, for he knew John's imagination was already creating not only the perfect bar, but the perfect woodworking studio. It would be another five minutes before either of them said a word. It wasn't until they were almost back to Kevin's house that John finally spoke.

"How much money are we talking?"

A wide smile formed on Kevin's face—on both their faces.

2

Less than a month later, the brothers once again stood at the vacant storefront. This time they were standing in the dead center of the building—proud co-owners of a new bar and studio.

Kevin handed John a Heineken, and as they clinked their bottles, he declared, "Here's to the next chapter of our lives."

"Cheers," smiled John.

They both took a long swig of beer then slowly looked around.

"And now the real work begins," said Kevin.

John nodded, and then couldn't help himself and said, "Are you sure we're gonna make it here? What if this neighborhood revitalization doesn't work? What if the bar has no customers? And what if…"

"Relax, bro. It'll be fine. If we build it, they will come."

John paused his pessimism long enough to shoot his brother a smirk.

"Really? You're gonna start quoting '*Field of Dreams*,' huh?"

Kevin returned his smirk and shrugged, knowing full-well that "*Field of Dreams*" was John's all-time favorite movie. Actually, it was both of their favorites. It was one of the few movies they had in common.

Kevin followed up his movie quote with a more heartfelt sentiment. He placed his hand on his brother's shoulder and confidently said, "I promise you this will all work out. I promise."

Kevin knew John's go-to emotion was worry. He also knew that John had a right to be nervous and worried. Not only would John have to eventually quit his steady job, but he had sucked up his pride when he borrowed a substantial amount of money from his in-laws. Bottom line, John had way more at stake than Kevin did.

Kevin's hand continued its encouraging grip on his brother's shoulder. But just as John allowed himself to buy into his brother's positivity, Kevin ruined the moment by saying, "Trust me, little bro, this place will be amazing."

It was the "little bro" comment which caused John to shake free of his brother's hand. He hated being called that. John was a year older, so technically, it was Kevin who was the little bro. Unfortunately for John, the "technically" part was all he had to hold on to, for as far back as he could remember, it was always Kevin who acted like the older brother.

Physically, Kevin was always the bigger of the two, and emotionally, he was always the more mature one. Whether physically or emotionally, it seemed like Kevin was always rescuing John. And although he never threw this into his brother's face, he did know referring to him as his "little bro" got under John's skin. To Kevin, it was just an innocent and playful jab, but to John, it was a cruel reminder of everything he wasn't.

Kevin was the first one to climb the giant maple tree in their backyard, the first to get picked in their neighborhood Wiffle ball games, and the first one of them to kiss, like really kiss a girl. More importantly, Kevin was the first, and pretty much the only one, who stood up to the man they referred to as HIM.

3

By the time Fourth of July weekend had arrived, the two brothers were literally knee-deep in their remodel. Their plan was to tackle the bar first, and once it was up and running, they would remodel John's woodworking space. The bar space was originally divided into three rooms, but John wasted no time in knocking down some of the walls to create a more open look.

With sheetrock dust still hanging in the air, John adjusted his trusty Cubs hat and peered up at the drop-ceiling.

"You're gonna rip that down too?" asked Kevin in a muffled voice.

The muffle was due to the dust mask covering his mouth. John let out a laugh when he noticed Kevin was also wearing goggles and an over-sized hard hat.

"What?" questioned Kevin.

"You look ridiculous."

"Safety first," Kevin muffled.

John shook his head and grabbed a step ladder. He then motioned to the other ladder.

"Shouldn't we clean up this mess first?" Kevin asked, pointing to the piles of sheetrock strewn across the floor.

"When doing demolition, it's best to just go for it all at once," John said, climbing the ladder.

Kevin followed with, "Just a thought... but what if we left the ceiling as is and just paint it black?"

Again, John shook his head at his brother. It was becoming more and more obvious that Kevin wasn't really accustomed to manual labor. Both brothers were extremely hard workers but in different mediums.

"No, Kevin, we're not leaving it and painting it black. An old historic building like this deserves to be exposed, not covered up with sheetrock and drop-ceilings. We'll paint the duct work and pipes above the ceiling black, but the ceiling's gotta go. It'll look amazing, trust me."

Hesitantly, Kevin nodded. Not only did he trust his brother, but he knew John had a specific image of how to turn this old building into the perfect bar.

Armed with sledgehammers and aided with step-ladders, the brothers spent the next hour smashing and pulling down the ratty, old ceiling. And despite Kevin's urging, John did the demolition without the proper safety equipment. When the entire metal frame had been pulled down, and when the final ceiling tile had fallen to the floor, the brothers climbed down from their ladders and stared around at the piles of rubble. Even though John had a specific plan and image of the finished product, the reality of the situation began to set in, and his glass half-empty attitude began to rear its ugly head.

"What the hell did we get ourselves into?" John said, wiping the sweat and dust from his forehead.

In his mind, Kevin was thinking the same thing, but he also knew this project would surely be doomed if they both had a defeatist attitude. Throughout the years, more times than not, it was Kevin who emitted positivity and encouragement over his pessimistic brother. This situation was no different.

"You just gotta look at the big picture, John. Think how cool it'll look when we're done. With my bar experience and your carpentry skills, it's a can't miss!"

John's initial reaction was to roll his eyes, but he paused a moment to let the words "can't miss" set in. The last time Kevin said that to him was eight years earlier. Ironically, back then they were also standing in a bar at the time. John was drinking and hanging out with some of Kevin's co-workers. One of them was a cute green-eyed blonde named Kristen. Well, blonde was her original color, but when John first met her, it was dyed black with a scarlet red streak running through it. He was immediately smitten and spent the entire night awkwardly flirting with her.

It wasn't until Kristen headed out that Kevin said to John, "What are you doing? Aren't you gonna ask her out?"

"Eh, she'd probably just say no," John shrugged.

"Are you kidding me? She's totally into you. Why else would she be laughing at your stupid jokes all night?"

"You really think I got a shot with her? I think she's out of my league."

"Oh, she's out of your league for sure," smiled Kevin. "But she's definitely into you. I can tell these things. Trust me, it's a *can't miss*."

John trusted his brother that night and ended up chasing Kristen down the sidewalk and asked her out. Eighteen months later they were married.

So as John continued to stare around at the piles and piles of debris, he knew he needed to once again trust his brother that this would all work out. Of course, he still rolled his eyes at Kevin and prepared a sarcastic response, but before he could utter a word, the large wooden front door slowly creaked open.

Seeing as they had covered all the windows with brown paper, the opened door allowed the only bit of sunlight into the space. The beam of light revealed and accentuated the dust-filled room even more. Up until then, the only light in the room was emitted from two spotlights.

The natural sunlight caused both brothers to shield their eyes. Through the dust and bright glare, all they could make out was two figures standing there.

"Is it safe to enter?" yelled a woman's voice.

"I don't know," Kevin announced. "Ask the man with the sledgehammer."

With the door now shut behind them, the appearance of the two figures came into clear view. They were John's wife and five-year-old daughter, Kristen and Hannah. Both were wearing hard hats, and they slowly crept forward, carefully avoiding the chunks of sheetrock and ceiling tiles.

"Hey, it's my two favorite girls… wearing hard hats… pink hard hats."

"Mommy and I painted them this morning," Hannah proudly said.

"I see that. I'm surprised you didn't put glitter on them too," joked John.

"That's a great idea, Daddy," Hannah said, wide-eyed. "Can we do that later, Mommy?"

"Of course, sweetie. And maybe Daddy wants his hard hat painted and glittered too."

"Yea, if he actually wore one," Kevin interjected.

"John Mathews!" Kristen sternly said. "Where in the H - E – double L is your hard hat?"

John shot Kevin a glare then turned his attention to his giggling daughter.

"What are you laughing at short stuff?"

"I know what bad word Mommy spelled," she said, continuing to giggle.

"Yea, Mommy has quite the potty mouth on her, huh? And she also doesn't realize you're getting to be such a good speller."

John reached out his hand and received a solid high five from his daughter.

Hannah quickly followed with, "But Mommy is right, you need to wear a hard hat. Safety first. Right, Uncle Kevin?"

"I couldn't have said it better myself," Kevin said, gloating at John. Kevin followed with his own high five with Hannah.

Meanwhile, Kristen was slowly taking in all the dust and debris that surrounded them.

"What did you guys get yourselves into?" she asked.

John took a page out of Kevin's book and said, "You've gotta look at the big picture, Kristen. Think how cool it'll look when we're done. Trust us, it's a can't miss! Right, Kev?"

Kevin smirked at his brother and said, "Yea, it's a can't miss."

"We were going to offer to bring you guys some lunch, but…" she paused and again gazed around at the rubble. "But maybe we should all go *out* to lunch."

"Sounds like a plan," Kevin eagerly answered.

"Thanks but no thanks," replied John. "We don't have time for lunch right now."

"We don't?" asked Kevin, clutching his stomach.

"No, we don't. We have way too much to do. The sooner we get this mess cleaned up, the sooner I can start the rebuild. And the sooner I start the rebuild, the sooner we can open and start making some money. Aaaand, the sooner we make some money, the sooner I can pay off my in-laws! And the sooner…"

"Ok, ok, enough. We get the picture," Kevin said, shaking his head towards Kristen.

"Don't look at me," she said. "He's your brother."

"Yea, but I didn't have a choice in that. You, on the other hand, chose to marry him."

Kristen looked at John and then back to Kevin.

"Good point," she smiled.

"What is this, pick on John day?" He then turned his attention to Hannah. "What about you? Are you gonna make fun of me too?"

Hannah widely smiled as she looked up at his dust-covered face and hair. His Cubs hat did little to protect his long, shaggy hair from looking gray from the dust.

"You look like an old man," she said. "Like Grampa Jack."

"Ouch! My own daughter hits me with a double-bladed insult. Not only did I get called an old man, but got compared to my *most favorite* father-in-law."

John's relationship with Kristen's dad, Jack, wasn't horrible, but it wasn't that great either. It just *was*. Mostly, it was just a case of no one being good enough for his little girl. John had long-since given up on trying to impress or prove himself to Kristen's father. Truth be told, if it wasn't for Kristen and her mom sweet-talking him, Jack would have never lent John the money.

Ignoring his sarcastic father-in-law comment, Kristen gave him a big hug and said, "Awww, but we still love you."

"You might wanna say that louder, Mommy. He *is* an old man."

As Kristen and Kevin cracked up laughing, John snatched up his little girl and began tickling her. Hannah's giggle echoed throughout the vacant building.

"John! You're getting her all dirty. I just washed that dress."

John placed his daughter back on the ground and admired her dust-covered dress.

"I think it adds character," he proclaimed.

"What's character?" asked Hannah.

"It's what makes you who you are," he said, ruffling her hair.

"Alright, kiddo," said Kristen, "let's leave the boys to their work. Are you going to be home for dinner tonight?"

John shrugged. "Depends how far we get. I'll let ya know."

As Kristen leaned over to give John a kiss, he pulled her against him, making sure he also covered her clothing with his dust. Kevin watched this playful exchange and couldn't help but be a little jealous. He wasn't jealous of Kristen per se, but jealous that John had a full-fledged family. Considering John's sarcastic and pessimistic demeanor, and considering John's original vow was to forever be a bachelor, Kevin just assumed he would have been married long before John ever was. Not only was Kevin not married yet, but he wasn't even seeing anyone. That being said, he loved his brother deeply and was genuinely happy for him.

4

As the summer rolled on, the brothers continued to work tirelessly on their dream bar. Ever since they were little, they had talked about going into business together. Ironically, owning a bar was never on their original list.

When Kevin was five, he wanted to go into the ice cream truck business. John loved this idea. Not so much for the profits, but more so for all the free ice cream. When Kevin was eight, they talked about one day owning a baseball card shop. Kevin took it one step further and suggested they have a batting cage out behind their shop. What got them totally excited was the idea of designing the batting cage to resemble Wrigley Field with an ivy-covered brick wall and everything.

Sadly, that was the last big idea they would have together. They were only eight and nine, but their innocent, child-like imagination would slowly be crushed and poisoned by HIM.

Most children have that light in their eyes; one that sparkles and glows, letting you know that their imagination is in full dream mode. That light had disappeared from John's eyes years ago—both brothers, actually. Kevin was always the more positive one, and although a year younger, he somehow felt it his duty to find ways to put that light back into John's eyes.

It would be Kristen who finally returned the light to John's eyes. That same light nearly tripled with the birth of Hannah. Yes, Kevin was more than a bit envious of John's happiness, but in his heart he knew it was well-deserved, especially after all the shit he had been through—all the shit they both had been through.

For as long as Kevin had been in the hospitality business, he dreamed of owning his very own bar, and although John never shared in his dream, he was secretly getting more and more excited by the day. Over the years, John worked one dead-end job after another and had more asshole bosses than he could count. Needless to say, he was looking forward to being his own boss. And if truth be told, he was also looking forward to working side by side with his brother. They were exact opposites, they were constantly razzing each other, but at the end of the day, they were best friends. And of course, John was most excited about getting his own woodworking business up and running. Finally, Mr. Kowalski's tools would be put to good use.

Neither of the brothers could afford to quit their jobs yet, so they were forced to do their remodel around their work schedules. This meant a lot of late nights and weekends. This also meant little or no quality time with Kristen and Hannah. Both girls loved the outdoors, so summertime was their favorite season. For the most part, Kristen kept to her usual summer routine, which consisted of: Playgrounds, parks, tending to her flower beds, and spending a lot of time at her parents' lake house.

John loved his family time and hated that he had to miss out on most of these things. Well, he wasn't that broken up over not hanging out at his in-laws. Many a night, John and Kevin would still be working on their bar long after 2 a.m.

No matter what Kristen had planned for the day, she always made sure to stop in and see the guys. Partly because, it was the only time she got to see her husband, but mostly, she wanted to make sure they were staying hydrated and eating. She also wanted to make sure no one had cut their fingers off with a power tool. This concern was mainly for Kevin, who wasn't very power-tool adept. Just in case, she made sure there was a fully-loaded first aid kit handy.

Sometimes she brought them takeout, but more times than not, she forced them to take a real break and go out to eat with her and Hannah. After they ate, Hannah always insisted they hit her favorite ice cream parlor for dessert.

Kevin was a black raspberry kind of guy, while John and Hannah were strictly chocoholics. Their flavor of choice was called Death by Chocolate, and of course, they added chocolate sprinkles on top. Kristen, on the other hand, was more on the basic side. Vanilla was her go-to flavor; just vanilla, no sprinkles or anything on it, and she didn't even have it in a cone. She had it in a cup with a cone on top.

Each and every time they went there, John and Hannah made sure to point out how plain and boring her order was. On most everything else, Kevin sided with Kristen, but when it came to vanilla ice cream in a dish, he was completely in John and Hannah's camp.

John was so focused and driven to get their bar remodeled and opened that even though he loved his family time, he was usually the one to end their ice cream date and head back to work.

As the summer moved on, it was obvious that the brothers were absolutely exhausted from burning the candle at both ends. They looked so tired and worn out that Kristen finally put her foot down and ordered them to take Sundays completely off. Make no doubt about it, it wasn't a request, it was an order.

Although John (more than Kevin) was originally against the idea, he quickly became a huge fan of it. Not only did he get to sleep in late, but he awoke to a full breakfast made by Kristen and Hannah. The rest of the day was spent in total relaxation mode. There were no honey-do lists from Kristen, no predetermined plans, and best of all, no requests to go visit her parents at their lake house.

On most Sundays, John simply lounged on the couch. He either watched the Cubs game or napped… or both. It was exactly the recharge his batteries needed. Sometimes the girls would hang out with him and watch the game; not that Kristen liked baseball or sports, for that matter. She just did it to spend some close family time with her two favorite people.

Hannah, on the other hand, liked watching the games with her father. She didn't have enough energy or focus to last an entire three hour game, but when she was focused, she was constantly asking questions about the game. They were usually good questions too, like: *Why did that guy bunt?* or, *Why did the pitcher intentionally walk that guy?*

Kristen was also full of questions, but they were more on the ridiculous side. Questions like: *How many points do you get for a home run?* or, *Who are we voting for in the game?*

Both John and Hannah would roll their eyes at each other, and it was usually Hannah who'd answer, "Mommy, it's not points, it's *runs*! And you don't vote for a team, you *root* for a team!"

If she left it at that, John would have been super proud, but Hannah followed it with, "And the team you're supposed to root for is always the Cubs… even when they suck ass."

Hannah immediately realized what she said and covered her mouth. Kristen's mouth fell open and her eyes widened.

"Hannah!" John said, fighting back laughter. "We don't talk like that!"

Kristen cocked her head and shot John a burning glare then said, "I wonder where she learned that?"

On John's following Sunday off, he was left to watch the game on his own while Kristen and Hannah spent the day shopping.

"Daddy, Daddy, look what I got today!" Hannah said, rushing in from the front door.

John opened his eyes from his nap and sat up just in time as Hannah jumped up next to him. She pointed down to her new t-shirt. It was a Beastie Boy shirt. Just then, Kristen walked through the door, and it was John's turn to shoot her a glare.

"What?" she knowingly smiled.

"You're worried about the phrases I teach her, yet you let her listen to that crap?"

"I pick and choose which songs I let her listen to," Kristen answered.

John shook his head, knowing he was outnumbered on this one. When it came to ice cream flavors and baseball, Hannah was all John. But when it came to her love of flowers and music, she was 100% Kristen. Before John could offer another comment, he noticed Kristen was holding a giant box.

"What did you buy?"

She placed it on the living room table and eagerly opened it.

"Voila," she said, revealing an old-fashioned record player. "I used to have one of these as a kid, and I've always wanted to get another one."

John scratched his head then pointed out, "You do know that only plays vinyl records, right? And if I'm not mistaken, we don't own any."

She smiled and held up a bag.

"Let me guess," John said. "We do now?"

Excitedly, she nodded and pulled out a bunch of records.

"The music store around the corner carries tons of vinyl. New and used."

John's face was less than excited as he flipped through them: The Smiths – *Louder Than Bombs*, Depeche Mode – *Black Celebration*, The Jesus and Mary Chain – *Darklands*.

John shook his head when he came across the Beastie Boys – *License to Ill*. And underneath that one was *Disintegration* by The Cure. The Cure was Kristen's all-time favorite band.

"Ah yes, The Cure. The guy with wild hair who wears more lipstick than most women."

"Don't you even start in on me, John Mathews! This is the best record of all time!"

John laughed, knowing full well not to make fun of her music, especially The Cure. Playfully, she snatched the albums from his hands.

"Keep it up, and I won't show you what else is in the bag."

John gave both girls a curious look. Hannah giggled in anticipation. Finally, Kristen handed him the bag. Inside were some more vinyl records consisting of: Led Zeppelin – *Houses of the Holy*, Pink Floyd – *Darkside of the Moon*, AC/DC – *Back in Black*, and Cheap Trick – *Live at Budokan*.

"Now this is some real music!... I mean, thank you, honey. I appreciate it."

"Yea, yea, yea," she smiled and leaned in for a big kiss.

* * *

By the time August 27ˢᵗ arrived, the old building that had once been filled with dust and debris had slowly been transformed into a gorgeous, quintessential neighborhood bar. The brothers stood in the center of the building, scanning the place for their next project. Kevin looked down at his clipboard to see what was next on their master checklist.

"So, what's next?" John asked.

"Umm, I think that's it." Kevin lowered the clipboard and smiled. "I think we're done. We totally did it!"

John matched his brother's smile and slowly put his arm around him.

"I still can't believe I let you talk me into this, but…" John's smile widened. "But I'm fucking glad you did. This place looks amazing. And it's ours… all ours."

"I'm telling you, John, it's all working out for us. We deserve this. We totally deserve this."

It was a simple phrase, but one that resonated deeply with both of them. John returned Kevin's nod and continued to gaze around. The lighting, which Kevin had personally picked out, perfectly accented John's beautifully handcrafted bar top.

"So when do we get the alcohol in, and when's our big opening?" John eagerly asked.

"Yea, about that…"

"John's excitement quickly changed into a nervous anxiousness.

"Relax," Kevin calmly said. "It's not the end of the world, but…"

"But what?"

"But the inspector is a little backed up and can't get to us for another three weeks."

"Three weeks?" John sighed. "I knew I shouldn't have quit my job yet. Not until we actually had this place up and running."

"Take a deep breath and relax, John. There's a chance we'll get lucky and the inspector will show up earlier than planned."

"Pffft. Lucky my ass. I bet my left nut it'll probably take longer than three weeks."

All Kevin could do was smile and shake his head. He was well-versed in his brother's pessimism.

Kevin gave John a nudge and said, "Let's go grab a drink and hit the batting cages. That'll take your mind off things."

Kevin knew John's soft spot. The only thing close to putting a shine into John's eyes as a kid was anything baseball—especially the batting cages. There were many times in their youth they honestly thought all they needed to be happy was a bat, a ball, a glove, and of course, each other. As kids, they spent hours on end playing catch at the park or hitting balls at the batting cages. Mostly, it was due to their love of baseball, but equally important, it kept them away from their house… and HIM.

John glanced at his watch and hesitantly said, "I might have to pass on that. Kristen and I are taking Hannah to meet her new kindergarten teacher later today."

"Kindergarten? Jesus! Where does the time go?"

"No shit. Seems like just yesterday I was feeding her a bottle and rocking her to sleep."

"We're getting old, aren't we?" said Kevin.

John nodded and both brothers made their way towards the large wooden front door. It was one of the only things left from the original building. It fit perfectly with the ambiance and design they had created.

Once they were outside on the sidewalk, they glanced above the door at their business sign. It matched the door and was hand-carved and painted by John himself. The sign read: The Wild Irish Rose.

"So where did you come up with that name again?" John asked.

Kevin shrugged. "Dunno. It kinda just came to me in a dream."

"A dream?" John dubiously laughed.

"I honestly don't remember how I came up with it, but as far back as I can remember, I thought it would be a great name for a bar. Why, don't you like it?"

"Oh, now you ask my opinion? Now that the sign is already made?" John said straight-faced. Before Kevin could respond, John cracked a smile and smacked him on his shoulder. "Just kidding. I like the name. I like it a lot actually."

A smile remained on both their faces as they stood staring and admiring the sign. Finally, Kevin broke the silence.

"So what time are you guys meeting with Hannah's teacher?"

"Early this afternoon."

As Kevin looked down at his watch, a sly smirk appeared on his face.

"So technically we have a little time to hit the batting cages, right?"

Of course, the question was rhetorical. Kevin knew John had a hard time turning down a trip to the cages.

5

By the time John reached his house, he knew he was running late. He was always running late. That was another big difference between the two brothers. Kevin's middle names were *punctual* and *responsible* and a few other names that John was not.

Slowly, John creaked open the front door. It was as if he was sixteen again and sneaking back into the house at three in the morning. He half-expected Kristen to be sitting in the living room with her eyes staring fixedly on him as she pointed to the clock.

To his surprise and relief, Kristen was not sitting there waiting for him. In fact, the living room was empty. Upon further inspection, he noticed the bathroom door was shut. Perfect, he thought. He'd quietly sneak into the bedroom and be changed before Kristen exited the bathroom.

He only took three steps before the bathroom door swung open. Kristen stood there in a cute white sundress, which accented her perfectly summer-bronzed skin.

Before she could say a word, John blurted out, "Kevin made me!"

"Uh huh," she said as her merlot lips curled into a smile. She shook her head, and as she carefully put her hair up, she gave John a look-over.

His sweat-soaked t-shirt clung to his body and strands of his shaggy hair were still matted to his forehead.

"Please tell me you're not wearing that to Hannah's school?"

John looked down at his clothes, and with a straight face said, "What's wrong with what I'm wearing?"

Before laser beams or daggers shot from her eyes, John followed with, "Kidding. Just kidding. I was just waiting until you were done in the bathroom so I could take a quick shower."

Without saying a word, Kristen stepped out from the doorway and motioned to the bathroom.

"Thanks," he smirked. "About time you got out of there. I've been waiting forever."

As he strutted by her, she gave a swift smack to his ass.

"Don't start something you can't finish," he joked.

"You're incorrigible, do you know that?"

"If by incorrigible you mean in need of a little afternoon delight then yes, yes I am."

Fighting back a smile, she simply pointed to the bathroom.

"Fine," he relented. "But you know where I'll be if ya wanna give me a hand… so to speak."

When the door shut behind him, she finally released her smile. She briefly let her mind reminisce on all the times she had joined him in the shower, but with an active and curious five-year-old roaming the house, those times were now very few and far between.

After John showered and dressed, he made his way towards Hannah's room. Before he even reached her door, the overwhelming scent of strawberry hit his nose. Hannah loved her strawberry air freshener and had no problem spraying everything in her room with it.

Her door was opened just enough for him to peer his head in undetected. Hannah lay on her bed perfectly still. With her hair in pigtails, she wore a light yellow dress and was clutching her favorite doll. Her normally happy face was replaced with a more serious expression as she gazed up to the ceiling.

"Hey pumpkin. You look pretty."

"Thanks," she quietly said, forcing a slight smile.

"What's wrong? Are you nervous about meeting your new teacher?"

Hannah shrugged and clutched her stomach.

"My tummy hurts."

"It's just butterflies, honey."

Her eyes widened. "I have butterflies in my tummy?"

"No," he laughed. "It's just an expression that means you're nervous, but there's nothing to worry about. You're going to love your teacher, and more importantly, your teacher is going to love you! And Mummy and I will be there with you, so there's nothing to worry about, okay?"

"Okay, Daddy," she said less than confidently.

"Do I have to tickle a real okay out of you?"

Hannah tightened her body and did her best not to crack a smile. Before John's fingers came anywhere close to her tickle zone, a smile and a loud giggle escaped her lips. Her tightened body squirmed to and fro, and her giggling became amplified as John's fingers tickled her sides.

"Stop, Daddy! Stop!" she squealed. "I'm gonna pee my pants!"

"John, stop!" urged Kristen from the doorway. "You're wrinkling her dress."

He stopped his tickling and looked from Kristen back to Hannah.

"Saved by Mommy again," he smiled.

Hannah clutched her doll and sat up in her bed. He watched as she straightened her dress out, but then turned his attention back to the doorway. As Kristen stood there putting on her favorite earrings, John noticed she had completely changed outfits. She was now wearing a fancier blue dress.

"Wow, you look beautiful, Mommy."

"Aww, thanks, sweetie. But trust me, underneath it all, I'm still the same ole plain Jane."

Hannah giggled. "Your name isn't Jane, silly."

"It's just an expression," explained Kristen.

"Oh brother, another expression," Hannah said, rolling her eyes.

John laughed then quickly turned his attention back to his wife.

"What's with all the outfits? Are we going to a meet and greet or a fashion show?"

"I'm too overdressed, aren't I?"

"You are if her teacher is a dude."

"Settle down, tiger. It's a woman. I just wanna look like I'm a good mother."

"Relax," he laughed. "You're an amazing mother no matter what you wear. There's no reason to be nervous."

"I think Mommy has butterflies in her tummy too," snickered Hannah.

After John and Hannah shared a laugh, he announced, "So, are we all ready to go?"

Kristen looked at her watch and answered, "We still have another hour or so."

Curiously, John looked over at the clock on Hannah's nightstand. Kristen's sly smirk said it all. John knew he had been duped. Knowing his propensity for always being late, she had told him the wrong time on purpose.

"I guess I'll have to remember that trick the next time you tell me to be somewhere at a certain time."

"Or you can just be there when you're told," she smiled.

John looked over at Hannah with a pretend look of shock.

"Did you hear that, kiddo? Mommy thinks she's the boss of me."

"She kinda is," giggled Hannah.

"That's my girl," laughed Kristen, pointing at her daughter.

"Oh yea? Well I think Mommy needs to be tickled too," he said, jumping off the bed and chasing Kristen into the living room.

Not wanting to miss a thing, Hannah grabbed her doll and scampered after them. John pinned Kristen into the corner and was tickling her sides.

"John Mathews, stop!" she laughed. "I just fixed my hair, and you're wrinkling my dress."

"Mommy is really ticklish under her arms too," added Hannah.

"Hey, whose side are you on anyway?"

Hannah scrunched her nose and offered an innocent shrug. Just then, John's cell phone rang. It was enough of a distraction to allow Kristen to break free.

"You better get that," she said. "It's probably Kevin. I mean, it's been a whole hour since you've seen each other. I'm sure he misses you."

As he removed the phone from his pocket, he shot her a playful glare and said, "Ha, ha. Saved by the bell… this time."

Kristen returned his playful look as she began fixing her hair and straightening out her dress.

"Hello," John answered, flipping open his phone. Before he could say another word, his look gave it away. Kristen laughed and gloated her way back into the bathroom, and as she stared into the mirror, her prediction was revealed.

"Hey, Kevin. Long time no chat," he said, glaring in Kristen's direction.

Kevin began the conversation with, "I hope you can live without your left nut."

"What are you babbling about?"

33

"Remember how you bet your left nut that inspector wouldn't get to us for at least another three weeks?"

"Umm, yea," John answered curiously.

As Kevin continued to talk, John's expression went from curious, to serious, to excited—very excited.

"Are you kidding me? What time? That's great! I'm on my way!"

By the time John snapped his phone shut, Kristen was standing in front of him with a questioning look.

"Great news! Apparently, the inspector is going to be in the building across the street from ours and decided to kill two birds with one stone."

Without missing a beat, John informed his puzzled daughter that this was yet another expression. He was also quick to point out there were no stones or real birds being killed.

"Can you believe that?" he said in Kristen's direction.

"I think that's great, honey, I really do, but… can't Kevin handle this on his own? Do you really need to be there? It's just an inspection."

"Well, yea, he can handle it, but it's my bar too. I just kind of wanna be there when we get the final license and approval to open the place."

"I get it, John, I do. I just thought we were going to Hannah's school as a family."

"We are," he reassured. "What time is our meeting with her teacher, like the *real* time?"

"It's at three thirty, but we're leaving at three o'clock sharp!"

"Then I'll be back by three… three o'clock sharp," he smiled as he saluted her. And before she could respond, he once again reassured her. "I promise I'll be back by three. I promise."

"I believe you, Daddy," announced Hannah from across the room.

"Why thank you, Hannah," John said with a wink. He then turned his puppy-dog eyes to Kristen. They were the same brown eyes she had fallen in love with years ago.

"Fine," she sighed, succumbing to his look. "Three o'clock and no later!"

"Yes dear," he smiled, planting a firm kiss on her cheek. He then rushed over to Hannah, and with one fluid motion, lifted her off her feet and kissed her square on the forehead. "I'll see you in a little bit, pumpkin." Before he set her back down, he rubbed her tummy. "Try to get rid of those butterflies before they turn into caterpillars."

"Butterflies don't turn into caterpillars, silly. Caterpillars turn into butterflies," she giggled.

John smacked his head. "Oooh yea! You're so smart. Why do we need to send her to school again?" he said in Kristen's direction.

He placed her back on the floor and snatched his keys off the table and hurried towards the door.

"Oh wait!" called Kristen. "Just in case we don't have time later, let's get a quick family picture."

Before John could respond, she offered up her own puppy-dog look. Like always, he took one look into her green eyes and became entranced. The next thing he knew, all three of them were pressed close together with Kristen's outstretched hand holding an old Polaroid camera.

"You do realize this isn't actually her first day of school? We're just going to a meet and greet."

Kristen ignored his comment as she continued fumbling with the clunky and outdated camera.

John smirked and looked over to Hannah. "Mommy and her pictures."

Hannah rolled her eyes and nodded in agreement.

"Oh hush! Both of you! One day you'll thank me for all my pictures. Today she's five, tomorrow she's eighteen, and next week she's… well, she's just growing up so fast."

John knew she spoke the truth. Their little girl was growing up way too fast. He clutched Hannah tightly and gave Kristen a warm smile. Although he'd never admit it, he loved her constantly snapping pictures. So much so, that he bought her a brand-new camera the previous Christmas. It was because of this that he laughed and shook his head at Kristen as she continued fumbling with her Polaroid camera.

"You also realize that I did buy you a camera for Christmas? A very expensive one… one with a timer?"

"I know you did, and I love it, but there's just something about the instant gratification of watching it develop before your eyes."

"Uh huh," he smiled.

"If you keep making fun of me, we're *all* going to be late today."

He placated her with a "Yes dear," and then he took the camera from her, and with his arm outstretched, he snapped the perfect Polaroid selfie. As the picture popped out of the front of the camera, Hannah excitedly grabbed it and began vigorously shaking it.

Before it had a chance to fully develop, John was already out the door and headed down the walkway. By the time he started the car, Kristen and Hannah had made their way onto the front porch.

"Hey!" yelled Kristen.

He rolled down his window, fully expecting her to hammer home the point about being back by three… three o'clock sharp.

To his pleasant surprise, she simply yelled, "Good luck."

"Yea, good luck," echoed Hannah then blew him a giant kiss.

John reached out the window pretending to catch her kiss. He pressed it against his heart and started to back out of the driveway. He didn't get but five feet before Hannah ran down the steps yelling at him.

"Daddy, wait!"

He gently pressed on the brakes and watched his daughter scamper closer to his window.

"What is it, Hannah? I really have to get going."

Hannah dismissed his comment and crossed her arms and began tapping her foot on the driveway. John couldn't help but laugh. At that very moment, it was as if there was a mini-Kristen standing in front of him. Slowly, she uncrossed her arms and pointed at the seatbelt.

"Seatbelt, Daddy. Safety first."

He continued to laugh. She was now less like Kristen and more like Kevin. He appeased her by putting on his seatbelt.

"Happy?" he asked.

She poked her head in as if to inspect if he had indeed clicked it. When she was completely satisfied, she stepped back and looked at her father.

"Happy!" she said as a smile broke free from her lips.

By now, Kristen had joined Hannah by her side. John smiled at them both, released the brake, and continued on his way. As he pulled out of the driveway, he caught a glimpse of his girls in his rearview mirror.

6

Almost a year later

John spent most of the night tossing and turning on the couch. A good night's sleep had long since evaded him. At this point, he would have settled for any sort of sleep, especially if it didn't involve dreams or nightmares.

When his eyes finally did close, the bottle of Jameson released from his grasp and fell to the floor. It didn't take long for one of his many reoccurring dreams to take hold. It was a dream he'd been having for as long as he could remember.

The gentle creaking of the wide barnboard floor…
A tiny hand being placed on an old paint-peeled six-paned window…
Raindrops quickly running down the exterior of the glass…
Complete darkness—with the exception of a faint red glow in the distance.
Complete silence—with the exception of the rain and a distant foghorn.

For a brief moment, John awoke, and with his eyes half-opened, his hand blindly searched the floor for the Jameson—his salvation. Before his fingers could get a full grasp on the bottle, his eyes fell shut and a new dream began:

Night had turned to day...

The rain had turned to sunshine...

The barnboard floor was replaced by green grass...

As the salt air hit his nose, he found himself standing on the edge of a cliff with a vast ocean before him. In the distance to his right was a lighthouse. It was perched high on a tiny rocky island.

Within the blink of an eye, he was transported to what appeared to be somebody's yard.

As a repetitive sound echoed in the distance, his eyes focused on a dirt path...

The next thing he knew, he was walking, almost floating down the path...

Through overgrown bushes and shrubs—moving closer to the sound...

When he finally exited the path, he was barefoot, standing on sand in what appeared to be a small cove—beach pebbles, driftwood, and seaweed strewn about...

The repetitive sound he had heard earlier was simply the waves gently lapping against the rocky shore of the cove...

Directly in front of him, an old lobster trap had washed ashore...

Inside it was a glass bottle...

He reached his hand in, grasping the bottle...

Just then, everything faded away and went pitch black...

When John finally opened his eyes, he was laying on his couch. His shirt was soaked in sweat, and clutched in his hand was the bottle of Jameson—empty. Pulling himself off the couch, he made his way into the bathroom. He was careful not to touch or move any of Kristen's makeup supplies. She was always leaving her stuff strewn about the bathroom counter.

As he stood there staring down at her makeup, he recalled that one time when he thought he was being helpful by putting all of her stuff in a basket and shoving it into the bathroom closet. Kristen didn't exactly see it as being helpful.

"I don't touch your stuff, don't touch mine."

Although she wore a smile on her face when she said it, John knew there was more than a hint of seriousness in her voice. From that point on, no matter how much clutter was on the bathroom counter, he refrained from touching any of it.

* * *

It was late afternoon when John arrived at the Wild Irish Rose. There were a handful of regulars sitting up at the bar, and as he swung open the front door, all eyes fell upon him. Not one of their looks was acknowledged by John. It wasn't that he didn't notice them. The hard truth was he just didn't care. He walked towards the bar with purpose—purpose being to get his hands on a bottle of Jameson.

He poured himself a shot, but before his lips touched the glass, he felt two eyes staring at him. It was a subtle, yet disapproving stare, and it wasn't from one of the regulars. It came from their twenty-eight-year-old bartender, Julie.

As if to interrupt his sip, she emptied the bucket of ice extra loudly into the bin. Unaffected and expressionless, he returned his lips to the glass and downed his drink. He filled the shot glass once again, but before lifting it, he turned his attention back to Julie.

"Where's my brother?"

"He had an appointment with the newspaper and then had some errands to run."

"The newspaper?"

"I think they want to do an article on this place."

John scoffed as he planted himself on a stool.

Julie noticed he had accidentally left his shot glass behind the bar. Her once disapproving stare began to soften. Before he could remember his shot, she quickly cracked a beer and slid it in front of him. She knew a beer was the lesser of two evils. Just happy to have alcohol in front of him, John completely forgot about the Jameson.

"How was your day?" she asked, pushing a strand of her dirty blonde hair behind her ear.

"Just another day, Julie. Just another day."

Although he left out the fact that he slept the whole day away, Julie had her suspicions. As she continued her polite small-talk, she nonchalantly placed an ice water next to his beer.

"The Cubs are doing pretty well, huh?"

"Pfft," he scoffed. "In the end, they'll disappoint like they always do."

"Ya never know. This might be their year."

John met her optimism with a huff and an eyeroll. He knew she meant well, so he held off on any further pessimistic comments and chose to concentrate on the beer in front of him.

Julie knew her small-talk was going nowhere, so she offered a slight smile and just let him be. From there, she moved down the bar making sure the other customers were taken care of. When everyone's drinks were refilled, each of their looks seemed to linger on her for a moment—a long moment.

It wasn't that she was overly attractive. As a matter of fact, in most people's opinion, she was considered just average looking. She was a no frills kind of girl who could care less about wearing designer clothes. She rarely wore makeup and never wore perfume, though that didn't stop her from smelling amazing. Her scent came from her favorite lotion from Bath and Body Works - Japanese Cherry Blossom.

Julie wasn't into fancy hairstyles either. "It is what it is," was her favorite comment regarding her hair. She had hazel eyes, was curvy, and she stood five foot two—two and a quarter if you asked her.

She wasn't overly flirtatious, but she just had a way of making people feel at home, and more importantly, making people feel special.

Some would say her beauty lay within her smile. Even if her smile wasn't directed at anyone specifically, one couldn't help but think it was meant for them. That in itself was truly a gift.

Despite having a stack of applications, it was all of these qualities that led Kevin to hire her on the spot without so much as an interview. Immediately, Kevin could tell she would be the perfect fit. And to his pleasant surprise, in the six months since she had been there, she had gone well beyond his expectations. Her welcoming yet unassuming personality was only trumped by her strong work ethic and her reliability.

By the time Kevin arrived, most every seat around the bar was occupied. Everyone had their own story to tell, and in true bartender fashion, Julie listened intently to each and every one.

"Sorry I took so long," Kevin said, entering the bar.

"No worries. I've got everything under control here," she said.

"I never had any doubts," he winked.

"Everything go okay with the newspaper?"

"Yea. They said they'd send someone in the next couple of weeks to do an interview or something."

"That's so exciting!"

Kevin just shrugged. She knew there was something on his mind. She also knew exactly what is was—who it was. Julie motioned to the bathroom door.

"He's here?" asked Kevin.

She nodded. "For about an hour or so."

"How bad is he today?"

Hesitantly, she answered, "Two shots and four beers."

Kevin shook his head then joined her behind the bar.

When John finished at the urinal, he made his way over to the sink, where his bottle of beer awaited him. One quick glance into the mirror was all he could handle. He looked down and turned on the faucet.

Vigorously, he splashed water over his face. With his eyes shut tight, and with the cool water running down his face, a familiar voice called to him from behind.

"Are you okay, Daddy?"

In one swift motion, John opened his eyes and spun around.

"Hannah? Hannah?" he called again.

He wiped the remaining water from his eyes and scanned the small bathroom.

"Pumpkin, where are you?" he yelled with more urgency, but there was no sign of his little girl. Her voice was now gone.

John turned back to the sink. The water was still running. Once again, he began splashing his face. It was as if he thought if he repeated the same actions, he would once again hear her voice. Over and over he splashed his face, but the sweet sound of his little girl never returned.

His hands were shaking as he attempted to reach for his beer. So much so, he accidentally knocked it off of the sink. John watched as the bottle smashed against the tile floor. As he stared down at the many shards of brown glass, his mind immediately transported him to a time and place he'd tried so hard to forget.

The gray tiled bathroom floor of the Wild Irish Rose morphed into a pale yellow linoleum. John was now standing in the kitchen of the O'Neil's. Out of the handful of foster homes John and Kevin had passed through over the years, it was the O'Neils' house that affected them the most. In this flashback, John was ten and Kevin, nine. They had just finished playing catch in their tiny backyard.

"I call dibs on the last can of Coke," John yelled, swinging open the fridge.

A disappointed look fell on Kevin's face when he saw all that was left to drink was beer, an outdated carton of milk, and one can of Coke.

John took pity on his younger brother and said, "Paper, rock, scissors?"

Kevin smiled and nodded. Actually, it was less about John taking pity and more about him finding ways to turn everything into a competition.

John lifted his Cubs hat, wiped the sweat from his brow, then turned to Kevin and asked, "Are you ready?"

Kevin nodded and both boys held out their fists and said in unison, "One, two, three shoot!"

Kevin smiled, knowing his paper defeated John's rock.

John gritted his teeth in anger then spouted out, "Two outta three!"

Not only was John competitive, but he hated, absolutely hated to lose—especially to his little brother. Unfortunately for John, it was Kevin who came out on top more times than not, which was ironic, considering Kevin didn't really even care about winning. He always just went along with whatever competition John had in mind.

Kevin appeased John by making their paper, rock, and scissors match a two out of three.

"One, two, three shoot!" they again said.

And once again, Kevin won. His rock crushed John's scissors.

With a stomp of his foot, John angrily whipped his baseball glove across the room. It landed on the kitchen table, sliding and knocking over a half-full bottle of Budweiser. As if in slow motion, the boys watched the bottle fall from the table and smashed onto the floor.

John stood frozen, panic-stricken. Kevin tossed his own glove down and quickly went into action. He grabbed the broom, dustpan, and roll of paper towels then hastily began cleaning up the mess. Just as John bent down to help his brother, it happened… HE entered.

The kitchen door swung open and towering above them was Richard O'Neil. John remembered every detail of what Mr. O'Neil was wearing. He remembered his blue jeans were ripped and dirty with paint splatters on them. He wore a white tank top which showed off several tattoos on his arms. On his head, he wore a ratty old NASCAR hat with the number 43 on it. And then there was the cigarette. Not only did he always have a cigarette dangling from his lips, but he always let the ashes build to the point where they'd break off.

Although it was Kevin who held the broom and dustpan, it was John who Mr. O'Neil laid his eyes on. John was the clumsy one. He was always breaking or spilling something, and Mr. O'Neil assumed this time was no different. Regrettably, this time it was Mr. O'Neil's beer that was spilled.

"You clumsy son of a bitch!" he yelled, moving closer to John, who remained frozen and frightened. John braced himself, expecting at any second to be hit. Instead, however, Mr. O'Neil chose a worse punishment. With his cigarette continuing to dangle from his mouth, he uttered the smoke-filled words, "No wonder why your parents wanted nothing to do with you… you're pathetic!"

This wasn't the first time he said these types of words, but they still cut right through the boys' hearts—especially John's.

To Mr. O'Neil's amusement, he watched as John did his best to fight back tears.

"Aww, is the little baby gonna start crying?" Mr. O'Neil raised his hand. "I'll give ya something to cry about!"

"It was me! I'm the one who broke it," Kevin yelled, jumping forward.

Kevin's pleas fell on deaf ears. It didn't matter who was to blame, for it was always John he focused his anger on.

Kevin tugged on Mr. O'Neil's shirt. "Seriously, it was me, not…"

Drunk and annoyed, Mr. O'Neil swung around, landing a solid backhand to the side of Kevin's face. John watched his brother fall to the floor. His heart raced, and his little fists clenched. He wanted so badly to defend his brother—but he couldn't. Instead, he remained frozen with fear as he watched the inch or so of ashes finally release and fall from Mr. O'Neil's cigarette.

"John? John!" Kevin yelled louder.

When John finally snapped out of his flashback, he turned to see Kevin standing there holding a broom, a dustpan, and a roll of paper towels. Kevin heard the glass shattering from out in the bar and knew what needed to be done. Without another word, Kevin began sweeping up the glass.

"What are you doing?" John knowingly asked.

"Cleaning up your mess."

Although Kevin left out the ending words *"as usual,"* John knew it was implied, which annoyed and angered him even more.

"I don't need you to clean up my messes!"

Kevin stopped sweeping and looked up at his brother and said, "No?"

John gritted his teeth and his face turned red, but he didn't say a word. Angrily, he turned and stumbled his way out of the bathroom and eventually out of the bar. Moments later, Julie knocked then opened the bathroom door to check on Kevin. With a frustrated and helpless look on his face, he looked up at her.

"I... I don't know what to do anymore."

Not knowing the right words to say, Julie offered a sympathetic smile and bent down to help him clean up John's mess.

* * *

The air outside the Wild Irish Rose was warm and still. It was the perfect late-summer's night. Not coincidentally, this all changed when John's bottle smashed to the bathroom floor. It wasn't a drastic change in weather, but it was a change nonetheless.

The temperature dropped, and a classic Chicago wind began to swirl up. Just then, the distinctive sound of footsteps echoed throughout the night air. Through the shadows on the sidewalk, a mysterious figure moved towards the Wild Irish Rose—slowly, yet with a purpose.

When the footsteps finally came to a halt, the dimly lit street light revealed the figure of a a man. He wore a brand-new Cubs hat, and in his right hand, he was clutching a cane. As newspapers and debris swirled around his well-worn black loafers, the man slowly peered upwards at the Wild Irish Rose sign.

It was at that point, John came rushing out of the bar, angry and mumbling to himself. He brushed past the man and stumbled his way to the corner. The man carefully watched John drunkenly wave down a cab, climb in, then drive away. He took another long look at the Wild Irish Rose sign then continued on his way.

❧

7

It had been forever since John had allowed those childhood memories to rear their ugly head. It was a lifetime ago, but the thought of Mr. O'Neil still sent shivers up and down his spine. Without even realizing it, his fists remained clenched the entire cab ride home. There was also a taste of blood in his mouth, which was caused by him angrily biting down on his lip at the mere thought of the O'Neil household.

John swung open his front door. Rather than turning on the light switch, he chose to blindly stumble his way over to the couch. The more he tried to push away the memory of the O'Neil's, the more the memories came flooding back. As he lay there in the dark, his mind took him back in time. He was around the same age as the previous flashback, but the details were so vivid, it was as if it was yesterday.

With their bunk beds behind them, John and Kevin sat on their bedroom floor in their pjs. John had baseballs, bats, and gloves all over his, and Kevin had rocket ships. The carpet between the boys was filled with hundreds of baseball cards. Despite Mr. O'Neil hating everything about baseball, Mrs. O'Neil would buy them a pack every time she went grocery shopping.

The boys organized the cards by teams and when they had collected an entire team, they arranged them on the floor with each card representing their position on the field. They would each chose a team and play make-believe games against one another. John, being the oldest, was always the Cubs. This didn't bother Kevin in the least, for he was just happy playing with his brother.

Speaking of the Cubs, the boys made sure to be extra careful with them. Not so much as a corner was bent on any of their Cubs cards. The Yankees cards were a different story. Even though they played in different leagues, the Yankees were still universally hated.

One of their favorite pastimes was drawing funny faces on the Yankees players. Whether it was putting cross-eyes on Catfish Hunter or devil horns and tail on Reggie Jackson, the brothers amused themselves for hours. John was so into the baseball cards, he had most of the players' stats from the back of the cards memorized.

As John continued tossing and turning on his couch, just the thought of defacing the Yankees cards all those years ago put a slight smile on his face. His smile would be short-lived as his flashback continued.

The baseball card game was interrupted by the familiar sounds of Mr. and Mrs. O'Neil fighting in the other room. Mostly, the sounds were from Mr. O'Neil. His swear words were accented by furniture being overturned or objects being thrown into a wall. If this was the extent of it, the boys would have considered it a good night, but sadly, on that night, the object being thrown around was Mrs. O'Neil.

Kevin watched as John blocked his ears and tightly closed his eyes. Even though the constant fighting affected both brothers, and even though Kevin was a year younger, he could tell it really, really affected John. Quietly, Kevin stood up and shut their bedroom door all the way, but this did little to mute Mr. O'Neil's loud, drunk voice or Mrs. O'Neil's cries and pleas.

The tossing and turning stopped as John abruptly sat up on his couch. He remembered thinking that as bad as he felt for Mrs. O'Neil,

he was secretly glad it was her taking the beating rather than himself…
or Kevin. Sweat poured from his face as a giant wave of guilt flooded
over him. He knew he was only a little kid at the time, but he still felt
horrible for ever having those thoughts.

As John sat in his darkened living room, he shut his eyes and
blocked his ears. It was his innate way of trying to prevent the final
part of his flashback. No matter how tightly he shut his eyes, and no
matter how hard he blocked his ears, his mind replayed the final scene
of that night.

With their little faces pressed against their bedroom window, John
and Kevin watched in dismay the actions of Mr. O'Neil. The full moon
illuminated the backyard and allowed them to see everything. They saw
Mr. O'Neil lift the lid of his charcoal grill and toss a match in it. Tears
poured down John's cheeks as he watched him throw every one of
their baseball cards into the fire. If that wasn't bad enough, the boys
watched Mr. O'Neil smugly unleash a half a bottle of lighter fluid onto
the cards.

Kevin placed his arm around John and forced him away from the
window. He spent the rest of the night consoling and attempting to
cheer up his broken-hearted older brother.

8

Anxiously, Kevin paced around the small waiting room. It had been years since he'd been to his therapist. Her location had changed, but the strong scent of incense brought him right back to all those years ago. The first session Kevin had with her was back in 1987. He was fifteen and had just been put into the Boys Home of Chicago with John. The State provided both brothers with a few sessions with a therapist. From the first moment John sat in front of her, he hated it. He simply leaned back with arms folded and barely said two words. There was no way he was going to be forced to open up to some strange woman about his feelings. This was another big difference between the two brothers.

Kevin was always more of a communicator. Even as a kid, he tried to face problems head on. John, on the other hand, was the master at ignoring and repressing his feelings. He kept everything inside, and no one was allowed in—even Kevin.

During those first few sessions, although Kevin said more words than John, there were no major breakthroughs or revelations for either one of them. The sessions weren't a complete failure, however. There was something about the therapist that Kevin liked. There was something about her that put him at ease.

Years later, when Kevin was nineteen, he felt as if his past was getting the better of him. All his feelings and thoughts regarding his childhood were bubbling to the surface, and he knew he needed to let them out. Even at nineteen, he was aware enough to realize he needed professional help, and he knew exactly who he wanted to contact.

He looked up his old therapist and thus began a two-and-a-half-year soul-cleansing journey with her. He found his sessions so useful, in fact, that he even attempted to get John to go see her as well. Of course, each and every attempt was unsuccessful.

"Kevin Mathews. Wow, it's been a while, hasn't it?"

Kevin stopped pacing, and there, standing in front of him was his old therapist. Before he could say a word, she embraced him. She was a hugger.

"You haven't changed a bit," she smiled.

"I don't know about that. I've gained some pounds… lost some hair… and on the verge of turning thirty-three."

"Age is just a number… that's what I keep telling myself anyway. Especially considering I'm on the verge of the big five-O," she winked.

He didn't verbalize it, but Kevin was shocked. He was amazed at how young she looked. As a matter of fact, she looked the same as the first time he met her seventeen years ago—right down to the long, flowing tie-dyed skirt.

She wore a loose, low-cut top, which was accented by a necklace made of seashells. Each of her wrists were adorned with colorfully hand-woven bracelets, and on her feet she wore nothing. From the first time Kevin met her, she was always barefoot.

It was her unusual approach and her free-spirited nature that drew Kevin in. She was completely unorthodox, but there was just something about her that he connected with.

She motioned him into her office, which was unlike any typical therapist's office. Three of the walls were sponge-painted in deep purples and blues. The other wall contained a large mural of The Tree of Life. Unlike the last time, there was no cushy couch to sit on. The old, comfortable leather couch was now replaced by a simple futon. Thrown across it was a Native American-style blanket.

"What do you think of my new space?"

"I like it," he said, continuing to gaze around. "It's quite… eclectic."

She took a deep breath, as if inhaling every ounce of air from the room. As she slowly exhaled, she said, "This space has a much better aura and vibe to it. Can't you feel it?"

"Um, yea, it's nice," he said, attempting to get comfortable on the futon.

Not only did she get rid of the couch, but she had replaced her large armchair with a simple Papasan chair. She took in and released one more deep breath before settling into her chair. She probably would have continued her small talk, but she could tell by Kevin's expression that his mind was firmly ready to tackle the problem at hand.

She crisscrossed her legs then calmly spoke. "What's on your mind, Kevin?"

He wasted no time, and before she finished her sentence, he unloaded on her. His stream of thought was choppy and rambling at times, but it was also very concise. Before she knew what hit her, he'd filled her in on everything since their last session years ago.

When he finished, she closed her eyes and once again took a long, deep breath. She held it for a moment then released. He assumed it was her way of processing everything he had just told her. Kevin watched as her mind and lips were attempting to form the perfect words to say. Not really knowing how long this would take, he stood up and continued to ramble on.

"I mean, John has always been distant and moody, but lately… it's like I don't even know him anymore. He's becoming more angry… more bitter. And his drinking is getting way out of control. It's like he's given up."

53

Again, Kevin watched as she contemplated the right words to say. And again, before any words could exit her mouth, he continued to speak.

"I know that John would never come see you on his own, so I was thinking maybe you could come by the bar and talk to him or something… maybe?"

She ran her fingers over the shells of her necklace, and with her kind eyes focused directly on Kevin, she said, "You can't force John to seek help. He has to want it. He needs to do it on his own terms… in his own time."

With that, she uncrossed her legs and arose from the chair. She walked over to a small table, and he watched as she reached her hand into a clay bowl. It seemed to contain a bunch of random crystals. As she tightly clutched a few of them in her hand, she once again closed her eyes. This time, Kevin didn't wait for her to open them back up.

"But what if he doesn't? What if he doesn't seek help? He's never been good at asking for help or talking about his feelings. You know how he is."

"Actually, I don't," she said, opening her eyes. "I only had a few brief sessions with him, and that was what, seventeen years ago? And if I remember correctly, he didn't say two words to me."

"But there's gotta be something I can do to help him."

Kevin was now standing directly in front of her. She released the crystals back into the bowl then gently placed her hand on his shoulder.

"You've spent your whole life being there for your brother… standing up for him… being his rock. Some things in life you just can't control… or fix. Sometimes, you just need to let the universe take its course."

Kevin dropped his head, letting out a big sigh. He knew coming to see her was a long shot, but still, her response left him disappointed and at a loss for what to do next. Over the years, he learned to respect and even believe in her quirky ways and her new-age philosophies, but letting the *universe take its course* was not what he wanted to hear. More importantly, it was a philosophy he had a hard time believing in.

* * *

Ever since she was hired, Julie had become more than just an employee. Her sweet, good-natured personality allowed her to be the perfect confidant and sounding board for Kevin. Although he found it easy and comforting to open up to her, he decided to leave out that he had just come from his therapist.

Back at the Wild Irish Rose, it was business as usual. Between five and six, most of the regulars had arrived from their jobs and were sitting up at the bar. Kevin and Julie served drinks while lending a kind ear to everyone's stories and complaints about their lives.

Ironically, listening to other people's problems was the best part of the night for Kevin. It was when his own problem walked through the door that his mood changed. His own problem, being his alcoholic brother.

Like clockwork, every evening John would walk through the door and immediately head behind the bar and grab a glass and a bottle of Jameson. And like clockwork, Julie would shoot Kevin a look, hoping this would be the night he stepped in and cut his brother off. Once again, this would not be the night.

Kevin hated, absolutely hated seeing his brother drink like this. But Kevin knew how much pain he was in, and he knew if he cut John off, there'd be a huge fight, which would just cause John to go drink somewhere else. At least this way, he could keep a close eye on him and do his best to make sure he made it home safely. Whether it was getting him a cab or bringing him home himself, Kevin had turned into a full-time babysitter.

John was already half in the bag when he arrived at the Wild Irish Rose, so it didn't take long before he was passed out with his head down on the bar. Kevin knew it was a bad look letting John sleep on the bar, but it was a better alternative than waking him up and watching him drink some more. It wasn't until the bar was closed that he finally attempted to wake John up.

"Come on, bro, I'll give you a ride home," Kevin said, helping John to his feet.

Once inside the car, John pressed his face against the window. The cool glass felt good on his hot, flushed cheeks. Although there were many things Kevin wanted to say to his brother, the words failed to fall from his mouth, and the entire ride home was done in complete silence.

It wasn't until Kevin helped John into the house and switched on the lamp that he knew he needed to say something. John's reaction to this was that of a vampire being hit with a ray of light. He quickly covered his eyes with the back of his hand and dropped his head down.

"Turn off the fuckin' light!" he ordered.

Kevin barely heard him. He was in complete shock at the disaster known as John's living room. Along with dirty clothes, there were endless amounts of take-out boxes and empty alcohol bottles strewn about everywhere.

"Light…off…now!" John repeated louder.

If this was my house, I wouldn't want to see it either, thought Kevin as he hesitantly switched off the light. The thin white curtains allowed enough moonlight in to dimly illuminate the interior of the house. Kevin put his arm around his brother and attempted to lead him down the hall and towards his bedroom. Realizing where they were headed, John stopped cold, broke free, and stumbled his way back to the living room and fell onto the couch.

The hallway was dark, but there was enough light for Kevin to see that John and Kristen's bedroom door was shut tight. Across the hall, he noticed that Hannah's door was also closed. Sympathetically, he approached the couch, where John was unsuccessfully fumbling with the blanket. Finally, the words began falling out of Kevin's mouth.

"You really should consider talking to someone."

John let out an unidentifiable grunt, turning his back to Kevin.

"I'm serious, John. I think you need some professional help."

This time, John's mumbling was more recognizable. "Pfft, like that hippy-chick shrink from years ago? No thanks."

Kevin persisted. "She's a little unorthodox, but…"

"Unorthodox? She was a fuckin' wacko," John said, turning to face his brother. "I'd hardly call her professional. The hippy-chick didn't even wear a bra. How professional is that?"

John laughed as he again fumbled with the twisted blanket. Frustrated and annoyed, John kicked the blanket to the floor. He turned on his side and began to doze off. Although his eyes were shut tight, he could still feel Kevin standing there staring at him.

John softened his tone and said, "Don't worry, Kev, I'm fine. I promise. I just need some sleep. Night."

"Kevin lowered his hand onto John's shoulder and quietly said, "Goodnight, John."

He then fixed the blanket so it was completely covering John's body. He took one last sad look around the place then headed out. Tears flowed freely down Kevin's cheeks as he drove home. His heart was breaking for his brother, and it killed him that there nothing he could do to fix it.

As usual, John spent most of the night tossing and turning. The cushions on the couch were now well-worn from months and months of being occupied by his body. Also, as usual, when he finally did fall asleep, his mind was invaded by strange and unsettling dreams. It all started with that same reoccurring dream. The one he'd been having for as long as he could remember.

The gentle creaking of the wide floor board…
A tiny hand being placed on an old paint-peeled six-paned window…
Raindrops quickly running down the exterior of the glass…
Complete darkness—with the exception of a faint red glow fading in and out.
Complete silence—with the exception of the rain and a distant foghorn.

Usually, in the next part of the dream, John would find himself wandering down a path which led to some sort of beach. The path in tonight's dream, however, didn't lead to a beach. There was no sand, no salt air, and no waves crashing against the rocky cove.

Instead, John found himself standing in a lush green park. The sky was the brightest of blue without a cloud in sight. The previous silence in the dream was now replaced by voices and laughter. They weren't random voices. They belonged to Kristen and Hannah.

John spun around, and there before his eyes were his two girls. They were both swinging on a swing set and were calling to him.

"Push us, Daddy, push us!" Hannah called out.

With a hand on each of their backs, John pushed his girls on the swings. He pushed them so high into the blue sky that he couldn't even see them at their apex. All John could hear was laughter and giggles.

"Higher, Daddy, higher!" Hannah yelled out as they returned to view.

Happily, John obliged by pushing them even higher than before. Again, only giggles were heard as they disappeared into the sun. John continued this for three giant pushes.

On the fourth push, everything changed. The blue sky and sun were taken over by a dark gray fog. This time, when they hit their apex, there were no giggles or laughter to be heard. And this time, when the swings returned to John, they were completely empty—his girls were gone.

Right before his eyes, the entire swing set was engulfed by the fog. His heart raced as he frantically attempted to scream out their names, but no sound came out of his mouth. It was as if the whole dream had been muted.

Fog or no fog, he was determined to search the entire park for them. He tried, but couldn't move. His legs were frozen in place. Again, he tried to call out their names, and again, no sound emerged. Just when he thought his heart would start beating out of his chest, the loud sound of a foghorn blared out.

John's eyes sprang open as he sat straight up on the couch. The sweat from his forehead poured down his face, mixing with the newly formed tears. His breaths were quick and sharp, as if in the midst of a panic attack. He quickly wiped his face then shielded his eyes from the bright rays of sunlight, which came bursting through the front window.

The blanket that Kevin had covered him with had long since been discarded, and it now lay crumpled on the floor. As John's heart continued to race, he knew exactly what he needed to help him calm down. He reached to the floor to where he kept his trusty bottle of salvation. His sweat-soaked t-shirt clung to him as he searched the floor around the couch. When his hand came up empty, he frantically scanned the messy living room. On the table in the center of the room sat his bottle of Jameson.

"Thank God," he mumbled, slowly peeling himself off the couch.

Still visibly shaken up from his dream, his legs wobbled beneath him. The path to the table was littered with empty bottles, pizza boxes, and half eaten bags of chips. Unaffected by these land mines, John desperately made his way towards the table. As he moved closer, he noticed something leaning against the bottle. Upon closer inspection, he saw it was a business card for that hippy-chick therapist.

"Fuckin' Kevin," he mumbled then crumpled and tossed the card onto the floor.

With his hands now shaking uncontrollably, he reached out and clutched the bottle. Just feeling it in his grasp sent a calming wave throughout his body. Quickly, he pressed it to his lips and tilted the bottle back. To his anger and dismay, it was empty—not a drop of liquid salvation was left.

"Fuckin' Kevin," he yelled louder, slamming the empty bottle down.

Before he had a chance to scour his house for another bottle, there was a knock at the door. Normally, John ignored all knocks and phone calls, but this one was persistent, and more importantly, it was interrupting his search.

"What do you want?" he yelled as he opened the door.

Standing in front of him was a clean-cut fresh-faced boy. He looked to be in his very early twenties.

"Good morning. How are you today, sir?" he politely said.

John took one look at the pamphlets the guy was holding in his right hand and knew immediately he was a Jehovah Witness.

"Are you fuckin' kidding me?" John said, more to himself than out loud.

"If I could just have a sec…"

That's all John allowed him to say.

"Unless you have some booze to give to me then get the fuck out!"

The poor boy was taken aback, and he knew it was pointless to continue his speech. Usually, he would have still tried to at least leave a pamphlet with the homeowner, but this time he chose not to. Quite frankly, he was scared where John might have shoved the pamphlet.

He put on his best polite smile and simply said, "I'm sorry to have bothered you, sir."

"Damn right you should be sorry!" he said, slamming the door.

John put his hands to his head as if to stop it from spinning. As he pressed his back against the door, he thought of Kristen. Neither one of them were big fans of being solicited by Jehovah Witnesses, but Kristen always allowed them in, and she always politely listened to their spiel.

Kristen was one of the sweetest and most kind-hearted people he'd ever met, and he knew she would be upset by how he just treated that poor boy. Slowly, he turned around and grasp the door knob. He had no intention on invited the boy in the house, but the least he could do was take a stupid pamphlet.

John opened the door, but the boy had already moved on to the neighbors across the street. He lowered his head and felt horrible for how he treated the boy... for how he'd been treating everyone lately. He was a mess and he knew it, but he had no idea how to fix himself. More importantly, he had no idea if he could be fixed. With his head still down, he watched his tears gently splatter onto the porch.

"I can't do this... I give up... I fuckin' give up."

Just then, John heard the ringing of a bell. Out on the sidewalk was a little girl riding her pink bicycle. Again, she rang her bell and offered John a smile and a wave. It was a quick wave, for she didn't trust herself enough to let go of the handlebars for long.

After he wiped away the tears that were clouding his eyes, the girl and her bike were gone. The neighbor across the way had let the Jehovah Witness inside, leaving the street quiet and empty. As John turned to re-enter his house, he heard the bell again. He shielded his eyes and gazed up the street. All at once, his eyes widened and his heart blew up like a balloon.

This time it was a different little girl—it was *his* little girl—it was Hannah. John stood frozen and watched a slightly younger version of himself pushing her from behind. His hands released the bike, and with a scared look on her face, her little legs nervously pedaled. He watched the bike wobble back and forth before finally tipping over. Hannah was fully padded and wore a helmet, so she wasn't physically hurt by the fall. Emotionally, however, was a different story.

Discouraged and upset, she uttered, "I give up! I'm never gonna learn how to ride a bike."

"Hey, that's not the right attitude," John replied. "What do I always say? Huh?"

Hannah sighed and reluctantly answered, "Whenever you fall down in life, you have to pick yourself up and try again."

"Because why?" he knowingly asked.

She let out another little sigh, rolled her eyes and said, "Because Mathews never quit."

"That's right," he smiled. "We never give up and we never quit. No matter what!"

Just then, a truck drove by, snapping John out of it. When the truck was out of sight, he looked up and down the road, but saw nothing. The air released from his heart, and as it sank deep into his chest, he knew the flashback was officially over. He took one more hopeful look out at the street before turning and heading back inside.

As if on auto-drive, he legs took him right back to the living room table. The next thing he knew, he was holding the crumpled business card. He did his best to smooth it out, and as he gazed down at it, he heard his little girl's sweet voice.

"Whenever you fall down in life, you have to pick yourself up and try again... because Mathews never quit."

9

Through the cab window, John fixated on the address numbers on the buildings. The next thing he knew, he was standing on the sidewalk in front of 337 Park Street, Unit 8.

He double-checked the address on the crumpled business card then mumbled, "What the fuck am I doing here?"

His answer came in the form of his little girl's voice, once again reminding him that Mathews never give up. His legs felt like they were stuck in cement. After a deep sigh, he plodded his way forward. Before grabbing the door handle, he pulled a silver flask from his pocket. The flask was a Christmas gift from Kevin years earlier and had the Chicago Cubs logo engraved on it. He took a long, calming swig.

John's apprehension grew even more upon entering her office. He spent the first few minutes just standing there looking at her crazy and eclectic décor. It was nowhere near how he remembered it from seventeen years earlier.

The memory of those initial three sessions was faint at best, but he did remember her cozy brown leather couch. Needless to say, he was less than pleased to find out it had been replaced with a futon.

"A fuckin' futon," were his exact words.

While John did his best to settle into the futon, the therapist was busy lighting some sort of incense in the corner. Once lit, she glided over and climbed into her Papasan chair. She reached down and grabbed a stainless steel water bottle, which had the yin and yang symbol on it. He watched her carefully as she took a giant sip and then crisscrossed her legs and settled in.

The first thing that caught his eye was her bare feet. It was so long ago, he couldn't remember if she had always been barefoot or was this a new quirk of hers. By the look of her office, he surmised that she had just gotten wackier over the years.

They weren't even clean feet. There must be some health code against that, he thought. When he was done being distracted by her feet, he gazed at her earth-toned hippy dress. He couldn't help but chuckle to himself when he noticed she wasn't wearing a bra. John made a mental note that if there was a sighting of unruly and unshaven arm pit hair then he was out of there!

"It really is nice to see you again, John. It's been a while."

A slight nod was all he offered.

"So, what can I do for you?"

It had only been two minutes, but he was already speechless. It was a simple question, but he honestly had no idea how to answer it. Nervous and anxious, he began fidgeting around the futon. He then adjusted his sunglasses and did his best to deflect her initial question.

"I have to tell you, Doc, my ass liked your old couch much better."

His deflection didn't exactly go as planned, for she continued to smile at him, completely ignoring his sarcasm. John waited for her to ask a new question or maybe repeat the first one, but she said nothing. Instead, she sat patiently, happily staring over at John. He could have offered her another clever deflection, but he reluctantly decided to answer her initial question.

"I don't know," he shrugged. "Trouble sleeping I guess."

"Would you like to talk about what's causing this trouble sleeping?"

"No," he quickly answered. "Honestly, I was just hoping you could write me a prescription or something. What I've been using isn't really working anymore."

Her fingers smoothed over her seashell necklace then asked, "And what might that be?"

"You mean what have I been using to help me sleep?"

She nodded yes, but her attention was more focused on her necklace.

"Jack, Johnny, and Jim," he answered loudly, in attempt to regain her attention. "Daniels, Walker, and Beam, that is. Although, I prefer their buddy, Jameson the most."

He chuckled at his sarcasm, but she didn't. She was completely unaffected by his attempt at humor. It was at that point, she uncrossed her legs and made her way to the opposite end of the room. On a small table sat a stuffed teddy bear. If that wasn't strange enough, it was wearing a tie-dyed Grateful Dead shirt.

Next to the bear was a lava lamp. John watched as she carefully plugged the lamp in. Between the incense, the tie dye, the lava lamp, and all the other weird paraphernalia, John felt like he was in Spencer's Gifts. It was as if she was ignoring him as she just stood there with a contented smile, watching the red blobs float about the lamp. John was seriously questioning his presence there.

Again, he spoke louder. "They used to help me sleep... help me forget."

With her eyes still gazing at the silly lava lamp, she asked, "And what are you trying to forget?"

Up until that point, the session was strange and unusual, but with her latest question, things just got real. John didn't do real.

"Look, Doc, I didn't come here to watch you play with a stupid stuffed animal or stare into a frickin' lava lamp. And I certainly didn't come here to be psycho-analyzed."

"Why did you come here?" she asked.

"I told you! I just need you to give me something to help knock me out. And while you're at it, something that'll get rid of the stupid nightmares too."

John lowered his head, knowing full well what her next question would be. She would ask about the nightmares. He was sure of it. After a solid minute of silence, he slowly raised his head to see why she wasn't questioning him further.

During that minute of silence, she had moved on from staring at the lava lamp. She was now watering the many plants around the room. John was a bit offended that she was focusing her attention on the plants rather than him. This was *his* session. He was even more offended and annoyed that she was whistling while she did it.

Determined to regain her focus on him, he joked aloud.

"I'm not even sure they're actually nightmares though. I mean, sometimes they occur when I'm wide awake. Hey Doc, is there a such thing as daymares?"

Again, she seemed unaffected by his attempt at humor, but she did stop watering her plants and made her way back over to her chair. John's competitive nature considered it a small victory that he was able to regain her focus on him. His victory would be short-lived however.

"These nightmares you speak of… your wife and daughter?"

John's face turned white and his fingers curled into a ball. The anger in his eyes burned through his sunglasses directly onto the therapist.

"How the hell do you know about that?"

The anger in his voice matched his eyes. Almost immediately, he answered his own question. It was all making sense. Kevin must have restarted his sessions with her. That's how he had a crisp new business card. John clenched his fists tightly at the thought of Kevin babbling to her about *his* personal life.

"Fucking Kevin!" he blurted out. "Looks like my big-mouth brother restarted his sessions with you, huh? He needs to learn to mind his own God damn business!"

John stood up from the futon and stomped his way over to the window. Rather than a typical curtain, she had a strung a row of colored beads across the frame. He rattled and clinked the beads aside in order to stare out the actual window.

"Don't you think what happened affected your brother as well?"

John paused a second then pulled his body back through the annoying beads.

"I knew this was a bad idea. Take care, Doc."

He flipped her a sarcastic peace symbol with his fingers then proceeded to storm out of her office. Moments after the door slammed behind him, she stood up and made her way over to her bowl of crystals. With the proper crystals clutched in her hand, she closed her eyes and pressed them tightly to her chest.

Within seconds of exiting her office, John pulled the flask from his pocket. He couldn't press it to his lips fast enough, but to his dismay, there was barely a swig left. After shoving it back into his pocket, he ran his fingers over his thick, scraggily beard and through his greasy hair. He couldn't even remember the last time he showered or shaved, nor did he really care. Right now, all he cared about was what his next move would be. And considering his flask was bone dry, the answer was simple—the Wild Irish Rose.

It would be a win-win situation for him. Not only would he be able to get a nice stiff drink (for free), but he'd be able to give Kevin a piece of his mind. How dare he blab to a complete stranger about John's personal life. He would most definitely let Kevin have it!

The Wild Irish Rose was only five blocks from the therapist, so he decided to hoof it there. During his walk, he kept replaying the entirety of his therapy session. Specifically, her final question to him: *"Don't you think what happened affected your brother as well?"*

By the time he reached the bar, his anger had subsided, and he decided to not ream his brother out after all. Partly because he didn't want Kevin to know he took his advice and went to the shrink, but mostly, he felt a little sorry for Kevin—guilty even.

Of course Kevin was affected by what happened with Kristen and Hannah. The more John thought about, the more he realized just how selfish and insensitive he'd been towards him; not just this past year, but always. John's feelings always trumped Kevin's. Even worse, John knew he'd been a huge burden on his brother, especially lately.

It was because of that, John decided to go easy on the drinking—at least in front of Kevin. Of course, in John's eyes, drinking beer versus the hard stuff was considered going easy.

It was late afternoon when he finally passed through the door of the Wild Irish Rose. Through his dark sunglasses he caught the look Julie gave to Kevin. It was an *Oh shit, here comes your pathetic, drunk brother looking for free drinks* kind of look.

He knew this was more or less true, but still, he resented Julie for the look. What made it worse was just how sweet, kind, and caring she was. It was hard to find a negative thing about her, which is what made him resent her even more. He resented that she had taken over his role at the Wild Irish Rose. Legally, he was still the co-owner, but physically and mentally he was completely vacant from the business.

Not only did Julie assume his responsibilities, but she was taking on even more. She was well-versed in QuickBooks and offered Kevin to take over all his bookkeeping—for free. Yup, yet another reason for John not to like her.

Despite their unapproving looks, John made his way straight behind the bar and cracked open a cold beer. For the moment, Kevin seemed to appreciate John's lesser of two evils decision by giving him a slight smile and an acknowledging nod. Julie took it one step further by pleasantly greeting him.

"Hey, John. How are you today?"

Her tone was sweet and genuine, which made John despise it even more.

"I'm stellar, thank you very much," he said, sitting on his usual stool at the end of the bar. His tone was the opposite of sweet and genuine.

As the sun went down on the small Chicago bar, so did John's idea of *taking it easy*. He put back one beer after another, but because his tolerance had grown over the past year, the beer-buzz just wasn't cutting it for him.

He knew if Kevin saw him getting something harder, there would surely be some sort of lecture, or even worse, a disappointed look from Julie. Because of that, he decided to choose his moment wisely. His big break came shortly after nine o'clock.

"Hey, Kev," asked Julie. "Can you help me move around some of those cases in the back room? I need to get to something."

"Sure. Of course."

And just like that, John had his opportunity. As soon as they were out of sight, he hurried behind the bar. He felt like a five-year-old sneaking behind his parents' back.

At the same time, outside the Wild Irish Rose, the wind began to pick up considerably. It whipped and swirled and brought a fall-like chill to the late August night. Through the whistling wind, the faint sound of footsteps could be heard as they slowly plodded up the sidewalk. Once again, the black shoes of the mystery man came to a halt in front of the Wild Irish Rose sign.

John quickly poured and pounded down a shot of Jameson. He was tempted to take the whole bottle back to his seat but decided against it. Instead, he settled on making himself a Captain and Coke with a little more Captain than Coke. With one eye on the pouring and the other on the back room, it was becoming more apparent that he was going to make it back to his stool without getting caught. A look of accomplishment filled his face. Only someone in his condition would consider the feeling of *not getting caught* an accomplishment.

With the glass firmly in his hand, he started to return to his seat. He only took one step when the front door creaked open. The cold chill from the outside wind quickly dispersed through the bar, but it was as if no one noticed—no one except John. While everyone continued laughing and drinking, John turned his attention towards the front door, and there, standing perfectly still was an older gentleman. He looked to be in his mid-sixties. He wore black shoes, an overcoat, and his right hand was grasping a cane.

For the moment, John forgot about his getaway from behind the bar. He simply stood there, fixated on the mysterious old man. Even when the door was fully closed, the man just stood there. A smile never left his face as he carefully gazed around at the entire room. Finally, after what seemed like minutes, the man set his eyes on an empty stool up at the bar. He approached slowly, but didn't appear to be relying heavily on his cane.

Over the past year, John had perfected the art of ignoring customers. His sole focus was on himself, and he left the customer service to Kevin and Julie. But this night was different. This customer was different. There was something about this man that held John's attention. So much so, that he decided to take the man's order.

John took a long swig from his Captain and Coke and looked at the man's Cubs hat. It was brand-spanking new, with the visor not even attempted to be curled and broken in. This was usually the sign of a bandwagon fan.

"What's your poison?" John asked.

The man watched John take another sip of his drink, pointed to it, then answered, "I'll have one of those."

John seemed pleased with the man's choice.

"One Captain and Coke coming up," John replied.

"Ohh, no, no," laughed the man. "I thought that was just a Coke you were drinking."

"So you just want a Coke?" John asked, offended.

"Yes, please. With extra ice if you don't mind."

"Who the hell comes into a bar and orders a Coke," he mumbled to himself, placing the drink in front of the man.

By now, Kevin and Julie were returning from the back. They stopped dead in their tracks when they saw John interacting with a customer.

"Oh shit! What is he doing?" Julie whispered to Kevin.

"I don't know, but we better get over there before he says or does something stupid."

From the corner of his eye, John saw Kevin and Julie standing there. He knew they were probably unhappy about him being behind the bar making himself a drink. He also knew they were probably uncomfortable with him talking and waiting on a customer. John hated that he was a disappointment and embarrassment to his brother, and he knew the right thing to do would be to dump his drink out and head home.

Unfortunately, his self-destructive path rarely included doing the right thing. Instead, John decided to do the opposite. He blatantly filled the rest of his glass with straight whiskey. And to get under their skin even more, he turned back to the man at the bar and started a conversation.

"So, do you think this is their year?"

The man returned John's question with a confused look.

"The Cubs," John said, pointing to the man's hat. "Are they finally gonna do it this year or what?"

"Ohhh," laughed the man. "I have no idea. To be honest, I don't really follow baseball… or any sports for that matter."

I fucking knew it! John thought to himself. *I knew he wasn't a real fan!* Between the man's non-alcoholic drink and his non-sports attitude, John was doubly offended.

"One of my nurses gave me the hat. I guess it was my consolation prize for all of my chemo treatments."

The older man continued to smile as he removed his hat, revealing his bald head. For a moment, John's attitude softened.

"Sorry. I didn't know."

"No worries, my friend. I've come to terms with it. That's life, right?" The man smiled and raised his drink to John.

"Ya… life," John repeated then clinked the man's glass with his.

By now, Kevin and Julie were standing directly behind John. They didn't say a word, but he knew exactly what they were thinking. Despite their presence, John pounded down the rest of his drink and continued his conversation with the man.

"I've never seen you in here before. You new in town?"

"Nooo," laughed the man. "I live a few blocks away. I've been in Chicago for nearly forty-five years. Originally, I'm from the Great State of Maine. It's been a tough year health-wise, so I haven't gotten out as much as I used to. Lately though, I've tried to venture out a bit more."

John was growing restless and bored, and he was only half-listening.

"I don't usually walk down this street, but for whatever reason, my feet have been taking me in this direction lately. Every time I've passed by this place, it always looked so warm and inviting. I kept telling myself I should stop in… and here I am!"

John's drink was empty, he had to go to the bathroom, and he was most definitely bored of this little exchange.

"Oh, and I love the name of this place," the man rambled on. "The Wild Irish Rose… perfect! Although, it's not like I'm Irish," he laughed. "I am part Scottish on my father's…"

"I need to take a piss," John rudely interrupted. "If you need anything else, I'm sure our *barkeep* can help you."

He made sure to emphasis barkeep. It was his way of letting Julie know her place. With that, John brushed past them and headed into the bathroom. In hopes of doing damage control, Kevin and Julie made their way over to the man.

"I'm sorry about my brother. He just has a lot on his mind."

The man offered a warm smile and said, "No need to apologize. I do tend to babble and ramble sometimes. I'm William, by the way," he said, extending his bony hand.

"Nice to meet you, William. I'm Kevin, and this is our *barkeep*, Julie."

Kevin also emphasized barkeep, but it was all done in fun. Julie gave him a smirk and a nudge. She knew it was Kevin's way of making light of his brother's insensitive comments. She also knew just how much Kevin appreciated all of her hard work.

"So, you and your brother own this place?" asked William.

Kevin hesitated then nodded.

"You remodeled it yourselves?"

Again, Kevin nodded. "Well, mostly John did. I just did my best to stay out of his way. He's the handy one. I'm more of the business side… and the day to day operations."

William gazed around then focused his attention on the bar top.

"He didn't do this, did he?"

"Yup. He designed and built it himself. I think out of everything he did here, this was his proudest accomplishment."

"As well it should be. It's absolutely exquisite," William exclaimed, running hand across the glossy finish.

"Do you need a refill?" Julie politely asked.

"Thank you, dear," he said, sliding his glass forward. "Just a Coke please… with extra ice," he said with a wink and a smile.

While Julie refilled his drink, William pulled out a handkerchief and began wiping the sweat on his forehead. Julie watched as he took off his hat and dabbed the sweat beads on his bald head.

She placed the Coke in front of him then sympathetically said, "I'm really sorry about your…"

"Oh, it's okay, dear. It's all part of God's master plan I guess."

"Pffft! You talk like he actually exists."

John had returned from the bathroom and was pouring himself a shot of Jameson.

William was quick to respond with, "God might work in mysterious ways, but he definitely exists, my friend. Life is all about doing the best you can with the hand you're dealt."

John rolled his eyes in disgust. "You're one of those people, aren't you?" In his best mocking voice, John said, "When life gives you lemons, make lemonade." He pounded his shot then added, "Bullshit, if ya ask me."

William chuckled at his comments.

"Looks like we have quite the pessimist here, huh?"

"Nope. Just a realist. There's no such thing as *God's master plan*… or *things happen for a reason*. It's all just a bunch of shit! Pure and simple, my friend, life sucks!"

Both Kevin and Julie shot John a stern glare. William, on the other hand, seemed amused by John's negativity. He took a sip of his Coke then focused in on John's wedding ring.

"Geez, your wife must be a saint to put up with your pessimism… I mean, realism."

William chuckled in the direction of Kevin and Julie, but their faces braced for John's reaction.

"Hey buddy! I'm sorry about your cancer, but don't come in here and lecture me about my attitude on life! And don't ever, EVER mention my wife again!"

He poured and pounded another shot, angrily slammed it down, then headed for the front door.

"John… wait…" Kevin called after him. But it was too late, John had stormed out the door.

"Shit," Kevin muttered, lowering his head.

He then looked up at Julie, and without saying a word, she gave him a nod. She knew he needed to go after his brother. Kevin tossed down the white bar rag and made his way towards the door. William sat there, confused as to what just went on.

"I was only joking…"

Julie turned her attention from the door to William.

"It's not your fault," she reassured him. "It's not your fault at all."

Moments later, Kevin re-entered the Wild Irish Rose—without John.

"He wouldn't let me drive him home. He jumped into a cab instead."

Julie's heart was breaking for him. Like so many times, she fought the urge to wrap her arms around him. Instead, she simply placed her soft hand on his, letting him know she was there if he needed her. When she felt his hand trembling, she squeezed even harder.

"He's in so much pain, Julie… and I have no idea how to help him."

The wrinkles on William's face formed a sad and sympathetic look as he overheard Kevin's comments. Quietly, William tossed some money onto the bar, grabbed his cane, and discretely disappeared into the Chicago night.

John fell into the backseat of the cab, and as it pulled away from the Wild Irish Rose, he angrily clenched his fists. There was a part of him that wanted to scream at the top of his lungs and punch out the windows of the cab. Fortunately, the better part of him didn't allow this to happen.

For John, the better part of him lied within his front pocket. As the cab sped off, he reached his hand in and pulled out a photograph. It was the Polaroid that Kristen had made him take of the three of them. His shaking hands did their best to smooth out the crinkled photo, and as he stared at it, his fists slowly unclenched. His anger was replaced by a sad and empty feeling in the pit of his stomach.

There was only one way John knew how to fill that emptiness. Leaning slightly forward, he removed the flask from his back pocket. Before taking a swig, he returned the photo to his front pocket. It was as if he didn't want his girls to see him like this.

In one fluid motion, he twisted off the cap and threw the flask up to his lips. He needed to taste that sweet burn. He needed his Irish whiskey to work its magic yet again. There would be no magic, however… no sweet burn. In his haste, he had forgotten to refill his flask while at the Wild Irish Rose.

"Just my fuckin' luck," he muttered to himself.

"What was that?" asked the cab driver.

"I said, can you stop at a liquor store somewhere?"

When John's alcohol supply was replenished, he made sure to take a few long pulls from the bottle before getting into the cab. With his bottle of Jameson tucked back into its brown bag and sitting on his lap, a sense of calmness fell over him. For now, the anger and sadness had dissipated, and the only thing he was feeling was pure exhaustion. So much so, that before he knew it, his head slumped forward and his eyes closed shut. Like always, his slumber was short-lived.

"Hello? Mister? Hello?"

It took a second for John to gather his bearings and realize he was still in the cab.

"This is your home, right?" asked the driver.

John nodded then reached in his pocket and tossed the man some money. He tightly clutched his bag of alcohol then stumbled his way to his front door.

Before he entered, the cabbie's words still echoed in his head. *"This is your home, right?"*

Although he had nodded to the driver, John knew this statement was far from the truth. He knew this place had stopped being a home a long time ago. To John, it was just a house. A cold, lonely, and empty house.

As usual, he didn't bother turning on the light. He'd become accustomed to the darkness, and he staggered his way towards the couch. He knew falling back asleep would not come easy, so he hunkered down with his whiskey and prepared for a long night of tossing and turning.

He placed the whiskey on the floor in front of him and then shoved the flask under his pillow. When that was accomplished, he began digging his hand around in the couch cushions until he found what he was looking for. It was a bottle of sleeping pills. He tossed a couple in his mouth, swallowed hard, then fell back onto the pillow.

Reaching to the floor, John grabbed the blanket and did his best to throw it over himself. Like always, it was twisted and bunched up. And like always, John didn't have the patience to properly straighten it out. So, with the blanket half on him, he burrowed his face into the back of the couch and let out a long exhale. John was never a praying man, but as he lay there drunk and exhausted, he prayed for just one solid, good night's sleep. One that didn't involve visions or dreams of his girls.

On that night, his prayers were answered. There were no visions of Hannah learning how to ride her bike, and there were no dreams of the fog-covered playground—no empty swings swinging back to him.

But to prove that God had a sick sense of humor, those dreams and visions of his girls were replaced with flashbacks of the O'Neils' house.

Earlier that night, when John was standing in line at the liquor store, his eyes quickly glossed over some posters that hung beneath the counter. His attention was more focused on purchasing his alcohol rather than examining the posters. But now, as he attempted to close his eyes on the couch, details of one of the posters began to crystalize in his head.

It was an advertisement for an upcoming local fair. What really resonated with John was what was written at the bottom of the poster:

Back by popular demand – Demolition Derby!

Those last two words were all it took to bring him back to the O'Neils' house. John was eight, and like before, he and Kevin sat on their bedroom floor. But unlike his last flashback, they weren't looking at their baseball cards. This time there were dozens of Matchbox cars scattered about. One at a time, they chose a car and added it to their pile. When all of the cars were equally divided up, both boys eagerly smiled in anticipation of their new favorite game: Matchbox Demolition Derby!

The derby consisted of them strategically picking one of their cars and then proceeding to smash them into each other. When one car flipped over on its hood, it would officially be eliminated from the competition. The process went on until all the cars from one team were completely destroyed.

Most of the smiles and laughter came from Kevin. He didn't really care if his cars won or lost, he just loved playing the fun new game John invented. Even though John was also laughing and enjoying himself, he was dead-set on winning. On that particular night, however, a winner was never crowned. Apparently, the boys' excited laughter was a little too loud.

About halfway through the Demolition Derby, the bedroom door swung open, and there, standing in the doorway was Mr. O'Neil. With a can of Old Milwaukee in his left hand, and his ash-filled cigarette dangling from his mouth, he glared down at the boys and their cars.

"Is this how we treat the stupid toys I buy you? Huh?"

The boys didn't say a word.

"I asked you a God damn question! Is this how we treat toys?"

All the boys could manage was a slight shake of their heads.

"Whose bright idea was this anyway? I bet it was yours, wasn't it?" he asked in John's direction.

John was too scared to utter a word. Kevin could see John's hands trembling—his entire body trembling.

"I asked you a question!" he yelled louder, taking a step closer to John.

Kevin sprung to his feet and blurted out, "It was both of our ideas, Mr. O'Neil."

"I wasn't talking to you, ya little shit," he said, grabbing Kevin's arm.

Just then, Mrs. O'Neil's voice entered from behind.

"Richard, the boys were just having fun, that's all."

Mr. O'Neil released Kevin's arm and straightened up. Slowly, he turned around and faced his wife.

"Smashing things is fun?" he asked as smoke bellowed from his mouth. His angry, annoyed tone switched to one of amusement. "Well then, maybe I should get in on the fun."

With his free hand, Mr. O'Neil reached over and snatched a small mirror off Kevin's dresser. Imprinted on the top of the mirror was the Chicago Cubs logo.

"Richard, no!" she exclaimed, stepping towards him.

It was too late. In one quick, forceful motion, he had smashed the mirror onto the dresser. Glass shards flew across the room, and John remembered looking over at his brother. Kevin didn't even try to fight back his emotion as tears flowed down his tiny cheeks. The more he cried, and the louder Mrs. O'Neil yelled at her husband, the more amused Mr. O'Neil seemed to get.

"Still think it's fun to smash things?" he smiled at his wife. "Let's go have some fun with *your* stuff."

She tried her best to prevent him, but his strength was no match for her. He pushed past her, and the next thing the boys knew, there were glasses and plates being smashed in the kitchen.

When the yelling, screaming, and the breaking of glass finally faded from John's flashback, he reached over and popped two more sleeping pills. He followed it up with one long, steady pull from his Irish whiskey.

When he woke up the next morning, his head was on the opposite side of the couch, and his blanket lay in a ball across the floor. His mind and body were exhausted. He did his best to straighten out his back, but it felt like a ton of bricks had been dumped on him.

Despite the curtains being closed, the thin white fabric still allowed plenty of sunlight into the room. John hated the daytime because it forced him to see everything he tried so hard to forget. Like the tan-colored recliner that Kristen used to curl up in and watch her ridiculous Lifetime movies. Or the end table next to the recliner, where she'd set her mug of hot tea. Ironically, she always made sure her tea was piping hot, but she never drank it until it was lukewarm at best. John lost track the amount of times he made fun of her for that.

Off to the side was Hannah's bright pink Hello Kitty beanbag chair. They bought it on one of her birthdays, and it was her go-to spot to watch cartoons and read. It was only a couple of years old but was well-soiled with juice and food stains. As John fixated on it, he could still see Goldfish crumbs strewn about.

In the far corner of the room sat the old-fashioned record player that Kristen had purchased. The lid was closed, which had protected it from the year-long gathering of dust. John knew he needed to stop looking around. With each new item he spotted, a wave of memories came flooding back. Each one was like a dagger cutting him deeper and deeper.

What he really needed was a drink, but before he could reach down for his bottle, something caught his eye. On the top of the TV cabinet was Kristen's Polaroid camera. John knew how much she loved that silly, old, outdated camera. Instead of reaching for the bottle, John's hand reached into his pocket and pulled out the Polaroid of the three of them.

10

The next thing John knew, he had once again found himself sitting on the futon in front of the therapist.

"The last time you were here, you mentioned you were having nightmares. How's that been going?" she asked.

John still wasn't ready to get into anything serious, so he turned to his sarcasm to delay the inevitable.

"Actually, Doc, if you were listening the other day, I said I was having daymares, not nightmares."

He looked up at her to see if she shared in his humor. She didn't. Well, if she did, she didn't show it. He wasn't even sure if she heard him. She was sitting back, fiddling with one of her many dreamcatchers. John was tempted to make a dreamcatcher versus daymare-catcher joke, but he held off. He knew there was a reason for him being there, and it certainly wasn't to just be a sarcastic prick. He settled into the futon and addressed her question.

"Between the dreams, and the nightmares, and the flashbacks, they're all getting worse."

She placed the dreamcatcher down by her side then picked up her yin and yang water bottle and took a long, slow, yet fulfilling sip. She carefully placed the bottle onto the floor then refocused her attention back to John.

"Talk to me about these flashbacks."

He shrugged. "They were just from a long, long time ago."

"Your childhood?" she asked.

He let out a little chuckle. He knew most people's childhood was filled with innocence and joy, and quite frankly, the best time of their lives. He was not one of those people.

"Pfft. You mean my lack of a childhood?"

"Would you like to talk about that?"

"No, I'm good. Besides, I'm sure my big-mouth brother filled you in already."

What John really wanted to do was reach into his pocket and pull out his flask. She carefully watched as he squirmed and fidgeted on the futon. She focused on the fingers of his right hand. They were nervously tapping and grasping at his front pants' pocket. The top of his silver flask stuck out just enough for her to notice. Behind his sunglasses, he could see exactly what she was looking at.

Immediately, John stood up to walk around. As soon as his back was turned from her, he shoved the flask deeper into his pocket. He knew, however, concealing it was pointless. She didn't need to see his flask to know he was a drunk. He was sure he smelled like a brewery, and considering he couldn't remember his last shower, he assumed he smelled like other things as well.

His sunglasses might have covered up his bloodshot eyes, but there was nothing to cover up the rest of him. Although he always tried his best to never look into a mirror, he could only imagine what his appearance looked like to others. If the outside was anything like how he felt like on the inside, he knew he looked like an exhausted, disheveled, empty piece of shit.

He made his way to the back of the room where a new item caught his eye. On a small table sat a brightly lit fish tank. Multi-colored stones lined the bottom of the tank. There were plastic castles and caves placed about the stones. The fish tank had all the bells and whistles—everything except fish.

John assumed the next time he was there (if there was a next time), there would probably be a bunch of guppies or goldfish darting around… or whatever type of fish a hippy new-age shrink would have.

Her voice pulled John out of his thought. "It must have been very hard on you to get passed on from one foster family to another? The chaos… the disconnect…"

John crossed his fingers in hopes of that being the end of her sentence. But it wasn't.

"… the abuse," she finished.

John hated that word. It made him feel like such a pathetic little victim. He turned from the tank and looked over at her.

"Sorry, Doc, but I'm not taking your bait. You're not gonna get me to talk about my shitty childhood."

She didn't need his sunglasses off to see the pain in his eyes. It was the same pain she had seen when he first sat in front of her years ago. She knew he wasn't ready to open up back then, but she felt he was very close now.

"Are you sure you don't want to talk about this *shitty* childhood?" she asked, putting air quotes around shitty.

"Yea, I'm pretty sure," he nodded confidently. "Besides, all those stupid families were just the effect—not the cause."

A curious look fell over her face.

"Our biological parents were the *real* cause."

The details of their abandonment were unknown by the therapist and unknown to the boys as well. All John knew was his real parents didn't want him, and they gave the boys up to the State when he was three. He and Kevin were much too young to remember details of that time, and neither of them even remembered the first foster family they were sent to.

John had a faint recollection of the second family – the Hawkins. The boys were there for two years, and although their recollection was hazy, they both remembered they liked it there. Mr. Hawkins was a huge Cubs fan, and John credited him for getting them into baseball. He bought the boys their first gloves and bats and would spend every evening playing catch with them after dinner. Mrs. Hawkins made the best mac & cheese and was known for her Saturday night root beer floats.

Those were probably the only two years of their childhood that John considered good. Actually, it was better than good, it was happy, fun, and most of all, peaceful. But like all good things, it came to a grinding halt when the Hawkins got a divorce. It came out of the blue and was a complete shock to the boys. Neither of them even remembered the Hawkins arguing. There were no loud fights or upturned furniture or any broken glass. And there were certainly no black eyes or broken arms. All of that stuff would be reserved for their third and final foster family - the O'Neils.

"Yup, our real parents are the true cause. If it wasn't for them ditching us then none of the other shit woulda happened!"

The therapist's eyes fell to the floor for a moment. It was as if she was having her own breakthrough. She had always just assumed John's anger stemmed from the abuse suffered at the hands of Richard O'Neil. So the fact that John blamed a set of parents whom he'd never met, seemed to surprise her a bit.

Slowly, she raised her eyes back up to him and said, "I see. So you believe that your biological parents are to blame for everything that's gone bad in your life?"

"Yup!" he said confidently.

"Your chaotic childhood?" she asked.

"Them," he answered equally confident.

"The abuse at the O'Neils'?"

"Them," he stated again.

"This whole pessimistic attitude you have on life?"

"Them!" His answers were becoming more and more emphatic. "And by the way, Doc, the word is realistic, not pessimistic."

John smirked at his wit, but she just sat there expressionless as she prepared her final question.

"How about the accident?"

Instantly, his smirk disappeared. A giant lump filled his throat, and a sick and empty feeling entered his stomach. This time, it was John's turn to let his eyes fall to the floor.

Without making eye contact with her, John stood up and quietly said, "No, that one's on me."

He then turned and walked out of her office. The therapist remained seated and still. When she was sure he wouldn't be returning, she climbed out of her chair. She took the two dreamcatchers she was working on and hung them in the window.

She then made her way over and lit a sage stick. After three long exhales, a peaceful smile formed on her lips. Although the session ended abruptly, she was confident that she was making progress with John, and she was even more confident that he would return again when he was ready.

John's feet barely hit the sidewalk, and he had already twisted off the cap of his flask. He took a long swig from it, but the satisfaction was minimal at best. He knew there wasn't enough whiskey in the flask, or the world for that matter, to calm his nerves from what just went down.

Why the hell would I pay someone, only to be tortured like this, he thought? He hated that she was digging up all those old emotions and feelings.

So, as he walked down the sidewalk, he vowed to never return to her office again.

It was the middle of the day, and John knew he couldn't go back to his house. He preferred to only do that when it was dark. Sadly though, he also knew all the darkness in the world couldn't prevent him from thinking of his girls.

Due to him storming out of the Wild Irish Rose and causing a scene the night before, he thought it best not to show his face there. With no destination in mind, John spent the afternoon just walking the streets of Chicago. He made quick work of his whiskey, making a mental note that he needed to buy a backup emergency flask.

Eventually, John found himself standing in front of a large stone church. He'd never been to church in his life, and he certainly wasn't going to start now. His feet were aching, for this was the most he had walked in months. He decided to take a little rest underneath one of the huge elm trees in the courtyard behind the church. The pavers leading to the courtyard were irregular, causing an already intoxicated John to mind his step even more. Tufts of soft moss hide the faults in the stone, which were created from years of wear.

The shade from the overarching trees and the quiet hum from the birds lent to a peaceful feeling. As John stretched out his body under the elm, he was surprised that a church in the middle of the city could actually be this quiet and peaceful.

As he lay there, he recalled the only time being in a church was for his wedding. Kristen wasn't much of a church goer either, but seeing as her parents paid for the wedding, they insisted on a *proper* church service.

Even as a kid, John and Kevin never attended church, at least not that he could remember. As he settled himself against the elm, he let out a laugh. He pictured Mr. O'Neil in church, sitting in the pew with his cigarette dangling and a beer in hand. John then pictured what it would be like if Mr. O'Neil got splashed by holy water. His mind went directly to the Wicked Witch on the Wizard of Oz. All he could hear was Mr. O'Neil screaming, *"I'm melting… I'm melting."*

Surprisingly, the rough bark against the back of his head along with the hard ground beneath him, felt more comfortable than his couch at home. As John closed his eyes, he continued to laugh at his make-believe scenarios. Before he knew it, he was out cold.

He fell asleep laughing at his silly scenarios of Mr. O'Neil, but the dream that followed was far from a laughing matter. Of course, it was less of a dream and more of a nightmare. It also revolved around Mr. O'Neil and took place fifteen years earlier. It was the final time John and Kevin would see the O'Neils ever again. That day had always been one of John's most repressed memories, and he never allowed his mind to replay it, and he certainly never talked about it—ever.

Subconsciously, John must have known he was dreaming, and he was able to force himself awake before the painful climax. He even let out a tiny scream as he woke up. Quickly, he gazed around to see if anyone was watching him. Luckily, he was the only one in the courtyard. John pulled himself up and continued walking.

It wasn't long before his feet took him to a familiar location—the Wrigley Field area. The Cubs were out of town, so the streets around the park were quieter than normal. The next thing he knew, his feet had taken him into one of their favorite bars – Murphy's Bleachers.

The last time they were there was nearly 15 months ago, and was the night Kevin revealed his big business venture. As John sat there now, drinking his cold draft beer, he wished to God he would have turned down Kevin's big idea. If so, maybe the nightmare of what transpired would have never happened.

11

Meanwhile, it was business as usual at the Wild Irish Rose. The stools around the bar were filled with regulars, and Julie was doing her best to keep the drinks and the laughter flowing. Julie was a huge movie buff and had become known for her imitations of certain scenes. From Uma Thurman in Pulp Fiction to Julia Roberts in Pretty Woman, she nailed the dialogue and voices perfectly. She even did a Stallone imitation from Rocky. On that night, she was taking requests.

"Marlon Brando – *The Godfather,*" yelled a middle-aged man, drinking a gin and tonic.

"Ohhh, that's a good one," the others said in unison.

This caused Kevin to curiously raise his head from the invoices he was working on at the end of the bar. He knew that Julie was more of an 80's and 90's girl; in particular, comedies and rom-coms. There was no way she had even seen *The Godfather*, never mind be able to imitate the great Brando.

Kevin laughed and pointed out, "You guys might wanna choose one that's more in her wheelhouse. Maybe *When Harry Met Sally* or some silly Adam Sandler flick."

Julie seemed surprised at his lack of confidence in her, offended even.

"Why Kevin Mathews, do you doubt my talents?"

The entire row of regulars turned their heads to see Kevin's response.

"No, I just doubt you've ever seen that movie. Not to mention, I remember you telling me how much you hated gangster flicks."

In unison, all heads turned back to Julie.

"Care to wager?" she said.

Again, all heads turned back to Kevin.

"What do you have in mind?" he smiled.

She pondered a second then giggled.

"If I nail it, then you let me choose the music in here for the next two weeks."

For most people, this wouldn't be that big of a deal, but Kevin knew Julie's affinity for boy bands and girl bands—the cheesier the better.

"And if *I* win?" he asked.

"Anything you want."

Kevin had no idea what he would choose if he won, but at that point, it didn't really matter. The group of regulars sat on the edge of their stools, eagerly awaiting his reply.

"Deal!" he finally said.

The small crowd cheered then turned their attention back to Julie. Unbeknownst to anyone in the bar, the wind outside had picked up quite a bit.

"Wait," Kevin interrupted. "Who's gonna be the judge whether you nailed it or not?"

"Pshhh, these guys, of course," she said, pointing to the collection of regulars up at the bar.

"Totally not fair! They're gonna be on your side because you're a girl… and you're prettier than I am," he joked.

"You got that right!" one of them yelled out.

"Fine," Julie replied. "I tell ya what, *you* can be the judge, Kevin. If you honestly think I did a shitty job then you win… no questions asked."

This is getting better and better, he thought as he nodded his approval. As soon as Kevin saw Julie ball up two napkins and shove them in her cheeks, he knew he was in for it.

Needless to say, Julie absolutely nailed the performance. Hoots, hollers, and whistling came from the crowd, and even Kevin gave her a standing ovation. For Julie, it wasn't really about winning the silly bet, it was about putting a smile on Kevin's face. She knew how much stress he was under with his brother, especially lately.

Next, Julie made an equally dramatic production of reaching into her bag and pulling out a few CDs. Kevin shook his head at her, continuing to smile as he returned to his invoices. No sooner did he sit down, did the (obnoxious) sound of NSync blare through the bar. The small group of regulars looked at each other in shock by the musical choice.

"See, this is what ya get," Kevin announced in their direction. "That'll teach you guys to cheer for her."

Ignoring his comment, Julie proudly bared her teeth and began dancing behind the bar. Kevin sat—officially smitten. She really did have it all. She continued dancing, all the while refilling everyone's drinks. Julie's dance moves were briefly interrupted by the opening of the front door.

"William!" she yelled. "You're just in time for our dance party."

All eyes turned to the old man. He wore a smile on his wrinkled face, but behind his eyes lied a more serious and somber look. With his cane in his hand, he made his way up to the bar. Two of the regulars tossed down some money then stood up.

"See, Julie," exclaimed Kevin. "Your music is already scaring off our customers. We're going to have no one here by the end of the week."

She shrugged and replied, "That'll teach ya to bet against me."

By now, William had settled into one of the vacated stools next to Kevin.

"Coke with extra ice?" Julie asked.

"Yes, please."

She filled a tall glass of ice with Coke then danced her way over and placed it in front of William. Kevin looked up from the invoices and noticed William anxiously scanning the bar.

"Don't worry, my brother isn't here."

William turned his head back towards Kevin and quickly blurted out what had been on his mind for the past twenty-four hours.

"I am so, so sorry for my comments last night. I…"

"Seriously, William, it's okay. You didn't say or do anything wrong. Like I said, John just has a lot on his mind, that's all."

For the moment, Kevin's reassurance seemed to lighten William's worry a little bit. His mood lightened even more when Julie decided to give him an encore performance of her Brando imitation.

"Bravo, bravo," William said, clapping his hands. "She's a keeper! Don't let this one get away," he said and smiled in Kevin's direction.

Both Kevin and Julie blushed at his comment. Kevin more so. It didn't take long for the heaviness and worry to leave both Kevin and William. Julie was truly the master of this. She definitely had the gift of gab, and more importantly, the gift and ability to take people's minds off their problems. Her gift was about to be put to the test. Everything came to a grinding halt, and the light, happy air of the room was sucked out upon the entrance of John.

"Shit," Julie cursed under her breath.

She just wanted Kevin to have one stress-free night—one John-free night. Kevin's stress level immediately reached a ten as he watched John help himself to a Captain and Coke.

John knew everyone's eyes were on him, but at that point, he didn't really give a care. With his drink in his hand, he headed for an empty stool on the opposite end from his brother. Julie was determined not to let him bring down the positive vibe she had created. She gave the top of the bar a quick wipe-down then approached William.

"So William, did I hear you correctly the other night? Did you say you're originally from Maine?"

"Yes, ma'am. Born and raised. Although that was a lifetime ago."

"I bet it's beautiful there. Did you live on the coast?" she asked.

"Directly on the coast," he winked. "The magical island of Applewood is directly on the Atlantic."

"Magical island, huh?" she asked more than a little curious.

"It is if you believe in the old Native American legend."

Julie moved closer and waited for William to continue. When he didn't, she pushed the issue.

"Well? I'm listening."

A hearty chuckle bellowed from his lips.

"Oh, you really don't want to hear me ramble on about some old Maine folklore. Besides," he quietly said, "I think I did enough rambling last night."

This time, it was Kevin who was determined to not let John's presence bring the vibe down.

"I'd spill it if I were you, William. Julie is a sucker for legends and folklore. As a matter of fact, her favorite movies are *The Dark Crystal*, the *Neverending Story*…oh, and *Legend* with Tom Cruise."

Julie's face turned red. It wasn't so much from the embarrassment of her love for these cheesy fantasy movies; it was more from her being impressed that Kevin remembered this obscure fact about her. She had only randomly mentioned this once, and it was way back in the first week she started working there. Even more than impressed, her heart was deeply touched.

"Come on, William," she urged. "We all wanna hear it."

She motioned to the remaining handful of regulars, and they all nodded in agreement. William gazed at their eager eyes, took a long, steady sip of Coke, and then prepared to tell his tale.

"As you all know, long before the English settlers came to America, the Native Americans inhabited much of the country… Maine was no exception. The land where Applewood now stands was once occupied by the Abenaki tribe.

"To the Abenakis, their ultimate Creator was known as the Great Spirit, but they also found solace in praying to multiple spirits. Animals were at the top of that list, as were the ocean, the sun, the moon, and the stars. There was one star in particular that hung high above their land. This was no ordinary star, mind you, but the brightest one in the sky. The Abenakis named the star Medillia, and they believed she gave direction to the lost."

"Pffft, it's called the North Star," John yelled, rudely interrupting.

William turned his attention to John and said, "No, son. You see, the North Star was used as a compass to those who were physically lost. Medillia was used to give direction to those who were more… emotionally lost."

John rolled his eyes and took another sip of his drink then sarcastically motioned for William to continue. Hesitantly, William turned back to the others and continued on.

"To the small Abenaki tribe, the radiance and glow of Medillia not only provided hope to the downhearted, but she provided the light needed for them to find their way again… their way back home."

When William said the word *home*, he patted his fist to his heart.

"Corny!" John yelled through his hand-megaphone.

Before he could say another sarcastic comment, Julie shot him a stern, scolding glare; stern enough to shut him up for the moment. Her glare switched into a warm, apologetic smile as she turned back to William.

"Go on," she winked.

He adjusted his hat then picked up where he left off.

"As the years passed, however, Medillia slowly started to lose her shine. The same brilliant shine that had guided so many lost souls was slowly fading out."

"How come?" Julie asked, refilling his Coke.

"Ironically, Medillia herself was losing hope. And as legend has it, on one fateful night, with all hope lost, Medillia plunged from the night sky and crashed just off of the coast of Applewood."

John couldn't help himself as he called out, "Oooooooo, a shooting star!"

"No, son, more like a fallen star. But as Medillia crashed into the rocks of Applewood, an explosion of the brightest and most beautiful stardust was emitted. The entire sky was lit up for a second… then went black. And as the legend goes, for the next nineteen sunrises, remnants of her stardust continued to fall onto the small Maine island. And it is said, during that brief moment in time, Applewood was turned into a magical place. This occurrence became known as Medillia's Lament."

Julie's elbows rested on the bar with her head perched in her hands. She was completely captivated with William's tale.

"What exactly do you mean by magical place?" she asked.

It was as if he was waiting for Julie to ask that. A smile crept onto his face, and with a twinkle in his eye, he leaned closer to her.

"It becomes a place where old wounds are healed… and a place where regrets find second chances. You see, during Medillia's Lament, time becomes irrelevant. The past, present, and future all get blurred together somehow, and within those nineteen sunrises, anything is possible... anything."

Everyone at the bar seemed to be enjoying William's story; no one more than Julie. Wide-eyed and beaming from ear to ear, she placed her hand on top of William's. Kevin was also smiling but not from the story. His was directed solely at Julie. He absolutely loved her child-like innocence, especially when it came to fairy tales and silly old legends.

William leaned back on his stool and finished with, "And supposedly, throughout the years, there's been other occasions where stars have lost their shine and have not only fallen into the same rocks of Applewood, but have emitted the same magical stardust."

"I love it!" Julie said as goosebumps ran up her arms. "That was a great story, William."

The small crowd nodded in agreement. Kevin and the regulars weren't as enthralled as Julie, but they raised their drinks in appreciation for his far-fetched tale.

John joined them by raising his glass and yelling out, "A toast - to Medusa's Lament! And while we're at it, a toast to The Tooth Fairy... and Santa Claus too!"

This time it was Kevin who turned an angry glare John's way.

"Enough, John!" he shot in his brother's direction.

With everyone staring at him, John rolled his eyes in disgust, polished off the rest of his drink, then stumbled his way out of the bar. Kevin did not chase after him this time, but rather tossed down his bar towel and stormed off into the back room. Julie wanted to follow him to see if he was okay but decided to give him some space. Instead, she turned her attention back to William.

"Have you ever seen it?" she asked.

William's head was turned, still preoccupied with John's abrupt departure.

"I'm sorry, what was that, dear?" he asked turning back to her.

"Medillia's Lament. Have you ever seen it?"

"I'm afraid not," he sadly smiled. "I have to admit, though, ever since I was a kid, I find myself looking for it every night. Pathetic, I know." William's revelation caused his cheeks to flush red.

"I don't think it's pathetic at all," she said, placing her hand once again onto his. "We all need something in this world to believe in."

He gave her a fragile squeeze with his soft bony hand.

"That we do, dear… that we do."

He slowly pulled out his wallet, but before he could even open it, Julie waved him off.

"It's on the house," she smiled.

He nodded in appreciation, grabbed his cane, then made his way out. Julie made sure everyone at the bar was taken care of then headed to the back to check on Kevin.

After John stormed out of the Wild Irish Rose, he found himself just wandering up and down the streets. He was too tired to head into another bar, but he certainly wasn't ready to go back to his house either. He was drunk and exhausted, and his legs and feet ached from all the walking he did earlier.

Further up the road, he came across a small park and stumbled his way over to a wooden bench. He crossed his ankles, leaned back, and with his arms outstretched, closed his eyes. It wasn't long before sleep took hold of him, and it also wasn't long before that same reoccurring dream popped into his head.

He watched the tiny hand press against the six-pane window as the rain ran down the glass. And like always, there was that red glow off in the distance. This time, however, John heard footsteps behind him. Slow, methodical footsteps. A chill ran up his body as he felt a cold wind swirling around him. The footsteps grew closer—the wind, colder. Then, just like that, everything was gone. The tiny hand, the window, the bright red glow—gone.

John's eyes startled open just in time to feel his Cubs hat being blown off his head. The swirling, brisk wind was not just in his dream. Slightly annoyed, he bent down and grabbed his hat. Just as he placed it back on his head, the wind subsided, and the faint sound of footsteps faded in.

John turned around and peered up the street. It was dark and all he could make out was the silhouette of what appeared to be a man. It wasn't until the man walked under the streetlight that John finally recognized him. It was William.

Almost immediately, John felt a twinge of guilt coursing through his veins. He felt like shit for how he treated this poor man. It was bad enough William was fighting a horrible disease, he certainly didn't need to be bombarded with John's callous sarcasm.

"Hey," he yelled in his direction.

William's unhurried stride slowed to a halt. Turning towards the voice, he strained his eyes to see who it was. It wasn't until John's second comment that William figured it out completely.

"I didn't mean to be such a jerk earlier. No offense."

William walked over to the bench, making sure he was face to face with John before replying.

"No offense taken, my friend. And I do believe I also owe you an apology… for my comments last night. I didn't…"

"It's okay," John quietly said, and then turned back towards the park.

Unsure what to say, William stood a moment before deciding to move along and head home. He only made it a couple of steps when John's voice cut through the darkness.

"You were right though… about my wife."

Without turning around, William continued to listen.

"She was a saint to put up with me. She was one of the best people I've ever met."

The fact that he referred to her in the past tense, led William to assume the worst. William made his way over and sat on the bench next to John. He didn't say a word. He just listened.

"Kristen had these eyes... these beautifully green and kind eyes. It was like she could make everything better just by the way she looked at you. I know that sounds stupid, but..."

"I don't think it sounds stupid. Not at all actually. I knew a girl with eyes just like that... once upon a time. Yup, she was the love of my life."

John didn't need to look over at William to know his face was beaming.

"Your wife?" asked John.

"Nooo," William chuckled. "I've actually never been married before."

"Really? Then who was she?"

"I met her back in school. She was so smart, and beautiful, and..."

"Wait," John interrupted, turning towards William. "You met her in school? That must have been like..."

"Like forty-five years ago. What can I say," he smiled. "She stole my heart."

John couldn't help but smile back as he asked, "So how long did you guys date?"

Slightly embarrassed, William answered, "Oh, we never dated."

John leaned his head back, letting out a loud laugh. Finally, he calmed himself and offered up an apology. "I'm sorry, William. I didn't mean to laugh so hard."

"Nope, I deserve it. Pathetic, I know. But I'll tell ya what, my friend, in my heart I know we could have been perfect together. To this day, I've never seen a smile like hers." William paused a second then continued. "If only I had asked her out... it would have completely changed my life."

"So why didn't you?"

"I was young... and way too shy. One of the problems with youth is we never think in terms of the moment. We just figure we'll have the rest of our lives to get that moment back."

Surprisingly, William's comment resonated deeply with John. It eerily reminded him of one of his favorite lines from his beloved *Field of Dreams*.

"Don't get me wrong, son," William continued, "I'm not complaining. I've lived a good life, and for the most part, I've smelled the roses along the way. No regrets."

As both men stared off into the Chicago sky, John felt a sense of sadness. He knew he couldn't say the same, for his life was filled with regrets. They sat staring at the sky for a little while longer. Finally, William broke the silence.

"Well, I suppose I should get going," he said as he grabbed his cane and struggled to climb off the bench. William glanced down at John and asked, "Are you going to be okay? Do you need me to call you a cab?"

"Nah. I'm fine... but thanks."

Although he didn't come out and say it, John was not only thanking William for his concern, but also for the brief chat and his kindness. John felt sympathy for the old man. It was the first time in a long, long time he'd felt sympathy for someone other than himself. Soon after William's footsteps faded into the night, John finally decided to head home.

12

Like clockwork, the very next night, William found himself back at the Wild Irish Rose. Julie made sure his Coke with extra ice was constantly topped off, and she also made sure to point out just how much she loved his story of Medillia's Lament.

Familiar faces filled most of the stools around the bar, but John's usual seat remained empty. When William entered the bar the previous night, he was a bit nervous about John being there. But now, twenty-four hours later, he was disappointed at John's absence. For a brief moment on the park bench, he saw a softer side of John. He knew there was more where that came from and hoped he would again make an appearance at the bar.

About an hour in, William's wish came true; John entered the front door. He wasn't as drunk as the night before, but he certainly had a good buzz going on. Ignoring the usual disapproving stares, he walked through the middle of the room. His face perked up when he saw William sitting up at the bar. William's face also perked up when he heard John's booming voice from behind.

"Well lookie here! It's my old buddy, William." John patted him on the back and sat next to him. "Looks like you're becoming quite the regular, huh?"

"I told you," smiled William, "there's just something about this place that I like."

"It's probably this beautifully handcrafted bar," John proudly said, running his hand across it.

William returned John's pat on the back and commented, "You are very talented, my friend. I don't have much of a yard, but if I did, I'd love to hire you to build me a gazebo."

"A gazebo?"

"We used to have one in our backyard in Maine. Whether it was reading a good book or doing a little writing, I used to love to relax in it… especially on a warm summer's day. Yup, if I had a big enough yard here, I'd definitely hire you to build it for me. You have quite the skill set, my friend."

John chuckled. "Unfortunately, carpentry is my only skill set. Well, that and being an alcoholic asshole. Right, Julie?"

Julie didn't dignify him with a response. She just continued washing the glasses.

"Speaking of alcohol, how about a drink, Jules?"

Without saying a word, Julie wiped her hands on the towel then filled a glass with ice.

John threw a snarky smile William's way. "I have her trained well, huh?"

No sooner did he finish his sentence, Julie placed a tall glass of ice water in front of him, and with an equally snarky smile, she tossed a lemon wedge in it. Normally, John would have snapped at her, but he held his tongue and turned his attention back to William.

"Ya know what, William, I was thinking about you today."

"Good thoughts, I hope?"

"I was actually thinking about what you said last night… about that girl of your dreams."

William acknowledged him with a polite smile.

"You said if you would have asked her out it would have completely changed your life."

"Well, if she would have said yes, that is," he winked.

"So you really think if you were with her your life woulda been that different?"

"I do," he matter-of-factly stated.

"As in you wouldn't have gotten cancer?"

William paused then answered, "No, son, I'm not that naïve. Cancer can find you whether your true love is by your side or not. But I will say this; my life would have definitely been happier… more complete."

John took a sip of the water, and his face contorted as if he was drinking a glass of poison. As he pushed it away, William continued on the subject.

"It's kind of silly, but I sometimes find myself creating these scenarios… scenarios of what our life would have been like together."

John was quick to point out, "Not to rain on your parade, but maybe the real thing wouldn't have lived up to your expectations, ya know? Hell, maybe things would have turned out worse for you. In my experience, there's always a greater chance that things can get worse rather than better. The happier you are, the more you have to lose - that's my philosophy."

"Ahh, ever the pessimist," William smiled then carefully contemplated John's words. He took the last sip of his Coke then said, "Perhaps you're right, my friend, but I tell you what, I'd love the chance to find out. How about we just leave it at that?"

John nodded in agreement. "Fair enough." He looked over at William's empty glass and asked, "You sure you don't want something stronger?"

"No thank you, son. I think I should be heading home."

William placed some money on the bar then did his best to slide off the stool. His legs shook beneath him and John placed his hand on William's back to steady him. With his other hand, he handed him his cane. When he was sure William was more balanced, he removed his hand. William appreciated John's assistance, but the thought of needing help standing up ate away at him. It wasn't that long ago he was running 5K races, and the use of a cane was the furthest from his mind. William had made a promise to himself that not only would he beat cancer, but he would once again be out running in the streets of Chicago. But now, as he slowly hobbled his way to the front door, he knew he was a shell of the man he intended to be.

As John watched William open and exit the large oak door, he too felt the same way. He was also a shell of the man he used to be, but for different reasons. John turned back around and knew if he wanted a drink, he'd need to go make it himself.

Kevin and Julie stood, talking directly in front of the bottle of Jameson. John was sure they did this on purpose. Rather than make another one of his famous scenes, John decided to take William's lead and simply leave. Of course, in full John-style, he couldn't leave without at least one parting shot.

He tossed down a five and loudly and obnoxiously exclaimed, "Thanks for the water. It was fuckin' delicious."

By the time John exited the bar, he noticed William had only gotten about ten feet down the sidewalk.

"Hey William, wanna share a cab with me?"

Without turning his head, he yelled back, "No thank you, I can walk it."

John recognized the stubborn pride in William's voice. He recognized it because he was full of the same.

"Wait up, William, I'll walk with you."

John quickly caught up with him, and the two unlikely friends headed down the sidewalk together. Sarcastic quips aside, over the past year, John had become quite accustomed to keeping to himself. On this night, however, he seemed to be in a rare, talkative mood.

"So you're originally from Maine, huh?"

"Yup, the Great State of Maine."

"Can't be that great if you've been in Chicago the last forty-five years."

"Touché," he chuckled. "Regrettably, another part of youth is we rarely appreciate where we're from. You know, the whole grass is always greener thing? Oh I love Maine, and Applewood, Applewood is an amazing place… just not when you're a teenager, I guess. I was out of the house and out of town as soon as I graduated."

"What did you do?" John asked, honestly curious.

A nostalgic smile crept over William's face. "Ah, yes, my master plan. My goals were simple, or so I thought. I wanted to travel and see as much of the country as possible… maybe even the world. And while I was in the process, I planned on writing the great American novel. And then… the best part of my plan. I was going to come back to Applewood and sweep the girl of my dreams off her feet. You know, the whole happily ever after thing?"

John allowed William's words to soak in before speaking.

"So what happened?"

"I only made it as far as Chicago before I ran out of money. I ended up taking a low-level job at the newspaper, and an even lower-level apartment. It was barely fit for humans," he winked.

John smiled along. He too remembered his first apartment. Although it was a one-bedroom shit hole, John was just so happy to be on his own. Of course, his independence didn't last long, for Kevin soon moved in with him. They had grown up sharing a bedroom, so it wasn't that big of a deal, but what was a big deal, was they were finally in control of their own lives.

William interrupted John's thoughts. "When I had enough money saved, I started taking some classes on the side. Over the years, I slowly climbed the ladder at the paper, and eventually, I became the Editor in Chief." A proud twinkle entered his eyes.

"And the great American novel?" asked John.

William shrugged and his twinkle faded a bit. "I wrote a handful of books, but they never quite turned out the way I had envisioned. I just wasn't happy with them… and obviously, neither were the fifty-two publishing companies I submitted them to."

"So you just gave up?"

Again, William shrugged. "I didn't consciously give up… I just lost my creative juices, that's all.

John didn't say another word, for he knew he was the last person to give advice about not giving up.

At the stop sign, William motioned for John to follow him left. The twinkle returned to William's eyes as he continued talking.

"I did, however, start writing again this past year. Maybe the chemo treatments triggered some sort of creative spark, I'm not really sure. What I do know, is that ideas and words have been flying out of me lately. I just need to come up with the perfect ending."

They walked the next block in silence, stopping a couple of times for William to catch his breath. John felt bad for the old man, and on multiple occasions, he was tempted to help William walk, but he didn't. John hated when Kevin had to help him out of the bar and into his house. Yes, he knew there was a big difference between being drunk and being sick, but the pride factor remained the same. As they continued walking, John thought about everything William had just shared.

"What about the girl of your dreams?" John asked out of the blue.

This time, the twinkle completely faded from William's eyes, and sadly, he answered, "I actually never saw her again."

John immediately regretted his question.

"Besides a few quick visits, I never really went back home. You see, when I left the first time, it was pretty much against my family's wishes—more so my father's. My mother didn't care so much that I wanted to be a writer, but she didn't understand why I had to leave Maine to do it."

Before continuing his story, William paused in front of a brownstone and motioned that this was his place.

"My mother was disappointed in my decision, but my father was furious. Well, maybe more embarrassed than furious."

"Embarrassed at what?" asked John.

William let out a sad chuckle then lowered himself onto his front step. John remained standing.

"Embarrassed that I wanted to be a writer. You see, Applewood is pretty much a fishing village, and my father, well, he was a fifth generation fisherman. Not only was he offended by my writing aspirations, but he couldn't for the life of him understand why I wanted to travel. He'd never been out of Applewood, never mind Maine. So, needless to say, I didn't leave on great terms." William ended with, "Oh well, it is what it is, right?"

John knew this was William's way of lightening the mood—of covering up his sadness. A part of John wanted to have a seat next to William and offer him some sort of sympathetic or positive remark. Instead, however, John's go-to pessimism kicked in.

"Yup, it is what it is, William. It's like I've been telling you, there's no master plan and no *things happen for a reason* shit! Life sucks then you die."

"I wouldn't go that far, my friend," William replied, and slowly raised himself up from the step. "Well, it's past this old man's bedtime. Thanks for the walk, son."

Without another word from either of them, they went their separate ways.

* * *

Over the next couple of days, William had become a fixture at the Wild Irish Rose. He didn't have a lot of close friends, and besides the nurses and doctors over the past year, he didn't really have a social life. The cozy atmosphere of the Wild Irish Rose suited him perfectly.

It didn't take long for Kevin, Julie, and the rest of the gang to realize what a great storyteller William was. With his Coke in front of him, he spun one yarn after another. William was as humble as they come, but secretly, he absolutely loved being the center of attention. It was a sense of importance he hadn't felt in years.

Throughout those same couple of days, John held true to his vow of not returning to, in his words, "the crazy hippy-chick shrink." It wasn't that he had anything against her, he just wasn't ready to revisit his past. Not yet.

There was no doubt that John thought she was as wacky as they come, but there was something about her; something calming, something safe. He would never admit this, but he understood why Kevin was drawn to her all those years ago. And John would also never admit this, but he was glad she had provided his brother with some peace—some closure.

During those next couple of days, John found himself hanging out with William more and more. Music, movies, and sports-wise, they had little in common, but somehow their conversations carried well into the night. Unlike the therapist, William never brought up John's past. And unlike Kevin or Julie, William was never judgmental. There was never a disapproving look or a comment regarding his drinking. Ironically, since he started hanging out with William, his drinking and obnoxious sarcasm had slightly subsided. This didn't go unnoticed with Julie.

"Do you wanna hear something crazy?" Julie whispered to Kevin.

"Besides this, you mean?" he joked, pointing to the speakers, which were playing the Spice Girls.

"I'm serious," she said, giving him a playful nudge. "Is it me or has John been drinking a little less lately? Not to mention, he's also been a little less of…"

"A miserable prick?" Kevin filled in the blank.

"Your words, not mine," she smiled. "But yea. I think it's because of William. He's like a good influence on him."

Kevin knew Julie didn't intend it, but he kind of took offense to her comment. Kevin had always been the good influence on his brother. Not to mention, he'd bent over backwards this past year to be there for him. Kevin was glad John and William were getting along so well, but he was quick to point out the reality of the situation to Julie.

"I wouldn't get your hopes up, Julie. I have a feeling things are going to get much worse… especially over the next twenty-four hours."

She gave him a puzzled look.

"Tomorrow's the day. The anniversary of the accident."

She looked over at John and then back to Kevin. Her heart broke for both brothers. Her hand found Kevin's, and with fingers intertwined, she gave it a comforting squeeze.

"We'll get through this," she whispered. "I promise."

Kevin returned the hand-squeeze and smiled at her comment. He was touched that she used the word *we'll*, but he was quick to point out this was his problem, not hers.

"Nonsense," she replied. "For months now, I've watched you be everything and everyone to your brother. You might have grown up carrying the weight of everyone's problems on your shoulders, but you need to know it's okay to share that weight." She squeezed tighter then said, "I'm not going anywhere. I'm in it for the long haul."

A feeling of warmth coursed through his body. He wasn't sure exactly what she meant, but it sounded a lot like a *more than friends* comment. If so, he was more than okay with that. So rather than ask her what exactly she meant, he simply locked his fingers tightly into hers and whispered back, "Good. I'd like that."

Another thing that was noticeable to Kevin and Julie, was William seemed to be looking weaker. It took him longer to make it from the front door to his stool, and he was relying more heavily on his cane for support.

William's deteriorating condition didn't go unnoticed with John either. He even tried to convince him to start taking a cab to and from the Wild Irish Rose, but William was still much too proud—much too stubborn for that. John made sure he was there to walk William home at night. Without completely realizing or understanding why, John had grown quite fond of the old man.

Besides that night on the park bench, not a word was said or brought up regarding John's wife. And even though he was still having dreams and flashbacks of the O'Neils, he never ever brought up his childhood to William.

Julie walked by and grabbed William's glass, preparing to get him his first refill of the young night. He looked at his watch then shook her off.

"Thanks, but no thanks, dear. I think I'm going to call it an early night. I want to try and get some writing in before I hit the sack."

This seemed to please Julie. "Working on a new book?"

He tried his best to be humble, but his excitement took hold as he leaned closer to Julie and said, "I think this will be my best work ever."

"When can I read it?"

"All in due time, dear. All in due time." He gave Julie his famous wink then carefully climbed down off the bar stool.

"Need me to hail you a cab?" John asked, already knowing the answer.

The look William shot him was exactly what John assumed.

"Fine, I guess I can call it an early night myself."

"You really don't have to walk this old man home, ya know?"

"Yea, I know," he smiled then helped William with his cane.

Julie couldn't help smiling herself as she watched this interaction.

"See?" she said, turning to Kevin. "Everything's going to work out."

He smiled back at her, but he was far less confident than he let on. As a matter of fact, there was a sick feeling beginning to grow in the pit of his stomach. He knew that tomorrow would be the true test for his brother, and worriedly, he feared the worst.

Something horrible was going to happen, he just knew it. He loved and appreciated Julie's innocent optimism, so he decided to keep his fears to himself. He would do what he always did, he would take care of his big brother—alone.

"Hey, John," Kevin yelled, "I was thinking maybe tomorrow you and I could go the Cubs game. I know a guy who can get us tickets on the cheap." Kevin held a hopeful breath that John would agree.

"Thanks, but I'm all set," John yelled back, without even turning around.

Kevin's hopeful breath released into a hopeless sigh. Before John reached the door, Kevin gave it a last-ditch effort.

"How about the batting cages then? It's been forever since…"

"I said I'm all set," John said more dismissively. He knew exactly what Kevin was trying to do, but he wanted no part of the pity party.

As the door shut behind them, Julie took note of the helpless look on Kevin's face. What really struck her to the core, was the look of utter fear that went along with it. And for the first time all night, she felt a chink in her formerly optimistic outlook concerning John.

13

In her heart, the therapist knew John would one day return to her office, but she didn't envision him to look as bad as he did. His ratty old clothes were unwashed and hung off his thinning frame. If it wasn't obvious before, it was certainly obvious now that he hadn't shaved or showered in weeks, maybe months. By the way he stumbled in and plopped himself onto her futon, it was also obvious that he was already drunk as a skunk.

With his Cubs hat pulled down over his sunglasses, he just sat there in dead silence. She also didn't say a word. For the longest time, she simply watched his body swaying back and forth and took note of his fingers nervously tapping on his leg.

On the floor in front of him sat his backpack. It was filled with bottles of alcohol he had previously purchased at the liquor store. His mission when he woke up that day was simple: drink as much as humanly possible. With that in mind, the irony of John going directly from the liquor store to his therapist wasn't lost on him.

The silence went on for ten solid minutes. What finally propelled her to speak was when John pulled out his flask, took a long pull from it, then offered her a sip.

"I find it quite funny, John, that you keep paying for sessions, yet you refuse to take it seriously."

Her comment nearly caused John to spit out his whiskey.

"Do you wanna know what I find funny, Doc? I find it funny just how many different cultures and stupid philosophies you buy into. Seriously, look at this place," he slurred, pointing around the room. "Ya got Chinese, Japanese, Indian... both Indians, as in feather in your headdress and dot on your forehead."

At this point, John climbed off the futon and headed over to her clay bowl.

"And then you have all this new-age crystal shit!" He grabbed a handful of crystals then tossed them back into the bowl. He did his best to keep his balance as he scanned the room. He focused on the tie-dye-clad teddy bear and lava lamp.

"And where did you get your degree, Doc, the University of Jerry Garcia? I think the only thing you're missing in here is a Magic 8 Ball and a Voodoo doll."

John continued to laugh at his humor as he once again plopped down onto the futon. He waited for a response from her, but she remained peacefully still and quiet. He hated the way she was looking at him. Actually, he could have handled it if she was *just* looking at him, but it went beyond that. It was as if she was looking *into* him—right into his soul. He was creeped out beyond belief and quickly attempted to escape her look with his sarcasm.

"And what the fuck is the deal with that stupid seashell necklace? Lemme guess, you got it in Hawaii from King Kamehameha? Oh wait, or did you get it in Atlantis from Aquaman?"

He continued to laugh at himself as he polished off the rest of his flask.

"Admit it, Doc, I'm too fucked up and too far gone to be saved?"

She ran her fingers over her necklace then finally spoke.

"Is that what you think?"

"Ahhh, answer a question with a question. Shrink 101, huh? Look, Doc, why don't you do us both a favor and just write me a prescription for something that'll knock me the fuck out."

Ignoring his request, she unfolded her legs and stood up. John watched as her bare feet glided over to the window. She pushed the beaded curtain aside and let the beam of sunlight hit her face. She closed her eyes and took a deep breath. It was as if she was attempting to suck in the sunbeam.

All John could do was sit there, shaking his head at her. *Where do I begin?* he thought. His mind immediately began thinking about his next sarcastic wisecrack. *Should I say something about her bare feet or maybe something about…*

"Can I ask you a question?" she asked, interrupting his train of thought.

"You always do, Doc. Shoot."

"Have you ever shared your experiences with anyone?"

"My experiences?"

"Your childhood… the O'Neils?"

"Pffft, what the fuck does that matter?"

"Have you ever told Kevin?"

"What the hell are you talking about? Kevin was there. He knows all about our shitty childhood."

"But have you ever told him how it made you *feel*… how it truly *affected* you?"

"This is pointless, Doc. I think it's time for me to be on my way."

Before he could pull himself off the futon, she hit him with a right hook.

"What about your wife? Did she know about your childhood?"

Her question staggered him enough to remain seated.

All John ever told Kristen was their parents abandoned them at a very young age and that they grew up in foster homes. That was it. He knew Kevin probably filled her in on more of the details, but he was determined to keep his dark past separate from his bright future.

She turned away from the window, allowing the beads to close behind her. John's silence confirmed what she had already suspected. Quietly, she stood there watching him slumping on the futon. He wasn't squirming or fidgeting, and even his fingers were refraining from that nervous tapping thing he did.

He was exhausted and beaten down. He was even too tired to come up with a sarcastic quip. Leaning forward, he removed his hat and ran his fingers through his long, greasy hair. He let out a shaky sigh then finally gave in.

"Today's the day… the accident."

He returned his hat to his head and awaited her response. Sympathy oozed from her eyes, and even she had to fight back a tear or two. Her heart broke for this poor soul. She knew he held a lifetime of pain, tragedy, and regret on his shoulders—maybe even more than his brother. She knew her next question would hit John even harder, and although she already knew the answer, she needed to ask it.

"Have you visited them yet… at the cemetery? Your wife and daughter?"

His fingers went from tapping to curling into a fist. Sweat began to form on his forehead as he regretfully looked down to the floor.

Without a word, she walked over to the small table, which held the teddy bear and lava lamp. She opened the drawer and pulled out a handful of rubber bands. Curiously, John watched her approach the brightly lit fish tank.

"Let's just say these elastics are your unspoken feelings… your inner demons, if you will. And let's say this fish tank represents you."

Behind his sunglasses, his eyes widened as he watched her plunge her hand deep into the tank. When her fist reached the colored pebbles at the bottom, she released the rubber bands.

"You can bury your feelings as deep as you want, but eventually…"

John watched as the elastics slowly floated to the top.

"… eventually they always come back to the surface. So the sooner you deal with this, the sooner you'll avoid, as I like to put it, *elastic overload.*"

And just like that, she headed back to her Papasan chair. She settled her body into the cushion, and John's look went from her to the tank, and then back to her.

"Umm, aren't you gonna take those out?" he hesitantly asked.

"Oh, no, it's okay. There aren't any fish in there. I just bought the tank because I like how peaceful and pretty it looks all lit up."

As she continued to happily stare over at the lit tank, she reached down and picked up her trusty water bottle, taking a long, satisfying sip.

Throughout his few sessions with her, John found himself playing a mental guessing game. He called it, *What exactly is she drinking out of her water bottle?* He was sure it was some sort of new-age healthy drink. A fancy iced Chai? A green tea? Some sort of green smoothie concoction? Maybe it was just water. Not regular water, of course. It was holy water blessed by the Dali Lama himself.

But now, as John watched the handful of rubber bands floating around the well-lit fishless fish tank, he was sure that she was drinking the same thing as him—whiskey.

Dumbfounded and a bit amused, John continued watching the rubber bands float and dance around the surface.

"You do understand the point I'm trying to make, right?" she asked. "You really need to start facing some of these issues that you've been burying all these years. I know it seems easier not to face this, but you need to start finding closure. Actually, I think you need to start coming to terms with a lot of things from your past."

John turned his attention back to her.

"Why? It's not gonna change things, will it?"

"Is that what you're hoping for… to change things?"

"Pffft, here we go again. Answering a question with a question. I told you, I hate that."

She decided to humor him by answering his original question.

"No, John, facing your demons won't change the past… but it's a great starting point for the healing process."

John's response was quick and firm. "Who says I want to be healed?"

Equally quick, she responded with, "You're here, aren't you?"

Nearly at his wits end with this psycho-analyzing repartee, he popped up from the futon and stood in front of her.

"Not for long I'm not. I have a bar stool with my name on it."

"Ah yes, the Wild Irish Rose," she said, smoothing her tie-dyed dress with her fingers.

"What? You think it's appropriate that someone like me owns a bar, don't you?"

"Is that what *you* think?" she asked.

John just shook his head and scoffed at her. He didn't bother reminding her just how much he hated her answering his questions with a question. He grabbed his backpack, threw it over his shoulder, then announced, "Keep up the good work, Doc. I'm outta here!"

She didn't try to stop him. She remained peaceful and still as he slammed the door behind him. A part of her was encouraged. She felt he was getting very close to a major breakthrough. Sadly though, a bigger part of her was worried—scared even. For she knew he was also close to a major breakdown.

She closed her eyes, took three deep breaths, then arose from her chair. Before she had a chance to light a sage stick or clutch a crystal, her office door reopened.

"And by the way," John announced, "you think *I* have issues? Who the hell buys a fish tank with no intention on owning fish? That's just weird, Doc. Even for you."

And just like that, the door closed and John disappeared into the streets of Chicago.

* * *

Despite claiming there was a barstool with his name on it, he had no intentions on going to the Wild Irish Rose—not today. So, with a backpack full of alcohol, he began aimlessly wandering down the sidewalk.

The way he looked, the way he staggered, and especially the way he was talking to himself, one could easily assume he was some crazy homeless guy. His mumbling was mostly incoherent, but every so often you could make out random bits and pieces.

He rambled things like: "rubbing the Buddha's belly," "the Grateful Dead," "stupid crystals," and even mentioned something about "a crazy black magic woman." And on more than one occasion, he mumbled things about a "frickin' fishless fish tank." He ended his mumble-fest with, "And for Christ sake woman, put a damn bra on."

When he was finished picking apart his wacky hippy-chick shrink, he allowed some of her questions into his head. Actually, he didn't really allow them, they just sort of entered his head, like an unwanted house guest that you just can't get rid of. He did his best to fight it, but her voice invaded his mind. One specific question of hers continuously looped in his head—

"Have you visited them yet… at the cemetery?"

"Have you visited them yet… at the cemetery?"

"Have you visited them yet… at the cemetery?"

The third time nearly knocked John over. He pressed his back against a brick wall, helplessly sliding down to the sidewalk. With his head in his hands, he just sat there, doing his best to rid himself of her question.

When his therapist's voice disappeared from his head, he slowly removed his hands from his face. He opened his eyes, but the bright sun made it hard to see anything. It took him a few moments, but when his eyes finally adjusted, they focused on the storefront across the street. It was an ice cream shop; the same one he and Kristen had taken Hannah to dozens of times.

As John remained slumped against the wall, all he could see was his little girl eating Death by Chocolate ice cream with chocolate sprinkles. And as it melted down the cone and onto her tiny hand, Kristen was quick to save the day with a handful of napkins. Then, for the hundredth time, she attempted to teach Hannah how to properly lick her ice cream to prevent this from happening again. And for the hundredth time, Hannah still did it *her own way*—melted ice cream and all.

A loud honking sound, snapped John out of his flashback. It was a yellow cab impatiently waiting in a long line of traffic. As the light turned green and the traffic dispersed, John knew exactly what he needed to do. He forced himself to his feet and made his way to the corner and hailed the next available cab.

Ironically, at that very same moment, William was also standing on a sidewalk. It was in front of his house, and as his shaky hand clutched his cane, he was also flagging down a cab.

Two different cabs in two totally different parts of town, but the one common thread was that both John and William were secretly dreading their ultimate destinations.

William's destination came first, but it lasted the longest. It was two o'clock when his cab dropped him off in front of Mercy Hospital. He was immediately greeted by one of his favorite nurses. She escorted him up to one of the exam rooms.

While in the backseat, John made quick work of the rest of his flask. Knowing he was going to need as much liquid courage as possible, he sloppily refilled it with one of the emergency bottles in his backpack. He then requested for the driver to make one quick stop before heading to his final destination.

Moving much slower than normal, William sluggishly undressed and slipped into his hospital gown. Just like at the Wild Irish Rose, William's positive and upbeat personality was infectious among the nurses and doctors. But on this particular day, it was the nurses that were forced to be the upbeat and positive ones. They all noticed the usual twinkle in his eyes had faded considerably. Still though, he wore his classic warm smile as the nurses prepared him for a battery of tests.

When the yellow cab finally rolled to a complete stop, John immediately felt sick to his stomach. At first, he didn't move a muscle. He kept his head down not even looking out the window. He might have sat there forever if the driver didn't call out to him.

"Hey buddy, is this this place or what?"

John slowly peered out the window and offered a hesitant nod. His hands were so clammy, they left sweat-prints on the well-worn black seat beneath him. His hand was shaking so much, he was barely able to grasp the handle.

"Can you wait here, please?" John quietly said to the driver.

Before shutting the door behind him, John reached into the backseat and grabbed two beautiful bouquets of flowers. His steps were short and purposely unhurried. His faded and filthy Chuck Taylor's came to a halt at a large iron gate which read: St. Boniface Cemetery. But that's as far as his feet would take him.

Sweat poured from his forehead, and his hands were trembling so much they nearly shook the petals off the flowers. His body stood frozen. It was as if he was completely paralyzed. Besides his trembling hands, the only movement on him was the string of tears streaming down his cheeks.

He stood there, for what seemed like forever, staring at the hundreds of headstones beyond the iron fence. John wanted to enter, he truly did, but he knew he still wasn't ready yet. Whether it was fear of the unknown or fear of the known, his whole life had been run by fear.

Brushing his tears away, John re-entered the cab. He kept it short and sweet.

"Nearest bar, please."

Exhausted and defeated, John closed his eyes and slumped down in the seat. He was passed out before the cab was even in gear. The next thing he knew, the driver was yelling at him.

"Hey, buddy, wake up! We're here."

John forced his eyes open and peered out the heavily smudged window. The cab was parked in front of a seedy dive bar.

"This what you had in mind?" asked the driver.

"It's perfect," he answered, tossing the man some money.

Before John could close the door behind him, the driver called out, "Hey, buddy, don't forget your flowers."

John stared in at the two bouquets sitting on the backseat. He knew if he stared too long at them his heart would break all over again.

"Keep 'em," John said, then turned and headed into the bar.

When William was fully redressed, he sat alone on the exam table and anxiously awaited the arrival of his doctor. His face was ashen and his posture had seen better days. His hands were so clammy, they left sweat-prints on the paper separator he sat on.

Finally, the door swung open and the doctor entered carrying a folder. They exchanged pleasantries, and he took a seat across from William. He then opened the folder and began reading through the information. William carefully watched the doctor's eyes. His expression said it all, and William didn't even wait for him to close the folder.

"How much longer do I have, Doc?"

By the time William exited the hospital, John had already been shut off and kicked out of two different bars. Worse than that, he had completely gone through his entire backpack supply of alcohol. All he had left was the emergency flask in his pocket, and even that was about to be polished off.

Stumbling across the busy street, John nearly got hit by multiple cars. He made his way into a darkened alley where he proceeded to toss his empty backpack into a dumpster. He had no use for it anymore. He had no use for anything anymore. The night was still young, but in his condition, he knew there wasn't a bar in the city that would serve him—except one.

The last place he wanted to be was the Wild Irish Rose, but as the night wore on, he was slowly drawn to the inevitable.

14

On three different occasions that day, Kevin swung by John's house to check on him. When he wasn't at home, and when he never showed up at the Wild Irish Rose, Kevin began to worry. He knew what this day meant to John, and he knew just how fragile he was.

Julie tried to convince Kevin to close the bar for the day, or at the very least, he should take the day off and let her run the show. She felt for John, she really did, but she also knew Kevin was just as affected by this tragedy.

Kevin appreciated her offer and concern, but just in case John showed his face that night, he needed to be there. Julie knew it was pointless to try and distract him with her silliness, and she also stayed away from offering upbeat comments. She did her best to give him space, but she made it clear to him that if he needed anything, she was right there.

Fortunately, it was a busier night than normal, which helped take his mind off of his brother, at least for a little while. More times than not, Julie would catch Kevin staring at the front door—waiting, hoping to see his brother enter.

"I'm sure he'll be here," she whispered, putting her hand on his shoulder. "I don't think a night has gone by without him showing his face here, right?"

Her encouraging smile was lost on Kevin, for he couldn't take his eyes off the door.

"Hey, he's gonna be here. I'm sure of it," she said, turning Kevin's face to hers. "It's gonna be okay. It'll all work out."

"I'm not so sure about that," he said, looking into her eyes. "But you're right, he'll definitely be here tonight. He partially blames this place for what happened. Yup, the Wild Irish Rose is the perfect place for him to drink himself into oblivion."

She released her hand from his shoulder, and without hesitation, wrapped her arms around him tightly. Although he was caught off guard, he found himself returning the gesture. He pulled her in close, taking in the familiar, intoxicating scent of her lotion. For a brief moment, her warm embrace seemed to melt away all of his worries.

Slowly, he pulled away and looked deep into her kind eyes. But before a word could be spoken, the front door creaked open. All at once, Kevin released his arms and quickly spun around, hoping to see the familiar face of his brother. Disappointment washed over him when he realized it wasn't John. It was, however, a familiar face.

"Hey, William," Julie called out.

William didn't offer his normal, cheery hello. Instead, he forced his lips into a slight smile. Almost immediately, Julie noticed something was off about him. His face appeared ghostly white, and his demeanor abnormally sullen. Even the way he made his way to the bar was different—slower, weaker.

When he finally climbed onto the barstool, Julie greeted him with a wide smile and a tall glass of Coke with extra ice.

"Umm, can I actually get a whiskey, please?"

At first she thought he was pulling her leg, but when she saw the sadness behind his eyes, she knew he was being completely serious. Even Kevin, who was still preoccupied with the front door, turned a curious eye towards William.

Over the next hour, Julie served William one whiskey after another, and although she was extremely tempted, she never once asked him what was wrong. Over the previous couple of weeks, they had developed a nice friendship, but Julie still didn't feel quite comfortable butting into his personal life. Like with Kevin, she gave him space, but made sure he knew she was there if he needed to talk. Julie never needed to actually speak these words. Her kind, compassionate eyes said it all.

After placing his fourth drink in front of him, Julie made her way over to Kevin on the opposite end of the bar.

"I've never seen him like this before. He just looks so weak… and sad."

Kevin nodded in agreement with Julie.

"I wonder what hap…"

Kevin stopped mid-sentence and his eyes widened. Julie followed his gaze, and there, entering through the door was John. It was obvious just how drunk he already was. He swayed to and fro, staggering his way towards the bar. The knees of his jeans were both torn and completely soaked from taking a digger in a puddle down one of the alleyways.

Kevin was relieved to finally see his brother, but seeing him in that condition, nearly falling over, broke Kevin's heart. John was so drunk, he didn't even notice everyone staring at him. Halfway across the room, he paused and focused his blurry eyes on the bar.

"Hey, it's my old buddy, William!" John yelled, making his way closer to William.

He attempted to sit next to him but had the hardest time climbing onto the stool. After nearly falling off twice, John settled in and glanced down at William's drink. A surprised, yet approving smile fell across John's face.

"Is that whiskey you're drinking?"

William slowly nodded as John gave him a congratulatory pat on the back. Shakily, William lifted the glass to his lips for one final sip. After placing the glass back onto the coaster, he addressed John.

"You know what, my friend, maybe you're right... maybe things don't happen for a reason. Maybe there is no master plan."

"I'll drink to that," John proclaimed, slamming his hand down on the bar. "Let me go get us another."

He started to get up, but William waved him off.

"No thank you, my friend. I think I've already had a little... a lot too much."

With that, William reached into his wallet and placed a crisp hundred dollar bill under his empty glass. A second later, Julie approached wearing her usual pleasant smile. Before she could say a word, William said, "Keep the change, dear."

"No, let me go get you some..."

"Seriously, dear, keep the change," he repeated then winked at her.

Julie was used to William winking at her, but this time was different. His winks usually gave her that warm and fuzzy feeling, but this one just made her feel sad—sad for whatever the sweet old man was going through.

"Are ya really gonna make me drink alone?" John laughed in William's direction.

William didn't answer. He simply gave John a smile, clutched his cane, then navigated his way towards the front door. Part of John wanted to help the old man out, but a bigger part of him needed another drink in the worse way possible. When William had finally exited, John slid off the stool and stumbled his way behind the bar.

After months of keeping quiet, Kevin finally took action. Before John reached for the bottle of Jameson, Kevin stepped in front of him.

"I think you've already had enough, John."

"Excuse me? This is my fucking bar," he loudly slurred, trying to push his way past Kevin.

Kevin didn't move an inch. Instead, he grabbed John's arm.

"It's my fucking bar too," Kevin said in a low tone. "I don't even know why you still own it except to punish yourself."

Again, John attempted to push past his brother, and again, Kevin tightened his grip on John's arm.

"I loved Kristen and Hannah too, you know?" Kevin lowered his tone even more. "And our parents abandoned *both* of us, not just you."

The tension to fight back seemed to lessen, and Kevin slowly released his grip on John's arm. Kevin wasn't drunk like John, but at that very moment, he was just as beaten down.

"And if you remember correctly," Kevin whispered, "it was *both* of us that went through that foster care nightmare."

The air and anger seemed to release from John's body, and as he fought back tears, he looked Kevin directly in the eyes and said, "Then you know I need that drink."

Kevin lovingly put his hand on his brother's shoulder.

"I'm sorry, John, but I'm not going to sit by and watch you do this to yourself... not anymore."

Just like that, John's anger returned.

"Whatever, I'll go drink somewhere else!"

He swatted Kevin's hand away then spun around to leave. In doing so, he lost his balance and drunkenly knocked over the entire row of glasses. Embarrassed and irritated, John proceeded to storm out of the bar.

Out on the sidewalk, the night air temporarily cooled down John's anger. It was cooled even further when he spotted William sitting on the curb. He was slouched over and appeared to have just gotten sick. As drunk as John was, he forced himself to sober up enough to help his new friend. He hailed a cab then helped William to his feet.

"C'mon, I'll take you home," John said, opening the cab door.

Despite his stubborn pride, William knew he was in no condition to argue. He gave an appreciative nod as John helped him into the backseat.

After the cab dropped them off, John carefully helped William up his steps and into his house. In the foyer, William leaned against the wall, struggling to take off his jacket. Again, his pride was forced to allow John to help him. John neatly hung his jacket on the free-standing iron coat rack.

William flipped on a light switch, and they made their way through the living room and down the hall towards the bedroom. The house was neat as a pin, but somehow, it wasn't exactly what John had pictured. Almost all the walls were painted an off-white with very little, if any, pictures hanging on them. The whole place in general was sparsely decorated.

The living room simply consisted of a fireplace, a brown leather recliner, and a 19" color TV. As John passed through, he couldn't help but smile. The simple and minimal décor reminded him of his first apartment. That all changed when he moved in with Kristen. She deemed his *basic* and *minimal* style as *boring* and *cold*.

John's smile faded when he thought of his wife. Without a shadow of a doubt, Kristen was the one who turned their house into a home. And she, along with Hannah, turned his life into one worth living.

As they entered the hallway, William's voice snapped John out of his thoughts.

"Did I ever mention that I hardly ever went back to Applewood after I moved here? In the beginning I used to go back for Christmas and then a few times in the summer, but… then I just stopped."

John's arms guided William down the hallway.

"I guess the longer you stay away from somewhere, the harder it is to return there, ya know?"

John nodded in agreement as he continued to support William's dead weight.

"At one point, I went nearly ten years without ever stepping foot back in Maine. When I finally went back, it was for my father's funeral."

"I'm sorry," John quietly said, entering the bedroom.

He flicked on the light and gazed around the room. Besides the bed and dresser, there was a large shelf filled with what seemed like hundreds of books. In the corner by the window sat a mahogany desk and chair. Centered perfectly on the desk was a typewriter. The small garbage can to the right of it was overflowing with crumpled papers.

"You don't still use that, do you?"

"Oh I most certainly do. I'm not really into the whole computer thing. Give me a pen and paper and a real typewriter any day. There's nothing like the sound of the keys or that beautiful ding sound as you complete a line."

John helped William onto the bed and again thought of his wife. The way William just described his typewriter was exactly how Kristen felt about her silly old Polaroid camera and her retro record player. John removed William's hat and hung it on one of the bedposts.

"When I finally went back," William continued, "I felt so out of place. I'd been gone for so long, it was like I was a stranger in my own town. It was like I didn't belong there… maybe I never did. I'm sorry, son, I'm not making any sense, am I?"

"You're fine, William," John smiled, propping a pillow under his head.

"The whole thing seemed so surreal. I felt so numb and… helpless."

John took a seat next to William and asked, "Why helpless?"

William looked to the ceiling, as if he was watching a movie of what once was.

"I was helpless because I had no idea how to console my mother. In all my years, I had never ever seen her like that. She was absolutely devastated. My parents had been together since they were little kids." Meekly, William let out a chuckle. "You've heard of high school sweethearts, right? Well, they were more like elementary school sweethearts."

John returned his smile and listened as William continued on.

"It was as if she had completely shut down. I had no idea what to say to her… how to make it better." He threw a look to John and said, "I'm not sure about you, but I'm not really good at emotional things sometimes… especially death and funerals."

A chill ran up John's spine and he forced himself to look away. It was as if William could see right through him.

"The whole thing just made me so uncomfortable; the funeral, my mother's sadness, and that feeling of being a stranger in my own town."

William's story was briefly interrupted by his hacking cough.

"You okay?" John asked, standing up from the bed. "You want me to get you some water?"

"I'm fine, thank you," he said, reaching out for John's arm.

John took that as a sign of William wanting him to sit back down beside him. It was obvious that William had a lot to get off his chest. In the two weeks they had known each other, this was the deepest William had been with him. John obliged and sat back down on the bed.

"I was so uncomfortable, in fact, that less than a day after the funeral, I made up some excuse and told my mother I needed to get back Chicago. She asked me if I could stay a while and help her get the house back in order. I guess over the years, they had slowly let some of the house repairs slide. It was definitely in need of some work, but

I think the real reason she wanted me to stay was just to be there with her. But I…"

William paused and before he turned his head away, John saw tears forming in the old man's eyes.

"I should have stayed. I should have been there for her." As he continued looking away, his voice broke, "That's the last time I saw her."

By now, William's entire body had turned on its side and faced away from John. The hunch of his shoulders reflected the shame of his actions. John had no idea what to say. He wasn't used to offering pity and sympathy. It was usually others who offered that to him. Quietly, John stood up and made his way to the foot of the bed. Without saying a word, he began removing William's black shoes.

"After my mother's funeral, I was notified that their house had been passed on to me." William slowly shook his head. "Owning that place was the last thing I wanted. I figured I'd just sell it and be done with it."

William turned his head and aimed his next comment in John's direction.

"Sometimes it's best to just let the past be the past, you know?"

John soaked William's words in as he neatly placed his shoes on the floor.

"But after a week of boxing up all their belongings… all their memories… I just couldn't bring myself to sell it." William fought to keep his eyes open. "So I ended up going back to Chicago with every intention of returning to Applewood and getting their… our house fixed up like it used to be—the way it should be. But… I never made it back." As his eyes fluttered shut, he mumbled, "I never made it back."

John grabbed the folded blanket at the end of the bed and spread it over William. When the blanket was firmly tucked around him, John quietly started to make his way out of the room. Just as he approached the door, William forced his eyes open.

"I kind of lied to you before, my friend."

John stopped and curiously turned back around.

"About me not having any regrets. I should have asked that girl out all those years ago. And I sure as hell should have been there for my mother when she needed me most."

Softly, John whispered, "We all have regrets, William. We all do."

He then turned off the light and closed the bedroom door. William's eyes were much too heavy to stay open. He let out a hauntingly regretful sigh then allowed his eyes to close for the night.

* * *

After the cab dropped John off at his house, he stood on his front porch. His hand was shaking as he clutched the doorknob. With each passing day, it had become harder and harder to bring himself to enter. And now, on the one year anniversary, it was nearly impossible.

When he finally was able to turn the knob and enter, he did something out of the ordinary. He turned on the light switch. He looked around the room at the disaster that was his living room. Kristen would be so disappointed in him knowing he allowed their house to come to this.

His embarrassment set off the need to find something to drink. Frantically, he searched through the many bottles scattered about on the floor. With each empty bottle, his desire to drink grew more and more, as did his anger.

He searched under the end tables—but nothing. Just before he ripped off the couch cushions, it hit him. A week earlier, he stashed a brand new bottle of Jameson in the kitchen. Worried that Kevin would come in and empty it out, John remembered hiding it in a cupboard.

As quickly as his drunken body let him, he stumbled into the kitchen and flipped on the light. He swung open cabinet after cabinet until finally he came face to face with his prized possession. The slow burn of the whiskey down his throat was exactly what he needed. Before he took a second long swig, he made the mistake of looking over at the fridge—like, really looking. Over the past year, he'd done his best to stay out of the kitchen, and if he did enter, he made it a point to avoid eye contact with the refrigerator, more specifically, its door.

Tonight, however, his eyes remained glued to it. The entire door was plastered with picture after picture, mostly from Kristen's Polaroid. As much as he wanted to look away, he couldn't. He found himself moving closer.

As his fingertips traced over each and every picture, tears flowed down his cheeks. It was the side of the refrigerator that really got to him. It contained multiple hand-drawn pictures by Hannah. Some were in crayon, some in colored pencil. Every picture she drew of John, she made sure to include his trusty Cubs hat.

Centered between Hannah's drawings was a calendar. The more he tried to fight it, the more his eyes focused in on the red circled date which read: Hannah's teacher - 3:30pm.

The longer he stared, the louder the voices became.

"We're leaving at three o'clock sharp!"

"Then I'll be back by three… three o'clock sharp." He remembered smiling as he saluted his wife. And then came his hollow words, "I promise I'll be back by three. I promise."

As his fingers touched the calendar, he heard his little girl say, "I believe you, Daddy,"

The voices were more than he could take. With his free hand, he snatched the calendar, throwing it to the floor. He then proceeded to angrily rip everything off the fridge. When his rant ended, there was nothing left but pictures, drawings, and magnets strewn about the floor beneath his feet. This was exactly why he had stayed away from the kitchen.

With the bottle tightly in his grasp, he stumbled back into the living room and fell onto his couch. He took another well-deserved swig of whiskey and then found himself digging into his front pocket. He pulled out the crumpled Polaroid of him and his girls. He sat up as straight as his body allowed then glanced down the hall towards the bathroom door. This time, it went beyond just hearing voices. The bathroom door opened and Kristen walked out wearing a blue dress.

"Wow, you look beautiful, Mommy."

John turned to his right and saw that Hannah was sitting next to him on the couch.

"Aww, thanks, sweetie," Kristen said, walking down the hallway towards John. "But trust me, underneath it all, I'm still the same ole plain Jane." By now, Kristen was standing directly in front of John on the couch. "I'm too overdressed, aren't I?"

As John watched his wife put on her favorite earrings, he heard himself saying, "You are if her teacher is a dude."

"Settle down, tiger. It's a woman. I just wanna look like I'm a good mother."

John reached for Kristen's hand to tell her what an amazing mother she was, but before he could touch her, she disappeared. He quickly turned to his right, but Hannah had also disappeared.

He was going crazy and he knew it. He also knew these voices and visions were just God's way of laughing at him—God's way of punishing him.

"Fuck, fuck, fuck!" he yelled out.

In one swift motion, John stood up and angrily overturned the coffee table, which sent his bottle of whiskey tumbling to the ground.

As John watched its contents spilling onto the floor, he lost it. He completely lost it.

Not one piece of furniture was safe from his drunken rage. Even the couch, which had housed his body over the past year, needed to be destroyed. The room began spinning even faster than before, and as John flipped the couch onto its back, he lost his balance and fell to the floor.

On hands and knees, John crawled across the room to where his bottle of whiskey lay on its side. He slumped against the wall and pressed the bottle to his quivering lips, and as the alcohol poured down his throat, the voices returned.

"Kristen Sanborn, will you marry me?"

"Yes! Yes, of course I will!"

John remembered it like it was yesterday. He proposed to Kristen in front of the Buckingham Fountain. It was one of her favorite places in the city.

That day was one of John's most treasured memories, but at that moment, it was just too much for him to handle. No matter how tightly he closed his eyes and covered his ears, the voices continued.

The loud sound of a crying baby echoed through his head.

"Do you want to hold your daughter?" Kristen said, handing him his baby girl.

"She's… she's so beautiful," he remembered saying. "I have a daughter! I'm somebody's father. Can you believe it?"

Without a doubt, that was the happiest day of John's life.

Slowly, he opened his eyes and everything disappeared. He was no longer proposing to Kristen or holding his brand-new baby girl. The only thing he was holding was his green bottle of Jameson.

Before he took a second swig, he reached into his pocket and pulled out his cell phone. For nearly a minute, he just stared at it. Finally, he flipped it open, hit a button, then hesitantly pressed it to his ear. He once again listened to the automated voice informing him of his one saved message. It was a message he had listened to a hundred times over the past year, and each time it brought him to his knees and filled his eyes with tears.

Upon completion, John closed the phone and let it slip from his hands to the floor. No matter how hard he tried, he couldn't stop the tears from pouring out his tired eyes. He brushed them away enough to look around the room at everything he had destroyed. His heart completely emptied when he spotted Kristen's Polaroid camera in pieces on the floor.

"No… no," he sobbed, knowing he must have smashed it during his fit of rage.

"I'm done. I'm so fucking done with everything."

Before he could take another swig, Hannah's voice stepped in.

"Whenever you fall down in life, you have to pick yourself up and try again because Mathews never quit."

"I'm sorry. I'm so sorry, Hannah, but I can't do this anymore."

It took all his energy, but John pulled himself to his feet and stumbled towards the bathroom. Halfway across the room, he bent down and retrieved the bottle of sleeping pills he had bought a day earlier.

He flipped on the bathroom light and stared down at the counter. It was littered with Kristen's makeup supplies and other various items. There was a thin film of dust on them, for they had remained there, untouched, for the entire year.

With one angry swipe, John knocked every last item to the floor. He then placed his whiskey on the counter and proceeded to empty the entire bottle of pills into his palm. Usually, he avoided looking into mirrors at all costs, but for whatever reason, he found himself gazing straight into it. He barely recognized the person looking back at him, and the longer he stared, the more he hated that person.

By now, his hand was shaking uncontrollably, and a few of the pills fell and rattled into the sink. John looked down and carefully placed them back into his palm. He tightened his grip on them then looked back up into the mirror. This time, it wasn't his own face looking back at him, it was Mr. O'Neil's.

With his cigarette dangling from his mouth, he looked at John and said, "You're pathetic! It's no wonder your parents didn't want you."

The reflection then began laughing at John, sadistically, almost taunting him to do something about it. John's blood boiled, and as he gritted his teeth together, his right hand clenched into a tight fist. This would be the last time Mr. O'Neil would laugh at him like that.

"Fuck you!!!" he yelled, slamming his fist into the mirror.

Mr. O'Neil's face slowly faded in the spiderweb cracks of the glass. John didn't stop there. He continued throwing punches until the entire mirror was covered in blood. His heart raced and he was nearly out of breath. The room began to spin, and as he looked down at the shards of glass sticking out of his bloody fist, the room spun faster.

He tried to reach for his whiskey, but his body was dizzy and his eyesight was too blurry to focus. So dizzy, in fact, his legs finally gave in and he fell to the floor. As he fell, his head smashed into the toilet, knocking him out immediately. Blood poured from John's forehead and pooled around the base of the white porcelain toilet.

At the same exact moment, on the opposite side of town, William was in the midst of a dream. It was so vivid and real, and one of the most beautiful dreams the old man had ever dreamt. When it ended, William's eyes popped open, and his body sprang up straight. His chest was tight and he couldn't breathe. It was as if someone had stolen his oxygen. When he finally exhaled, a smile filled his face, and a feeling of relief and utter joy washed over his frail body.

15

John slowly forced his eyes open only to be blinded by a bright light. It wasn't until he grumbled his displeasure that Kevin noticed he was finally awake.

"Hey, you," Kevin said, moving closer to his bedside.

As John raised his hand to block out the light, he noticed his arm was connected to an IV. Kevin closed the shade and turned his attention back to his brother.

"Where the hell am I?"

"You're in the hospital."

"What happened?"

"Apparently you beat up your mirror. After that, you must have passed out. You cracked your head open on the way down."

John looked down at the bandages covering his right hand. With his left hand, he reached up and touched the gauze, which was wrapped around his head.

"You found me?" John asked.

Slowly, Kevin nodded then spoke. "I went to check on you. I was worried you'd do something stupid, and it looks like you almost did."

John said nothing. He just lay there watching his brother fumble with what to say.

Kevin's voice was soft yet serious. "I found the pills, John. You had nearly a whole bottle of pills scattered by your hand. What the hell were you thinking?"

John remained silent and looked away from his brother's question.

"Do you know how lucky you are? Cracking your head and passing out probably saved your life."

"Oh yea, I'm real lucky."

Kevin was in no mood for John's sarcasm.

"This isn't a joke, John!"

Just as quickly, Kevin softened his tone. He knew how much his brother was hurting.

"You need some help. Like some professional help."

John shrugged and continued to look away. He knew Kevin was right, but he couldn't bring himself to admit it.

"I just need to get away from here... get out of Chicago. Just need to clear my head. There are just too many memories here, ya know?"

John turned and looked at his brother. Kevin knew exactly what he meant, and the pain in John's eyes made Kevin's heart ache even more.

"And you were right, Kev. I don't belong owning that bar with you. I probably never did."

"I didn't really mean that, John... that bar was our dream."

"More like my nightmare."

Not knowing what to say, Kevin reached over and placed his hand on his brother's. John knew he was beaten down. He had no sarcastic comments left, and he certainly had no answers.

As a tear formed in the corner of his eye, he quietly said, "I just don't know what to do anymore, Kev."

Kevin squeezed John's hand tighter as he formulated his thoughts. But before he could say a word, a voice floated in from behind them.

"I might have a suggestion."

Both brothers turned their heads, and there, in the doorway stood William.

"William? What are you doing here?" asked John.

"I went by the Wild Irish Rose to thank you for taking care of me last night. Julie informed me of what happened."

Relying heavily on his cane, William made his way into the room. He looked from John's hand up to the bandages on his head then politely asked, "How are you feeling, son?"

"Physically or mentally?" John half-smiled.

"Both," William smiled back.

Almost embarrassed, John lowered his head and confessed, "Not so good."

Kevin grabbed a chair from the corner and motioned for William to have a seat. He gave Kevin an appreciative nod and slowly lowered himself into the chair.

When he was completely settled in, Kevin curiously asked, "So what's this suggestion of yours?"

"Well, it's more like a favor," William replied, placing his cane across his lap. "Remember that house I told you about… the one I grew up in?"

A bit puzzled, John nodded.

"I think it's time… time to get it fixed up. A place like that… with so many memories… doesn't deserve to be neglected. But as much as I'd love to go, I'm in no condition to make the long trip. It's not in the cards, I guess. I've been putting this off for far too long. It'll be nice to have that peace of mind before my time is up. And if truth be told, I probably don't have much longer."

William wasn't trying to overdramatize or search for sympathy; he was simply being honest and matter-of-fact.

"Aw, William, don't say that," Kevin said.

"It's true, son, but it's okay. I've come to terms with it."

Kevin thought for a moment then again spoke.

"Are you insinuating that you want my brother to go to Maine to fix up a house you own?"

William smiled and nodded, and then turned his attention to John.

"I saw the amazing work you did at the bar. I know I've said this to you before, but you have a true gift, my friend. It should only take you a couple of weeks, and I'd pay you, of course." Both brothers were speechless as William continued his sales pitch. "And you said yourself, you needed to get out of Chicago and clear your head. Trust me, son, there's no better place to clear your head than Applewood—especially now."

When Kevin saw that John was actually considering this, he was forced to step in.

"I'm sorry, William, but my brother is in no condition to…"

"Maine, huh?" John pondered out loud.

Kevin threw John a look then attempted to plead his case to William.

"As I was saying, my brother isn't in any cond…"

"I'll do it," John announced.

William beamed with excitement and exclaimed, "Excellent! Then it's a deal."

John knew this didn't set well with Kevin.

"Think of it this way, Kev, I'll be out of your hair for a couple weeks."

It was obvious by Kevin's glare that he didn't appreciate John making light of the situation. Before Kevin could say a word, William had risen from his chair and had his cane firmly planted on the ground.

"I'll be in touch with the details," he winked then turned to leave.

"I'll be right back," Kevin said to John. "I'm just gonna walk him out."

When the door was shut, and when they were out in the hall, Kevin turned to William.

"Look, William, I appreciate you trying to help my brother out, I really do, but I'm not sure he's up for working, never mind a trip to Maine. He's just so… fragile right now."

Before William could address his concerns, Kevin continued.

"And what if he starts drinking and I'm not there to watch out for him?" Kevin paused and attempted to calm himself down. "Do you even know why he's in here… what he tried to do last night?"

William felt Kevin's pain and concern, he truly did, but at this point, he couldn't contain his excitement any longer. His bony hand clutched at Kevin's arm.

"I saw it! Last night I saw it!"

"Saw what?" Kevin asked, completely confused.

William's face beamed as he said the words, "Medillia's Lament."

"Huh?"

"It came to me in a dream."

When Kevin saw just how serious William was, his confused look turned to one of sympathy. The poor old man had also been through a lot lately. Kevin placed his hand on William's and softened his tone.

"John's not the only one going through some heavy times, is he?"

William pulled back, almost taking offense to his comment.

"You don't believe me, do you?"

"I'm sure you had a dream about it, but—"

"No!" William said sternly. "It *came* to me in a dream, but it was *real*… and it's happening right now in Applewood."

"Aw, William. Look, I enjoyed your little legend as much as everyone else, but this is my brother's life we're talking about. He's been through a lot… we both have."

Again, William clutched Kevin's arm. "That's exactly why he needs to go. I know you really don't know me, son, but you need to trust me."

Kevin looked deep into William's eyes, deep enough to hopefully make him understand just how serious John's situation was.

"You do realize, the only reason my brother accepted your offer is so he has a place to go drink himself to death with no one there to babysit him? I can't lose him, William. He's all I got."

"Never underestimate the power of the human spirit," winked William.

"It's my brother's spirit I'm worried about," Kevin said, looking at John through the door window.

William felt Kevin's love and concern for John, but he knew he needed to convince him. He joined Kevin at the window and put his arm around him.

"Trust me, if I didn't think Applewood would do him some good, I surely wouldn't send him. Trust me."

Kevin turned towards the old man, but before he could say a word, William continued.

"I didn't walk into your bar on accident, for there are no accidents in life. There's a reason for everything, we have to believe that."

Kevin let out a defeated sigh. He knew it was impossible to argue with the old man. With a warm smile and a twinkle in his eye, William threw Kevin a parting wink then turned and headed out.

* * *

Before he was released from the hospital, Kevin made sure that John's house was cleaned from top to bottom. He didn't want anything to remind him of what went on the previous night. Of course, he would offer John to stay with him, but he knew full-well the extent of his brother's stubbornness.

Against his wishes, Julie joined him in cleaning. He already felt bad enough for her being dragged into his brother's mess the past few months.

"Kevin, if I didn't want to help, I wouldn't," she said on the car ride over.

"I just feel so bad that…"

"Kevin, stop! You really need to stop apologizing all the time, and you need to start accepting people's help."

Out of the corner of his eye, he could see that she was smirking.

"What's so funny?"

"You and your brother are different in so many ways, but being stubborn and asking for help isn't one of them. I'm helping you. Deal with it."

* * *

Less than two days after John was released from the hospital, he had his duffle bag packed and ready to go. He had no clue what kind of repairs he would be doing, so he loaded the back of his truck with as many tools as possible. John was still exhausted and beaten down, so he really wasn't looking forward to the physical labor aspect of the trip. He was, however, excited at the thought of just getting away; away from Chicago, his worrisome brother, and hopefully away from all the memories of what once was.

Although William's health was deteriorating, he was also excited for John's trip but for different reasons. Kevin was the opposite of excited. Ever since William's proposal, Kevin had a bad feeling in the pit of his stomach.

Julie was split down the middle. She completely understood Kevin's worry, and she agreed the only reason John was going was to be by himself and drink. But there was another part of her that agreed with William and thought maybe, just maybe, a change of scenery and doing a little work with his hands would do him some good.

She did her best to calm Kevin's nerves and be a neutral voice of reason. Kevin was not a fan of this at all. He wanted... he *needed* Julie to be on his side on this one. Needless to say, he left out the part about William claiming to have had a dream of Medillia's Lament and that he believed it was happening right now. Yup, he knew if Julie heard that, her child-like belief in magic and fairy tales would shine through, thus causing her to take William's side completely.

After John was released from the hospital, Kevin insisted he come stay with him, at least until he left for Maine. Reluctantly, John agreed. Mostly, it was in hopes of pacifying Kevin enough to get him off his back regarding the trip. Besides a few swigs here and there, John remained sober. Again, it was just another way to pacify his brother.

Kevin held off on his badgering, but it certainly wasn't because John had him fooled. Kevin saw right through his brother, and only held his tongue to avoid a big fight. Besides, he knew the more he strongly suggested that John stay, the more strongly and stubbornly John would do the opposite.

Bright and early, on the morning of the trip, they all met at the Wild Irish Rose to say their goodbyes; they being Kevin, William, and even Julie. She was there more so for support of Kevin rather than the actual goodbye.

With his cane clutched in his left hand, William gave John a piece of paper. Not only did it contain detailed directions to his house, but it had a few other pieces of useful information on it. The smile never left William's face as he eagerly went over it with John.

"I believe the closest hardware store and lumber yard is in the next town over. If you need groceries or whatnot, there used to be an old general store a few miles from my house. Oh, and the Applewood Diner is in that area as well. But like I said, I haven't been back in years, so I'm not even sure if they're still around. Also, Applewood has its share of parks and scenic spots… I jotted some of them down as well."

It was at this moment, Kevin decided to attempt a last-ditch effort.

"Wow, Applewood sounds so good that maybe I should go too. I could definitely use a vacation. You can handle the bar, right?" he said, looking over at Julie.

She was completely caught off guard. She had no idea he was going to play that final, desperate card.

"Ummm…" was all she could get out before John jumped in.

"I'll be fine on my own, Kevin. Save your vacation for the Caribbean or something."

Kevin wouldn't let it go. "I'm just saying, you might need some extra help fixing up William's house, and you and I made a pretty good team once before." Kevin motioned around the bar.

This time, it was William who stepped in.

"He'll be fine on his own, son. Besides, it'll probably do you both some good to be apart for a bit," he winked.

Julie's mouth said nothing, but her mind whole-heartedly agreed. With no other ideas up his sleeve, Kevin let out a sigh and defeatedly hung his head. John folded the piece of paper then reached his hand out to William.

"Consider your house fixed."

William's bony, frail hand did its best to grip John's.

"Thank you again, John. I appreciate it."

John then reached his hand out to his brother. Kevin was slightly put off by the impersonable handshake versus a hug, but at that point, he took what he could get. As he tightly gripped John's hand, he pulled him in closer and whispered into his ear.

"Drive safe… and John, please, PLEASE, no alcohol, okay?"

"Yea, yea, yea, I know," he said dismissively.

John tried to pull away, but Kevin increased his grip.

"I'm serious, John. No alcohol."

When Kevin was sure he heard him, he released the handshake and let him go.

"Oh, and John, make sure you call me as soon as you get there… if not sooner."

John smiled at his over-protective brother, gave him a salute, then threw Julie a wave goodbye. As he climbed into his truck, Julie was quick to console Kevin by gently placing her hand on his shoulder. William stood off to the side and watched John's truck rumble down the street and away from Chicago.

"Good luck, my friend," he whispered aloud. "I hope there's enough magic left for you there. You deserve it."

16

Due to John's heavy alcohol consumption the past few months, it had been a while since he'd driven his truck. It felt good being back behind the wheel. He used to love just driving around and listening to tunes. He claimed he did his best thinking that way. Usually, this simply consisted of him driving around the city or up by the lake; a far cry from the sixteen-hour trek across the country to Maine.

Kevin made him promise not to push himself on the drive, and he hammered home the point to stop and sleep as soon as he got tired. Although John promised he would, deep down, he had no intention of stopping until he was there. Like with most things, John looked at this as a competition, and no matter how tired he got, he was bound and determined to get to Maine in a straight shot.

Gas, food, and bathroom stops were all he allowed for himself, and usually, he accomplished those all at once. On more than one occasion, he found himself itching for a drink—one that involved whiskey. Each time, he fought the urge and continued driving on. It certainly wasn't because Kevin had ordered him not to drink. John would never do something because he was ordered, especially from his brother. In his head, he was only holding off drinking until he got there. Once in Maine, all bets were off.

It was well after midnight by the time he crossed over the green arches of the Piscataqua River Bridge. He could barely keep his eyes open. The last few hours were the hardest, and he tried every trick in the book to stay awake. When coffee and loud music didn't cut it, he went from turning on the heat to cranking up the AC. At one point, he even rolled down the window and drove with his head sticking out.

On the other side of the bridge, he finally saw what he'd been waiting for. It was a big blue sign which read:

Welcome to Maine – The Way Life Should Be.

"The way life should be," he mumbled. "We'll see about that."

As he continued up I-95, he flipped on the interior light and glanced down at William's directions. The light remained on even after he got off the proper exit. There were a lot of turns coming up, and the last thing he wanted was to get lost in Maine, especially at this hour. He'd read too many Stephen King books and knew nothing good happens in Maine after midnight.

John was exhausted, and his eyes strained to read the handwritten directions. After what seemed like a dozen twists and turns, he found himself driving over some sort of causeway. Being the only car on the road, he stopped halfway across. The moon was nearly full and illuminated the ocean on either side of him.

This was the first time his eyes had ever seen the Atlantic Ocean. An accomplished smile crept across his face as he just sat there and stared. The moonlight glistened off the water and John was able to make out the many colored buoys on both sides of him.

Applewood was technically an island but was only a quarter-mile from the mainland with the short causeway being the only way in or out. As he crossed over the causeway, an old wooden sign greeted him. The sign read: Welcome to Applewood – Maine's Magical Island.

"Looks like William isn't the only one buying into this crap." He laughed to himself then continued on.

It wasn't long before John passed by the general store and diner William had mentioned. It was much too late for them to be open, but it definitely looked as though they were both still in business. After a few more turns, John found himself on a tiny dead-end road. There were no street lights, so seeing house numbers was a bit challenging. Luckily, William's directions were specific enough to easily find the house.

Before his headlights shut off, they revealed a small but heavily overgrown yard. John grabbed his bag, blanket, and pillow, then headed towards the front door. The moonlight through the trees was enough to allow him to see the keyhole.

He turned the key and pushed the creaking door forward. Unlike his own house, there was no need to navigate through the dark. He felt around on the wall until he found the switch. The overhead light had three bulbs but only one came on. Still, it was enough to illuminate William's living room.

On either side of the fireplace were two bookshelves, which were completely empty and void of books. Besides an armchair, a couch, and a large circular coffee table, the room was bare. John was way too exhausted to search out a bedroom, and just like home, he decided to simply crash on the couch. He moved closer and noticed both the couch and chair were covered in plastic. It immediately reminded him of Kristen's grandmother's house. She had every single piece of furniture covered in plastic. He laughed, remembering the first time he sat on her couch he slipped right off onto the floor.

He never understood the purpose of these silly coverings, but as he glanced down at the thick layer of dust, he was glad this one had it, for it had protected the couch from years of neglect. Slowly, he dragged the plastic off, but it wasn't slow enough to prevent a small dust cloud from forming in the air. John grabbed his blanket and pillow and fell onto the couch. As a matter of fact, before the dust had completely settled, John was already fast asleep.

* * *

It would be late morning before his eyes opened again. Not only hadn't he moved an inch during the night, but the blanket remained on him rather than bunched up on the floor somewhere. Sunlight beamed in from each and every living room window, causing John to briefly shield his eyes.

He stood up, stretched his arms to the ceiling, and gave his back a good crack. He couldn't remember the last time he had a good night's sleep like that. With the sunlight pouring in, the living room looked bigger than the previous night, or maybe it was just from the lack of items. There were no end tables, no lamps, and more importantly, no TV.

The first room he explored was the kitchen. It was fairly small and was also empty looking. Besides a few glasses and plates, the cupboards were completely bare. The only thing on the counter was a giant microwave, which looked like it was from the 80s. The refrigerator was spotlessly cleaned out and unplugged. Assuming he would need it while he was there, John plugged it back in.

The next room he entered looked to be the dining room. The classic old farmer's table was pushed into the corner with its chairs upside down on top. The rest of the room was filled with boxes. Each one was neatly taped up and properly labeled. There were also random pieces of furniture stacked off to the side: Tables, lamps, and even a TV, which also looked to be from the 80s.

As John stared at all the packed boxes and items, his heart went out to William. He knew how hard it must have been packing up all those years of memories. John knew he would need to do the same one day, but he also knew he was nowhere near ready for that yet.

Off the living room was a short hallway containing a bathroom, a hall closet, and a tiny bedroom. He assumed by the lack of a bed, it was just a spare room. He walked back into the living room and spotted a wooden staircase leading to the second floor.

With each and every step John took, the old boards creaked louder and louder. The upstairs was fairly small and only contained a bathroom and two bedrooms. Other than a bed and a dresser, both rooms were completely empty. Even the clothes in the closets must have been packed up. Again, John couldn't fathom packing up his girls' clothes. He hadn't so much as entered their bedrooms in the past year, never mind pack up their stuff.

Not wanting to think about this any further, he made his way back downstairs. William had explained that the majority of the repairs were on the exterior of the house, but John did notice a few rooms where the drywall needed to be patched and painted.

Before getting started on a master to-do list, he decided to first head into town and pick up some food and drinks. As soon as he exited the house, the faint smell of salt air hit his nose. Between that and the amazing night's sleep, John felt rested and raring to go.

The sign on the store boasted that it was one of the oldest family-run general stores in Maine. When he entered, it was as if he took a step back in time. Dusty old floorboards greeted his feet as his eyes glanced around at the small, well-stocked store. The smell of coffee and baked goods filled the entire place.

The woman behind the counter gave him a look-over then threw a polite, welcoming smile his way. The lack of many customers in the store made it easy for John to navigate through the narrow aisles. Just like back home, he had no intention of cooking any major meals, so he loaded up on as many microwave items as possible.

He also loaded up in the penny candy section. There were items there he hadn't seen since he was a little kid. He remembered when the Hawkins were their foster parents, they used to take the boys to a candy store in the city. Kevin used to love Pop Rocks and candy cigarettes, while John always went for the colored candy buttons on paper and root beer flavored Tootsie Pops. And both brothers had to have as many candy wax bottles as possible.

It was still morning, so John decided against purchasing any alcohol. He settled for a couple of six-packs of old-fashioned cream soda, making a mental note that the store not only carried beer, but had a small section of hard liquor as well. He would most definitely be back for that. On his way to the register, he grabbed a pad of paper and a pen to use for his to-do list.

Once back at William's, John put away the few items he bought at the general store. At the bottom of the grocery bag, he pulled out the pen and paper then made his way outside.

The first thing he wrote down was: Repair, scrape & paint front porch. As he walked around the small property, he focused most of his attention on the house itself. The wooden shakes were weathered and there were a dozen or so that needed to be replaced, but for the most part, they were in good shape.

John did notice that most of the wooden trim on the east side of the house was completely rotted. He stepped back as far as the treeline would allow and peered up to the roof. It was covered in pine needles and moss, but as far as he could tell, it seemed in pretty good shape. This caused him to breathe a sigh of relief. He was never a big fan of roofs, never mind heights.

Among the tall grass, a large pine tree lay sprawled out on its side. By the looks of the rot and decay, John assumed it must have fallen years ago, probably during a big storm. Upon closer inspection, he noticed the remnants of what appeared to be the gazebo William had mentioned. The giant pine had completely crushed it.

When he finished examining the entire exterior of the house, he looked down at his list. They were all the type of repairs that a local carpenter could have banged out. Why did William insist on *him* being the one to do the work? Maybe he just felt sorry for him and figured having him do a little handy work would make his problems just disappear. If that was the case, then William was just as wacked as that hippy-chick shrink.

The thought of being pitied never set well with John, but he knew the old man meant well. Not to mention, the smell of the salt air, combined with the utter peace and quiet, made it nearly impossible to be mad at anything.

John placed the pen behind his ear, closed the notebook then turned his attention to the yard. The grass was completely overgrown and nearly up to his knees. Weeds had infiltrated the cracks of the fieldstone pavers, making the walkway barely visible. It was settled, tackling the landscaping would be John's first project.

"A clean-cut yard is a happy yard."

That's what Kristen used to say. Their yard was a little smaller than William's, but John remembered spending many a Sunday doing yardwork with Kristen. He took care of the grass while Kristen weeded and tended to her many flower gardens.

He couldn't help but laugh to himself as he thought about little Hannah sitting next to Kristen pulling weeds. Hannah was the perfect mix of girly-girl and tomboy. She had no problem playing in the dirt, but she also had no problem doing it while wearing a dress.

He assumed if there was a lawn mower on the property it would probably be in the shed, which was tucked away in the corner of the backyard. The siding matched the house and was equally as weathered. Beneath pine needles, pine cones, and fresh fallen leaves, there was at least two inches of moss covering the shed roof.

The padlock on the door was so rusted, it practically disintegrated as he gave it a tug. The wooden door creaked open revealing multiple spiderwebs. John picked up a stick and began clearing the webs from the doorway. It was only a little 8X8 shed, but it was stocked full of tools, rakes, and random shovels.

"Good thing I brought my own tools," he said, looking down at them. Most of the tools were enveloped in spiderwebs and covered in mouse and/or squirrel droppings.

Again, John chuckled to himself as he looked at all the tools scattered about. Being this disorganized would never fly with Kristen. Every tool, rake, and shovel had a specific home in John's shed at home. Not only did Kristen print labels where everything went, but she outlined every tool with black marker. This was her way of making it dummy-proof, or in other words, John-proof. Sometimes he would put the hammer where the screwdriver went just to get a rise out of her.

He made his way to the back corner, where a blue tarp was draped over something. Half expecting an animal to jump out at him, he slowly lifted it off.

"Bingo," he said as he spotted an old push mower.

It had seen better days, but he was just thankful it was a gas push mower and not one of those old-fashioned reel mowers. He cleared the cobwebs and pulled it down the ramp onto the yard. With one foot on the mower and one hand on the handle, John gave the cord a quick pull. When nothing happened, he upped his game and pulled harder. He continued to pull; some with the choke half on, some with it fully on. By the time he yanked it for the tenth time, he was practically out of breath, not to mention, completely frustrated.

"Why won't this God-damn mower start!" he loudly mumbled.

Before he could give it another pull, a voice from behind him called out, "Whatcha doing?"

Startled, John spun around to see a little blonde-haired girl staring up at him.

"Ummm, I'm just trying to get this thing started," he answered.

"Why?"

"So I can cut the grass."

John gave the cord one last powerful yet unsuccessful yank.

"Did you put gas in the tank?" the little girl asked.

John thought a second then looked down at the tank. Before he could reply, she blurted out, "My name is Suzy. What's yours?"

"Umm, John," he answered, still pondering her gas tank question.

Before she could hit him with another question, a loud voice came from next door.

"Suzy! Get over here!"

Both John and Suzy turned towards the voice. It belonged to Suzy's mom. She looked to be in her early thirties and wore faded blue jeans with an over-sized Champion sweatshirt. She then turned her attention to her twelve-year-old son, who was swinging on a tire swing in their yard.

"Ben! I told you to keep an eye on your sister."

"I am. She's right over there talking to that guy."

She shot her son a look then continued marching towards John and Suzy.

"Suzy, get over here! You know better than to talk to strangers!"

"He's not a stranger, Mommy. His name is John, and he's just trying to get this God-damn mower started."

John quickly lowered his eyes as his face flushed red.

"Suzy! We don't talk like that."

"I'm afraid that was my fault," he said, looking over at Suzy. "She's just repeating what she overheard."

Suzy nodded in agreement.

"No need to apologize. It's not your fault my daughter is an eavesdropper. I'm Sara, by the way," she said, reaching out her hand.

John wiped his dirty hands on his jeans then hesitantly shook her hand and said, "John."

Sara glanced over at William's house. "I didn't know someone bought this old place."

"Oh I didn't buy it. I'm just fixing it up for a friend, that's all."

"I hope you're gonna fix and paint the front porch," Suzy blurted out. "Mommy says it's starting to look ass-ugly."

It was now Sara's turn to blush and look towards the ground. Suzy covered her mouth and let out a giggle when she saw John fighting back a smile.

"Okay, Suzy, that's enough. Go play with your brother."

Suzy continued giggling. "Bye, John. Good luck with the mower," she yelled as she scampered off towards her brother.

Still red with embarrassment, Sara shook her head and looked from Suzy to John.

"Sorry about that. Ya never know what they're gonna say next. She's five going on eighteen."

As her words hung in the air, John thought of his own daughter. A cloud of sadness fell over him, and he stood there completely still. Unsure what to say or do, John offered a polite smile then began fiddling with the mower. The uncomfortable moment of silence was also felt by Sara, and she thought it best to head back home.

"Well, good luck. Looks like you have your work cut out for you."

"Thanks," he quietly said as he continued nervously fiddling with the choke.

"Nice meeting you, John."

"You too," he said, lifting his eyes just as she turned and walked away.

After Sara and her two kids went into the house, John bent down closer to the mower. When he was sure no one was looking, he untwisted the gas cap and peered inside.

"Son of a bitch," he smirked, looking down at the bone-dry tank.

He entered the shed and grabbed the gas can from the floor. Before he made another trip to general store, he decided to come up with a way to move the downed tree out of the yard. John retrieved an old chain from the shed and used his truck to drag the meat of the mighty pine to the very back of the yard along the tree line.

It was when he unhooked the chain that he saw what appeared to be a path. It was overgrown and camouflaged, but there was definitely a dirt path leading into the woods. John froze, nearly dropping the chain onto his foot. This was no ordinary path, it was the same one from his dreams.

As he stood there staring at it, he began questioning his sanity. Maybe this wasn't the path from his dream. Or maybe this *was* a dream. Before he could pinch himself, a mosquito did it for him. John smacked his forearm.

"Nope, not a dream," he mumbled, looking down at the bloody trail of mosquito guts on his arm.

Finally, his curiosity got the best of him. He shut off his truck then stepped into the woods and onto the path. With each step and each turn of the path, he knew this was indeed the same one from his dreams. He had dreamt of this path so many times in his life, he felt as if he could close his eyes and still find his way.

About a hundred feet in, John stopped and listened. Off in the distance, he could hear the cawing of seagulls and the dull roar of the ocean. The closer he got to the end of the path, the more his heart raced. Chills ran up his entire body as he exited and stepped into a small cove.

The stones, the seaweed, and even the beached lobster trap; it was exactly like his dream. Without even thinking about it, John found himself reaching into his pocket for his flask. His hand began to shake when he realized his flask was still buried beneath his clothes in his bag.

As he stood there completely still, he debated whether he should rush back for his flask or continue walking. The longer he stood there, and the more he breathed in the crisp salt air, the less anxious he felt. Before he knew it, his feet were walking across the smooth beach stones.

Between the familiar path through the woods, and now, the familiar cove, John thought for sure he was going crazy. Ironically, as he walked the beach, the eerie déjà vu feeling became less and less unsettling. At one point, he even found himself smiling at two seagulls who appeared to be arguing over a stray crab shell. The louder they squawked, the wider he smiled as he couldn't help but picture him and Kevin fighting over the last chicken wing.

John then turned his attention to the water. This was the first time he had ever been to an ocean—a real ocean. Without hesitation, he slipped off his socks and shoes and let the cold salt water gently lap over his feet.

The Atlantic glistened under the bright September sun. Its beauty was definitely not lost on him. Wistfully, he smiled. He knew if Kristen was there now, she'd be snapping one picture after another. And there was no doubt in his mind that if Hannah was there, she'd be laughing and loudly squealing at how cold the water was.

It didn't take long before John's feet were completely numb. With his shoes in hand, he continued walking through the cove. He couldn't believe just how quiet and peaceful it was. It was almost like he had discovered his own private beach; one that no soul had ever walked on before.

He noticed the blue sky was now turning dark and gray, and the bright sun was completely covered by clouds. The cold breeze off the ocean caused chills to run up his arms. About a hundred feet in front of him, he spotted an old, abandoned fishing boat. It looked like it had been washed ashore and sat high up on the beach. The paint was all but peeled off, and there was a large hole on its side.

He headed towards the boat and was reminded of the endless childhood hours watching Gilligan's Island. This caused John to envision the old, dilapidated boat as the S.S. Minnow. As he moved closer, his imagination switched from Gilligan's Island to the Goonies.

He lost track how many times he and Kevin had watched that movie over the years.

Although the boat was nowhere near the size of a pirate ship, that didn't stop John's imagination from thinking there might be a treasure hidden on board, or maybe there was a map to a treasure.

Just then, a rustling from the other side of the boat caused him to stop dead in his tracks. Yes, for a brief second, the thought of One-Eyed Willie passed through his mind. The person who emerged from the other side of the boat wasn't an old pirate but rather an old fisherman.

The man had gray hair with a matching beard and looked to be in his seventies, maybe eighties. He wore a dirty white t-shirt with the classic fisherman suspenders over it. On his head was a faded blue captain's hat.

The old man didn't notice him standing there, and John wanted to keep it that way. He already had one awkward conversation today and didn't plan on making it two. He didn't come to Maine to be social. He only took William up on his offer because he wanted to help the old guy out, not to mention, he needed a place to be completely alone with no one to bother him—mostly the latter.

Hoping to remain unnoticed, John turned to head back to the house. It was too late - the old fisherman not only spotted John, but called to him.

"Mornin' young fella," the man called out.

John turned back towards the old man and politely nodded. He didn't want to, but he found himself walking a bit closer to the boat. As he neared, he noticed the old man was larger than he originally thought. His face was like an old piece of leather; wrinkled, cracked, and weathered from a long, hard life. Not wanting to stare at him for too long, John turned his attention to the equally weathered boat.

"Damn rocks got the best of her," the old man said, pointing to the damaged boat. "But I'll get her back as good as new."

John said nothing. He simply stood there looking around at his surroundings. By now, a heavy fog had filtered into the cove. Almost on cue, a foghorn sounded. The loud sound seemed to startle John.

"Oh, that's just from the lighthouse around the bend." The man peculiarly raised an eyebrow at John. "You're not from around here, are ya?"

"Umm, no. From Chicago."

"Ahhh, the Windy City."

John nodded at the man.

"Name is Clarence, by the way," he said, reaching his hand out.

"Umm, I'm John," he uttered as he shook the man's hand.

His hand was twice the size of John's and was calloused and as rough as sandpaper.

"Well, don't be a stranger, John. I could always use the extra help."

Again, John only offered a polite smile then turned to leave.

"I hope you find what you're looking for while you're here," the man called out.

John didn't turn back around, but with a puzzled look on his face, he slowly headed back towards the path.

"We're all looking for something here, son," mumbled the old man when John was out of earshot.

John's pace quickened as he made his way back down the path. He had dreamed of it so many times, he knew every twist and turn by heart. By the time he made it back to William's house, the fog had completely dissipated and the sun was back out. On his way out of the woods, he stopped at the shed and grabbed the gas can. He tossed it in the back of his truck and again headed to the general store.

He remembered seeing a lone gas pump there, but as he pulled alongside of it, he started to wonder if it actually worked. It was so old looking that John thought maybe it was just an antique show-piece. With the gas can in one hand and his credit card in the other, he stood in front of it dumbfounded. There was no way this could be a real gas pump. Not only did it still have the old rolodex numbers, but there was no place for a credit card.

"Cash only, Bub."

John turned to see another suspender-clad fisherman. He appeared to be in his thirties and was wearing a black woolen hat. He had just exited the store and was carrying a tin of Skoal. Before John could say a word, the man had already climbed into his beat-up Ford and was inserting a pinch of tobacco into his mouth.

In addition to the gas, John grabbed a Gatorade and a Clark's chocolate bar. Directly next to the candy were packs of Topps baseball cards. A sad smile fell on his face as he remembered him and Kevin saving up their money and rushing out to buy packs of cards. They barely made it out of the store before the packs were ripped open and the gum shoved in their mouths, and as they sat on the curb quickly flipping through the cards, they both uttered phrases like, "Got it... got it... need it... got it... need it."

For old times' sake, John tossed a pack of cards onto the counter, and yes, before he even lifted the gas pump, he had already ripped the cards open and shoved the stale strip of gum into his mouth.

Just before he reached William's road, he came upon a four-way stop. Normally, it was the type of four-way that one might do a rolling stop through, but John knew he was a stranger in a strange town. The last thing he wanted was some small-town, cocky cop writing him a ticket and asking questions.

Even though there wasn't a car around, he came to a complete stop. Before he accelerated, his eye caught an old, deteriorated sign off to his left. It had nearly fallen over and read: Island Air Tours.

He couldn't explain it, but a sick feeling immediately entered the pit of his stomach. He quickly shook it off then found himself focusing in on another sign. This one was on his right. It was slightly faded but in much better condition. It read: Harbor Cove Park, and it had a picture of a lighthouse on it. He recognized the name from the paper William had given him.

John stared long and hard at the sign, and without even thinking, he found himself turning right rather than continuing straight. The signs took him to a small, vacant dirt parking area. The final sign pointed up a steep hill. John began climbing the wooden steps, which were built into the hill.

With each step he took, the cool ocean breeze became more prevalent against his face; as too was the smell of the salt air. When he finally reached the top, John paused to take in the scenic park in front of him. From well-landscaped flower gardens to the winding paved paths, the park was beauty in its truest form.

The park was high above the ocean's edge and the views were the epitome of breathtaking. Like the cove, the park was quiet and peaceful, and by the lack of cars in the lot, it seemed John had the entire place to himself.

It was early September still, but autumn had already taken hold of some of the trees, turning their leaves to reds, oranges, and bright yellows. At one vantage point, it looked as though the park was an oil painting. It was literally picture perfect. Without a doubt, if Kristen was here, her finger would be cramping from all her picture taking.

John continued down the paved path and as he rounded a small bend, he stopped in his tracks. Down to his right, and off in the distance, was the lighthouse. He was too far away to tell for sure, but it eerily resembled the one from his dreams. The closer he got, the more he realized it was exactly the same lighthouse from his dreams.

"What the fuck is happening to me?" he said to himself. He reached up and pressed his hand against his forehead, as if to see if he had a temperature.

The path ended in a tiny cul-de-sac at the edge of the cliff. In its center was a large granite memorial. It contained an etched lighthouse and underneath it was an inscription, which read:

...... O HEAR US WHEN WE CRY TO THEE
FOR THOSE IN PERIL ON THE SEA ......

There were a few different types of flowers spread out on the grass beneath. His eyes didn't linger very long on the memorial, for his attention was solely on the lighthouse off to his right. It was perched on a small rocky island about a couple hundred feet away. John made his way over to one of the many scenic overlook benches on the grass. The wind picked up, and as the blue sky once again turned gray, a light fog rolled in. John noticed none of these—just the lighthouse.

The longer he stared, the more he searched for explanations. Maybe he wasn't going crazy. Maybe there was some sort of hallucinogen in the town water. Or maybe the salt air wasn't as good for you as people say. John ran through one reason after another why he was having all of these déjà vu moments.

Just then, a sound from behind him snapped him from his thoughts. At first, the sound blended in with the squawking of the seagulls, but slowly John distinguished between the two. The noise he was hearing was more of a squeaking sound.

He looked over his shoulder and saw an old lady slowly pushing a shopping cart down the path. Her shoulders stooped and her shuffled gait looked weary as she struggled to lift her heavy orthotic shoes. She wore a ragged cardigan sweater over a worn Calico floral dress.

He couldn't exactly tell what the cart was filled with, but he did notice she had her jacket slung over the end of it. Due to her extremely slow pace, and the fact that she appeared to have a bad back, John assumed she was quite old.

Being from Chicago, seeing homeless people pushing shopping carts was nothing new to John, but he was shocked to see it here in Applewood. And just like home, John made sure his eye contact didn't linger. He remembered the first time Hannah had seen homeless people on the streets. Like most kids, she couldn't stop staring and had a million questions.

"Why is that person sleeping on a piece of cardboard? Why does that person have all their clothes with them? Why is that person talking to himself? Why do they have signs asking for money?"

John did his best to answer her questions, but was adamant about not making eye contact. And ever the jaded one, John was always weary about giving his hard-earned money to *beggars*.

Kristen, on the other hand, always threw a little something in their cup. She was also quick to point out, "We should never judge someone until you walk a day in their shoes." John would give her a huff and an eye roll but secretly loved her optimism.

As he turned his attention back to the lighthouse, he felt a twinge of sadness… and guilt. He always assumed Kristen knew how much he loved her kindness and optimism, but he never actually told her. He had told her many things, but it was the words that were left unsaid that he regretted the most.

The squeaky shopping cart wheel was getting closer and closer, and John knew it was only a matter of time before she'd ask him if he could spare any change. Against his better judgement, he reached in his pocket and pulled out a ten. He knew this would make Kristen happy.

The bill never left his hand, however, for the old lady never approached him. Instead, she made her way over to another one of the overlook benches about twenty feet to his left. For whatever reason, John ended up breaking his number one rule and once again made eye contact with her. At first, she was too busy gazing out at the ocean to notice his look. She was close enough now for him to somewhat make out what was in her cart. It seemed to be filled with plants and flowers.

When John finally raised his eyes from her cart, he found her staring directly at him. He didn't say a word but offered a polite smile. With their eyes still locked, she fumbled with her glasses, which she had on a chain around her neck. Even with her glasses on, she squinted long and hard over at John. She then sat up as straight as her back allowed, and her eyes widened as if in shock.

Her look made John feel uneasy. *This is exactly why you avoid eye contact*, he thought to himself and quickly looked away. He tried his best to refocus on the lighthouse, but he could sense that the woman was still staring at him. It wasn't until she started to get up that John knew it was time to leave. The last thing he wanted was to listen to some old homeless lady babble to him and beg for money.

Before she even started to approach him, John had stood up and high-tailed it out of there. He stuffed the ten dollar bill back into his pocket, said a quick apology to Kristen, then headed back to William's.

* * *

It was mid-afternoon before he finally began mowing the yard. The previous couple of hours were spent moving the rest of the tree and stacking the broken gazebo off to the side. The grass was tall, but luckily, it wasn't very thick. John still had to go over it twice, but he knew it could have been much worse. When the grass was mowed, and when the walkway was weeded, John grabbed the clippers and did his best to trim the overgrown hedges on either side of the front porch.

It had been a long time since he had done this much manual labor, so he found himself taking frequent breaks. Although very tempted, his breaks consisted of water or Gatorade—not the whiskey from his flask. As a matter of fact, the flask still remained tucked away in his bag of clothes.

For dinner, he made his way back to the diner he had driven by the night before. While he didn't try their award-winning clam chowder, he did have more than his fill of Shephard's Pie. For dessert, he indulged in their "World Famous" apple pie. The slice was as big as his head, and the giant scoop of ice cream on top nearly did him in.

For months he'd been living on fast food, junk food, and whiskey. He couldn't even remember his last home-cooked meal. Actually, he could. It was a couple nights before... before the accident. Kristen made spaghetti and meatballs. Kristen made the meatballs and sauce completely from scratch. Hannah was in charge of the garlic bread and may or may not have overdone it on the garlic. John nearly choked to death on his first bite, but he told Hannah it was the best garlic bread ever.

As John finished off his apple pie, his thoughts turned to Kevin. He knew he had put his brother through hell this past year, especially the last month. He also knew he promised Kevin that he'd call him as soon as he got to Applewood. While John waited for the waitress to drop the check off, he reached into his pocket and pulled out his flip phone. Just like he thought; he had five missed calls and five new messages.

"More coffee?" asked the waitress as she placed the bill on the table.

John pondered a second then smiled. "Sure, why not."

She returned his smile and topped off his coffee. He closed his phone and placed it back into his pocket, promising himself to call Kevin later on.

The sun was on its final descent when John arrived back at William's house. He was so stuffed from his meal that he was tempted to just pass out on the couch, but he didn't. Strangely, he found enough energy to start another project.

From his truck, he grabbed a scraper and made his way over to the front porch. He planned on replacing the steps tomorrow, but the railings and deck itself were in desperate need of a good scraping. The paint was pretty much already disintegrated, so it didn't take a lot of effort on John's part. That being said, he was still able to work up quite a sweat. At one point, he was in such a zone and rhythm that he didn't hear Sara approaching from behind.

"Wow, the yard looks great," she said.

John jumped and nearly dropped the scraper.

"Sorry," she smiled. "I didn't mean to startle you. I thought you could use some lemonade."

He stood up from his crouched position and took the glass from Sara's outreached hand.

"Thank you."

"Don't thank me until you taste it," she laughed. "Suzy was in charge of the sugar, so it might be a tad sweet."

"I'm sure it'll be fine," he politely said as he took a sip then nearly spit it back out.

"Warned you," she smiled and watched John choke down another small sip. "You really don't have to drink it. Suzy strongly suggested I bring a glass over to you. And by suggested, I mean she ordered me. Yes, apparently I take orders from a five-year-old."

John returned her smile then forced down another sip.

"Seriously, you don't have to drink it. I usually just take a sip to appease my daughter then throw the rest away."

"It's okay. I can handle a tad sweet."

Sara gazed around the yard then said, "It's amazing how a simple mow can make such a difference."

He nodded in agreement, but stood there unsure what to say next. Fortunately, Sara was well equipped to carry the conversation.

"I noticed your license plate earlier… you're from Illinois?"

Again, he nodded then quietly answered, "Chicago."

"Cool! I would love to go there. I've never really been anywhere. Sometimes it feels like I'll be stuck here for the rest of my life."

John didn't really know how to respond, so he simply stood there sipping his lemonade.

"Wait, you drove all the way from Chicago just to fix up this little house? That's a long drive."

"Kind of a working vacation, I guess," he shrugged. "And it wasn't that bad of a drive."

"Still, I would have totally flown," she said.

John shrugged again then said, "I guess I've always kind of had a fear of flying."

"Bad experience?" she asked.

"No. I've never actually flown before."

"So is this what you do for a living? Drive around fixing up people's houses?"

"Umm, no. This is just a favor."

Sara remained persistent. "So what do you do back in Chicago? I'm sorry. I'm asking way too many questions, aren't I?"

Yes, yes you are, the voice in John's head answered. *I just want to be left alone to my scraping.*

John's real voice ended up saying, "It's okay. I kind of own a bar with my brother."

"Oh cool! That's similar to my career," she said.

"Really? You own a bar?"

"No," she laughed. "I'm a teacher, but sometimes alcohol plays a very important part in that."

John found himself laughing along with her.

"I'm just kidding. I actually rarely drink. I'm an English teacher. High school. A high school English teacher to be specific."

Realizing she was way more talkative than John, Sara paused her babbling and turned her attention back to her own house. Ben was in the front yard throwing a baseball up onto the roof then catching it in his glove. Little Suzy was riding her bike in the road and proceeded to ring her bell over and over.

"They're a handful, but definitely worth it," she smiled. "How about you? Any kids?"

As Sara's question hung in the air, John focused on Suzy riding her bike. And the more he focused, the more his mind took him back in time to his own daughter. He was once again standing on the sidewalk outside his house pushing Hannah on her bike. Her face contained the same scared and nervous look as his previous flashback.

"Don't let go, Daddy! I'm not ready yet."

"I'm not letting go, sweetie. I got you," John said, releasing his hands from her seat.

With his breath held, he stood back and anxiously watched Hannah pedal as she white-knuckle-gripped the handlebars. She was wobbly and unstable, but she was absolutely doing it on her own.

"Use your brake," he yelled.

Hannah slammed on her brakes, nearly skidding into a bush. She kept her balance, placed both little feet on the ground, then turned back around. When she saw John smiling and proudly rushing down the road towards her, she realized she had done it on her own.

"I did it! I did it, Daddy!" she excitedly screamed, jumping off her bike. She examined her skid mark then boasted, "And I laid some serious rubber too!"

John laughed and held out his arms.

"I did it, I did it!" she continued to scream as she ran to hug her father.

But just as she entered John's outstretched arms, she disappeared. When he snapped out of his flashback, he lost his grip on the glass, causing it to fall and shatter onto the porch.

"Oh shit!" he exclaimed. "I'm so sorry!"

The noise caused Suzy and Ben to stop what they were doing and look over.

"Are you okay?" Sara asked.

Visibly shaken, John just stood there watching Sara bend down to pick up the pieces.

"I can pick that up, Sara. I guess I'm still exhausted from the trip yesterday. I think maybe I should head in and get some rest."

"A trip like that, you definitely need a good night's sleep," she said, continuing to pick up the broken glass.

"I said I'll pick it up later!" he snapped.

His sharp tone caused Sara to slowly stand and back up. He'd become so accustomed to snapping at his brother for cleaning up his messes, it took him a second to realize who he was talking to.

"Oh my God! I'm sorry, Sara," he quickly apologized. "I didn't mean to snap at you."

"It's okay," she said, still taken aback. "You should get some rest."

"Yea, I will," he nodded then turned and grabbed the door knob. "Sorry again for the glass."

Before Sara could tell him it was okay, he had already entered the house and shut the door behind him. Sara stood there a second, picked up the rest of the glass, then returned to her house.

John leaned his back against the front door and placed his head in his hands. He couldn't believe he was still having flashbacks. It was as if he thought traveling hundreds of miles from home and being without a drink for four days would cure his broken heart and damaged past. Between the strange déjà vu moments of his day, and his flashbacks of his daughter, he knew only one thing could numb his pain.

He marched over to where he dropped his bag the night before. It took him a moment, but his jittery hands finally got it unzipped. He rustled through his clothes until he felt the cool-to-the-touch stainless steel flask. The only feeling more satisfying was when he twisted off the cap and emptied the contents into his mouth.

In eager anticipation, he leaned back on the couch and tipped the flask upwards. But instead of the soothing, familiar burn of whiskey, John cringed in disgust. His whiskey had been replaced with water. Fucking water. John knew exactly who was responsible.

"Fuckin' Kevin!" he mumbled aloud, slamming the flask back into his bag.

When he calmed down a bit, he remembered that the local general store had a small selection of hard alcohol. He kicked himself for not stocking up earlier. He knew the store would be closing soon, so he needed to get a move on if he wanted some whiskey flowing through his body before nightfall. The couch cushions had a different plan for him, however. They were old and dusty but extremely comfortable.

John's intentions were to just rest his eyes for a few minutes, but the soothing sounds from the wind chimes outside turned a few minutes into the entire night. Without a doubt, it was deepest and best night of sleep he'd had in what seemed like forever. There was no tossing and turning, no flashbacks or bad dreams, and even his craving for alcohol had subsided for the night.

17

Applewood high school was the typical small-town school. It was small enough for everyone to know each other's names, but big enough to have all the same cliques as a larger school.

Inside Sara's classroom, she had just finished reading the poem "Nothing Gold Can Stay" to her class.

"This is a perfect example how poems don't always need to be long and drawn out to get there point across. This one only has eight lines, yet within those lines, Mr. Frost uses nature's imagery as a metaphor for his deeper meaning. And although this one does, not all poems need to rhyme either."

One of the jocks in the back row blurted out, "Stay gold, Ponyboy!"

More specifically, it came from Don Cavanagh, the self-proclaimed king of the jocks. Not only was he the captain of the football team, but he was the captain of being loud and obnoxious as well.

"Yes, Don, this poem was featured in the *Outsiders*. It's nice to see you've actually read the book," she joked.

"There's a book? I was talking about the movie."

While Sara smiled and shook her head, Don exchanged high fives with his two sidekicks, Brock and Trevor.

Sara gazed up at the clock.

"And don't forget, people, each of you is to pick a favorite poem which you will read aloud in class."

Almost the entire class let out a giant groan; everyone except Bill. Bill was the shy, smart, shaggy-haired boy, who always sat in the front row. Partly, he did this to be as far away from Don and his friends as possible, but mostly, it had to with Rachel Letourneau.

Rachel was extremely good looking, popular, and as smart as they come. She wasn't the stuck-up type of popular or the type to hang out with Don and his immature friends. Her popularity stemmed from her being polite, friendly, and respectful to everyone. Of course, her drop-dead gorgeous looks didn't hurt either.

Bill sat two seats away from Rachel, and his eyes didn't leave her the entire time Sara was reading the poem. He'd had a crush on her for as long as he could remember. He liked everything about her; her smile, her laugh, her sweet smell, and yes, he even loved how smart she was. Everything about her was perfect. Bill was still fixated on Rachel when Sara addressed him.

"And I'm especially looking forward to the poem you pick out, Bill." Sara said in Bill's direction.

Sara's comment caused Rachel to turn and smile over at Bill, which also caused Rachel to catch Bill staring at her. The whole thing caused Bill to quickly look away as his face turned a bright red. Luckily, the period bell sounded off, saving Bill from further embarrassment.

His face remained red, and he slowly stood up and clumsily loaded his notebook into his backpack. He made absolutely sure not to look over at Rachel. When he finally peered out from the corner of his eye and saw that she had left, he let out a sigh of relief. His relief was short-lived, however.

"Hey, Bill," yelled Don, from the back of the room. "Are you going to the homecoming dance?"

Bill looked over at the three jocks then lowered his head and shrugged.

"I can't believe Rachel Letourneau is actually thinking of asking you to it," Don scoffed.

Bill's heart leapt up into his throat, and he raised his head to Don.

"What?" Bill hesitantly asked.

"We can't believe it either," said Brock. "But that's the rumor around school."

Bill's face remained stoic, but his insides were jumping for joy.

"Really? You heard that Rachel wants to ask *me* to the homecoming dance?"

The three jocks held their look for as long as they could. Finally, they all burst out laughing.

"Are you serious, Billy boy?" laughed Don. "Do you really think Rachel Letourneau would go to the dance with you?"

"Looks like you're stuck going with your mom," laughed Trevor.

Deflated and once again embarrassed, Bill lowered his head and threw his backpack over his shoulder.

"Okay, that's enough boys!" Sara scolded. "Get to class."

The three jocks snickered and laughed their way out the door. Before Bill could shuffle his way out as well, Sara called to him.

"Hey, Bill, do you have a second?"

"Um, yes, Mrs. Peyton," he said, slowly turning back around.

"Don't let those idiots get to you, okay?"

Bill looked down at his untied shoes and nodded.

"Besides, I'm chaperoning that dance, so you better be there."

His head remained lowered as he shrugged.

"And FYI, I heard that Rachel is going by herself to the dance."

Her comment perked him up enough to raise his head at her.

"How do you know that?" he asked.

"I'm a teacher. I know everything," she smiled and then winked.

Bill returned her smile and rolled his eyes at his favorite teacher.

"And it's none of my business, Bill, but I think you should ask her to the dance."

And just like that, his smile faded and his head once again lowered.

Before she could say another word, Mr. Goodwin entered Sara's room.

"Well, you better get to class," she said to Bill. "And just think about what I said, okay?"

"Yes, Mrs. Peyton," he said then turned to leave.

"Hey, Bill," Mr. Goodwin said as he walked by him.

When Bill was completely out of the classroom, Mr. Goodwin sat on the corner of Sara's desk.

"What was that all about?" he asked.

"Sorry, Paul," she smiled, "but teacher/student confidentiality prevents me from telling you."

"Yeah, yeah, yeah," he said, rolling his eyes. "So, how's your day going?"

"Not so bad. How about you?"

"Oh, you know, just another day of molding young minds."

"Is that what we're supposed to be doing?"

"Something like that," he smiled.

Paul taught history, and like Sara, this was his first year teaching at Applewood High. Also like Sara, Paul was one of the youngest teachers there. He had just turned twenty-seven, and due to his young, hip nature, he was by far a favorite among the students. He was kind and funny, and his teaching methods were more relatable to the kids compared to the tired old ways.

His clean-cut good looks also made him popular with some of the older female teachers; the single ones or otherwise. Whether he was humble or simply oblivious, Paul didn't seem to pay any mind to their flirting. From day one, he only had eyes for Sara. And from day one, she politely spurned all of his attempts at asking her out. It wasn't because she didn't like him or find him attractive, because she did, very much.

"By the way, you look great today," he said, looking her over.

"Thanks," she said then slightly blushed. "You do realize you tell me that every day, right?"

Without missing a beat he said, "Well, I guess you look good every day then."

It was true, Paul complimented Sara's outfit every single day, but the reason it still made her blush was his sincerity. Unlike most guys, Paul's comment wasn't intended as a pickup line, it was truly and genuinely meant as an honest compliment.

Secretly, Sara loved his compliments. And if truth be told, she loved hearing them in front of the other female teachers. Especially the ones who went out of their way to try and get Paul to notice or compliment them as well. Cliques, gossiping, and acting catty wasn't just relegated to the students.

"Hey, I heard there's a new Italian restaurant that just opened up. What do you say we check it out one night this week?"

With her cheeks still red from his earlier compliment, she let out a sigh and gave him a look. It was the type of look one might give to a child who asked a question that they already knew the answer to.

"Paul."

"What?" he asked and smiled knowingly.

"I told you, I just don't think it would be very professional of us, that's all."

"It's not like I'm one of your students asking you out. Now that wouldn't be very professional. But it's just two colleagues eating good food together."

"You're incorrigible," she smiled.

"Soooo? Is that a yes?" he asked hopefully.

"I'm sorry Paul, I just can't."

Before he could say another word, the bell rang.

Paul shot her a playful look then said, "Saved by the bell… this time." He stood up and started to leave. "I'm not giving up, you know?"

She returned his smile, blushed a brighter red, then turned her attention to the students who started to filter into her room.

* * *

When John finally awoke from his sleep, he couldn't believe how well-rested he was. The alcohol craving from the night before had subsided. Not only did he have the best night of sleep in forever, but he awoke with a clear, hangover-free head. It had been a long time for that as well.

Another rarity was John awoke with the sun. Actually, he was awake and ready to go before the sun even poked its head out. He knew the general store opened early, but as he pulled in for a coffee, he was shocked at just how busy it was at that hour. It was nothing like the previous day.

Almost the entirety of its customers were fishermen and lobstermen, and then there was John; a big city bar owner who had never even been on a boat in the ocean. Everyone was polite enough, but it was completely obvious that John was an outsider.

On that particular morning, he stuck out even more. While everyone there was clad in flannel, Carhartts, and fishing gear, John sported jeans, a white Cubs hoodie, and his classic blue Cubs hat. Yup, his appearance screamed outsider!

After John made himself a coffee and grabbed a blueberry muffin, he began to wander around the old general store. The next thing he knew, he was standing directly in front of the small section of hard alcohol. The bottle of Jameson glistened under the store's overhead lights. It stared back at John, almost whispering for him to pick it up. After a long, hard stare-down, he decided against it. He already felt like everybody's eyes were on him. He didn't need to give them more of a reason to look at him funny, and purchasing a bottle of whiskey before the sun even came up would certainly be cause for that.

Before walking away, he shot the bottle a look, as if to say, *Don't worry, I'll be back for you later.* John then headed to the counter to pay for his coffee and muffin.

"Anything else I can get ya?" asked the older woman behind the register.

"No, I think I'm all…"

Before he finished his sentence, his eyes fell upon a display of disposable cameras behind the woman.

"Actually, can I get one of those cameras?"

She turned and grabbed one of them off the shelf.

"Doing some sightseeing while you're in town?" she smiled.

At first, John was taken aback by her comment, but then he remembered how he was dressed. He was tempted to make a joke about how obvious it was that he wasn't from there. He could have filled her in on where he was from and why he was in town, but that would have required him being social—he wasn't ready for that yet.

He felt more rested than he'd been in months, but still, he wasn't looking to be social. He was there to fix up William's house, and when that was done with, he most definitely planned on getting reacquainted with his Jameson or whatever else he decided to drink. The quietness of Applewood would provide the perfect place to drink it all away. There'd be no Kevin or Julie giving him disappointed looks, and there certainly wouldn't be a wacky therapist shoving rubber bands into a fish tank talking about his buried feelings.

"Need batteries for it?" she asked.

"What?" John asked.

"Batteries… for the camera."

"Oh, yea, that'd be great. Thank you."

That's as much of a conversation as she would get from him. He paid for his items, climbed into his truck, then headed back to the house. It was still way too dark and early for him to start any of the repairs, so he decided to make his way through the wooded path and into the cove.

With his coffee in hand, he sat on a large rock and watched the sun slowly rise over the horizon. The sky was a pinkish purple and was one of the most beautiful sights he'd ever seen. He reached into his sweatshirt pocket and pulled out his new camera. Before he knew it, he was snapping pictures left and right. This is what Kristen would be doing, he thought. More importantly, seeing as she wasn't there, he knew this is what she'd want him to be doing.

When the pinks and purples faded, and when the sun was high enough in the sky, John climbed down from the rock and continued to walk through the cove. When he came upon the broken-down boat, he paused. The last thing he wanted was to strike up another conversation with the old fisherman. He had nothing against the man, he simply wanted to be on his own and enjoy the peace and quiet of the beach.

When he was sure there were no signs of the man, John continued forward. Less than twenty feet from the boat, he heard a scraping sound followed by whistling. Again, before he could turn and head back in the other direction, the old man came around the boat. A wide smile appeared when he saw John standing there.

"Ahoy, matey!" the man yelled out. "I see you're taking me up on my offer to help fix her up."

"Um… no… I was just taking a…"

"Oh come on. I'm sure you've got a little time to help an old man out."

Before John could say another word, Clarence tossed him a paint scraper.

"Go ahead, attack her. She needs a good scraping."

This was yet another reason John wanted to avoid social interactions with people. Not only was he now forced to enter into a conversation, but he got guilted into physical labor. He hesitated but couldn't bring himself to say no to the old man, so he placed his coffee on a rock and began scraping the side of the boat.

Besides Clarence whistling an upbeat tune, the sound of scraping paint was the only noise heard over the next ten minutes. John would gladly take the sound of whistling over conversation any day. When Clarence's whistling finally stopped, John knew it was only a matter of time.

"So, what brings a big-city boy to our little town?" Clarence asked, continuing his scraping.

"Um, I'm just helping a friend fix their house and tie up some loose ends. He's actually still back in Chicago… he was a little too sick to make the trip himself."

Clarence sensed this was a more serious type of sickness than John led on.

"I see," said Clarence, pausing his scraping. "Sorry about your friend."

John had no desire to go into details about William's condition. Nor did he have the need to explain that he barely even knew William. In hindsight, he should have told him. Instead, John's silence caused Clarence to ask another question; a question that John wasn't prepared for.

"You got a family back there in Chicago?"

John's heart stopped, and he nearly dropped the scraper. Completely caught off guard, he was speechless for a moment. The next thing he knew, his lips uttered, "Ummm, yea, a wife and daughter."

"Ahh, nice. Did they come out here with you?"

John just couldn't bring himself to clarify his original response, so he simply shook his head no and said nothing.

Sensing John's uneasiness, Clarence took in a deep breath of air then said, "Ahh, nothing like the salt air. It always helps me clear my head. It has a strange way of making people think straight." He winked at John then gazed out towards the ocean. "It's all out there, ya know?"

John followed Clarence's gaze but all he saw was a vast, empty ocean.

"What is?"

"The answers," Clarence responded expressionless.

John looked at the ocean and let out a slight skeptical laugh, but when he saw the seriousness on the old man's face, John decided to curb his laughter and resume scraping. While Clarence continued staring out at the waves, John moved to the other side of the boat. It was there, in faded, paint-peeled black lettering that he noticed the name of the boat: "*Medillia's Lament.*"

"Not you too?" John laughed out loud.

Clarence made his way over to John and smiled. "I see you've heard of the legend, huh?"

"Oh, I've heard it," John laughed again.

"Ahh, I see," Clarence said, rubbing his beard. "You've heard it but don't believe it, huh?"

"Something like that."

"Oh, it's true, my boy. It only lasts for a brief moment in time, mind you, but when this magical event occurs, it turns Applewood into a place where anything is possible."

John didn't want to be rude to the old man, so he held back his laughter and placated him with an agreeing nod.

Clarence saw right through it and said, "Ahhh, a pessimist, I see."

"Just a realist," John muttered and then pretended to check his watch. "I should probably get going. I have a lot to do back at the house."

He handed his scraper to Clarence and slowly made his way back around the boat. He grabbed his coffee off the rock, threw a wave to the old man, and then started to head off.

"Thanks again, son, for your help. I appreciate it more than you'll know."

John turned back around and gave him a polite nod.

"And in case you happen to wander by again, I take my coffee black with two sugars."

Again, John gave him a polite nod before turning and walking away.

18

When John returned to William's house, the wind had picked up significantly. It was cold and brisk, and brought the strong refreshing scent of salt air with it. Compared to Chicago, any kind of air was refreshing, but there really was something special about this ocean air from Maine.

Once back at the house, John replaced the front steps and finished scraping down the porch. By late morning, it was ready for paint. There were some paint cans in the shed, but they were much too old and dried up to use. He made his way to the local hardware store for some new paint and brushes.

Because of the heavy traffic in Chicago, it could take you twenty minutes to drive a few miles. But here in Applewood, John was lucky if he saw another car on the road. He loved how quiet and peaceful the island was.

After he gave the porch two good coats of paint, he checked it off his list and moved on to the next project: Replace and paint the trim around the windows. The windy conditions were perfect for helping the paint dry on the porch, but not so much for climbing up a ladder. Because of that, John decided to start on the first floor windows.

* * *

The rest of the school day, Bill couldn't get Mrs. Peyton's words out of his head: *I heard that Rachel is going by herself to the dance... I think you should ask her...*

Bill had a hard time believing that Rachel didn't have a date to the big dance, but he also had a hard time believing Mrs. Peyton would lie to him. She was his all-time favorite teacher. He had some great teachers over the years, but Mrs. Peyton was different; she *got* him, like really got him. She saw things in him that most people didn't.

There were times when he actually thought he'd have a better chance of Mrs. Peyton going to the dance with him rather than Rachel Letourneau. Unfortunately, the reality was that Don and his friends were probably right. He would have a better chance going with his mom than Rachel.

That being said, Bill had spent the entire day working up the courage to at least strike up a conversation with Rachel. So when the final bell rang, Bill headed straight for his locker, which was a few down from hers. As he walked down the long hallway, he noticed that she was already at her locker. Nervously, he thought about what he was going to say to her. He had come up with some bullet-point conversation topics while in Math class, but all that went out the window when she made eye contact with him and smiled.

His pace came to a halt, and he returned her smile. Or did he? In his heart, he was smiling ear to ear, but he wasn't sure if that actually transferred to his actual face or not.

He stood perfectly still, watching her from afar as she placed her things into her locker. He clutched his books, took a deep breath, and prepared to walk over and talk to her. Unfortunately, Bill didn't clutch his books tight enough, nor did he sense Don approaching him from behind.

In one swift motion, Don karate chopped Bill's arms, causing his books to tumble to the ground. Don and his friends just laughed and continued walking. Bill's face turned a bright red as he slowly bent over to collect his things.

He was way too embarrassed to even raise his head up. *Did Rachel see what just happened? Was she laughing with the rest of them?* When he finally did look up, Rachel was nowhere in sight. His plan for a real conversation with her would have to wait another day.

Sara spent her after school time in the office making copies. When she was finally finished, she made her way back to her classroom. A wide, curious smile fell on her face as she entered her room. There, on her desk, sat a small bouquet of flowers. She looked around, but she was the only one in the room.

Hesitantly, Sara approached her desk and lifted the flowers into her arms. She reached in and grabbed the small note, which was resting inside the bouquet. Her face flushed red and she continued to smile as she read the note: *Not giving up! ~ Paul*

Again, she looked around the room to see if anyone was there. When she was sure she was alone, she sat in her chair and raised the flowers up to her nose. Their sweet scent caused her to blush even more. If Sara was catty like most of her colleagues, she would have paraded the flowers into the teachers' room and nonchalantly placed them (and the note) on the counter for all to see. Although tempted, Sara knew she was better than that. She packed up her things, grabbed the flowers, and made her way out to her car.

***

It was a little after three o'clock when John noticed a car pull into Sara's driveway. Suzy and Ben jumped out of the car and sprinted towards the house. Well, Suzy sprinted. Ben's pace was more slow and mopey. The driver was an older woman, and John assumed by her age and resemblance that she was probably Sara's mother.

Before the woman even got to the front door, Suzy was already rushing out of the house with a handful of dolls. She planted herself on the grass with them then looked over and shot John an excited wave. Although more subdued, John waved back at her.

A few minutes later, Ben also exited the house. He was wearing ripped blue jeans and a black sweatshirt with the hood pulled over his head. He wore his baseball glove on his left hand, and John watched as he began tossing the ball onto the roof then catching it. Even though John had yet to have a conversation with Ben, he smiled at the fact that Ben completely reminded him of himself at that age.

John also could tell that Suzy and Ben were nothing alike. Suzy was very outgoing and full of life, not to mention, quite talkative. Ben seemed more reserved—more of a loner—more sad. It was all of those things that reminded John of himself years earlier.

Seeing as he had been up since sunrise, John decided to call it a day. He put away his tools then headed inside for a well-deserved shower. As he walked up the front steps, he paused a second to admire his paint job on the porch. These were all minor repairs, but he definitely felt a sense of accomplishment. It was something he hadn't felt in a long time.

He took an extra-long shower, making sure to let the hot water penetrate deep into his aching muscles. He was more than a bit embarrassed at just how sore he was, especially considering how little he had done. *Months of drinking and planting yourself on the couch will do that to a man*, he thought.

After his shower, he decided to drive over to his new favorite restaurant, the Applewood Diner. As much as he loved their Shephard's Pie, he decided to go with the specialty of the night - fish-n-chips. He was pleasantly blown away by the large portion of fresh haddock. It was a far cry from the tiny frozen fish sticks Mrs. O'Neil used to cook for them.

Ironically, fish stick night was one of Kevin and John's favorite meals. What they hated was Sloppy Joe night. Not because they disliked them, but because they were Mr. O'Neil's favorite. They were forced to sit there and watch in disgust as Mr. O'Neil chewed and talked with his mouth wide open. This wasn't really different from any other meal, but Sloppy Joe night just felt worse. Secretly, both brothers had their fingers crossed that one night he would choke to death on them.

Quickly, John shook the image of Mr. O'Neil from his mind. He wasn't about to let that asshole ruin his perfect and delicious fish-n-chips. When John was finished, he also decided to switch up his dessert choice and had their homemade coconut cream pie. It was a decision he wouldn't regret.

John actually loved that the diner was always packed. He considered it a win-win. He got to eat an amazing meal, and the waitresses were always too busy with customers to pay much attention to him. He knew if the diner was quiet, there'd be a better chance for the waitress to strike up a conversation with him.

You're not from around here, are you? Where are you from? Why are you here? What do you do back home? Married? Kids?

John wanted to avoid these questions at all costs.

He paid his bill and headed back towards William's house. Once again, when he came to the four-way stop, his eyes focused to his left on the deteriorated, knocked over Island Air Tours sign. And once again, that same sick feeling entered his stomach.

Sick feeling aside, his curiosity got the best of him, and he turned left. One side of the road was lined with nothing but pine trees, and on the other, as far as the eyes could see, was nothing but marsh land. Finally, after about three or four miles, he spotted another Island Air

Tour sign. It was in just as bad a condition as the first sign. It was barely visible behind a pair of overgrown bushes, and John actually drove by it before noticing it.

He slowly backed up and turned down a dirt road. The setting sun caused shadows from the trees to fall upon the road. At one point, the road got so narrow, and the branches were so low, that they creepily brushed against his truck. For a brief second, he wondered if he was a character in a Stephen King novel.

Just as quickly, however, the road widened and the trees lessened. The road took a sharp turn to the right, and that's when it was revealed. Up ahead was a large clearing. John pulled in front of a small, vacant building. There was a wide wooden sign hanging from the roof. Most of the painted letters were faded and peeled off, but it was still obvious what it said: Island Air Tours. The building itself wasn't in much better condition. There were weeds and vines growing up its side and most of the windows were broken.

John climbed out of his truck and took a walk behind the building. Eventually, he came across what he assumed to be its runway. Like the building, the old asphalt runway had seen better days. Weeds and grass poked their way through the many, many cracks, and in some cases, were nearly waist high.

As John gazed around, he couldn't shake the unsettling feeling coursing through his body. He had no clue what was causing it, but what he did know, was he didn't want to be stuck out there when the sun officially went down. Hastily, he walked back to his truck then high-tailed it out of there.

By the time he made his way back to the four-way stop, the setting sun had caused the sky to turn the brightest of pinks. Without even thinking about it, he found himself driving out towards Harbor Cove Park. After the creepy feeling he just experienced, he figured relaxing on a bench overlooking the ocean would be the perfect ending to his day.

Once again, his car was the only one in the small dirt lot. He couldn't believe a place as beautiful and peaceful as this wasn't packed with people. He couldn't believe it, but he certainly wasn't complaining.

After he climbed the wooden steps, he wound his way down the paved path towards the lighthouse overlook. The sun was setting fast, and with it, the pink hues had nearly faded out completely. John was still able to snap a couple of good shots of the lighthouse. He planted himself on the bench and made a mental note that he should come here one morning for the sunrise. *It would be the perfect spot*, he thought.

He still couldn't believe this was the same lighthouse from his dreams. Seeing as his mind had been so screwed up this past year, he started to question whether he really had those dreams or not. Maybe he just dreamed he had the dream. The longer he stared at it, the more he knew the truth. This was indeed the same lighthouse he had been dreaming about for as long as he could remember.

As he continued to gaze at it, he began laughing out loud. Between the visions of the lighthouse and the path to the cove, maybe God had had given him the gift of premonition. Of course, *if* God actually existed, this would totally be his style; to give John the ability to see useless shit. Why couldn't God have given him cool premonitions, like the Cubs finally winning the World Series, or what the winning lottery numbers would be. Yup, these were yet another reason why John had a hard time believing in the man upstairs.

"It is what it is," he mumbled to himself as he leaned back on the bench. He soon became mesmerized watching the waves crash into the rocks surrounding the lighthouse. So mesmerized, in fact, his eyes slowly closed, and he found himself in a peaceful sleep.

It wasn't until he heard the familiar sound of the squeaky wheel that he awoke. It was faint at first, causing him to assume he was just dreaming. But the closer and louder it got, the wider his eyes opened. By now, darkness had fallen over the park. John adjusted his eyes and slowly peered over his shoulder.

The cart was parked next to the granite memorial, and the old woman was kneeled down beside it. John told himself he needed to quickly look away as to avoid the dreaded eye contact, but it was too late; she looked up and their eyes met. Once again, she placed her glasses on her face and stared over at him. And once again, this creeped him out.

Like before, he threw her a polite smile then turned back towards the darkened ocean. He assumed at any moment the squeaky cart would make its way over to him and she'd be hitting him up for money. John reached for his wallet but realized he'd left it in his truck. In his head, he began rehearsing lines.

Sorry, ma'am, I'd love to help out, but I left my wallet in my truck.

No, that wouldn't work. What if she decided to follow him back to his truck? He decided it was best to just apologize to her and tell her he left his wallet at home. *Yea, that would work*, he thought.

Right on schedule, the wheel began squeaking. To John's surprise, instead of getting louder and closer, it got quieter and quieter. When he could barely hear it, he finally turned his head and saw that she was all the way at the other end of the park.

He immediately felt like shit and promised himself that the next time he saw her, he would offer her some money. Or maybe he might even offer to buy her a warm meal at the diner. Well, that might be pushing it, but he'd definitely offer some money. John carried that thought with him as he left the park and headed back to William's house.

Before he hit the couch and passed out for the night, he decided to finally call his brother. Kevin spent the first few minutes scolding John for not calling sooner. Normally, Kevin's chastising tone would have pissed John off and he would have gotten all defensive, but this time was different.

He knew how worried Kevin was, and he also knew he had every right to be. He'd put his brother through hell this past year. John apologized for his lack of consideration, which completely caught Kevin off guard. Kevin didn't come out and ask it, but John knew exactly what he was wondering. He wanted to know if John was drinking again.

Although the subject was never talked about, the sheer length of their phone call was enough to slightly ease Kevin's mind. The brothers stayed on the phone with one another for nearly thirty minutes. It was their longest conversation in over a year, phone or otherwise.

John did his best to describe Applewood and the coast of Maine. He filled Kevin in on the repairs he had done already to the house. Before getting off the phone, he told Kevin to tell William that everything was going perfectly.

"So when do you think you're coming back?" asked Kevin.

"Dunno. Another week or so maybe."

After they hung up with each other, John thought more about Kevin's question. The repairs weren't as bad as William had originally described, and because of that, John assumed he could have it all finished in a few more days. Usually, the thought of finishing a job earlier than planned was a good thing, but in this case, it saddened him a bit. He wasn't ready to go back to Chicago—back to his bar—back to his house.

Before John left Chicago, William gave him a check to cover the repairs and labor. Now that he was in Applewood and able to assess the repairs in person, he realized the check was nearly five times more than he actually needed for all the materials. John also remembered William saying, "Spend what you need to, and the rest is for you. I will *not* be accepting any money back," and then he winked and handed John the check.

John didn't like having so much money left over, and he certainly didn't like the idea of keeping it for himself. Bottom line is he would have done this all for free. Just the fact he was able to get away from Chicago and come to this beautiful place; *hell, I should be paying William for this*, John thought.

Over the next few days, he continued to plug away on the repairs. He also developed a daily routine. He'd wake up with the sun, drive down to the general store for a coffee and muffin, and then head back and start his work day. He did find himself avoiding the cove. It wasn't that John had anything against the old fisherman, not at all. He simply wanted to focus on his own projects, and he knew if he walked by the boat, Clarence would probably convince him to help out again.

It wasn't the helping part John minded, it was the socializing that he dreaded. Even though Applewood had relaxed him quite a bit, he still wasn't ready to answer questions or get into his personal life with anyone. He also avoided going out to Harbor Cove Park. He just didn't want to deal with that old shopping-cart woman making him uncomfortable and begging for money. Granted, she had yet to ask for a penny, but John knew it was only a matter of time.

And then there was Sara. John didn't need to avoid any interactions with her, for she was the one doing the avoiding. She was always quick to offer him a polite smile and wave, but she made it a point not to invade his space—with lemonade or conversation. John knew this stemmed from him snapping at her regarding the broken glass. He felt horrible about it, and he kept telling himself he needed to go over and apologize for his outburst, but he never did. Like most times in his life, he failed to say the words that needed to be said. Whether he was three or thirty-three, he had the hardest time admitting when he was wrong or saying he was sorry. This time was no different than the rest.

Little Suzy, on the other hand, had no problem saying what was on her mind. There were many times that she would yell across the yard, saying hi to John and asking how his day was. John usually just gave her a wave and a thumbs up.

Ben never waved or even acknowledged John. He was either too busy throwing and catching the baseball off the roof or taking walks by himself. John respected both. The more he watched Ben's sad demeanor, the more he was reminded of himself at that age.

Although John kept to himself, he did enjoy watching Sara interact with her kids. As a matter of fact, whenever Sara was home, he couldn't seem take his eyes off her. Sometimes he'd be sitting in the living room inconspicuously watching her through the window. Yes, he realized how creepy this was, but there was just something about her that he was drawn to. He didn't normally consider himself a nosy person, but his mind couldn't help but form random questions about Sara.

Was she married? If so, where was her husband? If not, then how come her ex never came by to visit his kids?

Sara was also intrigued by her new neighbor, and discretely, she found herself watching him as he worked hard on the house. John wasn't the only one with random questions floating about his head. He also wasn't the only one with a daily routine. Sara's daily routine was monotonous and even more tiring than John's.

Sara's schedule: Get two kids up and ready to go. Get them on the bus and then head to school for a long day of molding young minds. If she was lucky, she'd be home by four thirty. This was followed by cooking dinner, doing dishes, overseeing homework, trying to spend a little quality time with her kids, baths, and bedtime.

On a good night, after they went to bed, Sara would draw a hot bath, grab a book, and enjoy a little me time. If she was awake enough, she'd make a cup of tea and curl up on the couch with a movie. More times than not, though, she was fast asleep before doing any of those things.

Over those next few days at school, Paul continued to awkwardly flirt with her and not-so subtly hint at going out to dinner. Each day that week, she would leave school and find a flyer advertising the new Italian restaurant on her windshield. And each time, she would remove it, place it in her car, and blush the whole way home.

During those few days, Bill continued to work up the courage to talk to Rachel. He also couldn't shake the idea of her going to the dance alone. Almost every one of his classroom daydreams revolved around him not only talking to her, but asking her to the dance as well.

* * *

Besides the peace and quiet of Applewood, the best part of John's trip was the sleep. From the first night his head hit the pillow on William's couch, he had the best and most relaxing sleep ever. And despite his brief flashback of Hannah on her bike, John had been flashback and nightmare free. Even his urge to drink had significantly lessened.

He was really starting to think there was something to this whole salt-air theory. Maybe William was right. Maybe Applewood was the perfect place to recharge his batteries. All of that was about to change, however. Those rubber bands his therapist had warned him about were once again on the verge of floating to the surface of his tank.

19

It was late afternoon, and John had just finished another solid day of house repairs. He decided to reward himself with a trip to the general store for a six-pack of cream soda and a box of his favorite snack: Chicken in a Biskit. The brothers were introduced to this delicious cracker while living with the Hawkins. It was one of the few things John remembered fondly from his childhood; watching TV with his brother while sharing a box of Chicken in a Biskit.

As John's truck neared the store, his mouth watered in anticipation. Less than a mile from the store, he heard sirens blaring from behind him. He glanced into his rearview mirror and saw the bright blue lights of a police car. Slowly, he pulled his truck over to the side of the road. The police car sped past him and was immediately followed by an ambulance with its lights and sirens in full effect.

John's heart began to race uncontrollably. He put his truck in park, trying his best to catch his breath as he intently stared at the ambulance until it was out of sight. His hands trembled on the steering wheel, and his breathing was so fast, he felt as if he was on the verge of a panic attack.

John's mind started to take him back to a place and time that he had been repressing for far too long. He wasn't ready for these thoughts to surface yet, so he fought with all his might to clear them from his head. He slammed his fist against the dashboard, threw the truck into drive, cranked on the radio, and continued on his way to the store.

By the time he arrived at the general store, his breathing was almost back to normal. Anxious and visibly shaken, he briskly walked inside and headed straight for the alcohol section. And there, like an old friend staring back at him, was the bottle of Jameson. Shakily, he reached up for the bottle but fell short before grasping it. He was interrupted by a tiny hand tugging on his shirt.

"Daddy!"

John turned around and saw Hannah looking up at him.

"We never give up and we never quit. No matter what!"

He moved his gaze from his daughter back to the bottle. His outreached hand slowly lowered to his side. When he once again turned around to see his little girl, she was gone. Before walking away empty handed, he touched his shirt where her hand had been tugging. He grabbed his crackers and the six-pack of cream soda and approached the register. As always, it was the same woman behind the counter.

"Afternoon," she said, ringing up his two items.

John gave her a nod then looked down, fumbling with his wallet.

"Only fucking sissies drink cream soda," a man's voice said and laughed.

John froze and slowly looked up at the cashier, but it wasn't the cashier at all. There, standing behind the counter was Mr. O'Neil— glaring and snickering at John. John's wallet instantly fell from his hands onto the floor. Hesitantly, he bent over to retrieve it, but when he glanced back up, Mr. O'Neil was gone. It was just the woman behind the counter.

"Anything else I can get ya?" she politely asked.

John paused and turned his head back towards the shelf of alcohol.

* * *

Once back at William's house, he rushed inside and put the brown bag on the kitchen counter. He pulled out the crackers and placed the soda inside of the refrigerator. With the Chicken in a Biskits clutched in his hand, he glanced back at the brown grocery bag then took a seat at the kitchen table.

Before his butt hit the chair, he had the box ripped open and a handful of crackers shoved into his mouth. The more he tried not to, the more he found himself staring at the brown bag. He hoped the familiar taste of his favorite cracker would help clear his mind, but no matter how hard he concentrated, and no matter how hard he tried, he couldn't shake the image of Mr. O'Neil laughing at him.

Eventually, the image became too much, and John cracked under its pressure. He tossed the box aside and walked over and pulled the bottle of Jameson out of the brown bag. He grabbed a glass from the cupboard and filled it more than halfway up.

The house was on the cool side, yet as John stood there staring at the whiskey, he found himself sweating profusely. Quietly, he offered an apology to his daughter then reached over and grabbed the glass. Just as it was about to press against his lips, he stopped. He curiously turned around and cocked his ear. He was positive he heard some sort of noise from the other room. He listened intently, but when he heard nothing, he simply chalked it up as him going crazy.

Once again, he attempted to raise the glass to his lips, and once again, he stopped short as the noise returned. This time he knew he wasn't going crazy. He placed the glass on the counter and headed into the living room. It took him a second to realize that the noise was actually coming from his front porch.

A puzzled look fell over his face as he peered out the window. He opened the front door, and there, sitting on his freshly painted porch was Suzy and a band of her stuffed animals. She had them all in a circle with little plastic tea cups in front of them.

"Suzy? Ummm, what are you doing?" he asked.

"We're having a tea party," she said matter-of-factly.

"Yea, I see that, but… wouldn't you rather do this on your own porch?"

"Nope. Now that you fixed this one up, it's way better than ours. Mr. Bear likes the new paint."

"Ahh. Wait…who?"

"Mr. Bear, silly," she said, pointing to a stuffed teddy bear.

"Oh, right. That Mr. Bear," he smiled.

John took a closer look at Suzy's other party guests. There was a sparkly unicorn, a pink cat, a purple elephant, and even a Barbie doll wearing a fancy dress.

"One of my favorite dolls couldn't make it today. She was feeling a little sick, so she's in bed resting."

John played along. "Sorry to hear that. Hope she feels better soon."

"Thanks," she said, pretending to fill the little plastic cups. "This one is for you," Suzy said, handing it to John.

Hesitantly, he took the tiny cup.

"You are gonna join us, right?" she asked. "After all, it is your porch."

John looked into her big, round blue eyes and knew he couldn't say no. He lowered his body and sat crisscrossed in between Suzy and Barbie.

"Shhhh," John whispered to Barbie. "Don't tell Ken I'm sitting this close to you. He might get jealous."

This caused Suzy to look over at her stuffed bear and giggle, "You're right, Mr. Bear, John is a funny guy."

Over the next half hour, they joked, laughed, and thoroughly enjoyed themselves. Suzy even taught John the official tea party song. The whole time he was enjoying his fake tea, his glass of whiskey sat on the kitchen counter—untouched. Even better, John didn't think about it once.

Sara, on the other hand, could have definitely used a shot of whiskey. While Suzy and John were enjoying their tea party, Sara was in her house arguing on the phone.

"Hello?" she said, picking up the cordless phone. "Oh, hi Rick. Thanks for returning one of my dozen messages." There was no joking in her tone. It was pure sarcasm. "What time are you picking Ben up next weekend?"

Rick's response caused her sarcasm to take on a more bitter and angry tone. Knowing she was about to unleash on him, Sara moved into the kitchen and lowered her voice.

"Are you kidding me? Do you know how excited he is for this camping trip?" She paused a second and listened to Rick's typical excuses. "I don't care how busy you are at work! He's your son for Christ sake! You do realize it's been over a month since you've even seen him?"

Rick's next comments caused her anger to build to a crescendo.

"Me? Why would **I** go with him? It's a father-son camping trip, you idiot! All I can say, is YOU'RE telling him, NOT me!"

Sara removed the phone from her ear long enough for her eyes to shoot laser beams at it. When she returned it to her ear, her anger grew even more.

"What do you mean what do you tell him? Tell him his father is a deadbeat, selfish son of a bitch!"

With that, she ended the call and slammed the phone onto the counter. Her eyes quickly moved from the phone to the back door in the kitchen. There, sitting in the corner, was the pile of Ben's camping gear. Without thinking, she rushed over and began kicking and throwing the gear. Her body slumped into one of the kitchen chairs, and she placed her head in her hands.

When her anger had mostly subsided, she slowly removed her hands from her face. Her eyes widened when she saw Ben standing in the doorway. He took one look at his upset mother and at the thrown-about camping gear and knew exactly what had happened. Sara's heart broke as she watched Ben turn and sprint outside.

She rushed to the front door, but it was too late, Ben was already at the edge of the woods. Sara wanted to rush after her little boy, but she knew he needed some space. Besides, she had no idea the right words to say to him. As much as she knew Rick was a giant asshole and horrible father, she would never ever dream of telling Ben that. Her attention then turned to her daughter, who was sitting on John's porch having an unapproved tea party.

Suzy continued to giggle at John's big fingers trying to hold onto the tiny tea cup handle. John paused mid-sip when he saw Ben fly out of the house and head for the woods.

"I wonder what's up with him?" John asked aloud.

Suzy shrugged and said, "He always runs into the woods when he's sad or in a bad mood… which is like all the time."

While Suzy poured refills for her animals, John remained focused on Ben and the woods. He could totally relate to the poor kid.

As Sara continued looking out her front door, she felt as if she was losing it. She had one kid running into the woods, and the other having a pretend tea party with the stranger from across the street. Frustrated, and at the end of her rope, Sara yelled across the yard for Suzy to come home immediately. She then turned and headed back into the kitchen and grabbed the phone and dialed.

"Hey, Mom. I know it's last minute but can you come over and watch the kids tonight? I just need to get out for a little while."

Long after the tea party ended and Suzy had reluctantly gone home, John continued to sit on the steps of the porch. He sensed Sara's anger and frustration when she yelled over at Suzy, and he couldn't help but wonder what might have caused this.

He was still on the steps when Sara's mom pulled in their driveway. Soon after, John watched as Ben exited the woods, somberly shuffling his feet towards his house. About halfway across the yard, Ben stopped and looked over at John. Without thinking about it, John threw him a sympathetic nod. Ben returned his gesture then quickly lowered his eyes back to the ground and headed inside.

Moments later, Sara exited the house and climbed into her car. Her eyes were focused straight ahead, and she didn't even notice John sitting there watching her. By the look on her face and the way she sped off, he definitely knew something was up.

It was at that point, John remembered what was waiting for him on the counter in the kitchen. His desire and thirst for the whiskey had lessened over the past hour. So much so, that he decided to remove himself from the temptation and take a drive and maybe a long walk.

He grabbed his keys, hopped into his truck, and then headed out to explore more of Applewood. Besides the diner and general store, the only places he had been was the park overlooking the lighthouse and the eerie, abandoned airstrip.

It was dark and late at night when he originally entered Applewood a week earlier, but he remembered driving by a marina. The late-day sun was fading behind the trees when John arrived at the small marina. He parked his truck along the side of the road and walked towards the waterfront.

As usual, he felt out of place, for he seemed to be the only non-fisherman mulling about. At one point, thinking John was lost, a lobsterman approached him.

"If ya looking for the Rusty Anchor, it's that-a-way," he said, pointing across the road.

"The what?" John asked, confused.

"The Rusty Anchor Tavern," he clarified.

John followed the man's finger and spotted a rundown shanty-like tavern just up the road.

"Oh… no. I wasn't looking for that. I was just taking in the scenery, that's all. It's not private property here, is it?"

The fisherman spat out a wad of tobacco then shook his head and said, "No private property here. Just stay off people's boats and don't touch anyone's traps."

"Oh, of course. I would never…"

That's as far as John got before the old fisherman turned and walked away. John then made his way towards a long, wide weathered pier. He was careful not to touch any of the lobster traps, which were stacked on either side of it.

A thick, frayed rope hung from pylon to pylon, marking the end of the pier. For what seemed like forever, John just stood there, watching the last of the fisherman and lobsterman exit their boats from a long, hard day's work. He recognized some of them from his early mornings at the general store. Working twelve plus hours a day out on a rough, frigid ocean was not something he could ever see himself doing.

The salt air and the pungent smell of fish hit John's nose as he continued gazing at the many boats scattered about. His thoughts turned to the old fisherman, Clarence. He hadn't been by the cove recently, and he wondered how Clarence's boat repairs were coming. A part of him felt sympathetic, guilty even, for not going and offering his help to the old man.

He finally removed his gaze from the ocean then turned and headed back down the pier and into the parking lot. Now that he was facing west, he could see the sun setting behind the trees and couldn't help but admire the fire-like colors it was leaving in its wake.

From his left sweatshirt pocket, he pulled out his disposable camera, but the tall pines prevented him from capturing the sky's true color.

"The best place to snap your little pictures would be up at Algonquin Park."

Startled, John looked over to his right and saw that same lobsterman from before.

"Algonquin Park?" John repeated.

"A-yah. The best place for the sunrise is Harbor Cove Park, but for the sunset, ya wanna head to Algonquin Park," he said then spat his tobacco onto the pavement.

"Umm, how do I get there?" asked John.

The man pointed down the road. "First road on your left then follow the signs."

John turned to thank him, but like before, the lobsterman had apparently lost interest in the conversation and was walking away.

"Thanks," he called out to no reply.

John knew his time was limited, so he hopped back into his truck and sped off towards Algonquin Park. The park was set well off the road, and if John had blinked, he would have missed its sign. Luckily, he didn't blink.

It was smaller than Harbor Cove Park, but its scenery and views made it yet another hidden gem. Applewood, like Maine, was known for its pine trees, but as far as John could tell, there wasn't one pine tree in the park. Oaks and white birches were scattered about, and a giant weeping willow loomed in the center.

A narrow river wound its way around the park with multiple benches lining its banks. With no trees on the other side of the river, the sky was wide open and was indeed the perfect spot to view the sunset. He made his way over to one of the benches, pulled out his camera, and began capturing what was left of the orange-colored sky. The peaceful sounds of nature provided John the perfect soundtrack for his picture-taking.

Before he even knew it, he had gone through the entire roll of the disposable camera. He made a mental note to buy another one in the morning. John placed the camera in his pocket then leaned back on the bench gazing around at the park. As he took it all in, his thoughts turned to Kristen. She would have absolutely adored this place. She loved the outdoors, and she loved her parks.

While he was leaning back on the bench, his eyes slowly fell shut, but his thoughts continued to be of his wife. All at once, he was transported to one of Chicago's many parks. Kristen walked by his side, and they were in the midst of an argument. Although, it wasn't really an argument, it was just another occasion of Kristen wondering why John wouldn't let her in.

"What? What do you wanna hear, John?" Kristen said, throwing her hands up in the air. "That it still doesn't bother me that we've been together all this time and yet you still don't trust me enough to open up about certain things? Because it does… it does bother me. A lot."

John ran his hand down his face and let out an irritated sigh.

"I've told you a hundred times, Kristen, it's NOT a trust thing! I trust and love you with all my heart. But the shit that happened to me and Kevin as kids has nothing to do with you and me."

Kristen was quick to respond. "But it's a part of who you are. It's a part of your life. And now I'm a part of your life, so…"

"It's NOT a part of who I am!" he angrily snapped. "Some things are better left in the past." John took a deep breath, and his anger softened as he turned towards Kristen. "Besides, all I wanna do now is concentrate on my future… my future with you. Unless, of course, you're having second thoughts about marrying me? Because I'd totally understand if you did."

Kristen's frustration also subsided a bit, and a smirk fell on her face.

"Settle down, tiger. No second thoughts here. I love you John. I love you so much, and I can't wait to spend the rest of our lives together. All I'm saying is nothing would make me happier than for you to open up and let me in… like *really* let me in."

Her smirk faded into a warm, endearing smile as she clutched his arm and walked on. It wasn't long before John's pessimism reared its ugly head.

"You really can't wait to spend the rest of our lives together, huh?"

She nodded and continued smiling.

"You do know it's gonna be a challenge though? With my moodiness and negativity, combined with the fact that divorce rates are over fifty percent…"

Confidently, she interrupted with, "None of that matters or means anything. I know in my heart we are meant to be together."

"Oh yea?" he laughed then curiously pressed some more. "But how do you know? Like, *really* know?"

Kristen's smile grew from ear to ear as she gazed up to the night sky. "It's all in the stars."

Skeptically, John looked into the night sky. Chicago's bright city lights made it nearly impossible to make out any stars.

"It might be difficult to see sometimes, but you just have to look hard enough, that's all," she smiled.

As Kristen's voice trailed off, and as the memory faded, John's eyes slowly opened. The sun had long since set and darkness now blanketed the sky. He leaned forward and lifted himself off the bench and made his way across the park towards his truck.

With Kristen's flashback still fresh in his mind, he paused in the middle of the park and gazed up at the star-filled sky. They were the same stars Kristen had put her faith into… and ultimately, the same stars that ripped it all away.

John lowered his eyes from the sky, and without even knowing it, his feet began taking him down a path towards the south end of the park. It was there that he noticed four ground lights shining up at some sort of statue. Upon closer inspection, the copper statue was of a Native American chief, who appeared to be looking and pointing up to the sky. Underneath the chief was a small plaque which read:

May all lost souls find the peace they search for
and the path that leads back home.

On most occasions, a quote like this would have caused him to shake his head and laugh. But as he stood there gazing up at the giant chief, the words seemed to resonate deeply within him. John had always considered himself a lost soul, and whether he admitted it to himself or not, he spent his entire life searching for some sort of inner peace and for a place to call home.

He thought he found both when Kristen came into his life, and he was sure he found them when Hannah was born. But just when he allowed himself to be comfortable, and just when he allowed himself to feel happiness, it was all ripped away. In his heart, he desperately wanted to believe in the chief's quote, but sadly, his heart was still too empty and broken to ever allow those type of hopeful thoughts in.

By the time he reached his truck, tears were rolling down his cheeks, and as he twisted at his wedding ring, more thoughts of Kristen came rushing back. A wave of regret flooded over him as he thought of all the things he was never able to tell her. He knew how much she loved him, but he also knew there was nothing in the world she wanted more than for him to truly let her in.

In his head, he had always justified his lack of communication regarding his past. It was never a case of not trusting or loving Kristen enough to let her in, for he loved and trusted her with all his heart.

When the brothers were both eighteen and had left the Boys Home, Kevin claimed that this was their "new beginning"… their "brand-new day to start again." John was glad to leave the Boys Home but never felt this *brand-new-day* thing Kevin referred to—not until Kristen came along.

When she entered his life, it was like a beam of light, illuminating things he never thought possible. Without a doubt, she was *his brand-new day*. And because of that, he saw no reason to delve into his dark past with her and take a chance on it casting a shadow on her light. Kristen saw this differently. For her, it was a case of the person she loved the most not trusting her enough to let her in.

With his tears still flowing, and with his regrets still looming over him, John sped down the darkened road. It wasn't until he approached the marina that he slowed his driving pace. His eyes fixated on the Rusty Anchor Tavern, and without even thinking about it, he found himself exiting his truck and walking towards the front door.

He swiped away the last of his tears as he entered the bar. The interior was exactly as he imagined it to be. The rustic tavern was cluttered with ocean and fishing memorabilia. The walls were filled with lobster traps, buoys, and old fishing gear. There were also many framed pictures throughout of the locals showing off their *big catch*. The centerpiece was a large rusty anchor and chain, which hung on the back wall.

The clientele was also exactly how he imagined it to be. The crowd was almost entirely made up of fishermen and lobstermen. Needless to say, the crowd was 90% males. John was completely out of place, but at that point, he didn't think twice about it. He desperately needed a drink, and it didn't matter if it was the warm, cozy confines of the Wild Irish Rose or this cold, fish-smelling seaside tavern.

John dropped his head down and did his best to inconspicuously walk across the room to an open stool up at the bar. Although it was only September, most of the guys wore black wool winter hats or the plaid ones with the ear flaps. John was the only one sporting a baseball hat, and a Cubs one at that.

He lowered his hat and watched as the very large bartender approached him. He must have been 6'8 and 300 plus pounds. He had a black beard and moustache, wore a tight black shirt, and on top of his black hair, he wore some sort of blue sailor's hat. All John could picture was Bluto from Popeye.

"What can I get ya?" he called in John's direction.

John hesitated a second, before the words finally spilled out.

"A whiskey… straight-up."

The large bartender gave John a quick look-over then turned and reached for a bottle of Jack Daniel's.

"Umm, Jameson, please," requested John.

Without turning back around, the bartender paused then released the Jack Daniel's and grabbed the bottle of Jameson. As John watched him pour it, his heart raced and his mouth watered in anticipation. The drink was long overdue and John knew it. His anticipation was interrupted by a familiar voice coming from behind him.

"Well, well, if it isn't John from Chicago!"

He turned and saw Sara walking towards him—staggering towards him. John recognized the stagger and slur all too well. He had actually perfected it over the past year. Although commonplace for himself, he was shocked to see Sara in this condition. Judging by their first conversation and watching her from afar, he just assumed she was way too sweet and innocent to ever be this drunk, especially in a place like this.

"Hey, Tiny," she yelled over to the bartender. "This is my new temporary neighbor from Chicago. May I?" she asked, motioning to the empty stool next to John.

John nodded, but was still reeling from seeing Sara this drunk; not to mention, hearing that the bartender's nickname was Tiny.

"And if you ever need any house repairs, John's your man! Hell, he'll even fly all the way from Chicago to fix it."

Sara laughed at herself, and John didn't bother correcting her on the fact that he drove, not flew from Chicago.

"Oh, and if ever you need any help in here, John's your man as well. He actually owns a big bar back in the city."

Again, John failed to correct her on the actual size of his bar. He watched as she climbed onto the stool, nearly falling off. He could only imagine this is what he looked like over the past year—except not as funny or as cute as her.

"But I will warn ya, Tiny, he's good at breaking glasses. And definitely don't try to offer to pick it up either," she laughed.

Tiny gave a slight laugh, but it was more at Sara's drunkenness rather than her actual humor. He then placed John's whiskey in front of him.

"Hey Tiny, I'll have what he's having, and you can put them both on my tab."

"Thanks, but you don't have to pay for my drink," John said.

Before Sara could reply, Tiny interrupted with, "I think you've had more than enough tonight, Sara."

"Oh come on, Tiny. Just one more?"

"Sorry, Sara," he said, shaking his head back and forth. He then smiled and handed her tab to her.

She gazed down at her bill and saw just how much she actually had to drink throughout the night. She also figured there were probably a few more drinks which Tiny didn't charge her for. Reluctantly, she conceded then reached for her purse.

"Fine. I guess I should probably head home anyway. After all, it is a frickin' school night."

Tiny smiled then asked, "Need me to get you a ride?"

"Pffft, no! I'm very capable of getting home on my own, thank you very much!"

"Sara," Tiny sternly said. "You're not driving."

"Pfft! Who said anything about driving? My legs are very capable of walking home, thank you very much!"

With that, Sara tossed down a wad of money then turned and stumbled out of the tavern.

As the door shut behind her, John thought to himself, *Walk home? She lives like six miles away.*

As if reading John's mind, Tiny said aloud, "Walk home? Who is she kidding? She lives like six miles away at least. I better call for a ride."

As Tiny made his way over to the phone, John's eyes went from his drink, to the door, and then back to his drink. He stared long and hard at the glass of whiskey, practically tasting it. But then his thoughts turned to Sara. He knew something was up when she rushed out of the house earlier, and her drunken condition just now, confirmed it.

"I'll give her a ride," John sighed then motioned to Tiny, who was in the process of dialing the phone.

Before John reached the front door, he turned around and looked back at the bar. For the second time that day, he left an untouched glass of whiskey behind. It didn't take long for his focus to switch from whiskey to Sara. She had only made it as far as the parking lot. John spotted her slumped against one of the light posts. As soon as she noticed him approaching, she attempted to straighten herself up.

"What are you doing here?" she asked.

"Eh, not really my type of crowd," he smiled.

"Pfft, you and me both."

"Come on," he said, motioning over to his truck. "I'll give you a ride."

"Thanks, but I can't go home yet. Not in this condition. My mother will bombard me with questions... followed by a long lecture."

John let out a chuckle as she continued.

"That's right, I'm a grown woman who will still go to great lengths to avoid my mother's bullshit lectures. Sorry for my language."

Again, John chuckled. "So you're just gonna stand here against the light post until you sober up?"

"No, no I'm not. It's low tide, so I'm gonna take a nice long walk on the beach," she said, pointing across the street.

She pulled herself off the light post, slung her purse over her shoulder, then staggered towards the beach."

John watched her take a few steps then called out, "Do you want some company?"

Without turning around she said, "As long as it's because you want to and not because you feel sorry for me."

"Nah," he said, catching up with her. "I usually reserve that for myself."

She threw a smirk his way as they crossed the street. John helped her down the small set of wooden stairs leading to the beach. The moon provided just enough light to guide their way along the darkened beach.

Besides the faint sound of a foghorn and the waves gently lapping onto the shore, the only sound was the beach pebbles and tiny seashells crunching beneath their feet. Unsure what to say, he remained quiet and walked by her side, aiding her when needed.

John hated when people butted into his life, so he was very cautious about doing the same to Sara. If she wanted to talk, he'd listen, but he certainly wasn't going to initiate. That being said, after five minutes of dead silence, John found himself initiating.

"Bad day?" he asked.

Little did he know, that was all it would take to unleash her inner babble.

"Pfft, bad day, week, month… year."

Before he could respond, she began her long, rambling rant.

"He just pisses me off, ya know? Ben had his heart set on this camping trip. It's always one reason or another why Rick can't come see his own son! I'm so tired of making up excuses for him. Sometimes I just wanna tell Ben the truth; that his dad is a lying, cheating, selfish douchebag! Sorry for my language," she apologized. "And don't worry, I would never actually tell Ben that."

John started to respond but realized he had no idea what to say. It didn't really matter, for Sara was just getting going.

"I know, I know, I'm a hot mess. A teacher getting drunk by herself on a school night… two different kids by two different fathers… you totally think I'm pathetic."

She paused just long enough for him to get a quick word in.

"I don't think you're pathetic. I don't even know you."

"Pfft, trust me, that's probably a good thing," she said then stopped her pace.

In front of them was a four-foot wide gully of water running from the storm drain to the ocean. John knew she was in no condition to make the tiny leap over it, so he started to turn back around and head the other way.

"What are you doing?" she asked. "The best part of the beach is that way," she said, pointing straight ahead. "We're totally jumping this."

"I'm not sure that's such a good idea," he said.

"You're chicken, aren't you?" she said in his direction. "You don't think you can make it, huh? I bet you a dollar I can make it and you can't."

John stood there a bit torn. He knew he could make that jump in his sleep, and he also knew in her condition there was no way she could make it over. But the fact that she made it into a bet made him hesitate. John's competitive nature wasn't just with his brother. Whether it was a hundred or a measly dollar bet, he had a hard time turning down a challenge, even from a drunken single mother.

In this case, however, he decided to do the right thing and pass on her silly bet. But when she began taunting him with crazy chicken noises, John was forced to say, "It's a bet!"

"Age before beauty," she smiled as she motioned him to go first.

John took one step back then proceeded to easily jump across the water. He probably didn't even need to jump. He could have just long-stretched his legs over the gully, but he decided to go for the emphatic overkill. As soon as he nailed the landing, he raised his hands and did a fist pump. It was more out of habit than anything. He then motioned for Sara to go.

Sara chose to get a much longer running start—a twenty-foot running start. With each step she took backwards, John started feeling guilty about this whole challenge idea. She could barely walk straight, never mind make a four-foot jump. Out of the corner of his eye, he saw a long piece of driftwood.

"You know what, Sara, I think we should cancel the bet. Let me throw this piece of wood down for you to…"

It was too late. Sara was already in full sprint-mode. Of course, her full sprint-mode was more like slow and clumsy-mode. John couldn't bear to watch, and at the last second, he closed his eyes.

What he missed was Sara jumping way too early. What he heard was a giant splash and a loud shriek. The good thing was she landed on two feet and not flat on her face. The bad news was her shoes and jacket were entirely soaked from the splash.

The driftwood dropped from John's hands, and he just stood there looking over at this poor soaked woman. As she trudged out from the gully, she raised both her arms and pointed at herself.

"Yup… this is my freakin' life in a nutshell!"

John fought back a smile and said, "Oh Sara, I am so sorry. We should definitely get you home."

"Ohhh, no! I didn't make that jump for nothing. I'm gonna walk the rest of the beach, even if I have to do it barefoot."

John said nothing as he watched her take off her shoes and socks. When he saw Sara peel off her soaked jacket, his guilt got the better of him. He immediately slipped off his thick sweatshirt and offered it to her.

"Thanks but no thanks," she said, shivering.

"Sara. Please, I insist," he said and tossed it at her.

She was too cold to argue, so she politely thanked him and pulled it on over her head.

John then looked down at her bare feet.

"Are you sure you don't want me to bring you home?"

"Nah. I go barefoot all the time. As long as the rest of my body is warm, I'll be fine."

"Suit yourself," he smiled as they continued on their walk.

It didn't take long before Sara's drunken babble started up again.

"Oh, and if today wasn't bad enough, I ran into an ex-boyfriend tonight from years ago. We broke up because I walked in on him in bed with some blonde bimbo. After I reminded him of that fact tonight, he not only offered to buy me a drink, but he suggested we go back to his place. Is that not some effed up shit or what? Sorry," she apologized, "I tend to swear when I drink."

John smiled but said nothing. Not that he could have if he wanted to, for she quickly continued rambling on.

"Can you believe the nerve of him? I mean, what did he think, that I was some sort of bimbo too?"

He started to reply but was immediately cut off.

"Seriously, do I look that easy or what?"

He wasn't sure if this was a rhetorical question or not. He paused a second, fearing she was only going to interrupt him anyway.

When Sara saw John hesitate, she stopped in her tracks, and her mouth fell open in shock.

"You do! You think I'm easy!"

"Wait…what? No! I don't even know you, Sara. I don't think you're…"

"Pfft, whatever," she huffed then continued walking ahead.

Assuming he would only say the wrong thing, John decided to just keep his mouth shut. He was tired, he was getting cold, and for the life of him, he couldn't figure out how he got himself into this situation. All he wanted was to sit at the bar by himself and enjoy his glass of whiskey. Instead, he found himself walking on a beach with a babbling lunatic. A drunk one at that.

They walked the final stretch of the beach in silence. When they reached the end, John followed Sara up a set of wooden stairs to the small boardwalk. They reversed their direction and headed back to where his truck was parked. John assumed Sara chose to go this way to avoid being faced with doing the gully-jump again.

As they walked down the sidewalk, Sara finally broke the silence.

"I'm not, ya know?"

"What?" he questioned.

"I'm not easy… or a bimbo."

Her tone was quieter than earlier, more subdued… more sad.

"Sara, I never said or even thought that. At all."

"I am however, probably gonna end up an old maid. I'll be like the crazy cat lady."

John sympathetically smiled then said, "I'm sure the right guy is out there somewhere."

Sara shrugged. "Not one who wants to take on this kind of baggage. I mean, Paul is nice enough, but trust me, he has no clue what he'd be getting himself into."

"Who?"

"Paul. He teaches history. Don't get me wrong, he's super sweet and genuine, but…"

"But what?"

"But I'm sure I'd just screw it up. Besides, I had my one shot at happiness. I guess it wasn't meant to be."

John waited a second to see if she was going to expound on her last statement. She didn't, and he didn't pry. When they reached his truck, he unlocked and opened the passenger side door for her.

"Thanks," she said, climbing in.

He started the truck and immediately cranked the heat on. He made sure it was flowing out of the floor vents so it could warm up her freezing feet. Again, she politely thanked him. He wasn't sure whether to turn the radio on or not, but just in case she wasn't done babbling, he left it off. Very soon he would regret his choice.

As he pulled out of the parking lot, Sara said, "Ya know what, enough about me and my stupid problems. I wanna know more about you."

John's eyes widened and a lump formed in his throat. *Fuck! I should have turned the radio on when I had the chance*, he thought. Before he had a chance to deter any of her questions, she hit him—hard.

"What's your story? Married I assume?"

John's eyes remained wide open as he slowly looked over at her. She motioned to his left hand on the steering wheel; more specifically, to his wedding ring. John said nothing.

"Sorry, I probably shouldn't assume things."

The lump in his throat grew larger, and without even thinking about it, he found himself nodding his head.

"Um, yea… I'm married."

He immediately regretted his answer. Just like with Clarence, he couldn't believe that he lied to Sara. His fingers clutched the steering wheel tighter as his lies were about to grow bigger.

"Nice," she said. "Kids?"

"Um, yea… I have a daughter."

"No way! How old?"

"She's about the same age as your daughter," he answered.

"So you totally know what I'm dealing with then," she laughed.

He forced a small smile then quietly uttered, "Yea."

Luckily for John, they only had a short drive home, and Sara spent the last part of the ride with her face pressed against the passenger-side window. The coolness of the window felt good on her cheeks. So good, in fact, she passed out within seconds.

She was sleeping so soundly that she didn't even notice John pulling into her driveway and putting the truck into park. Although still reeling from his lies, his heart had slowed, and his grip on the steering wheel had loosened. He actually felt a sense of calmness as he sat there watching Sara sleep.

217

While he listened to her soft breathing, he thought about some of the things she revealed earlier in the night. Things like, how Suzy and Ben had different fathers, and how Ben's dad sounded like a total asshole for neglecting him. John would give anything in the world to hold Hannah in his arms one more time. There was no way he could ever dream of neglecting his child; not the way Ben's father did, and certainly not the way his own parents did.

John watched as Sara's slow exhale fogged up the window. He didn't know the details about Suzy's dad, but he assumed he was also in the asshole category. John began feeling sorry for this poor woman. He didn't know Sara very well, but she seemed like one of the good ones—definitely not deserving of all these asshole guys in her life.

Just then, Sara's eyes opened. It took her a second to realize where she was. It also took her a second to realize she had been drooling while she slept. Her face turned a bright red as she wiped her mouth and then used her sleeve to wipe the remaining drool off John's window.

"I'm so sorry about passing out on you… and drooling. I'm sorry about the whole night actually. You really must think I'm an unstable, babbling lunatic?"

"Nah. I don't think you're unstable… or a lunatic. You do talk a lot though," he joked.

She continued to blush and joined him in laughing at herself.

"Well, I guess I should head in," she said, grabbing her wet shoes from the floor. "Thanks again for the ride… and the walk… and listening to me yapping all night."

The last thing on John's mind when he left the house earlier was hanging out and being social with people, especially his cute neighbor. That being said, he surprisingly had a good time hanging out with her. Despite that sentiment, all he could manage to say to her was, "You're welcome."

"Goodnight, John from Chicago," she replied, climbing out of the truck. Before she shut the door behind her, she noticed she was still wearing his sweatshirt. "Oh, as soon as I wash my smell and drool out of this, I'll get it back to you."

"No hurry. Goodnight, Sara," he said, but wanted to say more—much more. This poor woman had poured her heart out to him tonight, and it was obvious she was going through a rough time. It was also obvious that she was a good person and didn't deserve any of it. He felt like he needed to say something more uplifting than just "*Goodnight Sara.*"

It wasn't until she had shut the door and was halfway up her front porch that John jumped out of his truck and yelled over to her.

"Hey, Sara."

"Yes?" she said, turning back around to him.

"About that baggage thing... umm, I wouldn't worry about it too much. As far as I can tell, your kids seem pretty great... and you seem like a really good mother. You're smart, and funny, and... talkative... definitely talkative," he smiled. "But in an endearing way."

Sara's cheeks flushed red and a huge smile filled her face.

"Why John, are you flirting with me?"

"What? No! Not at all," he quickly and defensively said. "I was just..."

"Settle down, tiger," she laughed. "I was just giving you a hard time."

The hairs stood up throughout his body as her choice of words struck a familiar chord.

"Are all you city boys this nervous and uptight?" she joked, and then swung open her front door and called out, "Goodnight, City Boy."

With her phrase, *settle down, tiger*, still echoing around his head, he climbed back into his truck and returned next door. Within minutes of entering William's house, his nerves had calmed. John wasn't exactly sure what it was, but there was just something about the house that put him at ease. Ironically, there was also something extremely mysterious about the house as well—about the whole town actually.

John flipped on the living room light then entered the kitchen. And there, staring right back at him was the untouched glass of Jameson from earlier. The desire and need to feel that sweet, familiar burn of whiskey down his throat had diminished hours ago.

Without thinking too heavily on it, John emptied the glass into the sink and chose a bottle of Poland Spring water instead. Although tempted to empty the entire bottle of Jameson down the drain, he didn't. His justification was: He'd rather have it and not need it, rather than need it and not have it.

20

The next morning at the crack of dawn, John awoke to a light but steady rain. Seeing as his main job that day was painting, he decided to sleep in. It didn't take long for the rhythmic pattern of the rain hitting the roof to put John back into a deep sleep.

Sara didn't have that luxury. Like always, she got herself and her kids up and ready for school. Unlike most mornings, she was still feeling hungover from the night before. On her way to school, she swung by the general store for a large coffee and a greasy bacon, egg and cheese sandwich. She hoped it would coat her stomach and hold her over until her first break, which wasn't until lunch.

She arrived in her classroom seconds before the first period bell rang. With just enough time to toss back a few Advil, she reached her hand into her purse. The longer her hand searched, the more desperate the look on her face became. At one point, she had the entire contents of her purse emptied onto her desk. When she realized she had left her Advil at home, she let out an exasperated sigh.

"Shit!" she uttered in unison to the ringing of the bell.

Sara was still stuffing items back into her purse as her first period students filed in. Advil or not, it was game time. Thankfully, her purse contained a bottle of eye drops. The students wouldn't notice her head pounding, but they would certainly notice her bloodshot eyes.

The first period class, as well as the entire morning, was a giant blur to Sara. More times than she could count, Sara found herself just staring at the clock—hoping and praying it would move faster. Usually, it was the students that were guilty of this.

By the time her fourth period class shuffled in, she was feeling a little more like herself. She still had a pounding headache, but her energy level was much better. That level was about to improve even more. Today was the day her fourth period students were to stand up in front of the class and read their favorite poem.

It was a win-win for Sara. Not only was poetry one of her favorite units, but on that particular day, she knew she didn't need to exert much energy teaching. She could just sit back and relax while her students stood up and read. Her only hope was that she didn't fall asleep at her desk. Or even worse, fall asleep and start drooling. Her mind went to the embarrassing events from the night before, and she made a promise to herself to never ever drink on a school night again.

When everyone was settled in their chairs, Sara put on her best cheery teacher smile and said, "Are we all excited for poetry day or what?"

Her comment was met with predictable groans.

"Not the exact enthusiasm I was going for," she smiled. "The bigger question is, who wants to be the first lamb to the slaughter?"

Also predictably, not one hand went up.

"Oh, come on people. Just think, if you get it over with first then you have the rest of the class to relax and watch everyone else shaking in their boots."

Again, no hands went up.

"Ok, fine. I guess we'll have to do it the old-fashioned way—I get to choose."

Sara actually liked this way the best. She loved looking around the room and watching her students sweat and squirm, in fear of being called on. She found it quite hilarious watching them do their best to not make eye contact with her, or even better, watching them slouch in their chairs in an attempt to make themselves smaller. She even saw some of them crossing their fingers and mouthing a quick prayer to God.

Silly kids, she thought. *Not even God is gonna save you from poetry week*, she laughed to herself.

As she slowly and carefully gazed around the room, her eyes stopped on Bill. The poor kid was attempting to do everything just mentioned: No eye contact, slouching deep in his chair, lips mumbling to God, and to top it off, he was sweating, literally sweating. Sara's heart went out to him. There was no way she could watch him do this for the entire class. She knew she needed to put this poor guy out of his misery.

"Bill, how about you go first."

Just like that, twenty-three students let out a collective, relieved exhale. And then there was Bill, who looked like he was going to throw up. If Bill wasn't so polite, he probably would have thrown a curse God's way.

He fumbled through his backpack and pulled out a small book of poetry then slowly made his way up to the front of the class. His legs were like spaghetti, and he felt at any moment he could lose his balance and fall over. Sara's heart oozed with sympathy.

"Whenever you're ready, Bill," she whispered to him.

Sheepishly, he looked from Sara back to his book. His hands shook as he flipped to the book-marked page. He hadn't even started to read, yet it felt like he'd been up there for an eternity. Finally, he cleared his throat, took a deep breath, then began to read.

"This is called 'Love's Deity' by John Donne."

Even though God had just let him down, Bill threw another quick prayer up to the big guy. He prayed for God to prevent him from stuttering, or even worse, his voice from cracking, like it always did when he did public speaking. The last thing he wanted was for the jocks to start making their pre-pubescent jokes at his expense— especially in front of Rachel.

"I long to talk with some old lover's ghost
Who died before the God of Love was born.
I cannot think that he who then loved most,
Sunk so low as to love one which did scorn.
But since this God produced a destiny
And that vice—nature, custom, lets it be,
I must love her who loves not me…"

Bill paused and mentally thanked God for making it through the first stanza without completely embarrassing himself. Even though his voice didn't stutter or crack, it didn't prevent Don and his friends from snickering in the back of the room. Sara shot them a stern glare then waited for Bill to continue. Although he told himself not to, his eyes looked over at Rachel. She wore a big smile and gave him an encouraging wink. It didn't show up on his face, but make no doubt about it, he was most certainly smiling on the inside as he continued reading the rest of the poem.

"…Falsehood is worse than hate,
And that must be,
If she whom I love, should love me."

With his hands still nervously shaking, Bill closed the book, lowered his head, and walked back to his desk.

A huge smile formed on Sara's face. "Excellent, Bill! That poem has always been one of my favorites. Okay, who's going to be next?"

she asked, looking out at her class. And just like before, everyone's eyes looked away from the her, and the squirming and slouching began once again.

Bill settled into his chair and let out a relieved sigh. He was actually glad Mrs. Peyton called on him first. He was also glad he didn't embarrass himself - not completely anyway. As he placed his poetry book back into his bag, he stole a quick glance over at Rachel.

His heart nearly jumped out of his chest when he saw her looking back at him. She gave him an approving thumbs up then smiled and looked away. Bill held onto the moment as long as he could, before he finally turned his attention back to Mrs. Peyton and watched as she chose the next victim.

Before the class was over, more than half the students had stood and read their poems. And while Bill's eyes were focused on each and every one, his mind was elsewhere. He spent the entire class rehearsing the perfect words to say to Rachel. Today was the day. He was definitely going to strike up a conversation with her after class, and maybe, just maybe, he might even ask her to the dance.

Bill's thoughts were briefly interrupted when he heard Mrs. Peyton call on Don to come up and read his poem. Bill wanted to give Don his full attention; not out of respect, but more out of curiosity. In Bill's eyes, Don was about as dumb and shallow as they come. So naturally, he was quite curious as to Don's choice in poems.

Don did not disappoint. In true dumb-jock style, he made a mockery of the assignment. He stood up in front of the class and pretended to get all emotional as he read "One Fish, Two Fish, Red Fish, Blue Fish" by Dr. Scuss.

To Bill's dismay, he watched as the class erupted in cheers and laughter. Bill quickly looked over at Mrs. Peyton. Surely, she didn't approve of this. And surely, she'd give Don a big fat zero—maybe even a detention. But once again, to Bill's dismay, Mrs. Peyton had a smile on her face as she shook her head.

"Cute, Don… real cute."

Those were the only words she could say as the period bell loudly sounded. Bill was tempted to approach Mrs. Peyton to make sure she was going to fail Don for his little stunt, but he knew it was none of his business. Besides, Bill had more important things to take care of; like strike up a conversation with Rachel.

Actually, this might work out perfectly, he thought. This could be his ice breaker. They could talk about how Don was an immature and shallow idiot for choosing Dr. Seuss. After that, maybe she'd tell Bill how much she loved his poem; how it was deep and thought-provoking.

With that in mind, Bill quickly gathered his things and headed straight for Rachel's locker. By the time he got there, Rachel was talking and laughing with her two best friends, Brittney and Erin. It was hard enough for him to strike up a conversation with Rachel on her own, never mind when she was with friends.

He opened his locker and pretended to be loading and unloading books. Secretly, he was hoping Rachel's friends would leave her alone long enough for him to make his move. Bill's plan came to a crashing halt as the obnoxious sound of Don's voice echoed down the hall.

"Excellent, Bill! That poem has always been one of my favorites," Don said, mocking Mrs. Peyton.

Bill turned to see Don and his crew strutting down the hall towards his locker.

"I hope you have a whole case of Chapstick for all that ass kissing you do," laughed Brock.

Bill's conversation with Rachel would have to wait. The last thing he wanted was for Don and his friends to further embarrass him, especially in front of Rachel. He quickly gathered his things and closed his locker. Fortunately for Bill, Don didn't say anything to further embarrass him. Unfortunately for Bill, Don's attention was also focused on Rachel. He watched as Don smugly moved closer to her, leaning against her locker.

"So Rach, I was thinking you and I should go to the dance together next weekend."

"Oh really?" she said in jest.

"Yup," he said, running his fingers through his perfect blonde hair. "My dad is letting me borrow the Beamer."

"I see," Rachel said, looking at her friends and then back to Don.

"And because I'm such a nice guy, I'll even take you shopping for a new dress or whatever else you might want. My treat of course." He boasted as he waved a credit card in front of her face.

Bill's heart sank. There was no way he could compete with Don; not with his good looks, or his hip and expensive fashion sense, and definitely not with his money. Bill didn't even have his own car yet, never mind have parents that owned a Beamer.

His heart wasn't the only thing that sank. His head, his eyes, his hopes - all sank to the ground. Before he turned and shuffled off to his next class, he heard Rachel laugh. It wasn't the kind of endearing, infatuated laugh that most girls gave Don. It was more of a mocking laugh.

"Wow, that's quite the proposition, Don… and I'm sure I'll probably regret this," she giggled. "But I think I'll pass."

Bill's eyes, head, and spirits all perked up. The king of the jocks had just been served!

For a second, Don was taken aback, but he quickly recovered with, "Pfft, whatever. Like I'd wanna go with a stuck-up goody two-shoes anyway."

Brock added to Don's defense with, "Yea, she's so stuck up, she'd probably drown in the shower."

"Yea, no shit, she'd probably drown in the shower," repeated Trevor.

"Your loss, chickie," Don said to Rachel. He then turned to his friends. "Let's bounce."

"Yea, let's bounce," repeated Trevor.

Rachel and her friends watched as the three jocks strutted their way back down the hall. Bill continued to stand there, still. Part of him was furious with Don for labeling Rachel as stuck up. She might have been super-popular, but Bill knew she was the furthest thing from stuck up. A bigger part of him was through the roof with excitement. He loved how Rachel put Don in his place by turning him down cold.

"Can you believe that guy?" Rachel said to her friends. "He has some nerve."

"Yup," said Brittney.

Erin nodded in agreement. "Yea, but you have to admit, he's like the hottest guy in Applewood... maybe even all of Maine."

Hesitantly, Brittney also nodded in agreement. "Erin speaks the truth. Not to mention, I saw his dad's new car and it's frickin' sweet."

Erin added, "And didn't you say the dress you wanted was way out of your price range?"

Rachel looked back and forth between her two friends, shaking her head in disbelief.

"I'm thinking you two should go to the dance with him then."

All three looked at one another and then simultaneously began cracking up laughing.

"Trust me, I'll make due with a cheaper dress. I don't need to be bribed with Don's money, or should I say, his daddy's money. Besides, I would much rather receive something from the heart than the wallet. Is that too much to ask for?"

Both Brittney and Erin answered, "In this school? Yes!"

All three of them giggled. Rachel shut her locker and as they walked past Bill, she smiled and called out, "Nice poem today, Bill. Wish me luck on mine tomorrow."

It wasn't until the girls were halfway down the hall that Bill returned her smile. And it wasn't until they were out of sight that Bill finally managed to reply to her. "Good luck, Rachel" he murmured to himself.

It didn't matter that his words fell on deaf ears, for he considered his little interaction with Rachel a huge success. The sky was the limit from here.

Back in the classroom, Sara was getting ready to enjoy her free period. Normally, she would use the time for prepping or grading, but today was definitely reserved for a quiet little nap at her desk. She thought about walking down to the nurse's office to get something for her pounding headache, but she was much too comfy in her chair. So, as she rested her head on the desk, her fingers gently massaged the sides of her temples.

"Rough night?"

Sara let out an eek and popped her head up.

"Did you just eek?" Paul asked, walking towards her desk. "Like, literally an eek?"

Sara's cheeks turned red. "You scared the crap outta me!" she said in a hushed tone.

"I was watching you through the door window, and I thought you could use these," he said, handing her a Poland Spring water and a bottle of Advil.

"Oh Paul, you're a savior! A little creepy that you were watching me through the window, but today, I'll let it slide," she smiled, popping two pills.

Paul watched her quickly unscrew the water, nearly chugging the entire bottle.

"Why, Sara, you're not hungover, are you? On a school night?"

Again, her cheeks turned red.

"Long story," she said, finishing off the water.

"Well, you could always fill me in on that long story over dinner one night this week," he smiled.

Although Sara did her typical eye roll at Paul, she really did love how he smiled at her. She also loved how he always checked up on her throughout the day. He had a knack for popping in and saying the right things at the right time to put her in a better mood.

"I know, I know," he said as he started to leave, "I believe the word you used was incorrigible?"

"Definitely incorrigible," she smiled.

She also could have used the words sweet, thoughtful, genuine, or easy on the eyes, but she knew her life was way too complicated to say any of those words to him. She would only disappoint him or break his heart in the end.

"But I really do appreciate the water and Advil," she called out to him.

"Yea, yea, yea," he joked. "Use me for my medication and hydration, why don't ya." Before he exited, he turned back around and said, "And just to clarify, I wasn't creeping on you through the window... I was just checking on you, that's all. Feel better, Sara."

"You too," she smiled back.

It wasn't until he closed the door behind him that Sara shook her head and muttered, "Why the heck did I just say *you too*? I really am a hot mess."

* * *

A light fall rain fell for most of the day causing John to remain indoors. He took full advantage of this by relaxing in front of a roaring fire in the living room. In one of the boxes in the dining room, John found an old transistor radio and placed it beside him on the couch. As hard as he tried, he could only get two stations – country and oldies.

The choice was easy. Both John and Kevin despised country music. It wasn't that they had anything personal against the artists or the genre in general, but they hated it because HE loved it—Mr. O'Neil. It was even worse when he listened to country music while watching NASCAR.

Mr. O'Neil's favorite song to listen to on repeat was "The Gambler" by Kenny Rogers. Even to this day, every time John or Kevin heard it being played, a sick feeling entered the pit of their stomachs.

It wasn't his favorite genre, but it didn't take long for John to be tapping his fingers and toes to the Beatles "Hard Day's Night." It also didn't take him long to pick up the notebook and a pencil and begin sketching some ideas for a brand-new gazebo for William.

By mid-afternoon, the rain had let up, but the sky remained gray and gloomy. Whether it cleared up or not, John had no intentions of doing any physical labor that day. He was quite content lounging on the couch with his sketch pad and a warm fire crackling in front of him. He was so content, in fact, that he soon found himself sound asleep and snoring.

The radio station remained on the oldies, but in his dream, it was country music that blared out. John found himself on his bed with Kevin sitting next to him. In the other room, Mr. O'Neil was watching a NASCAR race with his favorite country station cranked on. When he wasn't yelling at the TV, he was loudly singing out of tune. This completely annoyed the brothers. But when the TV and music were shut off, they went from annoyed to scared.

The brief silence was interrupted by the crack of a beer tab, followed by Mr. O'Neil's heavy, plodding footsteps down the hall. But just before Mr. O'Neil entered their bedroom, John forced his eyes open and awoke from his nightmare.

When he finally composed himself, he noticed the fire was just about out and a chill filled the living room. Without even knowing it, John's notebook had fallen to the floor, and the pencil in his hand had been snapped in two. As he sat up on the couch, the wise, yet annoying words of his therapist echoed around the room.

"You really need to start facing some of these issues you've been burying all these years. I know it seems easier not to face this, but you need to start finding closure. Actually, I think you need to start coming to terms with a lot of things from your past."

"Fuck closure!" he yelled, throwing the broken pencil across the room. "And fuck your stupid fish tank," he added for good measure.

He climbed off the couch and headed into the kitchen and straight for the bottle of Jameson. He untwisted its cap, grabbed a glass, but paused a second before pouring it. He took a quick glance down at his watch and realized it was nearly three thirty. Sara's kids were already home from school, and seeing as the weather had cleared, there was a good chance Suzy would be heading over for another one of her famous tea parties. The last thing he needed was for his drinking to be interrupted yet again.

His new plan of action was to fill up his flask and head directly out to the cove behind the house. He could already picture the exact set of rocks where he could sit and drink without ever being bothered. He thought about bringing the whole bottle with him, but decided against it. With the flask, he was simply just having a little drink to take the edge off, that's all. He'd become great at making up justifications for his drinking; for all his actions actually.

When the flask was filled, he tucked it into his pocket and bolted out the back door. John's pace slowed when he entered the path in the woods. It was still extremely muddy and slippery from all of the earlier rain. He came to a complete stop when he heard a loud thud about thirty feet in front of him. An animal, maybe? A moose? A black bear? John had never seen either one of them before, in a zoo or otherwise.

He stood perfectly still with his eyes straight ahead. A few seconds later, he heard it again. It seemed to be coming from the large pine tree. A second later, it happened again. It wasn't an animal. It was something being thrown at the tree. The longer he stood and observed, the more he realized the sound was someone throwing rocks at the pine tree.

Was this path not part of William's property? Was the rock thrower a crazy redneck neighbor trying to scare him off? Either way, John was in no mood for a violent confrontation. He started to turn back towards the house, but stopped when he heard a rustling off to his left. He silently prayed not to see a plaid or orange hunter's hat.

To his surprise, the only hat he could see through the trees was a Red Sox hat, and it didn't belong to a hunter or a redneck. As the figure emerged from behind a large boulder, John saw that it was Sara's son, Ben.

Ben reached into his sweatshirt pocket and pulled out another rock and proceeded to whip it at the large pine tree across the way. It smacked dead center on the tree.

"Nice shot," John called out.

Ben spun around and saw John standing down the path.

"I'm sorry, sir. I didn't mean to be throwing rocks on your property."

"Eh, it's okay," John said, making his way towards Ben. "I'm not even sure if this is my property."

The closer John got, the more nervous Ben seemed.

"I… I should probably get back home anyway. Sorry again, sir."

Before Ben could rush off, John yelled out, "It's okay. You don't have to leave. I'm just headed into the cove. Feel free to keep chucking rocks."

By now, John had reached the young boy. Ben threw his hoodie on and shyly looked away, avoiding eye contact. John had an important date with his flask, but there was something about Ben that seemed off. Not that John had ever met Ben before, but the boy seemed nervous and was avoiding any sort of eye contact with John. It was also obvious that Ben just wanted to be left alone. John, of all people, could totally appreciate and respect this. That being said, for some reason, John continued the conversation.

"I don't think we've officially met. I'm John."

He reached out his hand to the boy. Hesitantly, Ben turned and reciprocated.

"I'm… I'm Ben," he meekly answered.

As Ben faced him, he could tell the boy had been crying. John felt a little uncomfortable and knew, now more than ever, he needed to just walk away and give this kid his space. He knew this, yet his mouth continued to speak.

"I know it's none of my business, but is everything okay, Ben?"

Embarrassed that John noticed his condition, Ben swiped at his tears and turned away.

"Yes, sir. I'm fine."

As they both stood there in an awkward silence, John reached into his pocket and felt the cool steel of his flask. He raised it slightly higher in his pocket. It reminded him he had places to be and whiskey to drink.

"Well, I'll let you be then," John said, turning and starting to walk away.

Before he made it five paces, Ben's voice quietly called out, "It would have been a stupid camping trip anyway."

John stopped walking. He pushed the flask deeper into his pocket then let out a quiet sigh. He knew Ben was calling out for help, and he knew he needed to turn back around and be the one who listened. He motioned for them to sit on a couple of tree stumps behind the large boulder. After a few moments of silence, John spoke.

"Your mom mentioned something about the camping trip. I'm sorry your dad had to work."

Ben kept his head down and eyes to the ground as he spoke.

"He's always too busy to see me. I overheard my mom say it was because he was a selfish SOB."

John remembered hearing Sara vent about Ben's dad, and selfish son of a bitch was probably the kindest thing she said about the guy. It wasn't John's place to judge. At that moment, he knew he needed to do his best to cheer Ben up.

"Well, I don't know about that, but I'm sure your dad really wanted to go camping with you."

Ben slowly shook his head back and forth.

"He never likes spending time with me. I... I think it's because he's embarrassed of me."

"Embarrassed of you? Why do you say that?"

Ben shrugged then said, "My dad was a super-cool athlete when he was younger, and every time he comes to my Little League games... well, the two times he came to my games, I struck out every time... and I made like two or three errors in the field."

"Oh, Ben, I'm sure he's not embarrassed of you. Trust me, we've all struck out with our parents watching."

John's mind flashed back to his Little League days. Mrs. O'Neil made it to most of their games, but Mr. O'Neil only showed up to one. It was bad enough that he hated sports, but the one game he came to, John had his worst game ever. He struck out four times, and his error caused the other team to score the winning run.

John never heard the end of it from Mr. O'Neil. The rest of the night was one comment after another at how unathletic John was and how much of an embarrassment he was as well. Mrs. O'Neil did her best to stop his hurtful comments, but this only caused yet another huge fight at the O'Neil house.

What made matters worse was Kevin had an amazing game. Normally, John would have been happy for his brother, but on that night, he absolutely resented Kevin for it. Kevin never threw his good game in John's face. As a matter of fact, Kevin did his best to cheer John up.

As John sat on the stump in front of Ben, he felt ashamed at the way he treated his little brother that night. He also knew there were dozens of other occasions where he had resented and treated Kevin unfairly.

"I'm not cool enough to be his son. He thinks I'm a loser."

"What? He told you that?"

Again, Ben shrugged and said, "No, but... but that's what some of the kids at my school say."

And just like that, John was once again transported back in time. He was around Ben's age and was sitting in his school's cafeteria. Kevin was absent that day, and John was forced to sit with some random kids—random and mean kids.

John sat at the very end of the table and did his best to keep to himself. He had barely made a dent in his Sloppy Joe when the first shot was fired at him.

"Hey, you," called out the blonde boy wearing a Chicago Bears jacket. "Aren't you the kid with foster parents?"

John hated confrontations and secretly wished with all his might that Kevin was there with him. When John said nothing, a not-so bright boy yelled out, "What the hell are foster parents?"

John remained quiet as his fork nervously ran circles around the kernels of corn on his tray.

The silence was quickly interrupted by Jacob Harrigan. Jacob was perhaps the most popular kid in John's class... also the most sarcastic and rude.

"It means his real parents didn't want him anymore," Jacob announced to the table. "Him and his loser brother weren't cool enough for them."

As they all chuckled and repeated Jacob's comments, John's fingers clenched into a fist. He desperately wanted to lash out at the little punks; not only for their comments about his parents, but mostly because they called his brother a loser. He wanted to lash out, but like always, he didn't. He chickened out and simply sat there and continued taking their verbal abuse.

John never told Kevin about that day at the lunch table. He rarely told Kevin anything that was truly bothering him. Like always, John vented to no one but himself. When John came out of his flashback, he noticed his fingers were clenched into fists.

"Don't listen to those little shits at school!" John blurted out, and then threw his own rock over at the large pine. It was a direct hit, and as the loud thwack echoed through the woods, Ben sat straight up. He was a little surprised at this crazy rock-chucking stranger from Chicago.

"I'm sorry," he said, realizing how Ben was looking at him.

John hated letting people in, especially into his past, but he felt the need to tell Ben about the flashback he just had. He hoped his shitty childhood would help Ben feel better about his own situation.

Over the next thirty minutes, John painted a brief picture of his own childhood; of being passed on to one family after another. He didn't go into graphic detail of just how bad it was at the O'Neil's, but it was enough to make Ben's problems seem a bit smaller.

"So don't ever blame yourself, Ben. The truth is, you should feel lucky. At least you have a Mom and a sister who love you."

Ben's mood had improved, but still, he shrugged off John's comments and said, "Pfft, a bratty and annoying sister, you mean?"

John laughed. "I don't know about that. She just has a lot of energy, that's all."

"And she never shuts up."

John smiled then replied, "She does talk a lot, doesn't she?"

Finally, a big smile formed on Ben's face.

"Ya think? Try living with her," he laughed.

After they finished laughing out loud, they sat there in silence. It wasn't necessarily uncomfortable, it was just silence.

John gazed down at the pile of rocks by Ben's feet. It reminded him of his own youthful venting. The O'Neils didn't have any woods around them, but John remembered running to an old vacant playground down the street. There, he would gather rocks and whip them at one of the old metal signs. Sometimes he would imagine the sign as a catcher's mitt as he pitched the Cubs into a World Series title. Other times, he imagined the sign was Mr. O'Neil's ugly and smug face. Either way, he always felt a little better afterwards.

"Okay, the first person to hit the pine tree five times wins the World Series. I'll be the Cubs and you the Red Sox."

Ben smiled at John then they both reached down for a handful of rocks. Although it went against John's highly competitive nature, he let Ben win five to four.

"Ah, nice shot, Ben. Well, it looks like the Red Sox win their first World Series in like a hundred years."

"And it looks like the Cubs will have to wait a hundred more," laughed Ben, in a much better mood than earlier.

"Oh I don't know about that," snapped John. "I definitely want a rematch." Before Ben could reply, he heard his mom's voice yelling out.

"Ben! Dinner!"

"Looks like we'll have to wait until later in the week for our rematch," John said. "Come on, I'll walk back with you."

As they headed back down the path, John didn't think twice about the flask in his pocket or his drinking destination in the cove. As a matter of fact, the main thing on his mind was his future rematch with Ben. There was no way he would let him win next time. Nope, not a chance in hell.

It wasn't until they exited the path in William's backyard that Ben finally spoke.

"Were you mad at them?"

"Mad at who?" asked John.

"At your real parents… for abandoning you?"

Caught off guard, John paused a moment before uttering, "Um, yea, I was."

Ben also paused then followed it up with, "Are you still?"

Luckily for John, he was saved by Sara once again calling out to Ben.

"Come on, honey. Dinner is ready."

Sara and John exchanged polite waves. Sara was quick to turn away, for she was still embarrassed about what transpired the night before. As she entered the house, she crossed her fingers that John didn't tell Ben about how much of a train wreck his mother was last night. She assumed Ben already knew how much of a mess she was, but still, she didn't need John confirming any of this to him.

Ben and John went their separate ways. Ben, to go eat dinner with his mother and his talkative sister, and John, to head back into William's house. Ben's mood and demeanor wasn't the only one that improved over the afternoon. John felt lighter, less angry than before, and even though Ben's question about John's parents still echoed in his mind, his desire to drink had all but disappeared.

Upon entering the living room, John reached down and picked up the sketch of his gazebo. And just like that, he made up his mind. He would order the lumber and get started on it in the morning.

After he placed the delivery order, he headed into the kitchen to see if he had anything good to eat. Besides a few odds and ends, he really didn't have anything, so he decided to drive over to the diner for another home-cooked meal.

When John returned from dinner, he lit another fire in the fireplace and continued to fine tune the plans for William's new gazebo. It was these thoughts and the sound of the crackling fire that John fell asleep to that night. As he snored soundly on the couch, his bottle of Jameson and his still untouched flask sat on the kitchen counter. Little did he know at the time, but his lips would never take a sip of whiskey, or any type of alcohol ever again. Also, when he awoke the next morning, he would begin to experience just how magical this little Maine town truly was.

21

Slowly, John peeled his eyes open, looked around and listened. After a few seconds of hearing nothing, he just assumed the knocking sound he heard was in his dreams. The fire had long since gone out, and the sun was just coming up. His lumber delivery wasn't coming for a few hours, so John allowed his eyes to once again fall shut.

An early morning chill had fallen over the house, so he reached down and pulled the blanket directly over his head. That's when he heard it again—the knocking. It was coming from his front door. For some strange reason, his first thought was his brother. Kevin had gotten so worried about him that he must have gotten the address from William and tracked him down. On their last phone call, Kevin made John promise to check in with him more often.

He whipped the blanket to the floor and made his way to the door. For a split second, before opening it, he thought about rushing into the kitchen and hiding the bottle and the flask. But as the knocking became louder, John decided to just face the music with his brother.

He swung open the door and uttered, "Dude, you really didn't need to check up on..."

His sentence died there when he realized it was Sara and not Kevin. Unsure who he was referring to, Sara just stood there for a moment.

"Sara? Is everything okay?"

"I'm so, so sorry for bothering you this early, but… I could really use a favor. I have a mandatory staff meeting before school today and I can't miss it. I'm already on thin ice from missing the last one."

John stood there holding the door, wondering where she was going with this.

"My mother was supposed to come over to get the kids off to school, but she has a 102 degree fever and can't get out of bed. I don't really know or trust my other neighbors very well… I mean, not that I know you very well either… but for whatever reason, I have a good vibe about you."

"You want me to take your kids to school?" he asked, wiping the remaining sleep from his eyes.

"No. Just make sure they're all dressed and fed and out to the bus stop by seven thirty. Trust me, I wouldn't ask if I wasn't desperate. I just woke them up, so they should be getting dressed now. You know how it goes though, you still might have to crack the whip," she half-laughed.

John sensed the desperation in her laugh and took pity on her. He couldn't imagine what it would be like to be a single parent juggling all these responsibilities.

"Uh, yea, sure. I'll get them off to school."

"Oh my God, you're a savior! Thank you, thank you, thank you!"

"It's okay. You look like you could use a break."

"What gave that away?" she asked. "My wild, desperate-looking eyes?"

"That and your socks aren't matching," he smiled, looking down at her feet.

Sara threw her hand over her face. "Ugh. You really must think I'm a raving lunatic, don't you?"

"No more than the rest of us," he smiled. "Get going. I'll take care of your kids."

"Thanks again, John. I owe you big time." She started to head off but stopped and turned back around. "Oh, and speaking of socks, you might wanna put on something more than *just* socks before heading over to my house." With that, she winked and rushed off.

Slowly, John lowered his eyes down his body. His face turned red when he realized he was only wearing white socks and a ratty old pair of black boxer briefs. He quickly shut the door and dressed for his babysitting duties.

When John arrived next door, Ben was already dressed and sitting in front of the TV with a bowl of cereal. John sat down on one of the arm chairs.

"Suzy is awake and getting dressed, right?" asked John.

"Yea, but it takes her forever to get ready though. I think it's a girl thing."

"It is definitely a girl thing," John laughed.

Just then, frantic screams echoed down from Suzy's room. John sat straight up and his eyes widened in panic-mode.

"Relax," calmed Ben. "She's probably just having a code red in the fashion department. Ya know, can't find shoes to match her dress and nail polish type of stuff. I'm sure glad I'm not a girl."

Before John could agree with Ben's comment, Suzy let out another scream.

"I should probably go check on her," he said, standing up.

"Good luck," Ben called to him as John walked upstairs towards Suzy's room.

He knocked twice on her door and asked, "Is everything okay, Suzy?"

When he entered the room, he saw that Suzy was wearing a pink dress and was sitting in front of her mirror.

"Things are *not* okay," she whined. "Look at my hair! It's like a rat's nest!"

"Wow, a rat's nest, huh?" he laughed.

Suzy spun around in her chair and clarified her statement.

"There's not really a rat's nest in my hair. It's just a figment of speech."

"You mean a figure of speech?" John said, continuing to laugh.

For a brief moment, his thoughts turned to his own daughter. Hannah was always intrigued and amused by silly expressions and figures of speech. Before he could get too sad or deep into the thoughts of his daughter, Suzy let out another frustrated growl.

"Mommy was supposed to fix my hair this morning! Now I'm gonna be the ugliest girl in school!" Suzy slouched her shoulders and anguished at her reflection.

"Well we wouldn't want that," he joked. "Don't worry, kiddo. I think we can figure this out. Brush," he ordered, sticking his hand out. Suzy handed him her brush. "Detangler," he said, sticking out his other hand. Unsure of his hair capabilities, Suzy hesitantly handed him the bottle of detangler.

Over the next few minutes, Suzy watched in amazement as John carefully and successfully detangled her rat's nest.

"There! Now you will certainly not be the ugliest girl in school. As a matter of fact, you'll probably be the prettiest."

While looking at her reflection in the mirror, Suzy ran her fingers through her soft, smooth hair. John noticed her look was still a bit unsatisfied.

"What's wrong? I think your hair looks great," he said.

"Yea, but…"

"But what?"

"Mommy was supposed to French braid my hair today too."

A smile fell across John's face.

"Well, looks like you're in luck, kiddo. That's my specialty."

Suzy's look said it all. She was sure that John had lost his mind. There was no way he knew how to do that, she thought. Before she could voice her concern, however, John was already working his magic on her hair. When he was finished, little Suzy's eyes were nearly bulging out of her head.

"Holy cow!" she exclaimed into the mirror. "Don't tell Mommy, but I think you do it better than she does."

John proudly smiled as he stood back admiring his handy work.

"How do you know how to do that? You're a guy."

"I used to help my daughter with her hair," he answered.

"You have a daughter? What's her name? How old is she? And how come she didn't come here with you?"

A bit overwhelmed by her barrage of questions, John paused a moment and looked into Suzy's wide, innocent eyes. Without thinking too heavily on it, he answered her—honestly.

"Um, her name is Hannah… and she would be pretty close to your age right now. She didn't come with me because… because… she's up in heaven now."

John's heart beat loudly inside his chest. It was the first time he had ever verbally admitted this.

"In heaven? With God?" she softly asked.

Sorrowfully, John nodded.

"Do you think people turn into angels when they go to heaven? Mommy said that my daddy turned into one when he went to heaven."

Chills ran up and down his body as he just stood there in shock. Sara had mentioned her kids had two different fathers, but until now, John never knew anything about Suzy's dad. He just assumed he was also just another deadbeat father.

The moment got so surreal that John had to sit on the bed in attempt to collect his thoughts. The whole situation was unnerving; not necessarily in a bad way, just in a weird and mysterious way.

"Five minutes before we gotta go!" yelled Ben from downstairs.

"Well, we should probably get going, kiddo," he said to Suzy.

She nodded, and before she grabbed her little pink backpack, she admired herself one more time in the mirror.

"Thanks again for fixing my hair, John."

"You're welcome," he warmly said, placing his hand on her shoulder.

As they walked out of her room, she paused and said, "Can I ask for a favor?"

"Sure. What do you need?"

"Can you not tell Mommy I was talking about my daddy? It makes her really sad when I talk about him. Sometimes, I hear her crying in the middle of the night. I'm pretty sure it's because she misses him so much."

At that very moment, John's broken heart seemed to break into a million more pieces. As he fought back his own tears, he gave Suzy a nod.

"You got it, kiddo. It'll be our secret."

"Thanks," she sadly smiled. "And I won't tell her about your daughter either. That would probably make her sad too."

"Good idea," he quietly said as they walked down the hall.

On their way down the stairs, Suzy threw one last question John's way.

"Do you miss your daughter like I miss my daddy?"

He stopped on the second to last step, looked down into Suzy's eyes, and answered, "Very much. Very much."

Outside, John's mind was still reeling. He stood between Suzy and Ben and watched a handful of other kids arrive at the bus stop. Ben gave John a look then quietly whispered to him.

"Um, Mom usually lets us stand by ourselves."

John looked around and noticed the other parents were congregated about fifteen feet away from the kids.

"Ahh. Got it." John winked and stepped backwards. He continued backing up until Ben seemed content with his distance.

He had never been to a bus stop as a parent. As the kids talked and mulled around, John thought deeper on the subject. He remembered how excited he was at the thought of taking Hannah to the bus stop for the first time. Again, he did his best to fight back the tears from forming in his eyes. He also did his best to stop his body from doing that nervous fidgeting thing.

Luckily, the school bus came roaring around the corner, stopping in front of the kids. Before Ben got on the bus, he turned and gave John a subtle nod goodbye. John smiled and returned his nod. What happened next completely caught John off guard. Suzy started to climb onto the bus, but stopped. She turned around and rushed over to John, briefly wrapping her arms around his waist.

"Thanks again for making me pretty today."

He didn't get a chance to say a word, for Suzy quickly released her hug and sprinted back up the stairs of the bus. When the kids were all finally settled in their seats, the bus slowly pulled away. John had lost track of where Ben was, but there, in the front was Suzy. She pressed her little face into the window, smiled, and waved to John.

He smiled and waved back, and as the bus faded out of sight, he could no longer fight his tears. They flowed freely as he made his way back over to William's house. He climbed onto the couch and tried to fall back asleep, but it was impossible. The strange events of the early morning had shaken him to the core.

He was sad and most certainly broken-hearted, but it wasn't the type of sadness to drive him to drink. As a matter of fact, the thought of alcohol never even crossed his mind. Instead, he headed out back and prepared the proper space for where the new gazebo would be built.

* * *

Between school meetings and going over to take care of her ailing mother, Sara and the kids were rarely home over the next few days. She was so tired and run down that she didn't even get a chance to thank John for his kind favor the other morning. She also hadn't even officially thanked him for babysitting her the other night at the tavern.

The few times that Sara and the kids were at home, she didn't want to disturb John. The fervent pace at which he was working, Sara could tell he was on a mission. And on the couple of occasions she did walk over to thank him, he wasn't there. Although he was bound and determined to finish all of the house repairs along with the gazebo, John began taking an hour or two each day to head out to the cove and give the old fisherman a hand fixing up his boat.

There wasn't a lot of talk while they worked, so fortunately for John, the topic of his family was never brought up again. When they did talk, it was usually Clarence telling John one outlandish fishing story after another. Either that, or they made small talk about baseball; about just how pathetic both their teams were. That being said, they both held blind faith that this would be the year.

John even made some time to drive over to Harbor Cove Park. Sometimes, he found himself just sitting and staring out at the lighthouse and ocean for hours on end. Between the sights, the sounds, and the smells, he found himself becoming more and more relaxed.

Each time he went to the lighthouse that week, he spotted that same homeless-looking woman. Each time, however, she was on the other side of the park. She appeared to be weeding random flowerbeds. Part of him thought he should walk over and see if she needed any help; financial or otherwise. But he never did. Instead, he simply kept to himself, gazing out at the vast ocean. He also found himself constantly snapping pictures of the beautiful scenery around him. Before he knew it, he had gone through four disposable cameras.

By the end of the week, he was putting the finishing touch on William's gazebo. It turned out exactly the way he envisioned it. John had forgotten how accomplished and proud one could feel after completing a project. Especially a project he created with his hands and imagination.

As he walked around the entire property admiring all of his handywork, he realized how much he missed working with his hands. And for the first time in a year, he began thinking about the vacant space next to the Wild Irish Rose. He started thinking seriously about getting it fixed up, so he could move all his equipment and tools into there. He wasn't a hundred percent sure if he was ready or not, but the passion for working with his hands had most definitely returned over the past week or so.

* * *

Due to the fact, there were multiple school assemblies and other various interruptions, Sara's poetry unit lasted the entire week. Last but not least on the reading list was Rachel Letourneau.

"Okay, Rachel, you're our final reader," Sara announced.

The students let out a mock cheer. More for the unit being done rather than for Rachel, who was approaching the front of the class.

Bill, who usually slouched, straighten up in his chair. He was excited to hear her poem choice, and he wanted to give her his full attention. And just in case she got nervous and stumbled over words, Bill was prepared to pay her back by giving her an encouraging wink and a smile if needed. It wasn't needed. From the moment she opened her mouth, she read with passion and the utmost confidence.

"This is called 'Tears, Idle Tears,' by Lord Alfred Tennyson." She took a measured breath then began reading from her book.

"Tears, idle tears, I know not what they mean,
Tears from the depth of some divine despair
Rise in the heart, and gather to the eyes,
In looking on the happy Autumn-fields,
And thinking of the days that are no more..."

At the same time across town, John made his way into the cove and was helping Clarence repaint his boat.

"After all the days and long hours, she's finally coming together," Clarence boasted, stepping back to admire his boat.

John also took a moment to proudly admire the nearly new-looking fishing vessel. Quickly, John's mind reflected back to when he first started dating Kristen. He remembered how he used to get lost for hours working at Mr. Kowalski's woodshop. Kristen used to get a little jealous of his time there and would joke that he was having an affair.

John smiled and joked to Clarence. "I bet your wife must get jealous of all the time you spend down here with your boat?"

Clarence returned his smile and took a long gaze out to the ocean.

"There are two loves in my life; my family and this ocean. Sadly, not always in that order."

His voice trailed off as he continued staring out at the crashing waves.

"Well, you must be doing something right," John interrupted. "Didn't you say you guys have been married forever?"

The lines on the old fisherman's face softened as he slowly nodded and said, "Nearly sixty years."

"Holy shit," John exclaimed. "I didn't think that was possible in this day and age."

Clarence turned his attention from the ocean back to John.

"Did you know that in all our years together, neither one of us ever had to say the words *I'm sorry?*"

"What?" laughed John. "Are you telling me you two never argue?"

A chuckle bellowed from Clarence.

"Oh I didn't say that, son. Trust me, we argue plenty. But ya see, neither one of us were ever good at saying *I love you* or *I'm sorry*. You might say we had our own unique way of expressing them."

A puzzled look fell on John's face, and he curiously awaited Clarence's explanation.

"The Red Sox," Clarence uttered, matter-of-factly.

"The Red Sox?" laughed John.

"Yup! Our best communication was done through the Sox. I think it all started when we were first married. Me and the Missus got into an awful fight… sleep on the couch kind of fight, if ya know what I mean?"

Knowing exactly what he meant, John's smile grew as he nodded along.

"I say it was awful, but to be honest, I can't even tell you what it was about. But I do remember we didn't speak to each other for most of the week. Then, one night while I was watching the Sox game, she walked in, sat next to me, and without a word, she grabbed my hand. We sat there and watched the rest of the game together. Trust me, she had no interest in baseball. She couldn't tell the difference from Ted Williams to Ted Kennedy. But as we sat there watching the game together, it was as if nothing had ever happened… as if everything was forgiven. The Sox won five to four, by the way," he winked.

John smiled and continued listening to the old fisherman.

"So, from that point on, it didn't matter how mad we were or who was to blame, as soon as one of us joined the other to watch the game—we knew all was forgiven. So, our *sorrys* and *I love yous* were expressed through the Red Sox."

John stood there, shaking his head in disbelief.

"Strange, I know, but it worked for us."

John pondered then laughed. "Wouldn't wanna see you guys in the off-season I guess."

Both men stood on the beach laughing at one another.

So if it wasn't for the Red Sox…" John began.

"Then we would probably woulda been divorced a long time ago," chuckled Clarence. "Of course, if it wasn't for those damn Sox, I probably wouldn't have had that anxiety attack back in '75… and I wouldn't have thrown my TV out the window in '86."

"Hey, at least the Red Sox have tasted a little success," John pointed out. "Think how us Cubs fans feel!"

Clarence nodded in commiseration then smiled and added, "I suppose it could be worse."

Both men looked at one another then simultaneously said, "We could be Yankee fans."

There was something *uplifting* knowing the Yankees were universally hated across the country.

* * *

Back in Sara's classroom, Rachel was putting the finishing touches on her poem.

"Dear as remember'd kisses after death,
And sweet as those by hopeless fancy feign'd
On lips that are for others; deep as love,
Deep as first love, and wild with all regret;
O Death in Life, the days that are no more!"

Rachel closed her book and looked over at Sara.

"Thank you, Rachel. That poem is another one of my favorites," Sara said, moments before the bell rang. "Okay everyone, no homework this weekend."

Miscellaneous cheers erupted as they gathered their things and hurried out of the room.

"Oh, and I expect to see everyone at the big homecoming dance tomorrow night!"

She accented the word *everyone* directly towards Bill. He immediately lowered his head to avoid eye contact with his favorite teacher, but her words were not lost on him. He'd been thinking non-stop about the dance, and more specifically, about asking Rachel to go with him.

He knew it was now or never to make his move. He stuffed his books into his bag and headed straight for Rachel's locker. As he neared her locker, that perfect speech he'd been rehearsing all week, all but disappeared. His mind went blank, and as he stood there watching Rachel close her locker, he panicked. He had no idea what to say to her.

With her friends by her side, Rachel started to walk away.

"I… I really liked your poem, Rachel," Bill called out.

She stopped and slowly turned back around. She was a little surprised at Bill's comment. Bill was more than a little surprised that words actually emitted from his mouth.

"Why thank you, Bill," she smiled. "I know it's kind of sad and depressing, but it's always been one of my all-time favorites."

"I love sad and depressing," he blurted out then blushed. "I mean… I love poems that make you think," he clarified.

"Agreed," she smiled. "By the way, I really loved your choice too. Who was the poet again?"

"John Donne," he answered.

"Yea, Donne… he rocks," she winked.

Bill stood there, completely in awe at her beauty and her utter coolness. His cheeks were still red, but nothing compared to the shade they were about to turn.

"Well, catch ya later, Bill. Hopefully I'll see you tomorrow night. Make sure you save a dance for me, okay?"

Bill's heart nearly stopped. His body froze, and any sort of words his mind was forming, died within the lump in his throat. All he could offer was a slow nod.

Long after Rachel and her friends headed out, Bill continued to stand by the lockers. He wasn't sure if the giant smile in his heart had manifested its way onto his face. By the weird looks of the people walking by, he assumed it had. Normally, Bill would have taken their weird looks personally, but at that very moment, all he could think of were Rachel's words… *"Hopefully I'll see you tomorrow night. Make sure you save a dance for me, okay?"*

He didn't actually ask Rachel to the dance as planned, but in his mind, this was just as good. The only thing left to worry about was the actual dancing part. Whether fast or slow, Bill had never danced in his life.

22

Friday night marked the end of the school week for Sara and her kids. It also marked the unofficial end for John and his projects. When he returned from helping Clarence, he did a thorough sweep around the entire property. Everything he had written on his original list had been completed and checked off. There were probably dozens of tiny projects and repairs he could have tackled, but John knew it was time to go home.

That being said, he had been thinking a lot lately about this little town of Applewood. What if he moved here? He could sell his house, find a small place down by the ocean, and live a quiet, unbothered life. Besides his brother, what was really left in Chicago for him?

The more serious John thought about this plan, the more he heard his therapist's voice in his head.

"You can't outrun your problems. No matter how far you go, if you don't deal with them head-on then all you're doing is packing them in your suitcase with you."

Whatever he ended up doing, he did know he needed to head back to Chicago first. John purchased his fifth and final disposable camera and used it to take pictures of all the improvements he'd made to the house. He was excited to see William's reaction. He knew William would be more than pleased with his work, especially the beautiful new gazebo.

While John was snapping pictures around the property, Sara was just finishing up washing the dinner dishes. As she wiped and hung up the pots and pans, her eyes focused on Ben's pile of camping gear, which was still sitting in the corner. That's when it hit her.

"Hey, guys," she called out, making her way into the living room.

Ben was on the couch watching TV while Suzy sat on the floor coloring.

"I have a great idea. How about we put that new tent to use and have a little backyard campout?"

"Yea!!!!" squeed Suzy.

Ben's response was less than enthusiastic. He shrugged and continued watching TV. Sara knew a campout with his mom and little sister was a far cry from a guy trip, but she was willing to try anything to snap Ben out of his funk.

"Come on, honey. It'll be fun."

"Can we have a fire and roast marshmallows?" Suzy asked excitedly.

"Of course. Whatever you guys want."

"Yippee!" Suzy yelled, jumping up and down.

Sara turned her attention to Ben.

"Come on, Ben. What do ya say?"

Ben knew his mother was only trying to cheer him up, and he did want to see what his new tent looked like all set up. Reluctantly, he shrugged and nodded in agreement.

"Excellent! Why don't you guys go get sleeping bags and blankets and I'll go set up the tent."

"I can do it by myself," Ben announced, sitting straight up.

Sara smiled. "Well okay then. You go set up the tent, and we'll meet you outside in a bit."

While the girls rushed upstairs to gather their things, Ben grabbed the tent and headed out back. In between taking pictures of his new gazebo, John paused to watch Ben attempt to set up the tent. He chuckled to himself, for it quickly became obvious that Ben had no clue what he was doing. Finally, John took pity on the young boy and walked over to offer a hand.

"Need a little help?"

Ben's face was red in embarrassment, but he knew he was in over his head. He also knew it was probably better to take John's help rather than admit to his mom that he couldn't do it.

"Umm, yea… if you don't mind," Ben quietly said.

"Don't mind at all," John said, shoving the camera into his pocket.

Inside the house, Sara grabbed her and Suzy's sleeping bags out of the closet.

"Hey Mom, can I bring some of my stuffed animals to the campout?"

"Sure, sweetie," Sara answered then turned around to see Suzy standing there holding at least a dozen animals and dolls. "Is there gonna be room in the tent for me and Ben?" she laughed.

Little Suzy scrunched her nose, smiled, and shrugged.

"Why don't you put them by the door and go look for the marshmallows."

"Okay, Mommy."

After Suzy scampered off, Sara stopped at her bedroom window and looked down into the backyard. She shook her head and began laughing to herself as she watched Ben and John fumble with the tent assembly. It was apparent that neither one of them had a clue how to set up a tent.

When the girls finally made their way outside, little to no progress had been made on the tent.

"Hi, John!" Suzy yelled out.

"Hey, Suzy," he replied, still focused on the tent poles.

"Do you two boys need some help with that?" Sara asked.

"No!" they stubbornly said in unison. "We got it."

"Okay," she smiled. "Well, maybe Suzy and I will go gather some wood for the fire."

The boys barely heard a word. Their attention was already back on the tent poles. By the time the girls gathered wood, built a firepit, and started the fire, the boys were no closer to setting up the tent. At that point, Sara shook her head, rolled up her sleeves, and showed them how it was done. It took her seven minutes to be precise. Ben and John stood by and watched in awe.

The night was filled with a warm fire, marshmallows, hot cocoa, and lots and lots of talking from Suzy. And as the cold fall night set in, it was also filled with laughter and ghost stories.

"Your turn to tell a ghost story," Ben said, looking over at John.

An unsure look fell on John's face. He'd spent much of the night as a quiet observer and was hoping to remain that way.

"Yea, your turn to tell a ghost story," echoed Suzy. "And make it super-scary!"

Both Ben and Sara shot Suzy an incredulous look.

"Yea, right," Ben laughed. "You couldn't handle a real scary story. You get scared watching the Wicked Witch on the Wizard of Oz."

"No I don't!" she yelled defensively.

"Do too!"

"Okay, enough you two." Sara could tell the last thing John wanted to do was come up with a silly ghost story or to be put in the middle of two arguing kids. "I think that's enough of the ghost stories for the night. As a matter of fact," she said, looking at her watch, "I think it's time for you guys to head into the tent and go to sleep."

Her words were met with loud moans and groans.

"Why do I have to go to bed the same time as Suzy? I'm like way older than her."

"You don't have to go to sleep, Ben, but I just want you inside the tent now, okay?"

"Fine," he relented. "Can I bring a flashlight and read my comic books?"

"Me too," yelled Suzy.

"Pfft, you don't even know how to read."

"Do too!" Suzy said, scowling and crossing her arms.

"Guys, enough! You both can read with flashlights. Just no more bickering. Understand?" When neither kid responded, Sara repeated with more emphasis. "Understand?"

"Yes, Mommy," Suzy finally said.

Ben was too cool to answer, but he gave his mother a look that told her he understood.

"Come on, ya clowns, I'll tuck you in," Sara said, standing up from her chair.

Ben unzipped the tent, but before they entered, Sara loudly cleared her throat.

"Aren't you guys gonna tell John, goodnight?"

Without making much eye contact, Ben mumbled goodnight then climbed inside the tent. Suzy was more animated with her response.

"Goodnight, John from Chicago!" she yelled while smiling and waving.

"Goodnight, kids," he responded.

"Wait!" Suzy said, poking her head back out of the tent. "Are you going to sleep in the tent with us?"

"No, silly. John is gonna sleep in his own house," Sara said, guiding her talkative daughter into the tent.

When they were both tucked into their sleeping bags, Sara handed each of them a flashlight then kissed them on their foreheads.

"Did you guys have fun?"

"Uh huh," Ben mumbled, but was more concerned with flipping through his comic book.

"It was wicked fun!" smiled Suzy. "The marshmallows were my favorite part… and the fire… and the hot chocolate… and the ghost stories…and the tent."

Ben paused his reading long enough to give his sister an annoyed look.

Sara laughed and ruffled the hair on both their heads. "Well I'm glad you had fun. Goodnight, guys. I love you."

"Love you more!" Suzy loudly pointed out.

Ben's annoyed look firmly remained on his little sister. Sara turned and crawled out of the tent, but before she completely zipped it back up, Ben called out.

"Hey, Mom… do you think sometime we can go on a real camping trip? Like way out in the woods?" And maybe with a place we can go fishing?"

"You bet, kiddo. You bet."

With that, she gave Ben a wink, zipped up the tent, and walked back to her chair. John was in the process of adding a couple more logs to the fire.

"Everything okay in there?" he asked.

"So far," she smirked. "I'm sure I'll have to go play referee a few more times before the night is out."

He tossed one more log onto the fire then sat back in his chair.

Without the kids there, especially Suzy, the fireside chat grew much quieter. At one point, a long silence filled the air as both John and Sara struggled for something to talk about. Finally, Sara let out a little laugh and leaned in closer to the warm fire.

"I suppose I owe you a couple of big thank yous," she said in John's direction.

"For what?"

"For babysitting me the other night at the tavern and for getting my kids off to school the other morning. I really do appreciate it."

"You're welcome. It wasn't that big of a deal."

"And thanks for hanging out with us tonight."

"Thanks for inviting me," he said. "You have great kids, Sara."

Lovingly, she looked towards the tent, which was dimly illuminated by their flashlights.

"It was really nice seeing Ben with a smile on his face tonight. I'm used to him being so sad and withdrawn. He sees all of his friends doing things with their dads, and I can't imagine how it must make him feel." She paused then said, "I suppose I should also thank you for talking to him the other day... in the woods."

A bit surprised, John looked over at Sara.

"Oh, he told you about that? Not really sure if I helped any."

"You totally did. I think you helped him realize that things can always be worse and that he should be thankful for what he has."

As the fire crackled, John wondered just how much Ben told her about their conversation. Sara's next comment answered his question.

"So, is it true you spent your entire childhood in foster care?"

John poked at the fire and nodded. This was certainly not the type of fireside conversation he wanted, but for whatever reason, he found himself expounding on his nod.

"I was three when we were first placed into the foster system."

"We?" she asked. "Do you have siblings?"

"I have a brother. We're a year apart."

From that point on, John let his guard down and allowed Sara into a place where very few had ever been. Over the next hour, he filled her in on all three of the foster homes they had been through. Due to his young age, details about the first family were vague at best. He had a lot more details of the second family and was able to point out some random memories that had stuck in his head.

The detailed portion of his foster care story came with the introduction of the O'Neils. John surprised himself at just how detailed he got with her. Every so often, Sara would interrupt with a question or comment, but for the most part, she simply sat still and listened intently.

The more John talked, the easier the words became. Before he knew it, he had pretty much filled Sara in on everything regarding the O'Neils; the arguments, the brutal fights, and he even told her about the night Mr. O'Neil sadistically torched their baseball cards. Sara was beside herself in shock and disgust.

"Apparently the State didn't have much of a screening process, huh?" she asked.

"Apparently not. Personally, I think they were just happy to get us placed in a home together."

"Still, I can't believe they let people like that be foster parents."

John shrugged. "There are plenty of shitty biological parents out there… so what's the difference?"

Sara pondered a second then nodded in agreement. "And you said Mrs. O'Neil was nice?"

"She was actually a very nice lady."

"Why would a nice woman like that stay married to a monster like him?"

"That same question always ran through my head as well. Unfortunately, the older I get, the more I see it all the time; nice women caught in toxic relationships. Either they're too scared to leave or too scared to be on their own I guess."

John noticed his comment had struck a chord with Sara.

"I'm sorry, I wasn't talking about you."

"You might as well have been. I've had more than my share of toxic relationships. Ben's father was a prime example. I guess in his case, I always thought I could change him."

John looked over at Sara and said, "I'm sorry."

"It's okay. Eventually I smartened up."

John went on to tell her his theory on Mr. and Mrs. O'Neil's marriage. From what Kevin and him had gathered over the years, it seemed the reason the O'Neils chose to have foster kids was that good ole Richard was incapable of having kids on his own. John assumed the whole foster kid thing was Mr. O'Neil's way of pacifying his wife. It was kind of a win-win for Mr. O'Neil. His wife got her make-shift family, and he got to collect a stipend check each month from the foster care system. A check which he had no problem using on alcohol.

"I remember he used to come in our bedroom each month with a big, smug smile on his face. He would wave the check in the air then tell us, 'Thanks, boys! Looks like this weekend's beers are on you!'"

"That's horrible!" exclaimed Sara.

"That was nothing. He was famous for barging into our bedroom saying mean things." John stared into the fire and recalled another long-lost memory. "I remember one time, I must have been around Ben's age. I wasn't doing so hot in school, and he came bursting into my room... drunk of course. After he slapped me around a bit, he got right in my face and said, 'Either you're not trying hard enough, or you're just plain stupid.' He then pounded the rest of his beer and said, 'My bet's on stupid. No wonder your real parents wanted nothing to do with you!'"

"He said that? Seriously, how can they let people like that be foster parents?"

John slowly shrugged as he continued staring into the fire.

"He was a giant asshole, but he was kind of right. Our real parents didn't want us."

Sara was quick to jump in. "John, I'm sure there must have been a good reason."

"Is there ever a good reason for ditching not one, but two kids?"

Sara sensed his anger and resentment and knew she needed to choose her words carefully. She sat quietly for a few moments before hesitantly asking, "Did you ever think about searching for them? Your real parents?"

He took a long pause. It was long enough for Sara to regret her question, but before she could apologize for getting too personal, John spoke up.

"I thought a lot about it, actually. I remember telling Kevin as soon as we turned eighteen that we should go to the foster care office and get their names and addresses. Do you realize we don't even know what our parents' names are. I'm assuming Mathews is our real last name, but who knows."

"Did you? Ever look them up?"

Slowly, John shook his head no. "Kevin was always against the idea. He thought we needed to just let it be and concentrate on our own lives and future. I'm sure he was probably right, but still… there were many times I was tempted to get some answers. But to answer your question, no, I've never actually looked them up."

John stood up and grabbed two logs and tossed them onto the fire. When he returned to his chair, Sara handed him another cup of hot chocolate.

"Thanks."

As he got the fire roaring again, Sara sat in silence, still thinking about all of his horrible childhood experiences. She promised not to keep prying, but she just couldn't help herself.

"He would really smack you guys around?"

"Yup. Unfortunately, Mrs. O'Neil and Kevin took the brunt of it. Apparently, they thought it was *their responsibility* to stand up for me."

The way he said the words *their responsibility*, and the way he was aggressively poking at the fire, Sara could tell how this affected him. She tried her best to spin it positively, but it only ended up backfiring.

"Well, I suppose that's what a mother and older brother are for."

"She wasn't my mother! And Kevin is my younger brother, NOT older. I didn't need them to defend me."

Knowing she hit a nerve, Sara softly offered an apology, which caused John to offer one right back.

"No, I'm the one who should be sorry. I didn't mean to snap at you. I guess I just always hated the fact that I was… was too scared to stand up to him. I hated that Kevin thought it was his job to protect me."

John took a deep breath then exhaled. He couldn't believe he just said those words out loud. Actually, he couldn't believe most of the words he had revealed that night to this stranger next door. The subject of John's childhood was briefly changed, but during the next long moment of silence, Sara once again found herself prying.

"Did you or your brother ever think about reporting Mr. O'Neil? Like, to your teachers or to the State?"

"All the time," John quietly laughed. "I remember one time in middle school, Kevin came to school with yet another black eye. I guess the teacher thought it was a little suspicious and sent him down to the guidance counselor. She asked if everything was okay at home. Kevin told them I had thrown a baseball at him when he wasn't looking."

"Did you?" Sara asked.

"All the time," he smiled. "I was kind of a mean older brother to him." John paused then continued. "But in that particular case, it wasn't me. Mr. O'Neil clocked Kevin in the eye the night before."

A puzzled look fell over Sara's face.

"So why didn't he just tell them the truth?"

John took a long sip of his hot chocolate then looked over at Sara and answered.

"Mr. O'Neil might have been a drunk son of a bitch, but he was no dummy. He was well aware that at any moment we would say something to an adult and get him in deep trouble. That's why he made it a point to constantly put the fear of God in us."

"He threatened worse violence to you if you ever told?" she asked in shock.

Slowly, John nodded. "But I don't think that was what really kept us from reporting him." Again, Sara gave him a puzzled look. "He told us if he ever got in trouble that Mrs. O'Neil would get in just as much trouble for allowing it to happen."

"Well that's a bunch of bullshit!" Sara blurted out.

"We were just kids," he shrugged. "We didn't know it was bullshit. And even worse than that, he told us if the State ever removed us, that because of our ages, we would definitely get separated and sent to different foster families. He told us we'd never see each other again. And yes, I know it's bullshit, and it probably wouldn't have happened, but... but like I said, we were just two scared kids. The only family we ever had was each other... so we couldn't ever take the chance of losing that."

Sympathy poured from Sara's eyes, but it went unnoticed. John's eyes were intently focused on the fire. She knew it was best to hold off on any further questions. The poor man had said enough, she thought. She used the break in conversation to go check on her kids in the tent.

When she returned to her chair, she was determined to change the subject to something cheerier. To her surprise, however, John picked up where they had left off.

"So needless to say, Kevin and I kept our mouths shut. Right up until I was sixteen. That's when we were finally removed."

Although she promised herself not to pry further, John's comment left her beyond curious, and she couldn't help herself.

"What happened when you were sixteen?" She quickly followed with an apology. "I'm sorry. It's totally none of my business."

"It's okay. I just don't talk about it much. Much at all actually."

By now, John had the fire roaring again, and Sara welcomed the heat against her cold cheeks. She sat back in her chair hoping he would continue his story. John also leaned back and stared long and hard into the fire. It seemed the longer he stared into the flames, the further his mind took him back in time; back to that late spring day when John and Kevin spent the afternoon at the batting cages. He continued gazing into the fire as he began his story.

"The batting cages was one of our most favorite places to go. That and the ball field at the park. They were like our little pieces of heaven."

Kevin stood outside the cage while John was inside crushing one pitch after another. Nervously, Kevin looked down at his black Casio watch.

"Come on, John. We gotta go. We're gonna be late."

"No way, Kev! I'm totally on a roll here. Just one more round."

One more round turned into two, and by the time they finally left the cages, they were a half hour late. It wasn't until they were almost home that John's carefree attitude completely switched. The gravity of just how late they were going to be was finally sinking into John's head.

As they rushed down the sidewalk, both boys silently prayed that Mr. O'Neil was either not home yet or was already passed out on the couch – neither would be true.

"We hadn't even made it up our walkway when we heard him screaming and throwing things," John said to Sara.

Hesitantly, the boys walked up the front steps, and through the screen door they could see some of the upturned furniture. Mrs. O'Neil met them at the door. Her lip was bleeding and her mascara was streaked down her face. She did her best to get them to leave, but it was too late. Mr. O'Neil spotted the boys and looked up at the clock on the living room wall.

"Don't you two idiots know how to tell time? Or are you even too stupid for that?"

John dropped his glove and bat and slowly took a step back on the porch.

"Where the hell do you think you're going?"

Angrily, Mr. O'Neil stumbled towards John, but Kevin stepped in front of him. Mrs. O'Neil stepped in front of both the boys in attempt to shield them from his drunken rage. She was nearly as tall as her husband, but she was nowhere near as strong as he was.

In one swift motion, he shoved her off to the right and onto the ground. Kevin rushed forward and grabbed him by the shirt. Mr. O'Neil staggered backwards but was still able to swing his right fist forward. It connected solidly on the side of Kevin's face, knocking him to the ground. John clenched his fists, but all he could do was stand there, frozen with fear.

"What are ya gonna do, Johnny boy? You want a piece of me?"

John remained frozen, and his fists were now shaking uncontrollably. Mr. O'Neil took one look at this frightened little teenager and began to laugh.

"That's what I thought. You're too much of a pussy to do anything. You always have been."

He took one last puff of his cigarette, flicked it at John's feet then took a step closer to the scared boy. Mrs. O'Neil had gotten to her feet and once again attempted to step in front of John. This time, Mr. O'Neil didn't shove her aside. Instead, he gave her a drunken backhand, which was hard enough to knock her into the wall.

He returned his attention to John, but before he could take another step closer, Kevin picked himself off the ground and lunged onto Mr. O'Neil's back. He began choking him in a headlock, and all Mr. O'Neil could do was flail his arms and spin around in circles in attempt to get Kevin off of him. The whole time this went on, John's fists remained clenched, but his feet and body stayed in the same spot.

With one last-ditch effort, Mr. O'Neil violently pushed backwards, sending them both crashing through the picture window and onto the front yard. All at once, John's eyes widened and his fists unclenched as he looked out at the two of them laying on the grass with a million pieces of glass shattered around them.

"The fall knocked Mr. O'Neil out," John said, looking away from the fire.

"Oh my God," exclaimed Sara. "What happened to your brother?"

"He just lay there... motionless. I swear I thought he was dead," John said, finally making eye contact with Sara.

His eye contact was short-lived as he gazed back into the fire and once again went back in time. When his mind returned to the O'Neil house, the driveway was full of flashing lights from the police cars and ambulances. As two officers hauled Mr. O'Neil away in cuffs, John anxiously watched the paramedics tending to Kevin and Mrs. O'Neil.

"I know I should have been relieved that the whole O'Neil nightmare was over, but..."

"But what?" Sara asked, leaning forward in her chair.

"I was just so pissed at myself. I just stood there that day and did nothing. I was always so scared to stand up to him like Kevin did... like Kevin always did. I hated myself for that. And if truth be told, I kinda hated Kevin for that as well. I know, I know, that sounds horrible."

Sympathetically, Sara shook her head no. "The whole situation was horrible. That's what I think. There's no embarrassment in being scared. He sounds like a monster." Slowly, John nodded in agreement. "So what happened to you and your brother?"

"We were placed in the Boys Home of Chicago until we were eighteen. It wasn't exactly a warm and cozy place, but it wasn't the O'Neil's either. And at least we got to stay together."

That was the last thing spoken that night regarding John's childhood. Any further questions Sara had, she kept to herself. She could tell John had stepped out of his comfort zone by telling her as much as he did, and she certainly didn't want to push it any further.

She reached down and picked up her thermos and attempted to refill her cup. When only two measly drops of hot chocolate fell out, she turned and looked over at John.

"Should I make some more?"

He glanced down at his empty cup and said, "Sure."

"Don't feel like you have to hang out here all night. I'm sure you have better things to do than keep me company."

She offered him an out, but secretly crossed her fingers that he'd stay. He did.

"I don't mind hanging out, as long as you don't mind having me. It's actually kind of relaxing out here. It's been a while since I've sat around a fire like this."

John quickly flashbacked to the last time. It was at his in-laws a couple years earlier. They had a very expensive and elaborate fire pit built into their large back patio. He dreaded hanging out over at Kristen's parents' house. They were nice enough to him, but he always felt out of place. That night by the fire was no different. He was constantly checking his watch and biding his time before they could head home. The sooner they left, the sooner he could hit the couch and catch the end of the Cubs game.

But now, looking back on it, John would have given anything to be back at his in-laws. He'd given anything to be sitting by the fire with his wife by his side and his daughter on his lap. Anything.

While Sara headed inside to make more hot chocolate, John gathered more wood for the fire; enough to keep it going well into the night. When Sara returned and saw how big the fire was, a wide smile fell on her face. She knew he planned on hanging out there for a while, and for whatever reason, this made her happy. John reached out his cup and watched Sara carefully fill it to the brim.

"Thanks."

"You're welcome. If you want something stronger, I might have some liquor up in one of my cabinets."

"Nah. This is perfect."

Sara nodded and filled her own cup. Completely relaxed, she sat back in her chair. "Ahh," she said, soaking in the heat of the fire. "Hot chocolate and a warm fire. This is like the height of my social life this past year. Pathetic, I know."

"You mean the other night at the tavern wasn't?"

Sara blushed then threw her hand over her face.

"Ugh, don't remind me of that night."

"I'm just kidding," he smiled. "You were actually pretty funny."

"And by funny, you mean overly talkative and emotionally unstable? I really am sorry you had to witness my pity party. I've tried to hold it together for so long, I guess I just needed a night to release some of it. It's just... ever since my..."

Sara paused and looked away. The huge flames illuminated her face enough for John to tell she was getting emotional. It was obvious she was having trouble getting the words out, and after a few moments of uncomfortable silence, John spoke.

"I'm sorry about your husband."

Completely surprised by his knowledge, she turned and gave him a curious look.

"Suzy kind of mentioned him the other morning when I was getting her ready for school."

"She did? What did she say?"

He shrugged. "Not a lot. Just that her daddy was an angel in heaven now."

John watched a tear run down her cheek as she sadly gazed over at the tent. Although he was curious about the details, he kept his questions to himself. If Sara wanted to tell him, she needed to do it on her own terms… in her own time.

Over the next few minutes, the only sound was the fire crackling into the night. John kept his eyes on the fire, but he could tell Sara was doing her best to compose herself and formulate what to say next. Finally, she took a deep breath and softly spoke.

"I've spent most my life dating one loser after another… especially Ben's dad. I had pretty much lost all faith in love… then I met Suzy's dad. He was definitely one of the good ones. We dated, we fell in love, and we got married. He even treated Ben like his own. Then, Suzy was born, and things were finally working out."

Sara paused and took a long emotional sigh before continuing.

"Then boom… he's gone… just like that. This past year has been like a blur to me. Sometimes I still can't believe he's gone. It's almost like the best part of me died that day too. For my kids' sake, I do my best to keep it together on the outside, but the truth is, on the inside I still feel so…"

John stepped in. "Empty? Lost?"

Sara nodded then gazed down at her finger.

"I just recently took off my wedding ring, but it's still sitting there on the nightstand by my bed. I have no idea what to do with it. It's hard to explain, but part of me feels by me taking it off, I'm…"

"Dishonoring his memory?"

Sara looked at John and shrugged. "Yea, kinda. But I know by me continuing to wear it, it makes it…"

"Hard to move on?"

Again, Sara looked at John then slowly nodded.

"I know exactly what you mean," he said, and then looked away and focused in on the flames, which were wildly flickering about. He took a deep breath of his own and then continued.

"I kind of lied to you before, Sara… about my wife and daughter… they died in a car accident last year."

"Oh my God, John!" she exclaimed, covering her mouth in shock. "I'm so sorry."

He paused and did his best to blink back the tears that were forming in his eyes. That was the first time he had ever said those words aloud.

"It was on the day we were supposed to go meet Hannah's kindergarten teacher for the first time. We were supposed to go as a family, but…"

As his voice trailed off, Sara stepped in and said, "John, you really don't have to talk about this with me."

"It's okay," he said then looked to the ground and began his story. "My brother and I were in the process of opening up our bar. For months we had put our blood, sweat, and tears into renovating it. All that was left was for the inspector to sign off on everything. It was all supposed to be so cut and dry. Meet with the inspector, be back home by three… go meet Hannah's kindergarten teacher… as a family."

John paused long enough to give the logs a poke then continued.

"I guess I just lost track of time. The next thing I knew, it was ten after three."

John closed his eyes for a moment, and when he opened them, he was standing in the middle of the Wild Irish Rose a year earlier. He gave Kevin a congratulatory high five then glanced down at his watch.

"Shit! I gotta go. I'm late," he said, rushing out the front door.

John sprinted down the sidewalk and jumped into his truck. As he pulled onto the road, he reached over to the passenger seat and grabbed his cell phone. He saw that there were two texts and one voice message.

The first text read: *It's five of three… where are you?*

The second text was five minutes later and simply consisted of four question marks in a row.

John grimaced then pressed the phone to his ear to listen to the voice message.

"John, where are you? It's after three. We'll give you five more minutes… if not, then I guess you'll have to meet us there. Bye!"

The way she said the word *Bye* and quickly hung up, John knew she was beyond perturbed.

"Fuck!" he yelled out and tossed the phone back onto the seat.

His foot pressed down harder on the gas as his truck roared down the street. Minutes later, he found himself at a complete stop in the middle of a traffic jam. He glanced at the clock in the truck: 3:30 p.m.

Before he could yell out another curse word, his cell phone rang. He quickly reached over and answered it.

"Kristen, I'm soooo…" he paused. "Oh, hi Kevin. No, I'm still not there yet. Just my frickin' luck, a traffic jam a couple of blocks from the school."

Impatient and irritated, John jerked his wheel to the right and pulled into a random driveway.

"Hopefully these people won't mind if I park here for a bit. Hey, let me call you back, Kev. Looks like I'm gonna have to hoof it to Hannah's school… Alright, talk to you later."

John jumped out of his truck, slamming the door behind him. Briskly, he made his way past all of the stopped cars. As he came closer to the giant intersection up ahead, he could see the blue flashing lights of police cars. There was also a fire truck parked at the intersection. Just then, an ambulance came screaming from the scene.

He decided not to approach any further and to take a short cut to the school. As he turned to his right, he stopped and gave another glance towards the accident scene. That's when he saw it. In the middle of the intersection, he saw a black Escalade with its front dented in. Before he continued on his way, he caught a glimpse of the other car. It looked a lot like Kristen's car. A sick feeling entered his stomach as he focused in on the front license plate. It *was* Kristen's car.

The entire driver's side was completely smashed in. With his heart in his throat, John rushed over to get a closer look. The scene was in the process of being taped off, but he ducked under and headed straight for his wife's car.

By the time officers got to him, he was already examining Kristen's smashed car. The inside was covered in broken glass. The officers tried to control John, but he was an emotional wreck.

"Where's my wife? Where's my daughter?"

The more he repeated himself, the louder he got. The officers did their best to subdue and calm him down.

Back at the campfire, Sara sat stunned with her mouth gaped open. The cup of hot chocolate began shaking in her hand.

John gave a log a violent poke then said, "Some idiot driver thought they could speed up and run the red light… my wife was pronounced dead on the scene. My little girl hung on in a coma for almost a week before she…"

John stopped short as tears began falling from his eyes. He looked over at Sara and said, "If only I had been home when I promised…"

Sara got out of her chair and kneeled by his side, grabbing his hand.

"John, you can't blame yourself. It's not your fault. It wasn't your fault."

He clutched her hand tighter as tears fell from both their eyes. Nothing else was spoken regarding the accident. For what seemed like forever, they both just sat there in silence, crying and staring into the fire.

When the tears finally stopped, and when they both had composed themselves, their conversation resumed. They spent the rest of the night talking about everything under the sun. From that point on, there were more laughs than tears. And speaking of the sun, they talked so deep into the night, that they were still awake as the sun was coming up.

One of the things they had talked about was Sara's coworker, Paul. She talked fondly of him and pointed out all of the sweet and kind things he had done for her throughout the school year.

By the time the sun was fully up, the wood had run out, and all that was left of the fire were embers. Both of them had double blankets thrown over their shoulders to keep warm. John poked at the embers then turned to Sara.

"I know this is none of my business, but maybe you should give that Paul guy a chance."

"He really is a sweet guy, but… it's just so hard letting someone else in… even harder to let myself feel happy again. It's like, any time I start to feel happy, I can't help but feel…"

"Guilty?" John interrupted. "I know exactly what you mean, but… but I'm sure your husband would want you to be happy again."

Knowingly, she looked into John's eyes and gave him a shrug and a smile. Not long after the sun was up in the sky, there was stirring going on inside the tent. A few minutes later, the door was unzipped and Ben and Suzy both exited, still sleepy-eyed.

"You guys are already awake?" Suzy asked.

"Actually," Sara said, looking over at John, "we've been up all night talking."

Suzy didn't seem impressed. She had more important things on her mind.

"I'm cold… and hungry. What's for breakfast?"

"Oh you are, are you?" Sara said, pulling Suzy under the blanket with her. "How about we head inside and make some blueberry pancakes?"

"With bacon too?" Ben asked.

"Well, duh," Sara laughed. "That's a given."

"Hey, John. Did you know that bacon comes from pigs?"

Before John could answer Suzy, Ben interrupted. "Of course he knows that. Everybody knows that!"

Suzy ignored her brother and continued to address John.

"It's kinda sad for the pigs… but bacon really is delicious though."

John laughed and agreed with her. "I can't argue with that."

Less than an hour later, they were all sitting in the kitchen stuffing their faces with pancakes and delicious bacon. Just as Ben polished off the last piece, there was a knock at the front door.

A puzzled look came over Sara's face.

"Who the heck could that be?" she said aloud.

"Yea," echoed Suzy. "Who the heck could that be?"

Sara entered the living room then slowly opened the door.

"Paul? What are you doing here?"

"I was just passing by and thought I'd see if you and your kids wanted to go out to eat. They're doing that big charity breakfast over at the…"

Over Sara's shoulder, Paul watched Suzy and Ben exit the kitchen— followed by John. Paul tried his best to remain expressionless, but his shock and disappointment were quite apparent.

"Oh… I'm sorry. I didn't mean to interrupt, "Paul said, trying not to make eye contact with John.

"No, not at all," she said as she motioned for Paul to come in. "This is our neighbor, John."

Politely, Paul offered a smile and reached out his hand to John. No sooner did they finish shaking hands, Suzy blurted out, "John spent the night last night."

This time, Paul wasn't the only one with a surprised and uncomfortable look on his face. Sara glanced over at John then tried her best to explain the situation to Paul.

"He didn't really *spend* the night," she pointed out. "It was more of a campout... kinda."

Suzy started giggling, and once again randomly blurted out, "John couldn't get it up, so Mommy had to help him."

John's eyes widened, and Sara spit out her coffee.

"Suzy!"

"What? You're the one who put the tent up, Mommy. Right?"

John and Sara both smiled at Suzy's wording. Paul was still clueless and very much feeling uncomfortable. Sara tried to clarify her daughter's comments, but she only got herself in deeper.

"Suzy was referring to the tent. The kids and I had a campout in the backyard, and John was having a hard time, so I helped him pitch his tent."

This time it was John who spit out his coffee. Sara realized what she just said and immediately tried to reword it.

"It was an *actual* tent that I helped him erect."

John fought back a smile as he placed his hand over his face.

"Oh boy," Sara said as her face turned a bright red. "I should probably just shut up."

Ben had kind of caught on to his mother's accidental sexual innuendoes, but Suzy had no clue what was going on. For different reasons, they both began laughing out loud. Paul wasn't laughing. There was no hiding the uncomfortable look on his face, and his desire to get the hell out of there as quickly as possible.

"I think I should head out," he said, stepping back towards the door. "Sorry again for stopping by unannounced."

"No need to apologize, Paul. I still have some food in the kitchen if ya wanna join us."

"Nah, that's okay," he politely smiled. "I'll see you at the dance?"

"I'll be there."

Before heading out, Paul said his goodbyes to the kids and to John. Sara shut the door behind him then turned and embarrassingly shook her head in John's direction.

"I think that went really well," he said, fighting back laughter.

23

Not long after Paul left, John also headed home. He spent the rest of the morning and early afternoon catching up on his sleep. When he finally awoke, he decided to take a drive up to Harbor Cove Park. He knew he'd be driving back to Chicago in a day or two and wanted to soak in the ocean and lighthouse views as much as possible. He still had a handful of exposures left on his camera and figured the park would be the perfect place to use them up.

It was a gray and gloomy fall day, and by the looks of the dark clouds rolling in, he knew his time would be limited. As usual, he was the only one there. As he walked towards the bench overlooking the lighthouse, he felt the wind start to pick up. The clouds became darker and moved at a steadier pace across the sky. Quickly, he pulled out the camera and was able to catch the perfect picture of a large ominous cloud formation hovering over the lighthouse. As soon as he snapped the picture, he found himself stealing a line his wife often used.

"That's a keeper," he said aloud then gazed down at the camera.

He couldn't help but think about all the times he heard that from his wife. He continued to smile, remembering how Kristen loved her silly old Polaroid camera. His smile turned into a laugh when he thought about Hannah dancing around shaking the picture. Her excitement was the same each and every time she watched the picture develop right before her eyes. Kristen was right, one hundred percent right. It really was the little things that mattered most.

For John's final picture, he decided to get a bit creative. His goal was to time it perfectly so that he could not only capture the rotating red light of the lighthouse, but also get the splash of the giant waves against its rocks. Patience was never his strong suit, but he was determined to wait as long as it took.

If this was the digital camera he had bought Kristen, he could have easily captured it by doing a burst of shots. But this was a disposable camera, and he only had one chance at getting it right. The wind picked up and the skies darkened even more, but John held his ground. Like most things, he looked at this photo-challenge as a competition. And like most competitions, he refused to back down or lose.

His finger anxiously tapped on the button as he waited… and waited… and waited. Finally, after what seemed like forever, it all fell into place. Just as a huge wave sent a giant spray of water into the air, the red light appeared front and center. Without hesitation, his finger firmly and confidently pressed down. Not only did he nail it, but he got the added bonus of capturing a seagull flying directly over the lighthouse as well.

With his hands raised in victory, he announced, "That's a keeper!"

No sooner did the words leave his mouth, a familiar noise was heard off in the distance. It was the squeaky wheel from the shopping cart. John looked over his shoulder and watched the old lady slowly make her way up the winding path.

Normally, the thought of her approaching and giving him that weird, creepy stare of hers was enough to make him get up and remove himself from the uncomfortable situation. But as a light rain began to fall, his demeanor softened a bit. Not only was he still reveling in his photography skills, but he knew this was probably his last visit to the park—his last run-in with the strange homeless looking woman—his last chance to offer her some assistance. Without a doubt, this is what his girls would want.

As the squeaky wheel grew louder, John reached into his pocket and pulled out his wallet. He still had quite a bit of money left over from William's check. It was money he felt like he didn't deserve. In his heart, he knew William only offered him to come to Maine as a way of helping him clear his head and recover.

The fact that William was basically a stranger to John, and yet reached out and offered his help, well, it made John realize that maybe he needed to do the same with this old shopping-cart woman.

With his wallet tightly clutched in his hand, he noticed the wheel had stopped squeaking. He peered over his shoulder and saw that she had paused in front of the memorial. She placed a handful of different colored flowers at the foot of it and stood there for a moment.

She then left the cart parked on the grass as she slowly made her way towards the edge of the cliff. She had yet to make eye contact with John, and it was as if she hadn't even noticed him. He found this odd and continued to watch her as she gazed out at the ocean.

The rain was picking up, and he knew it wouldn't be long before the storm would be right on top of them. He couldn't believe the woman wasn't even wearing a jacket to protect her against the oncoming weather. Sadness and sympathy filled his heart, and as he looked down at his wallet, he knew what he needed to do.

He stood up from the bench and looked back over at the old lady. Her attention had turned from the ocean to him—directly at him. That same weird, creepy smile appeared on her face. He fought the urge to look away, and instead, offered a polite nod hello. As he slowly made his way towards her, her eyes continued to stare directly into his. John shook off his uneasiness and tried to formulate exactly what he was going to say to her.

"Afternoon," was all he could come up with.

The woman said nothing. Instead, her smile grew wider, and she cocked her head, leaning in closer to John. It was as if she was carefully inspecting his face. It was enough to cause John that same uncomfortable feeling as before, and it was certainly enough to make him second guess what the hell he was doing there. He should have just kept to himself and avoided any sort of interaction with the woman. What she said next emphasized that point even more.

"I knew you'd come back to Applewood one day… I just knew it!"

John's uneasiness quickly turned into sympathy for the old lady. Not only was she probably homeless, but she must be suffering from some sort of dementia, maybe even schizophrenia.

Again, he offered a polite smile and said, "I'm sorry, ma'am, I think you have me confused with someone else."

She continued to smile and shook her head side to side.

"Ohhh no… I never forget a face. It's been a long, long time, but I'd recognize those brown eyes anywhere."

John was torn. Should he play along with her delusions or should he continue being honest? He didn't want her to think she was losing her mind, so he decided the polite thing to do was play along, and hopefully he could find the perfect way to offer her some financial assistance. That moment would never come, however. From that point on, the conversation turned from awkward to strange—extremely strange.

"Yup, I'd recognize that baby face anywhere," she said as she ran her bony fingers across his face. "I'm so glad you came back, John."

A chill ran up his spine, and he took a step backwards and curiously asked, "How do you… how do you know my name?"

"I used to be friends with your parents," she softly said.

Her latest comment cemented the fact that this woman had indeed lost her mind. John knew he should be polite and compassionate, but the fact that she knew his name, and the mere mention of his parents, caused him to resort to sarcasm.

"My parents, huh? Would that be foster family one, two, or three?" he half-laughed.

Her smile faded and her eyes widened.

"Oh, you poor boys!" she exclaimed.

Boys? Was she referring to my brother? If so, how the hell did she know about him? Before he had a chance to question her on it, she spoke.

"I'm sorry you had to go through all of that, but I was friends with your *real* parents... Caitlin and Robert."

By now, John had lost all sympathy and patience for this woman.

"Those names mean nothing to me. We never even knew their names. My *real* parents wanted nothing to do with us. They abandoned us when I three."

The old lady's eyes glossed over in sadness as she clutched at her heart.

"Abandoned? Who told you that? That's not true at all! They died in a tragic plane crash right here in Applewood."

Chills ran up and down John's entire body as he just stood there frozen, not knowing what to say. He thought about the eerie, unexplained feeling he had at the airstrip that day, and for a brief moment, he almost believed what she was telling him. That brief moment was quickly taken over with skepticism and anger.

"Look, I have no idea what the hell you're talking about or how you know my name, but I think this conversation is over!"

With that, John shoved the wallet back into his pocket and turned and walked away.

"You have to believe me!" she called after him. "I swear I'm telling the truth, John."

He should have just continued walking away, but his anger got the best of him and he turned around and yelled back, "The truth, huh?

This coming from a crazy old lady who spends her days pushing around a stupid shopping cart of flowers!"

By the time John climbed in his truck, the skies had opened up, and the rain poured down. The rain was so hard, he had to pull over halfway home. When he finally made it back to William's, the wind had also picked up substantially. It was a short distance from the truck to the front door, but nevertheless, John was completely soaked from head to toe when he entered the house.

He didn't bother changing into dry clothes. Instead, he found himself pacing around the living room, muttering to himself.

"Fucking crazy old lady... pfft, plane crash, yea right... and how the fuck did she know my name!?!"

John's anger took him from the living room into the kitchen. It was there that he came face to face with his old friend—Jameson. So, as the rain loudly pelted the roof, and as the wind practically shook the house, John reached over and grabbed the bottle off the counter.

This time there was nothing to interrupt him. Shakily, he began untwisting the cap. It would only be a matter of seconds before that familiar and comforting burn of whiskey would enter his mouth. But just as he tossed the cap onto the counter, a loud smashing noise was heard from upstairs. It sounded like glass being shattered. John looked from the bottle up to the ceiling and then back to the bottle.

"Mother fucker!" he said, slamming it back onto the counter.

He stormed out of the kitchen and marched upstairs. He searched each and every room but found no broken windows or glass anywhere. Just when he entered the hallway, and just when he thought he might be going crazy, he heard it again. It was definitely the sound of glass falling to the floor.

John looked up and saw a rope hanging from what appeared to be an attic door in the ceiling. He reached up and carefully pulled on the rope until the stairs were completely unfolded. Halfway up the stairs, he could feel a cold draft blowing down on him.

When he reached the attic, he squinted his eyes in attempt to adjust to the darkness. There was a window in the far corner, but seeing as the skies outside were still stormy and black, it allowed little light in the large attic space. John took a step forward onto the wide, dust-covered pine boards and was immediately startled by something hitting his face.

He swiped at it with his hand but quickly realized it was only a chain attached to the light above him. He gave it a tug and was surprised that the lightbulb actually came on. It wasn't tremendously bright, but it was enough to illuminate most of the attic. There were countless boxes stacked against the walls, some had a half an inch of dust on top of them.

Every corner of the attic was filled with endless amounts of cobwebs. He carefully made his way towards the window, and with his eyes looking down, he couldn't help but notice the wide pine floorboards. They seemed so familiar.

He approached the window and noticed the floorboards were covered in broken glass. That must have been the sound he had heard, and its culprit was a tree branch. With every powerful gust of wind, the branch would swing against the lower half of the window causing glass to shatter everywhere.

Two of the window's six panes were completely smashed out. A chill ran through his body as he stared at the window. The chill wasn't caused by the cold draft blowing in, it was the window itself. As John watched the rain run down the outside of the window, he found himself raising and pressing his hand against the glass.

Chills continued to course through his body as he leaned in closer and peered out the window. There, in the distance between two trees, he could faintly see the red glow of the lighthouse.

The floorboards, the six-paned window, the lighthouse in the distance, it was all exactly like the dream he'd been having since he was a kid. The only difference was the hand in his dream was that of a toddler.

John quickly snapped out of his déjà vu moment when the branch once again slammed against the window, causing a third pane to shatter. He jumped back, startled and still in shock over the familiarity of the attic and window.

Not caring about the thick layer of dust, John sat on one of the boxes and tried to collect his thoughts, all the while staring mesmerized at the window. Between the crazy old lady claiming to know his parents, and now, his strangest déjà vu moment yet, he thought for sure he was losing it.

"What the hell is going on in this…"

Before he could finish his sentence, a huge gust of wind blew in through the broken window. It was so strong, it caused a stack of old newspapers to blow about. But just as quickly as the wind blew in, it stopped, leaving dozens of newspapers strewn all across the attic floor. John's trance-like state was snapped. He then found himself bending down picking up the scattered papers.

When they were all restacked, he placed them back onto the floor and searched for something heavy to prevent them from getting blown again. In the corner, he grabbed a couple of small pieces of two-by-fours, but before he could place them on the stack, the headline of the top newspaper caught his attention. It was the Applewood Weekly, and as he read the headline, his eyes widened and his mouth fell open.

The headline read: Tragedy at Applewood Airfield.

Before John read any further, he gazed up at the date on the paper which read: July 20, 1975. He grabbed the paper and swiftly moved closer to the sole lightbulb and began reading the article.

Kyle Blaisdell, pilot and owner of Island Air Tours, was killed when his plane crashed off the coast of Applewood soon after takeoff. His two passengers, Robert and Caitlin Mathews of Chicago, were also killed in the crash. The cause is still unknown and under investigation. Kyle Blaisdell was a lifelong resident of Applewood and had provided scenic tours of coastal Maine for the past 20 years. He leaves behind a wife and four children. Robert and Caitlin Mathews were regular summer visitors to the island for the past five years. They leave behind two young boys.

John's heart raced, and his face turned white as he read and reread the article three more times. The old woman was telling the truth. Still dripping wet from the rain, John stood there for the longest time talking to himself.

"This can't be… this can't be… there's just no way," he muttered.

By the time he finally climbed back down the ladder, the storm had completely ended. Without thinking twice about it, he tucked the newspaper under his arm and jumped into his truck and headed back to the lighthouse. He needed the old woman to be there, and he desperately needed more answers.

He rushed up the steps and sprinted the paved path until he reached the benches overlooking the lighthouse. There was no sign of the woman. There was no sign of anyone. John was completely alone staring out at a lighthouse that he had seen so many times in his dreams. He glanced at the newspaper, and once again wondered if he truly was going crazy.

His hand reached into his front pocket in hopes of feeling the cool metal flask. When it came up empty, he remembered he had left it on the kitchen counter. Before he had a chance to let out an exasperated sigh, he heard it—the squeaky shopping cart wheel.

He turned his head and watched as the old woman slowly made her way up the winding paved path. At first, when they finally stood face to face, not a word was spoken. After a few moments of silence, John held up the newspaper then spoke.

"You… you were telling the truth."

All at once, images flashed through his mind: The dirt path behind William's, the cove, the lighthouse, the six-paned window.

"I've really been here before, haven't I?"

She nodded, and a kind smile filled her face. The woman then reached into her cart, and in between the bundles of flowers, she pulled out a small towel. After she wiped off the excess water from the rain, she motioned for John to have a seat next to her on the bench. She glanced at the newspaper then gazed out at the ocean as if to collect her thoughts.

"Your parents started coming here before they were even married. Applewood had turned into one of their favorite vacation spots. Something about the magic of the salt air, they'd say. They ended up returning here every year after that. For one week every summer, they'd leave their problems back in Chicago and enjoy the beauty and peacefulness of Applewood."

She paused a second to take in the ocean view. Off in the distance, there were more storm clouds heading their way. But for now, there was a hint of blue sky hanging above them, and for the most part, the waves had calmed considerably. It was hard to believe that a storm had even passed through. As her eyes went from the ocean to John, her smile grew bigger.

"And then, one summer, they showed up with their new bundle of joy… you." She placed her hand on his leg and continued to sweetly smile. "And the very next summer, we were introduced to your brother. They absolutely adored you two."

John did his best to return her smile, but his focus turned back to the newspaper.

"How come we weren't on the plane?"

"Your father had planned a romantic date for your mother. They went out to dinner at a picturesque restaurant up on the cliffs, and then he had booked a scenic sunset flight with our friend Kyle Blaisdell. He owned the Island Air Tours. We happily agreed to watch you and your brother for them." She took a long, sad pause before continuing. "I remember exactly where I was when my husband told me the news. He had heard it over his marine radio."

John's mind was swirling with questions. He started with the crash.

"So… they never found out what caused the plane to…"

Sadly, the woman shook her head.

"They assumed it was the engine, but they never found out for sure. Most of the plane's remains sunk to the bottom of the ocean."

John's eyes moved from the woman to the sea. He still couldn't believe what he was hearing.

"This is a tight little community, and the crash shook everyone to the core."

"Is that why the airfield closed?" he asked.

The woman nodded and said, "Kyle and his family owned all that land. A few years later, his wife had an offer from a company who wanted to build a giant shopping plaza there, but she turned them down flat. Mrs. Blaisdell knew the last thing this town needed was a shopping plaza, and more importantly, she knew her husband would definitely agree. So, the airfield might be abandoned and all rundown, but Kyle would much rather have that than a silly shopping plaza."

John remembered walking around the airfield, and he also remembered that sick, eerie feeling in the pit of his stomach. He now knew why. The old woman knew John's head must be spinning, but she sat in silence and awaited his next question.

"But… why foster care? Didn't we have any other family that could have taken us?"

"Your parents didn't really have any family around, certainly no one who was capable of taking care of two young boys. Your father's parents both passed away when he was young, and he didn't have any siblings."

"What about my… my mother?" A shiver ran up his spine. This might have been the first time he'd ever said the words *my mother* without it being in disdain.

Again, she placed her hand on John's leg.

"As far as Caitlin's parents were concerned; her mother's health was failing and she was in assisted living. Your mom's father had been out of the picture since she was a little kid. So, besides some distant uncle who was in and out of jail, there was really no one to take you in. The courts felt it best for you boys to return to Chicago while everything was getting sorted out."

She paused, grabbed his leg tighter, and looked at him with sad, remorseful eyes.

"I swear, if we would have known that you were going to be passed on from one family to another, we would have taken you in ourselves."

John could sense the regret oozing out of the old woman's eyes. Because of this, he decided to leave out a more detailed description of the families—especially the O'Neils.

"All we ever knew was that our last name was Mathews. We never even knew our parents first names. We were always told that they had abandoned us and that they didn't want us, and we never questioned it. We never questioned it."

"Oh, you poor, poor boys! I can't believe someone would tell you such a lie!"

John looked down to the ground then quietly said, "I've spent all these years being mad at them, actually hating them for what they did to us…"

She was quick to interrupt with, "You and your brother were their pride and joy. Their pride and joy!"

Her words brought a slight smile to John's face.

"I'm… I'm sorry for calling you a crazy old woman. I didn't really mean it, ma'am."

"Oh sweetie, it's okay," she said, grasping his hand. "And please, call me Mary."

And just like that, the wind picked up, and those dark clouds off in the distance were quickly approaching. Seeing this, Mary stood up and walked over to her cart.

"I tell you what, why don't you come back tomorrow, and I'll tell you more about your parents."

John nodded. "I'd like that." He stood up from the bench as a light rain began to fall. "Do you need a ride… or a place to stay?" he asked.

"Thank you, dear, but I'm all set. I don't have far to go."

"Are you sure? I can fit your cart in the back of…"

She smiled and cut him off. "Just meet me back here tomorrow afternoon, okay?"

Again, he nodded and watched her push her cart back down the path. John folded up the newspaper and shoved it inside his jacket to prevent it from getting wet. He then turned his attention back to the ocean and lighthouse. His was still trying to wrap his mind around everything he had just seen and heard.

The rain never really picked up in intensity, and the dark clouds slowly dissipated and went out to sea. By the time John returned to William's house, the sky had turned a pale blue and the wind had completely diminished.

When he pulled into the driveway, he noticed Sara out at the road checking her mailbox. They gave each other a wave, and as he climbed out of his truck, she made her way over to him. His hair and clothes were still wet from the earlier storm.

"Do they not believe in umbrellas in Chicago? Or simply staying out of the rain, for that matter?"

He looked down at his wet clothes and gave her a shrug and a smile.

"Some storm earlier, huh?" she asked. "At one point my whole house was shaking. But luckily, I don't think there was any serious damage. You?"

"Besides a broken attic window, I think the house held up."

Sara gazed over at William's house and yard.

"The place really does look amazing. It's like a hundred percent improvement."

"Thanks."

"Looks like you're pretty much finished. When are you heading back to Chicago?"

John looked around and shrugged. "Monday maybe."

They both seemed a bit disappointed by his answer. She then returned her attention to John's wet clothes.

"Seriously, did you get caught out in the storm or what?"

For a brief moment, John thought about filling her in on everything he had learned that day: The old lady, his parents, the plane crash. But he decided against it. He was having a hard enough time believing it himself, and seeing as he only had a few days left in town, the last thing he wanted was for Sara to think he was a giant nut job.

"Yea, something like that," he replied, and then changed the subject. "So, any big plans tonight?"

"Kinda," she smiled.

"Good for you."

She continued to smile as she said, "Speaking of which, I could use a huge favor."

"Let me guess, you want me to be your designated driver again, huh?"

"Ha, ha. No!" she said, smacking his arm. "I'm actually chaperoning our big homecoming dance tonight."

"Ahhh, sounds fun."

"I'm glad you think so, because we could use another chaperone."

Assuming she was putting him on, John just stood there and laughed.

"I'm actually kinda serious. There's a huge flu bug going around the school and most of the volunteers are sick in bed. We could really use an extra body."

Sara put on her best, most convincing smile and said, "You said yourself it sounded fun."

"I was kidding. It sounds horrible."

"Oh, come on. It won't be that bad. All you have to do is make sure nothing shady is going down in the bathrooms and in the dark corners of the gym. That's all."

"Like I said, it sounds horrible," he smiled.

"Where's your sense of adventure? Besides, you can hang out with me most of the night. It'll be the perfect way to end your little vacation here in Applewood."

John cocked his head and smirked at her.

"Wait, isn't that Paul guy chaperoning too?"

"Uh huh."

"You don't think that will make for another awkward moment... you and I showing up together?"

"First of all, you and I are not going as a couple, silly. And I already called Paul and explained the whole misunderstanding about earlier."

"Ahhh," he smiled. "You mean about you trying to help me get it up... the tent, that is?"

Again, she smacked his arm as her face flushed red.

"Sooo, is that a yes or what?"

"You're really not gonna take no for an answer, are you?"

"You're just realizing that now?" she said then winked and turned to walk away. "Be ready to go by a quarter to seven," she called over her shoulder.

"Wait! What should I wear?"

"Dry clothes."

24

John had less than two hours to get ready. Normally, this would be an hour and forty-five minutes more than he needed, but this silly little school dance had him panicked. When he originally packed, he assumed he was coming to Maine strictly to work and not to socialize, especially at some school dance. So, for the most part, all he packed was grungy work clothes.

The nearest clothing store was at least thirty minutes away, and he didn't want to risk being late. He then remembered he had packed one button-down shirt, but it was stuffed at the bottom of his bag and was wrinkled beyond belief. Luckily, William had specifically labeled the boxes in the dining room, so John was able to find an iron. Knowing how to use it was a different story. He picked out his cleanest pair of jeans then slipped on his Chuck Taylors. They had certainly seen better days, but it was either that or his clunky work boots.

John spent the final forty-five minutes taking care of something that was long overdue. He jumped into his truck and drove towards the diner. The diner wasn't his destination, but rather the business next door. There, in the tiny storefront was the local barbershop.

Before he knew it, the two hours were up, and Sara was knocking on his door. He absolutely knew this was not a date, yet his heart nervously pounded as if he was twenty again and going out with a girl for the first time. His heart pounded even more when he opened the door and saw Sara dressed in what looked to be a new black dress.

Before he could even think of complimenting her dress, she blurted out, "Holy smokes! Where is John, and what have you done with him?"

Self-consciously, he ran his fingers over his smooth face and through his short hair. "Bad, huh?"

"No, not bad... just different, that's all."

John spent most of the ride apologizing for his lack of proper attire. Sara spent most of the ride laughing and telling him he needed to chill out and relax. When they arrived at the school, they still had a half an hour before the dance actually started. There were a handful of students finishing up decorating the gym, and the DJ was already cranking out some pre-dance tunes.

Sara introduced John to a couple of teachers, and as he stood there making small talk, a single phrase ran through his mind: *Why the hell did I agree to this?* As if on a loop, the phrase ran over and over in his mind. He told himself that as soon as the teachers walked away, he'd tell Sara he didn't belong there and that he just should bail. Unfortunately for John, he never got the chance. As soon as the teachers dispersed, one of the students approached Sara.

"Mrs. Peyton, do you know where we can get some more tape? We just ran out."

"Yea, sure. Let me run into the school and scrounge you guys up some."

Please don't leave me standing by myself. Please don't leave me standing by myself. The voice in John's head was working overtime.

"I'll be right back, okay?" she said to John.

John didn't say a word, he simply nodded and prepared to stand there by himself. The dance hadn't even started yet, and he was already dreading the next few hours of his life. Not to mention, standing there all alone, he couldn't help but feel self-conscious. Maybe it was the fact that he was completely and totally out of his comfort zone. Or maybe it was the fact that he felt naked without all his facial hair. Or maybe it was because he had never actually been to a school dance before. Even after the boys were removed from the O'Neils, John spent his high school years with his head down keeping to himself. He never even went to his own prom.

John saw how nicely dressed the students and teachers were and really felt self-conscious as he gazed down at his jeans and wrinkled shirt. He shook his head in disgust and wondered if this night could get any worse. Ten seconds later, his question was answered. Walking through the gym door was Paul.

It wasn't that John had anything against Paul, not at all. Besides the quick interaction earlier that morning, he didn't even know the guy. From everything that Sara had told him, Paul seemed like a real stand-up kinda guy. That being said, John couldn't help but feel a twinge of jealousy towards him. In his head, he knew how crazy that sounded. It wasn't like John had designs on Sara. She was sweet, funny, attractive, and there was certainly a strange air of familiarity about her, but he knew nothing could ever come of it. Without a doubt, he knew that, but it still didn't prevent a hint of jealousy from rearing its ugly head.

John watched Paul greet two other teachers and then shot a wave over at the students of the decorating committee. He noticed that Paul was also wearing jeans, albeit a much nicer pair. That's where the similarities ended. Paul wore a crisply-ironed white shirt with a navy blue blazer over it, and his hair was, well, it was perfect.

If John wasn't self-conscious earlier, he certainly was now. Just then, both men made eye contact with each other. Paul gave John a quick look-over, and although he was obviously the better dressed one, he still had his own share of jealously running through his head. After all, Paul had been unsuccessfully asking Sara out for weeks, yet she had no problem inviting John to a campout and breakfast in her house.

As the two men stood there staring at each other, it was like *they* were the ones in high school; both in competition for the pretty girl. But they weren't in high school, and although there was something very special about Sara, John knew he was leaving in two days, and a future with her just wasn't in the cards. So ultimately, there was no competition, and John knew he needed to be the bigger man and that he needed to go over and say hi. Paul, however, beat John to the punch and approached him with his hand outstretched.

"Hey, thanks so much for helping us out tonight," Paul said, shaking his hand. "I'm sure there were a million other things you'd rather be doing."

"I don't know about a million... but at least a thousand," joked John.

And just like that, the tension was cut. From that point on, John could tell exactly why Sara talked so highly of Paul. He was charming and funny, and most of all, he was genuine. Any feelings of jealousy that either man had, quickly went out the window.

It didn't take long before the conversation fell right into John's wheelhouse—baseball. Paul told him that he had attended a Cubs game a few years earlier while on a guy trip to Chicago.

"In college, me and a couple of friends set a goal to see a game in as many classic stadiums as possible. Unfortunately, we only made it to four. Marriages and kids have a way of putting a crimp on guy trips," laughed Paul.

"Yea, I'm sure," John nodded. "But still, four is pretty good."

Internally, he was extremely jealous. John and Kevin had once set that same goal. Dodger Stadium, Camden Yards, Fenway Park, and yes, even the dreaded Yankee Stadium were all on their list. Not to mention, John's longing to make the pilgrimage out to Iowa and the *Field of Dreams*.

Just like he did with Clarence, John and Paul compared one story after another regarding the disappointments of their respective teams. What really made John laugh and relate to Paul was when Paul revealed the two most popular phrases of a Red Sox fan.

"This is gonna be our year. And we'll get'em next year."

John continued to laugh then said, "And here I thought we trademarked those phrases."

They were so into their baseball conversation that they didn't even notice Sara walking up from behind them.

"Hey, Paul," she said.

"Oh, hey Sara," he answered as he gave her a look-over. "Wow, you look great tonight."

She rolled her eyes and turned to John and said, "He says that every day."

This might have been true, but John could tell by her red cheeks that Paul's compliment still resonated with her.

"Just because he says it every day doesn't make it any less true."

"Exactly!" Paul proudly smiled and nodded.

This only made Sara blush even more. Luckily, she would be saved any further embarrassment as a student approached and addressed Paul.

"Excuse me, Mr. Goodwin, but can you give us a hand hanging the final banner?"

"Oh I see," Sara interrupted, "I'm good enough to go get you tape but not to help you hang a banner?"

The student smirked then quietly responded with, "You're kinda too short to help us, Mrs. Peyton."

Paul smiled and shrugged at her as he headed off with the student.

"Pfft, whatever," she said, pretending to be offended.

After they walked off, John looked at Sara and said, "You are pretty short."

Sara ignored his comment, for she had more pressing things to discuss with him.

"Sooo, what were you and Paul talking about?"

Without missing a beat, he answered, "We were talking about different techniques of pitching a tent."

"Cute, real cute."

"If you must know, we were talking about baseball."

"Boring!"

"If you want, Paul and I can revolve our next conversation around you?"

Sara looked at him and just shook her head. "The sad thing is you actually think you're funny, don't you?"

John thought for a second then gave her the *little bit* gesture with his fingers.

"Come on, funny guy, let's go check on the refreshments."

It wasn't long before the gym was filled with loud dance music and hormone-infused teenagers. John and Paul were the only male chaperones there, so they took turns patrolling the men's bathroom. Luckily, the night went on without an incident. There were, however, a few dark-corner make-out sessions, but most of the chaperones didn't have the heart to break them up. The unwritten rule. Kissing was fine as long as there were no hands up shirts or down pants. John prayed he didn't have to enforce this.

Sara knew that he felt more than a little out of place, so she did her best to stay by his side. At one point, a disappointed look came over Sara's face as she scanned the crowd.

"What's wrong?" John asked.

"I was really hoping one of my favorite students was going to be here."

Sara went on to tell John all about Bill; at how sweet and smart he was, and yes, how shy he was too.

"I've never seen him at a dance before… but I thought for sure this would be the one."

As they continued looking out at the students, John couldn't help but notice pockets of cliques.

"I can't believe there are still cliques in high school. I would have just assumed that was an 80's/ John Hughes thing."

Sara laughed and said, "The only things that have changed since our day is fashion, music, and the lingo they use."

John settled his eyes on Don and his buddies. They were surrounded by a handful of girls.

"Lemme guess, the jocks?"

Sara nodded. "Yup. And between you and me," she hushed her tone, "the jerks as well."

"Those chicks they're with look really young."

"First of all, they're girls, *not* chicks," Sara said straight-faced.

John couldn't tell if she was serious or not. Her next comment answered his question.

"But yea, those chicks are freshman," she smirked. "They're the only ones naïve enough to fall for their cheesy lines."

John laughed as he watched the girls giggling at Don and his friends.

Sara looked at him and asked, "You were totally a jock in school, weren't you?"

"Me? Nah. I was into sports, but... never really played them in school."

"Ahh. So which clique were you?" she asked.

"Dunno," he shrugged. "I don't think I really had one."

Her question caused John to think back to his high school days. When they were placed in the Boys Home, they were forced to attend a completely different school than they were used to. There's nothing worse than being the new kid, especially when your new school is one of the biggest in Chicago. Most of his high school years were spent sitting by himself or with Kevin and his friends. Kevin was always better at being social.

John's train of thought was interrupted when Sara exclaimed, "Awww, he showed up."

"Who?"

Sara pointed to the front door. "Bill... my student I was telling you about. And he got his haircut too."

John looked over at the boy standing just inside the door. Bill was wearing pleated khaki pants with a light blue shirt and tie. His once shaggy hair was indeed cut. It wasn't drastically shorter than before, but it was enough to make him self-consciously run his fingers through it every few seconds. John could totally relate.

"I'm gonna go say hi to him. I'll be back in a few, okay?"

"I'll be here," John smiled.

Soon after she walked off, Paul joined him.

"Wow," Paul said, looking over at Sara and Bill. "I can't believe he actually came."

"That bad, huh?" John asked.

"One of the smartest and nicest kids in school, but yeah, definitely a wallflower."

Both guys watched as Sara slowly made her way back from saying hi to Bill. Paul's look was a bit more mesmerized and somewhat smitten. He wasted no time in throwing her another compliment.

"That's a new dress, isn't it?"

It was absolutely a new dress, but in true female fashion, Sara played it off as if she had it for years.

"Well, either way, you look amazing in it," he said, still mesmerized by her beauty.

Once again, Sara's cheeks turned red and she rolled her eyes.

"Thanks, Paul. But trust me, it must be the dress, 'cuz underneath it all I'm still the same ole plain Jane."

John, who was focused on the dance floor, heard Sara's comment and immediately flashed back to when Kristen said those exact same words. His arms filled with goosebumps as he turned and stared over at Sara. John's eerie trance was quickly broken when Paul asked Sara to dance.

"We can't do that, Paul. We're chaperones."

Paul smiled and pointed to the dance floor. There were other teachers out dancing with the students. Sara knew she was running out of excuses. She then turned to John.

"You're definitely not getting *me* on that dance floor," he said. "I'll be over there getting some punch."

With that, John walked off, and Paul held his hand out to Sara.

"You really are incorrigible, aren't you?" She smirked then hesitantly took his hand.

No sooner did they hit the dance floor, the fast song faded out and was replaced by a slow one. This couldn't have worked out more perfectly for Paul or worked out more uncomfortably for Sara. It wasn't uncomfortable because she didn't want to be dancing with Paul, for she had actually grown quite fond of him. What made it uncomfortable was the last time she had slow-danced was years ago with her husband.

When John arrived at the refreshment table, he saw that Bill had finally moved from his spot by the front door and was drinking some punch. John grabbed himself a cup then joked, "You didn't spike this, did you?"

Bill looked at him as if he was serious. "Um, no sir. I didn't."

"I was just kidding," he laughed. "It's Bill, right?"

Puzzled, Bill slowly nodded yes.

"I'm friends with Sara… I mean, Mrs. Peyton."

"Are you her boyfriend?" asked Bill.

"Boyfriend? No, not at all. We're just neighbors… sorta."

Without acknowledging, Bill lowered his eyes back to the ground.

John poured himself some punch then searched for something else to say to fill the quiet void.

"Mrs. Peyton has been raving about you all night."

Bill looked up. "She has?"

"Well yeah. You're like one of her all-time favorite students."

A sheepish, embarrassed smile formed on Bill's face.

"She was really hoping you'd show up tonight."

Out on the dance floor, Paul was thoroughly enjoying his slow dance with Sara. He didn't even attempt to hide how he was feeling. The beaming smile on his face said it all. He loved the way she smelled, and he really loved having his hands on her hips.

Her expression was more subdued, but Sara was also very much enjoying herself. She was, however, a bit self-conscious and felt as though everyone was staring at them. There were definitely more than a few students looking over at them, but it was only because they always thought Mrs. Peyton and Mr. Goodwin would make a cute couple.

By the lack of conversation, it was apparent that both of them were nervous. Finally, about halfway through the song, Paul broke the silence.

"So, I know of this really cool cabin in the woods about two hours north of here."

Sara looked up at him, wondering where he was going with this.

"I was thinking maybe we could go up there next weekend." Before she had a chance to thwart his idea, he added to his proposal. "It's a beautiful drive, and I heard the leaves are already changing color up that way."

Sara met his proposal with a smirk.

"You go from asking me to dinner to going on a little getaway in the woods?"

Paul knew he was taking a big leap but smiled and continued to persuade her.

"It's a super-cozy cabin with a wood stove and everything."

Sara wore a smile, but inside, her stomach was in knots. She loved Paul's arms around her, and she loved the idea of a nice weekend getaway, but... but she couldn't help feeling guilty. For months now she'd been telling herself it was too soon—too soon to move on—too soon to be with someone else. Nervously, she looked away and found herself glancing over at John. He was still standing with Bill over at the refreshment table.

"Sooo?" Paul asked hopefully.

Sara let out a little sigh and then made eye contact with him.

"It sounds wonderful, it really does, but maybe another time, okay?"

She wanted to let him down easy and not come across as cold, so she did her best to come up with a legitimate excuse.

"Besides, I don't think my mother could watch the kids next weekend."

When she saw Paul grinning, she knew her excuse had backfired.

"Sara, I meant you *and* your kids come up to the cabin."

A blushing smile slowly came over her face. It wasn't a nervous or uncomfortable smile, it was happy and content. The fact that Paul wanted to include her kids on their getaway completely sealed the deal.

"Really? You want my kids to come too?"

"Of course. I think your kids are great. And did I mention there's a lake there too? Perfect for fishing or boating. I mean, I'm not sure if they're into that or not, but..."

Without hesitating, she said, "They would love that... we all would."

Paul's hands moved from her hips to her back as he pulled her in a bit closer. Neither one of them could contain their happiness.

Back at the refreshment table, John and Bill's small talk had come to a grinding halt. When Bill wasn't staring down at the ground, he was looking over at Rachel, who was talking and laughing with her friends.

"You gonna ask her to dance, or what?" John joked.

Bill's eyes widened and his face turned red as he quickly looked away from Rachel.

"Seriously, you should go ask her to dance."

Bill lowered his eyes, shrugged, and then slowly shook his head no. John thought for a second then looked over at Rachel and said, "Yea, probably best. Being that good looking, she's probably stuck up, huh?"

"No!" Bill blurted out. "She's like the coolest girl in here. Prettiest too," he said a bit more quietly.

John smiled at Bill's emphatic comment. It was the most animated he had seen him.

"Let me guess, she has a boyfriend?"

Bill looked up at John and shook his head no.

"So what's stopping you? Go ask her to dance."

Bill shrugged and forced his eyes to look back over at Rachel then said, "She'd probably just say no anyway. Besides, I just get so… so nervous around her."

As the slow song ended, John searched for something motivational to say. Before he could come up with anything, Bill let out a sigh and said, "Well, it was nice meeting you, sir."

As Bill started to walk away, John called to him.

"It's none of my business, Bill, but… we only regret the chances we didn't take… my wife used to tell me that all the time."

He wasn't sure, but he thought he saw a slight smile on Bill's face before he nodded at John and walked away. The moment was interrupted by the DJ's voice booming over the speakers.

"Alright, guys, only about a half an hour left. I want to see everybody on the dance floor!"

Just then, "Hey Ya" by Outkast blared out. Although the song had been out for a year, this was the first time John heard it. He hadn't really listened to anything the past year, not to mention, it wasn't his type of music at all. The students seemed to be enjoying it, for the dance floor was now fully packed.

Over his shoulder, John glanced back and saw that Bill was once again standing alone against the wall by the front door. John then turned back to the dance floor and watched the students dance around as they loudly sang along with the song. It was right then and there that one of the lyrics caught his ear, nearly making his heart beat out of his chest.

The crowd sang out, "Shake it, shake it, shake it like a Polaroid picture."

John immediately thought of Kristen and her camera. He also thought of his little girl and how she loved to watch the picture develop before her eyes. One of the last memories he had of Hannah was in the living room the day of the accident.

For the past year he did his best to block out those type of memories. It was just too hard for him to remember. But now, a smile formed on his face as he thought of Kristen holding her silly camera and begging him to take a family picture. An even bigger smile formed on his face when he remembered Hannah snatching the photo from the camera and shaking it as she excitedly danced around the room.

"Uh, hello? Earth to John."

John snapped out of his nostalgic trance and glanced over to his right, where Sara was grinning at him.

"What? What are you smiling at?" he asked.

"Me? You're the one staring out at the dance floor with a big grin. Is this song your jam or what?"

"Yea, something like that," he said, continuing to smile.

"What were you and Bill talking about?"

"Oh, I was just trying to give him a little pep talk. Trying to convince him he should go over and ask that girl to dance."

Sara looked across the room at Rachel.

"Bill coming here tonight is one thing, but him asking Rachel to dance would be nothing short of a miracle."

"Well, it looks like I'm a miracle worker then," John grinned as he gazed over her shoulder.

Sara turned around and saw Bill very slowly walking towards Rachel and her friends.

"Oh my God," Sara whispered. "He's gonna do it. He's actually gonna ask her to dance."

John proudly crossed his arms and boasted, "Must have been my sage advice."

No sooner did John finish his sentence, Bill's pace slowed to a complete stop.

"Come on, Bill, don't stop now," urged Sara.

Bill was halfway across the gym, but they could tell his hands were trembling as he stood there frozen still. Despite their quiet encouragement, they watched Bill's shoulders and head droop down, and then he defeatedly turned and walked away. Not only did he walk away, but he walked straight out the front door leaving the dance.

"Poor kid," Sara said, letting out a sympathetic sigh.

After the disappointment of watching Bill exit the gym, John tried to lift Sara's spirits back up.

"So, how was your dance with Paul?"

That was all it took for her to start turning red. "It was... good," she smiled.

"Hmm, I would have assumed by your glowing face it would have been considered more than just good."

She shrugged and continued to blush. "He might have invited me and my kids for a little getaway next weekend."

"Aaaaand?"

"And I might have said yes."

"Good for you."

As the dance was winding down, Paul joined Sara and John.

"Well, looks like it was a successful night," Paul said, motioning out to a packed dance floor. He then reached his hand out to John. "Thanks again for helping out tonight."

John shook his hand then said, "No problem. Despite being pressured into it by a certain someone, it actually wasn't as bad as I…"

John stopped mid-sentence as he looked over Sara's shoulder.

"Holy shit!" he exclaimed.

"John!" Sara scolded, and then turned around to see what he was looking at. When she saw it was Bill re-entering the dance, she echoed John's sentiments. "Holy shit!"

Just then, the DJ faded the song out and picked up the mic.

"Okay, Applewood High, this is the final dance of the night. Make it count."

As Sheriff's "When I'm With You" began to play, John, Sara, and Paul were focused on Bill. Although he still looked nervous, his pace was more purposeful. It was as if he was on a mission.

"What's he holding?" Sara whispered.

Bill's right hand was clutching what appeared to be some sort of wrapped present. His timing couldn't have been more perfect. Both of Rachel's friends were being escorted onto the dance floor, leaving Rachel standing by herself.

When he was about ten feet away from her, his pace once again came to a halt. Sara thought for sure Bill would chicken out again, and he probably would have if it wasn't for Rachel turning around making eye contact with him.

"Hey, Bill!" she said with a warm smile on her face. "Nice haircut. Spiffy," she winked. "Have you been here all night?"

Bill didn't respond. Instead, in hopes of gaining confidence, he took a deep breath. When he finally released his breath, he hesitantly moved forward and handed Rachel the present.

"For me? Really?" Her face beamed with curiosity.

As she carefully began to unwrap the brown paper, Bill tried to downplay it.

"It's… it's really nothing major… at all actually. I just thought…"

"Oh my God, Bill!" she interrupted, holding up his gift.

It was her favorite poem, "Tears, Idle Tears," and was beautifully framed.

"I love it!" she said with her entire face glowing.

What happened next would be forever emblazoned in Bill's mind. Rachel stepped forward and gave him a huge, heartfelt hug and whispered, "This is the sweetest thing anyone has ever given me." She then pulled away and said, "Wait here. I'll be right back, okay?"

His heart was too full, and the lump in his throat was too big for him to properly respond. He simply nodded and remained standing still. Rachel rushed over to Sara, holding up the poem.

"Look, Mrs. Peyton! Look what Bill gave me!"

"Aww, he framed your favorite poem," gushed Sara.

"Isn't that the sweetest thing ever?" Before Sara could respond, Rachel asked, "Can you hold this for me?"

Rachel handed Sara the poem and then rushed back over and grabbed Bill's hand and took him out onto the dance floor. There were only two plus minutes left in the song, but for Bill, it was as if time stood still.

When the song finally faded out, Sara, Paul, and John made their way to the front door and watched as the students slowly filed out.

311

Rachel retrieved her poem from Sara but remained in the gym talking to Bill for a while longer. Besides the students on the clean-up crew, Rachel and Bill were two of the last to leave. A few moments after they exited the gym, Bill returned and addressed John.

"Thanks again, sir… for the pep talk."

After Bill walked back outside, John turned and gloated to Sara.

"See, I told ya. It was my pep talk that did the trick."

Sara rolled her eyes then motioned for them to join in with the clean-up crew.

25

John had the hardest time falling asleep that night. His tossing and turning weren't caused from flashbacks or even nightmares. His trouble sleeping had more to do with it being his final night in Maine. Part of him was sad to leave such a beautiful and peaceful place, but a bigger part of him knew it was time to head back home and start to face things he had long since put off.

There was also a sense of anticipation about the following afternoon. That was when he was supposed to head back to the lighthouse and see Mary again. She had promised him more details about his parents, and John was more than excited and curious to hear her stories. So needless to say, with all the crazy and unbelievable events of the previous two weeks swirling around his head, it was nearly impossible for John to get a good night's sleep that evening.

Despite not falling asleep until well past three, he still found himself waking up with the sunrise. He was exhausted, but he wanted to make the most of his final day in Applewood. Before heading back to Chicago later that day, John knew he needed to not only carve out some time to meet with Mary, but to fix the broken window in the attic. He also hoped Sara would be home throughout the day so he could say goodbye to her in person.

Before any of that, John drove out to the general store for his final morning coffee in Maine. He purchased two large coffees and decided to head out the cove and say goodbye to Clarence. It'd been a few days since his last trip to the cove, and he figured he could offer up part of his morning to help the old man with his boat repairs.

With coffees in hand, John wound his way through the path and leisurely walked across the quiet cove. The beach pebbles crunched and slid beneath his feet. He stopped just short of the boat and stood back admiring it. Its nearly pristine condition was night and day from when John first saw it two weeks earlier.

"Ahoy there, matey," Clarence announced, poking his head out from behind the boat.

John moved closer, handing him one of the coffees. Clarence nodded in appreciation then said, "Well, what do ya think?"

"I think it looks amazing."

"She. She looks amazing," Clarence corrected.

John smiled and rephrased. "I think *she* looks amazing. You've definitely made her sea-worthy again."

John took a sip of coffee and continued to admire the boat. Clarence took note of the look on John's face.

"Is that a smile? I see the salt air has been good to you. Find those answers you were looking for?" he asked, motioning out to the sea.

John paused a second, let out a chuckle and said, "You wouldn't believe me if I told you."

"Oh, you'd be surprised at what I'd believe. I told ya, Applewood can be a magical place."

Although John shrugged, he was certainly more of a believer now in the magic than he was weeks earlier.

"I haven't seen you around. How's your house project coming?"

"I have one final repair this morning and that's it."

"Ahh, I see. So when ya heading back to Chicago?"

"Probably sometime later today."

Clarence gazed out at the ocean then outstretched his hand to John.

314

John shook the old man's large, calloused hand.

"In case I don't see ya again, have a safe trip home and take care of yourself." As Clarence's grip grew tighter, his voice dropped lower. "And thanks again for helping an old fisherman out with his boat."

"You're welcome," John said, releasing his hand. "I didn't really do much though."

"More than you know, son. More than you know."

There was a brief, awkward moment of silence as they both just stood there in front of one another. Finally, John said, "Well, I guess I should get going. I've got a window to fix."

He gave Clarence a polite nod goodbye then turned to walk away.

"Oh, John," Clarence called after him. "Tell your friend he picked a good man to come fix up his house... and I wish him the best of luck with his health and all."

Again, John smiled and appreciatively nodded before turning and heading back to William's house.

26

The window repair took a bit longer than he expected, and it was just after noon when he finally finished. Sara's car had been gone most of the morning, and he hoped she'd be back before he officially left for Chicago. John did a quick clean up and then jumped in his truck and headed towards the park. He kept his fingers crossed that Mary would once again be there. He was very much looking forward to learning more about his parents.

That being said, when he arrived at his spot on the bench, he was more than a little disappointed to see no trace of Mary. Doubts and negative thoughts took hold as John began to wonder if this whole thing was just a dream. Maybe he had only imagined the old woman.

He stared out at the lighthouse, frequently looking over his shoulder for any signs of Mary or her shopping cart. He pulled his phone out of his pocket to check the time. What he saw was yet another missed call and message from his brother. He'd been calling for the past three days wondering how John was doing and when he'd be back home. John had been meaning to call him back, he really had, but with all the crazy events of the past few days, it just slipped his mind.

He started to dial Kevin's number, but stopped. He'd waited this long, he might as well just surprise him when he returned to Chicago tomorrow night. No sooner did he slide the phone back into his pocket, he heard the squeaky shopping cart wheel. He spun around and anxiously awaited as Mary methodically made her way up the path. It wasn't a dream. It was the real deal, he thought.

He watched her park the cart on the grass. Not only was it filled with her usual assortment of flowers, but the front basket contained an old, worn out shoebox. She carefully picked up the box and walked over and took a seat on the bench. When she was settled in, John took his place next to her.

"You didn't think I'd show up today, did you?" she asked.

"No, I knew you'd be here," he answered then hesitated. "Well, I was kinda wondering if it was all just a dream. You... our conversation... my parents."

She warmly smiled and said, "Well, maybe this will help."

She handed him the shoebox and watched as he slowly took the lid off. There were a couple dozen old pictures scattered about the box. One at a time, John picked them up and closely examined them. The first picture was of a man and woman in their late twenties.

"These are my parents?" he softly asked.

"Yup. This was taken at the beach the first year they came here, so you weren't even born yet."

A sad smile formed on his face as he stared long and hard at the photo.

"God, she was beautiful."

"That she was. And your father certainly thought so. He was always great at giving her compliments. Too bad none of that rubbed off on my husband," she laughed.

John turned his attention onto his father. He could definitely see parts of himself and Kevin in his father.

"What was he like?" John asked.

"Your father? Oh, he was a good man... and a very, very hard worker."

"What did he do for work?"

"He worked long, hard hours at some factory back in Chicago. He definitely loved and took full advantage of his vacation time here in Maine."

John continued looking at his father. "A factory, huh?"

"My memory isn't what it used to be, so I forget exactly what kind of factory it was, but I do know he hated it. But he did it to pay the bills. Your father was pretty multi-talented though. He was a brilliant carpenter. I even had him build a few things for us."

The fact that his father was a carpenter struck a deep chord, and he did his best to fight back a tear. Before looking at the next picture, John looked out at the ocean and shook his head.

"Kevin is never gonna believe this."

"Aww, Kevin was such a sweet little baby… you both were. And you were a great big brother to him. You two were only a year apart, but you were always looking out for him. I'm sure that hasn't changed."

Although he smiled back at Mary, he didn't bother telling her the roles had been reversed for some time now.

"Did Kevin come here with you?" she asked.

"No. He's back in Chicago. We actually own a bar together… sorta."

A giant grin fell on her face as she laughed out loud.

"A bar, huh? Yet another pipedream of your father's."

John gave her a puzzled look.

"Like I said, he was extremely talented with his hands, but if you asked him, his real dream was to open a bar… or a pub as he referred to it as."

"Really?"

Mary nodded and continued. "Your father was definitely a dreamer. He always had big ideas and even bigger dreams. Your mother, on the other hand, was always the more practical one. She was constantly pointing out that a bar was just too big of a risk." Mary paused, letting out a chuckle. "Although, one summer he almost had her swayed."

"How so?"

"Did I mention your father was also quite the sweet talker? He told your mother that if she let him buy a bar that he'd name it after his pet name for her."

Curiously, John smiled and awaited her response.

"He used to call her his Wild Irish Rose."

John's smile turned to a look of shock as chills ran up and down his arms. He was so taken aback, he didn't even tell Mary that was also the name of their bar. Still reeling from her comment, John returned his gaze to the photo of his parents.

"My husband and I were very, very fond of Caitlin and Robert."

"Where's your husband now?"

With her eyes to the ocean, she softly answered, "He passed away a while back."

"I'm sorry," was all John could manage.

"Like pretty much everyone around here, he was a fisherman. He was nearly sixty-five and was still going out every morning. I kept telling him to slow down, but he never listened. It wasn't 'til I heard they were calling for a huge storm the next day that I really put my foot down. I practically forbid him to go out, but being the stubborn ole goat that he was, he insisted that no little storm would defeat him. We fought deep into the night. The more stubborn he was, the more furious I became… and the more furious I became, the more hurtful things I'd say. More than anything, I think I was just jealous… jealous of him choosing that damn ocean over me yet again."

Mary paused and just sat there, staring out to the lighthouse. John didn't want to pry, but his curiosity got the best of him.

"What happened?"

She let out a deep sigh then turned to face him.

"When he woke up that morning, I literally begged him not to go… but it was no use. His mind was made up. So, on his way out the door…" Mary paused and John noticed tears welling up in her eyes. "… on his way out the door I said, 'If you walk out that door, don't bother coming back 'cuz I won't be here waiting.' "

At that point, the tears released and ran down her wrinkled cheeks.

"They found his boat a day later… and his body a few days after that."

John's heart sank, but all he offered was a sympathetic look.

"I didn't really mean it," she said, clutching at his hand. "Of course I was still going to be here. Of course I was!"

Not knowing the right words to say, John simply sat there holding the woman's hand and listening to her pour her heart out.

"We've probably said a million words to each other over the years, but those were the last words I spoke to him… and I have to live with that for eternity."

They both just sat there, staring out at the ocean in silence. Eventually, Mary turned her attention back to the photo. She looked from John to the photo and then back to John again.

"You have your father's nose and cheekbones, but you definitely have your mother's eyes."

Warmly, John smiled at the kind old woman. He then found himself glancing over at her cart of flowers. Mary took note of this.

"After he passed away, it took a while for me to leave the house. When I finally did, I went to visit him at the cemetery and saw that his headstone was all grown over… neglected. Headstones, like people, shouldn't be neglected. It bothered me so much that I soon found myself placing flowers on not only his, but all the neglected stones I came across. Did you know that each of the flowers have a specific symbolism?" she asked.

When John shook his head no, she began pointing at each of the flowers.

"The pink carnation — *I will never forget you*. The pansy — *remembrance*. And the iris — *faith and hope*. Of course, these vary depending on your culture or religion, but those are what they symbolize to me. I know, I know, I'm just a crazy old lady, right?"

"No, not at all," he quietly said, feeling guilty for ever calling her that.

He turned his attention back to the shoebox and flipped through a few more pictures of his parents. One of them caught his eye. It had the lighthouse in the background, and it looked as though it was taken very close to where he was sitting. Just the thought that his parents were once standing right here, was enough to make him smile. It was also enough to make him feel a bit regretful.

"I spent my whole life so angry with them… actually hating them for abandoning us. But now… now…"

"Now you know the truth," she said, grabbing his hand tighter. "And now you can spend the rest of your life knowing how much they loved you… both of you."

The next handful of pictures caused John to let out a laugh. They were random pictures of him and Kevin, ranging from newborn to three years old. There was a family picture where Mrs. Mathews was holding Kevin and Mr. Mathews was holding John. It looked to be in some sort of park.

There was a picture of a toddler happily building a sand castle at the beach. In the very next picture, that same boy was in tears, crying at his crumbled castle.

"Ha! Just like Kevin to be a little cry baby," laughed John.

Mary looked at the picture then giggled and pointed out, "Actually, that was you."

John's laughter halted.

"Whether it was sand castles or building blocks, you always hated when things didn't go your way. Not to mention, even at three, you were always so competitive with everything."

Knowingly, John shrugged and smirked.

There was another family picture of the four of them standing on the beach.

"I took that one," Mary boasted.

All four of them had big smiles on their faces.

"Kevin and I looked so happy. Mom and Dad looked happy too."

A warm feeling filled John's heart when he realized that was the first time he had used the words Mom and Dad in a loving way.

"Why wouldn't they be happy?" Mary smiled. "You two were the love of their lives."

She continued smiling as she reached her hand into the shoebox.

"Let's see what else we have in here."

She dug around the bottom and pulled out a few more. Her smile quickly disappeared and a surprised and sullen look fell over her face.

"What? What is it?" asked John.

Without taking her eyes off the picture, she softy answered, "I don't know how this got in here, but… it's a picture of me and my husband."

John's eyes nearly popped out of his head, and his mouth fell open when she showed him the picture. It was of Mary and Clarence with their arms around each other under a large weeping willow.

"That's your husband? But… but I know him," John exclaimed.

"Oh, I'm sure you can't remember that far back. You were only three the last time you saw him."

"No… like now… I know him now. I've been hanging out with him down at the cove the last couple weeks."

She snatched the picture away from John, and for the first time since they met, an angry look fell over her face.

"Why would you say such a thing? I've been nothing but nice to you! I know you think I'm just a crazy old lady, but you don't have to…"

"Mary, I'm not lying! I swear. I don't know what the hell is going on in this place, but I've been helping Clarence for the past two weeks."

Surprised, Mary hesitantly said, "I never told you his name."

"I know."

John couldn't sit still any longer. He stood up and ran his fingers through his short hair. Learning the truth about his parents was one thing, but finding out he had been talking to a ghost was quite another. With his hands on his head, he took a couple steps towards the cliff and began mumbling to himself.

"He can't be… I talked to him… I shook his hand…"

Mary interrupted his mumbling. "Wait… what have you been helping him with?"

John turned back to her and said, "I've been helping him fix up his boat."

"His boat?" she hesitantly asked.

"Yea, the Medillia's…"

Stunned, she finished his sentence. "Lament?"

John slowly nodded. Realizing he might actually be telling the truth, Mary leaned forward on the bench.

"You're serious, aren't you?" she asked as her eyes glazed over.

"I swear, Mary, I'm telling you the truth," he said and shook his head and looked around. "This place is getting stranger by the day."

"Does he… talk to you?"

Again, John nodded.

"About what?"

He shrugged. "Mostly about his many, many adventures out at sea."

"Yup, that's my Clarence," she sadly smiled. "Does he… talk about me?"

"Umm…" John hesitated a second, trying to recall everything he and Clarence had talked about. Mary, however, took his hesitation as her answer.

"It's okay," she said, waving him off. "Like I said before, I always knew he loved that ocean more than me."

This time, it was Mary who climbed off the bench and walked to the edge of the cliff. She stared long and hard out to the water then rubbed her arms trying to fight off the cold breeze. While John desperately searched for the right words to say, Mary looked down at the photo of her and her husband.

"He probably doesn't talk about me because he's still mad at what I said to him that day."

"No, of course he's not mad at that," John said, moving closer.

"Did he tell you that?" she asked, looking him dead in the eyes.

John started to speak but no words came out. Again, his hesitation caused Mary's head and body to hopelessly slump lower.

Gently, John placed his hand on her shoulder and took a chance by asking, "It's none of my business, but… have you forgiven him? You know, for not listening to your pleas and for leaving that day?"

Mary was quick to respond. "Of course I forgive him!" She paused then looked back out the sea. "I guess in my heart, I always knew this ocean was his passion… his true love." She let out a mournful sigh and softy repeated, "Of course I forgive him."

She continued staring out at the waves, and John could tell just how devastated and heartbroken she was.

After a long silence, she shook her head and said, "Fixing up his boat, huh? Even in death, he's in such a hurry to hit that stupid ocean again."

Perturbed, yet sad, she continued shaking her head at the sea.

John was never good at talking about his feelings, and he was even worse at coming up with the right words for other people's feelings. Somberly, Mary turned and started to make her way back to her cart. John knew he needed to say something to help this woman's broken heart.

"You're right, Mary," he called after her. "He is in a hurry to get his boat fixed. But it's not because he misses the ocean."

Without turning back around, Mary skeptically rolled her eyes.

"I'm serious," John continued. "He actually said something about... being in a hurry to..." John's mind scrambled for the perfect words. "...being in a hurry to get back home and watch the Red Sox game with his wife."

Mary's body froze, and she stopped dead in her tracks. As she slowly turned back around, John could tell his comment resonated deeply within her. Her voice quivered as she spoke.

"He said that? My Clarence said that?"

John nodded then said, "I'm not sure if that means anything or not to you, but..."

"It means everything. Everything."

As happy tears filled her eyes, she glanced back down at the photo of her and her husband and smiled. John also smiled, knowing that at least once in his life, he had come up with the right words.

At the same exact time, somewhere in the middle of the ocean, Clarence steered his boat through the churning waters. And as the cold salt air hit his weathered face, he said aloud, "Thank you, my friend. I couldn't have said it better myself."

Wistfully, he smiled and gazed back towards the coast of Maine.

"And you had it wrong, Mary. This ocean might have been my passion, but you... *you* were my true love."

27

Eventually, John and Mary said their goodbyes. She kept the photo of her and Clarence but gave John the shoebox with the rest of the pictures. The first thing he did when he returned to William's house, was rush down the path and into the cove. He needed to see this ghost one more time.

To his surprise, when he arrived at the cove, the boat was gone. There wasn't even a trace left behind that it had ever been there at all. Once again, this caused John to question his sanity.

When he arrived back at William's house, he was relieved to see Sara's car parked in her driveway. John had no idea what he'd say, but he knew he couldn't leave town without saying some sort of goodbye to her.

He gave the inside of the house a once-over, making sure everything was as he found it. This included emptying the rest of his Jameson down the drain and tossing the bottle in the garbage along with his flask.

After he locked the door behind him, he took a walk around the outside of the property. Part of him felt as though he really hadn't done a lot to the house while he was there, but the more he looked it over, it was apparent he was leaving it in a much better condition.

Before heading across the street, he tossed his bag in the front seat. Just as he closed the passenger door, Sara's front door opened. A second later, Sara and Suzy walked hand in hand across the lawn towards John.

"Are you leaving to go back home?" asked Suzy.

"Yup, I am."

Just then, a panicked look came over Suzy's face.

"Wait! Don't leave yet… I have something for you!"

Both Sara and John curiously watched as Suzy scampered back into her house.

John looked around the yard and asked, "Where's Ben?"

"Paul took him to the batting cages a couple towns over."

"Good for him… and for you. You deserve to be happy."

"So do you, John."

He politely shrugged off her comment.

"Maybe you should follow your own advice and allow yourself to be happy again too. I know there's someone out there who will fill your heart again. I just know it," she confidently smiled.

"Oh yea," he chuckled. "Ya think?"

"I don't *think*—I **know**. You just have to keep your eyes open for the signs, that's all."

"The signs, huh?" he laughed. "I don't know about that."

"Well I do. It's all in the stars. It might be difficult to see sometimes, but you just have to look hard enough, that's all." She sweetly smiled at him and followed it up with a wink.

John's heart nearly stopped and chills shot up through his entire body as Sara had once again repeated an exact quote from his wife. All he could do was stand there, curiously and deeply staring into her eyes. It was Sara who made the first move. With arms outstretched, she took a step forward to hug John goodbye. Their embrace was long and tight, and most of all, it was cathartic.

Before pulling away, Sara whispered in his ear, "Thank you, John. Thank you for letting me in. Like, really letting me in."

Tears formed in both of their eyes. John turned and started walking towards his truck.

"Wait! Wait! Don't leave yet!" yelled Suzy, rushing across the street. She stopped just in front of John.

"This is one of my favorite dollies. She's the one that was sick during our tea party, but she's much better now."

She handed John the raggedy old doll.

"I want you to have it," she quietly said.

John could no longer fight back his tears. It looked exactly like Hannah's favorite doll. Hesitantly, John took it from her and held it tightly in his hands. He then leaned down and gave Suzy a big hug and whispered, "Thank you. I'll take good care of her."

John smiled at Sara and Suzy then climbed into his truck. He backed out of the driveway and slowly drove off.

28

John was so wired, and there was so much running through his head, he found himself driving deep into the night before stopping at some cheap motel. The solace of driving by himself gave him a chance to think about everything that had just happened. He thought about each and every strange occurrence of the past two weeks, and he couldn't help but once again wonder if this was all just a dream?

The whole thing was crazy. The two weeks flew by, yet it seemed like forever ago he had made the drive from Chicago to Maine. That earlier drive was hazy at best. At that point, all he knew about Maine was Stephen King lived there, and that a lot of his weird and creepy stories took place there. Now, reflecting back, John wondered if maybe over the last two weeks he'd actually been trapped in a Stephen King novel. Either way, the whole thing was indeed crazy.

Eventually, John's thoughts turned to William. *Did William know about my past in Applewood… about my real parents? He must have. If not, then that would have been the biggest coincidence ever. He must have known! But how?*

John was eager to see William face to face and get some direct answers. He was also eager to show him pictures of the work he did on his house. John couldn't wait to see William's expression when he saw the brand-new gazebo in the backyard.

Talking to William would be easy, especially if he really *did* know about the history of John's parents in Applewood. But Kevin, Kevin would be a different story. There was no way Kevin would believe him. Luckily, John had the shoebox of pictures to help prove his case. But the whole *talking to a ghost thing* would be a much, much harder sell. Kevin would certainly think John had been drinking heavily again.

Unlike the rushed trip out to Maine weeks earlier, he decided to take his time driving home. He had no idea if he'd ever do this again, so he wanted to take full advantage of the road trip and its scenery.

* * *

It was mid-afternoon when John's trusty old pickup truck entered downtown Chicago. He parked along the side of the street and opened his door. As soon as he climbed out, he reached his hands to the sky, stretching out his tired body. He gave his back and neck a crack then headed up the sidewalk towards the Wild Irish Rose. He inhaled deeply, sucking in the familiar Chicago air. It wasn't as crisp and refreshing or as salt-filled as Applewood, but it was his home, and despite everything, he was actually glad to be back.

He knew not everyone would feel the same way about his return. He assumed the regulars were beyond sick and tired of his rude, drunken antics over the past year, and he was positive that Julie shared in their opinions. Julie, along with Kevin had taken the brunt of his behavior. Kevin was blood, so John knew the whole unconditional thing would cause Kevin to eventually forgive him for his words or actions. Julie was a different story. She had every right to hold a grudge. John knew he had been rude and mean to her on more than one occasion. He also knew, she absolutely didn't deserve it.

"Here goes nothing," he said aloud as he slowly opened the front door to his bar.

Luckily, it was early enough that most of the regulars hadn't shown up yet, so there weren't a lot of stares in his direction. There was no sign of his brother, but he noticed that Julie was behind the bar. He also noticed she was looking directly at him.

He quickly lowered his head as to avoid the inevitable *Julie glare*. To his surprise, however, he didn't get halfway across the room before she rushed out from behind the bar and greeted him with a big hug.

"Hey, you!" she said, wrapping her arms around him.

John lifted his arms but didn't fully embrace her.

"Hey," he replied, still a bit surprised at her embrace.

"So? How was Maine?"

"Umm, Maine was… good. Interesting, but good."

"More importantly, how are you?"

John paused a moment then said, "Better… I think."

Julie took a step back, giving him a look-over. She motioned to where his scraggly beard and long hair used to be and said, "You look better… and smell better too, if I may say?"

They both cracked a smile. John thought this would be a good time to throw an apology her way, but she interrupted his thought.

"I'm just kidding with ya, but you do look good… refreshed. We missed you."

John gave her a dubious smirk.

"I know, I know, it's hard to believe, but we actually did… especially your brother. He missed you, but even more than that, he's been worried sick about you."

Right on cue, Kevin walked out from the back room and stopped in his tracks when he saw his brother had returned. A relieved look washed over his face. Before John approached him, Julie whispered a warning.

"Just a heads up, he's a little pissed that you haven't returned any of his calls this week."

"I know," he sighed in preparation.

"Look who finally returned," she yelled over to Kevin as John walked towards him.

Kevin also gave him a look-over and said, "Kind of looks like my brother, but I'm not sure."

"Fuck you," John smiled.

"Yup, that's my brother," Kevin laughed, giving him a hug.

John reciprocated a little more than with Julie but not much.

"Ever heard of returning a phone call?"

"I know, I know. I'm sorry. It's just been a crazy week."

"Yea, yea, yea."

Kevin continued to look John over then his tone switched a bit more serious.

"How are you doing?"

"Good."

"Seriously, John. How are you *really* doing?"

"I'm being serious. I'm doing good… maybe a little better than good actually."

Kevin shot him a curious look and said, "What's that supposed to mean?"

John's smile grew. There were so many things he couldn't wait to tell his brother. He peered over Kevin's shoulder and noticed four or five customers entering the bar.

"I tell ya what, how about we wait until the bar is closed, and I'll fill you in on everything? I promise."

"Not even a hint?"

John shook his head. "Not even a hint."

"Fine," Kevin replied, letting out a resigned sigh. "So, did you accomplish everything you needed to at William's?"

"I think so," he nodded. "I believe William will be very happy with the place. Speaking of which…" John said, gazing around the bar, "where is the old fella?"

"Actually, I haven't seen him in a few days, but I do know he's been very curious as to how you were doing. I could have filled him in, but, well, you know… someone never returned my calls."

John rolled his eyes and said, "And on that note, I think I'm gonna head over to William's."

"Tell him I said hi."

John nodded, but before he walked off, he paused then initiated another hug with his brother. This, along with John's comments, caught Kevin completely off guard.

"Thanks," he whispered. "For always being there for me… and always watching out for me. I really do appreciate it."

When John released his embrace, Kevin gave him a puzzled look and asked, "Are you sure you're okay?"

"Yea, I am. Oh, and by the way, I was thinking maybe sometime in the near future, I could start turning next door into my workshop… if that's alright with you?"

"Sure," smiled Kevin. "I think that's a great idea… just like we always planned."

John nodded and headed towards the door. On his way by, he stopped at one of the tables Julie was wiping down.

"Here, I got this for you."

He reached into his jacket and pulled out a postcard. Julie's eyes beamed and she smiled widely. The picture on the card was the lighthouse at night with stardust falling around it. The caption read: Applewood, Maine – Home to Medillia's Lament.

"Awww, thanks so much, John," she said, giving him another hug. This time he reciprocated and fully embraced her.

"No, thank you, Julie… for putting up with my shit the last few months. And most of all, for being there for my brother. He's lucky to have you. We both are." Over her shoulder, John watched as Kevin waited on a customer. "You guys make a good couple."

Julie stepped back and gave John a look of pretend confusion.

"Oh, come on. I might have been a drunk a-hole the past few months, but I wasn't blind."

Julie grinned and blushed, and both her and John glanced over to Kevin.

"Well, I'm off to see William. I'll be back in a bit."

"Say hi for me," Julie called out, still beaming and blushing.

When John left the Wild Irish Rose, the sun was nearly set, and the wind had picked up. He zipped up his jacket and began his short walk to William's house. He wanted to show William the pictures of everything he had done to the house, but he hadn't yet developed any of the disposable cameras he had purchased on his trip. He could have waited to visit William another day, but the questions he had for the old man far outweighed the urgency of the pictures.

John paused before walking up the steps to William's brownstone. Curiously, he looked up at the front door. He had only been there twice, and although he was drunk both times, he could have sworn the door was brown, not red. There was something else different about the place. It took him a second, but he finally realized it was the flowerpots on either side of the small porch. They were filled with mums and looked very well-taken care of.

John gazed around and counted houses. He was positive William's place was four houses after the stop sign. Feeling a bit unsure, he headed up the stairs. Maybe William was feeling creative and painted the door and added the flower pots. John rapped three times on the door and waited.

After a few moments, the door slowly opened, but instead of William's kind face, John was greeted by an older woman. She looked to be in her sixties, and she had light brown hair with hints of gray.

"Can I help you?" she asked with a polite smile.

John hesitated, thinking maybe he did have the wrong house after all.

"Umm… is William here?"

Her smile faded, and her brown eyes saddened.

"I'm sorry, dear, William passed away a few days ago."

John's heart sank like a stone. He knew William was sick, but there was no way he could be gone… not yet… not before John could show him the new and improved Applewood house… not before John could tell him everything that had happened… and certainly not before he could ask William his many questions.

The woman could see how shocked and devasted John was. Softly, she asked, "Were you a friend of his?"

"Umm, kind of, I guess," he shrugged. "I've been in Maine fixing up his house for him."

Her face lit up, and the smile returned to her lips.

"Ahh, so you're John… from the Wild Irish Rose? I've heard a lot about you. That was a very nice thing you did for my husband."

A stunned and puzzled look fell on John's face, wondering if he just heard what he thought he heard.

"He always talked about going back to Applewood to fix…"

"I'm sorry," he interrupted, "but did you say husband? As in William?"

She let out a quiet laugh and shook her head.

"He never mentioned me, huh? I mean, I know he loves to talk about his writing and whatnot… and I know it's not the cool thing to do to talk about your wife when you're out at the bar with the guys, but geesh, you'd think he woulda at least mentioned his wife of forty years." She smirked and continued to playfully shake her head.

John remained frozen, still stunned and speechless. She noticed his look and asked, "Are you okay, dear? Would you like a glass of water or something?"

His mouth was too dry to even answer. Slowly, he just nodded his head yes.

"Come on in and let me get you something."

He took two steps into the foyer and once again stopped. He could have sworn the foyer wall used to be white, but now, it was a warm coffee-type color. And there used to be a free-standing iron coat rack, not this horizontal pine one attached to the wall.

John's confusion continued as he walked into the house and looked around. It was completely different from what he remembered before. The white and beige walls were now painted with muted colors, and what was once bare, was now filled with paintings and pictures. John paused at an antique end table. It was full of framed photos, mostly of William and this woman.

Before John took another step, one of the pictures caught his eye. He reached over, carefully picking it up. His mouth fell open and his eyes widened. It was a photo of Clarence and Mary.

"Those are William's parents," the woman smiled.

Slowly, John looked up at the woman and said, "These are his parents? But... I thought William said they *both* passed away?"

She nodded. "They did... a while ago. His father died in a boating accident during a horrible storm, and sadly, his mom passed away not long after. The doctors said it was natural causes, but if you ask me, it was from a broken heart. Clarence was her whole life. They'd been together since they were kids."

By now, John's hand was trembling as he held the picture. She took one look at his face and said, "You look like you've seen a ghost. Let me go get you that water. Make yourself comfortable."

John placed the picture back on the table and shook his head in disbelief. She was right, he had seen a ghost—two actually. *Impossible,* he thought. *This whole fucking thing is impossible.*

John's head began to spin wildly. It was as if he'd been binging on whiskey all day. Still reeling from the thought of talking to two ghosts, John made his way into the living room. His head continued spinning, and his confusion didn't improve any as he saw that the living room was also different than before. The room was filled with furniture, which was most definitely not there the last time. What was once cold and sparsely decorated, was now more welcoming... more lived in... more homey.

John gazed around the room, but quickly became fixated on the fireplace mantle. More specifically, what was on the mantle. He moved closer, and for the nth time, his eyes widened in shock. He carefully grabbed it off the mantle and saw that it was the framed poem Bill had given to Rachel. As he stood there staring in disbelief, William's voice entered John's head.

"You see, during Medillia's Lament, time becomes irrelevant. The past, present, and future all get blurred together somehow. And within those nineteen sunrises, anything is possible. Anything."

The woman re-entered the room and saw John holding the framed poem.

"That was his very first gift to me. First of many," she smiled. "He gave it to me at our homecoming dance. I guess you could say that was the beginning of it all."

A chill ran up John's spine, and he smiled as he thought to himself, *Bill... William.*

The woman handed him the water, and watched him quickly pound it down.

"Would you like some more?"

He shook his head no and returned the poem to its rightful place.

"Actually, I think I should probably get going," he said, handing her the empty glass.

When they were back in the foyer, she reached out her hand and sweetly said, "Well, it was very nice to finally meet you, John."

He shook her soft hand and said, "It was very nice to meet you too... Rachel."

"Sooo, William *did* mention me?" she smirked.

"Of course he did. You were the love of his life."

Rachel gave him a sad, yet appreciative smile. He reached for the door knob, but stopped short.

"Oh, wait," she called after him. "I have something for you. Wait here, I'll be right back."

When Rachel returned, she was carrying a 9x14 manila packaging envelope. She handed it to John and said, "William wanted you to have this."

A bit curious, he politely took it from her.

"Thank you."

"No, thank you, John," she said, staring into his eyes.

He opened the door and stepped onto the porch. Before taking another step, he turned back around.

"Oh, I almost forgot," he said, reaching into his pocket. "Here's the key to his house in Maine."

Rachel looked at the key and then looked up at John and said, "Why don't you hold onto it. I think William would like that... I think we all would."

John offered an appreciative smile then placed the key back in his pocket and headed off. Although he was very curious about the contents of the package, he didn't open it until he returned to the Wild Irish Rose. He spent the entire walk trying to decipher everything that had just been revealed to him. Up until that point, John had chalked up the events of the past two weeks simply as unlikely and utterly strange coincidences. But now, for the first time in his life, he started to believe that maybe things really do happen for a reason, and maybe, just maybe, the magic of Medillia's Lament really did exist.

But even more than magic, ghosts, and strange occurrences, John's mind focused on William. He'd only known him for a few short weeks, but his heart mourned as if he'd known him forever.

When he arrived back at the bar, he broke the sad news to everyone. Julie took it the hardest. Like most people who had ever crossed his path, Julie felt a close connection to William.

At one point, she offered a bar-wide toast for William. In honor of his old friend, John's drink of choice that night, and every night forward, would be a Coke with extra ice. He perched himself on a stool at the end of the bar, took another sip of his Coke then slowly looked around. He stared at every inch, recalling all the blood, sweat, and tears that him and Kevin had put into the place over a year ago. He was never able to fully experience or appreciate just how beautifully it turned out, for John had mentally checked out long before the doors officially opened. He ran his hand across the high-gloss sheen of the bar top and immediately remembered just how much he enjoyed designing and building it.

"What's in the package?" Julie asked.

John removed his hand from the bar top and looked to his left. He had almost forgotten about William's package.

"William left it for me," he softly replied.

Julie was extremely curious as to its contents, but she knew this was between William and John. She sweetly smiled at John and placed her hand on his arm.

"William was one of the good ones. Definitely one of the good ones."

He nodded in agreement and watched as Julie slowly made her way over to tend to another customer. He stared long and hard at the package before finally picking it up and opening it. The first thing that fell out was a note. Carefully, John peered closer and began to read it.

John,

While my only hope was that there would be enough magic left in Applewood for you, I never in my wildest dreams thought that same magic could affect so many lives. Words cannot express how grateful I am for what you did for me, and more importantly, what you did for my parents. I truly hope that one day you can find the peace and happiness that you so desperately deserve. Remember, my friend, everything happens for a reason, even if we can't see it at the time!

Your friend,
William

P.S. Do you remember those scenarios I used to create in my head of what it would have been like if Rachel and I would have been together? Well, as it turns out, the real thing was so much better...better than I could have ever dreamed of. And because of you, John, I found the perfect ending to my novel; the novel that took me a lifetime to write, but more importantly, the novel that I was born to write!

A sad smile fell on John's face and his eyes glazed over. He reread the note three more times before folding it back up and placing it next to him. He paused a moment then reached his hand into the envelope and pulled out a thick stack of neatly bound papers. His sad smile curled into a more happier one when he realized it was the finished manuscript of William's novel. John's smile grew even more when he read the title: *"Medillia's Lament."*

Soon after the bar closed and Julie headed home, John sat down with Kevin and did his best to explain everything. As expected, Kevin kept smelling John's breath to see if he'd been drinking. It wasn't until he pulled out the shoebox of pictures and the newspaper article that Kevin finally started to believe John's fantastical story.

The brothers stayed at the bar well into the early morning just talking... at times laughing... and at times even crying. All in all, it would go down as one of their favorite memories together.

29

It took John a few days, but since his return to Chicago, he slowly started putting the pieces of his life back together. He knew there were still many things he needed to face head on and decided it would be best to return to his therapist. Before he restarted his sessions, however, there were some things he needed to do.

After sleeping at Kevin's the first two nights back, John returned to his house. It took all the strength he had, but he finally found the courage to open the doors and enter both bedrooms. A thick layer of dust had settled over each and every inch of their rooms. It was almost as if the layer of dust had preserved things just as they once were. Maybe it was just in his mind, but John swore he could still smell Kristen's perfume hanging in the air. Hannah's room was no different, as the strong smell of strawberry air freshener immediately hit his nose.

He remained in their rooms for most of the afternoon, allowing the memories to wash over him. The more memories he thought of, the more he felt like the pieces of sadness and regret were lifting from his heart.

From the bedroom, he moved into the kitchen. On the counter sat the stack of photos that John had angrily ripped off the fridge the night he attempted to end it all. He grabbed the stack and made his way into the living room. Before he sat down on the couch, he walked over to the corner of the room and stared down at Kristen's retro record player.

Neatly stacked underneath was her collection of vinyl records. John flipped through them until he found what he was looking for. Slowly, he pulled out *Disintegration* by The Cure. He placed the record on the turntable and carefully lowered the needle onto track two – "Pictures of You" – Kristen's all-time favorite song off her all-time favorite record.

He cranked up the volume and returned to his seat on the couch, where he did his best to smooth out some of the more crumpled and crinkled pictures he had destroyed earlier. As the song echoed through the house, John looked through each and every one of Kristen's photos.

"One day you'll thank me," she used to say regarding her picture-taking.

She was right. She was absolutely right, he thought as he continued flipping through the many photos.

With each and every picture, his smile grew more and more. He lost track of how many times he used to make fun of Kristen for listening to her boring alternative bands, in particular, The Cure. But as he sat there in an empty house, he allowed the sad, haunting lyrics to seep into his head, and he allowed happy, cathartic tears to fall from his eyes.

Reopening the doors and the memories in his house weren't the only things he knew he needed to do. It was long overdue, but he knew he needed to find the courage to finally go visit his girls.

***

When John's truck came to a rumbling stop on the side of the street, he threw it in park and just sat there. He took several deep breaths before finally exiting his truck. With him, he carried two bouquets of flowers. The white lilies were Hannah's favorite, and the yellow tulips were Kristen's. Slowly, he made his way towards the entrance. It was a raw fall day and dark gray clouds loomed over the cemetery. It felt like a cold Chicago rain was inevitable.

Just like before, he found himself standing frozen in front of the large iron gates of St. Boniface Cemetery. If he couldn't enter the cemetery when he was drinking, he had no clue how he'd do it stone-cold sober. The flowers trembled in his nervous, sweaty hands, but John dug deep and refused to turn and walk away. He wouldn't chicken out—not this time. Again, he took a few deep breaths then placed one foot in front of the other and entered the cemetery.

Multiple times after the funeral, Kevin had offered to go to the cemetery with John and show him where the girls' plots were. John refused each and every time, so Kevin finally gave him a detailed map of their exact location, in case John ever wanted to go on his own. Eventually, John threw it away, but he had studied the map so well, it was emblazoned in his head.

He wound his way through the cemetery paths, until he finally arrived at the proper location. Immediately, his eyes focused on each of the headstones. Just seeing their engraved names staring back at him, caused an aching in his heart he had never felt before. It was almost as if the names made it more real. On the ground beneath their graves, he noticed there were already lilies and tulips strewn about. They could have been left by Kevin, but more than likely, they were from Kristen's parents. He propped his own flower bouquets against each of their stones.

Once again, he turned his attention to the engravement. Hesitantly, he kneeled down, and with his hand still trembling, he reached out to touch Kristen's cold stone. As his finger traced the engraved letters of her name, tears began to roll down his cheeks. By the time he did the same to Hannah's name, his tears had become uncontrollable. He found himself apologizing for everything he'd ever done wrong— especially their final day.

"I should have been there on time… I should have been there on time. I'm sorry… I'm so, so sorry." Tears poured down his face, splashing onto the flowers beneath their stones.

For what seemed like forever, John sat there crying and apologizing to his girls. When he was finally all cried out, he wiped his face then neatly organized the flowers around their graves. Before he stood back up, he reached down to his left hand and hesitantly twisted off his ring. He gave it a kiss then carefully placed it on top of Kristen's headstone.

John then leaned his head against the stone and closed his eyes. Within seconds, he found himself standing in a fog-filled playground. It was the exact same one from his earlier nightmares. Up ahead, he could hear the familiar squeaking of a swing set. Against his will, his legs moved him forward, and like always, he found himself standing directly behind the swing set.

John did his best to fight the urge, but just like always, he found himself pushing his girls on the swings. They giggled louder and louder as they swung higher and higher. John knew exactly how this would end, but no matter how hard he fought it, he continued pushing them.

The fog thickened, and just like the previous nightmares, the girls briefly disappeared at their peak only to return back to John. On the third push, John knew the inevitable was about to happen, yet he gave them one last push and watched them disappear into the fog. John held his breath, as the moment seemed to last forever. Predictably, yet sadly, when the swings returned to him, they were empty. He knew it was pointless, but like always, he scanned the playground for any sign at all of his girls.

Strangely, unlike before, instead of the fog growing thicker, it slowly began to disperse. And when it was all but cleared completely, John saw them. Standing off in the distance were Kristen and Hannah.

Hannah gave her daddy the sweetest, biggest and brightest smile. John returned her smile and then looked over at his wife. They both stood there in silence as they shared a beautifully sad yet cathartic look. Both girls gave John a wave goodbye then turned to go. As they began walking away, Hannah spun back around and blew a big kiss his way. He reached out and caught it in his hand, and as he pressed it tightly against his heart, the girls slowly faded away.

When John finally opened his eyes and pulled away from Kristen's headstone, the rain clouds had passed by, and all he could see in the distance were blue skies. He gave one last, longing look at their headstones then slowly walked away. After only a few steps past their graves, he stopped and glanced back over his shoulder. That's when he saw it. There, on the backside of each of their headstones were more flowers. Upon closer inspection, they were the exact same types that Mary carried in her cart back in Maine. A warm feeling filled his heart as he glanced up to the sky.

30

"It's nice to see you again," the therapist said, crossing her legs.

John twisted and squirmed, trying to adjust himself. Even sober, the futon was nearly impossible to get comfortable in.

"You didn't think you'd ever see me again, huh?" he asked.

"I wouldn't say that at all. I never lost faith in you."

John had no idea where to start or what to say, but he knew he needed to be there.

"So how have you been?" she asked.

"Good… better… I think. I kinda took a little vacation."

"A vacation, huh? Good for you."

"It was sorta like a working vacation. But it kind of gave me a chance to work on my…" John smiled then finished, "My elastics."

She returned his smile then followed with, "Would you like to talk about this vacation of yours?"

John leaned back and deliberated. He knew this topic would come up, but he decided against telling her the entire fantastical story of Applewood. She might have been a wacky, off-the-wall hippy-chick shrink, but there was no way she would believe what he had to say. Sometimes, it was still hard to believe it himself.

"Where did you go?" she asked.

"I actually went out to Maine… to help a friend fix up his house."

Her face beamed. "Aww, that's where I'm from."

John's face went blank. "You're kidding, right?"

"Well, I actually have never been there," she smiled. "But that's where my ancestors are from."

"Really?" John leaned forward, attempting to process her comments. "That's kind of a weird coincidence. Small world, I guess."

She gazed over her shoulder at the two dreamcatchers hanging in her window.

"My family line can be traced back to a Native American tribe in Maine." She then ran her fingers over her seashell necklace. "These shells are from Maine… given to me by my great, great grandmother. I'm actually related to a famous chief there."

John's face turned white, and his mind went directly to the statue of the chief in the park.

She took a long sip from her mystery drink then turned to him and said, "Oh, and by the way, John, I don't really believe in coincidences. Everything happens for a reason."

She gave him a wink then made her way over and lit a stick of incense. As John sat there stunned and speechless, a smile slowly crept onto his face. He still had no intentions on filling her in on the events of Applewood, but he knew he didn't need to.

When the session was over, and as John started to walk out the door, he peered over to the fish tank. To his bemusement, she had finally added fish to it.

"Nice fish, Doc," he smirked as he exited her office.

Once on the sidewalk, he laughed and mumbled, "Now she just has to work on wearing a bra."

31

One year later

Day by day, week by week, and month by month, John slowly started filling his heart up with acceptance, and more importantly, with hope. Although his sessions became less and less, he still made it a point to continue seeing his wacky therapist.

For Christmas, he surprised her by blowing up and nicely framing the photo he took of the statue of the Native American chief in Algonquin Park. He also bought her a glow-in-the-dark Grateful Dead poster with a blacklight and everything. Not surprisingly, she loved both presents equally.

What also helped John move on was the fact that he finally remodeled and opened his woodworking business. It quickly became his home away from home. Business was slow at first, but over time, his talent, reputation, and client list began growing at a more rapid pace. He supplemented his income by still working part time next door at the Wild Irish Rose. Mostly, he did it to give Kevin and Julie some well-deserved time off.

* * *

It was early evening and John had just called it quits from sanding a new custom-made kitchen table for a customer. With his hair covered in wood dust, he went next door and grabbed himself a Coke then sat up at the bar. He watched Julie wiping down the counter, and also watched as she paused to admire the diamond ring on her finger.

"Still not too late to back out, ya know? I'm telling ya, I think you can do much better."

Julie giggled.

"Don't laugh at him. It only encourages him," Kevin said, shooting a playful glare his way.

Like most nights, John sat up at the bar and bantered with the regulars. Unlike the previous year, he did this completely sober. Not only had he become friends with most of the regulars, but a few of them even hired him to do some custom work: A beautiful entertainment center for one, an antique looking desk and chair for another. One of them even hired John to completely transform their basement into the ultimate man cave with a smaller version of the bar top from the Wild Irish Rose. Ironically, this customer still spent the majority of his time at the actual Wild Irish Rose.

As the night passed, and as the bantering continued, John couldn't help but notice a cute woman sitting up at the opposite end of the bar. Even from across the way, he took notice of her piercing blue eyes. They were in direct contrast, yet extremely complimentary to her scarlet-dyed hair.

Throughout the next hour, he found himself continuously staring over at her. He also couldn't help but notice the stool next to her remained empty. She had placed her coat on it earlier as if to save it for someone.

Was she meeting one of her friends here? Her boyfriend? Her husband? Why hadn't he seen her around here before? These thoughts and more kept running through John's mind. Finally, he motioned Julie over.

"Hey, what's the deal with that chick over there?"

Julie glanced over at the woman then said, "I think she was supposed to meet her date here, but it looks like he stood her up. Poor girl."

"Wow, who the hell would stand that up," John said to himself as much as to Julie. "Was it like a blind date? Or was it one of those dating sites? Or did one of her friends set…"

John paused when he noticed Julie staring at him, smiling.

"What?"

"Maybe you should go sit with her and ask her?" Julie said, continuing to smile. Before he could respond, Julie winked and walked off.

He pondered her suggestion, but quickly pushed it out of his mind. It had been a long, long time since he had found himself staring at a woman like this. There was just something about her look that caught his eye. She wasn't overly made up or dressed too fancy, but there was something about her look that kept him mesmerized.

Even if he wanted to sit next to her, what would he say? He assumed his conversational and flirting skills had long since gone by the wayside. And the last thing this woman needed after getting stood up was for John to awkwardly and pathetically attempt to flirt with her. So it was settled, he would simply continue to gawk and admire her from a safe distance.

Over that hour, John witnessed not one, but three guys try to talk, flirt, and/or buy her a drink. Albeit politely, each time she spurned their feeble attempts. John momentarily took his eye off the woman when he saw Julie approaching him.

"Hey, would you mind watching the bar for a bit? I need to go out back and get some inventory done for tomorrow's order."

"Where's Kev?"

"I think he's laying down in the office. He's not feeling very well."

"Really? Um, yea, sure. I'll watch the bar."

"Thanks," Julie said. Before she headed off, she turned back to John and mentioned, "Oh, by the way, I think the woman at the end needs a refill."

As he climbed off his stool and made his way behind the bar, he had a sneaking suspicion that he was being set up. When he walked by the woman, he noticed that her drink was empty and that she indeed needed a refill.

"Can I get you another one?" he asked.

The woman hesitated a moment, looked at the empty stool next to her, then slid her glass John's way and replied, "Sure, why not."

"What did you have?"

"Cranberry and vodka."

While John filled a new glass with ice, the woman leaned forward and asked, "When does it go from him just being late to him probably not showing up at all?"

John looked into her swimming-pool blue eyes and asked, "How long has it been?"

She glanced down at her watch and answered, "An hour and sixteen minutes."

His look and hesitation were all she needed to answer her own question.

"Yea, that's what I thought," she sighed.

"I'm sorry," he said. "But if it's any consolation, your drinks are on the house tonight."

He immediately regretted his comment. He was sure she didn't think a free drink or two would be an appropriate consolation for getting stood up. Even worse, what if she thought he was just trying to hit on her? Before his mind could over-analyze his comment, she gave him a sweet smile.

"I appreciate the gesture, but it's really not necessary. Besides, the way my last two dates ended, getting stood up is a major improvement."

"That bad, huh? The same guy?"

"Oh no. Different guys. I'm in the process of trying one of those online dating services. Or I should say, I'm in the process of *ending* my online dating service. I've been out of the dating scene for a while, and my friends said this was the new way to go."

"Sounds like your friends should be the ones buying your drinks then," John smiled.

She raised her drink and said, "That they should!"

He took a chance and pried a little deeper. "So, how long have you been out of the game?"

"A few years. I was in a long-term relationship and let's just say, it didn't end too well. I kinda shut down for a while, but recently decided I needed to pick up the pieces and move on with my life."

A couple of regulars were in need of a drink refill, but John's focus was solely on the cute, blue-eyed woman.

"Although, I'm starting to think if this online dating thing is the only way to meet people at my age then I'm probably screwed."

John laughed and said, "At your age? You make it sound like you're ancient."

She slowly nodded and said, "Thirty... well, thirty-ish."

Again, he laughed. "For what's it's worth, you don't look a day over twenty-nine... well, twenty-nine-ish. And whoever stood you up tonight, it's definitely his loss."

Not believing he just uttered those words, John turned away to avoid any sort of eye contact. When he did finally turn back around, the woman was smiling and blushing as she took a sip of her drink.

Before he could embarrass himself any further, he noticed Julie and Kevin laughing as they headed towards the bar. Kevin didn't look sick, not at all. And come to think of it, why would Julie need to do inventory… on a Saturday? The delivery didn't come until Wednesday. It was at that point, John knew Julie had set him up. She just wanted him to interact with this woman in hopes that something might come of it. *Ridiculous*, John thought. *Completely and totally ridiculous.*

"Thanks for covering," smiled Julie. "We got it from here."

"Yea, why don't you sit back down and relax," echoed Kevin.

Just then, a new customer sat down on the stool where John had been sitting.

"Whoops, looks like you lost your seat at the bar, bro."

The only seat available was next to the woman. She noticed this and quickly removed her coat from the stool and motioned for John to have a seat. He threw a smirk at his brother and Julie then slid onto the stool next to the woman.

John assumed they only had enough in common to last for a short conversation at best, and he predicted that within ten minutes an awkward silence would set in. John assumed wrong. Not only did they have plenty in common, but they ended up talking and laughing the rest of the night. Their biggest talking point was baseball – more specifically, the Cubs. Though John would never admit it, at one point, he thought she might even be more fanatical about them than he was. She recited statistics, random facts, and could even name their batting order from fifteen years ago. Needless to say, John was impressed with her… and smitten, completely smitten.

They avoided cliché topics like past relationships, and they stuck to more upbeat subjects. John explained that he along with Kevin were the owners of the bar.

"The Wild Irish Rose, huh? Is there a story behind that name?" she asked.

"You might say that," he laughed.

John was vague at best about the name, but was more detailed and passionate about his woodworking business. She was extremely jealous of his creativeness, and quite frankly, the career freedom he had. She worked a corporate job in downtown Chicago, which she explained, translated to long, tedious hours with no creativity to speak of.

"Why don't you do something different?" he asked.

She twirled her straw in her drink, shrugged then said, "I've thought about it."

"What would you wanna do?"

"I originally went to school to be a teacher, but while I was actually looking for a position to open up, my dad hooked me up with a job at his company. I guess I just got used to the security and the really good paychecks, and eventually I stopped applying for teaching jobs. Now, I kinda wanna teach again, but... I'd have to go back and take classes and get recertified."

"And?"

"I kinda feel like I'm too old for that now."

John immediately shot her a look. "Are you kidding me? You're nowhere close to being too old for school. I think you should do it. At least give it a try. Worst case scenario, you get your job back at the company, right?"

She smiled and hesitantly nodded. "Maybe I will. I tell you what I definitely want to start doing soon... roadtrips."

"Oh yea?"

"Yup. There are so many places I want to see, but whenever I get my vacation time, for whatever reason, I always end up just sticking around here."

"Like, where would you wanna go?" he asked.

"Anywhere and everywhere. The Pacific coast would be cool: Seattle, San Francisco, San Diego. New York City is definitely on my list as well. And I'd love to go up to the New England area, especially in the fall. I heard it's gorgeous that time of year."

As the woman continued listing her travel spots, John's mind couldn't help but picture himself accompanying her on these trips. He chuckled to himself at how ridiculous that seemed, especially considering they'd known each other less than a few hours.

She paused a second then let out a little laugh and said, "Do you know what else is on my list? I mean, it's not really a vacation spot, but more like point of interest."

"Where?" he asked, intrigued.

"To the actual *Field of Dreams* in Iowa. You know, where they filmed the movie?"

John said nothing. He simply sat there wide-eyed and grinning ear to ear. If she hadn't won him over yet, she certainly just did. John also revealed his love of the movie and expressed his life-long desire to also visit the field.

"It's only like four hours from here too," John said. "For years now, my brother and I have kept saying, 'One of these days… one of these days.' Yet we still haven't made the trek."

"We should totally go," she said, finishing the rest of her drink.

John wasn't sure if that was an actual invite or just a blanket statement, but either way, it didn't stop him from getting his hopes up. And it certainly didn't stop him from smiling at this intriguing blue-eyed, scarlet-haired girl.

Their first real lull in the conversation came when she noticed that they were the only customers left in the bar.

"Wow," she said, glancing at her watch. "I can't believe how late it is."

John smirked then said, "I guess it's safe to say your date's not showing up."

She smiled back at him then shrugged. "Eh, everything happens for a reason, right?"

John had no words. All he could do was slowly nod in agreement.

"Well, I should get going so you guys can close up."

Before she could grab her credit card out of her wallet, Julie called over, "You're all set, hun. Your drinks are on the house."

"I wouldn't argue with her," John pointed out. "She rarely loses an argument."

"True story!" echoed Kevin.

"Thanks guys, I really appreciate that," she said, putting on her coat. She then reached her hand out to John. "Thanks for the conversation tonight. It was nice. Hopefully I didn't babble your ear off too much?"

"Nah," he said, shaking her soft hand.

She then waved to Kevin and Julie and headed out the door. Just then, John felt an ice cube ping against his head. He turned to see both Kevin and Julie staring at him.

"Go get her," Julie said, pointing to the front door.

John looked to his brother, who was already nodding in agreement. He returned their smiles, and without over-thinking it, he rushed outside after the woman.

She was only a few steps up the sidewalk when he caught up to her.

"Hey… ummm, I was thinking… if you're not sick of babbling yet, maybe we could go grab a bite to eat? There's an all-night diner a couple blocks away."

She paused long enough to get him nervous then sweetly smiled and said, "I would love that."

With both of their faces beaming, they continued up the sidewalk. After a handful of paces, he abruptly stopped then turned to her and let out a laugh.

"What?" she asked.

"Do you realize we've talked all night but haven't actually introduced ourselves?"

She pondered a second then nodded in agreement.

"Wow, you're right," she said, reaching out her hand. "I'm Jain… spelled J-A-I-N. My parents thought they'd give the name a fancy twist."

"Nice to meet you Jain, I'm John… just boring ole J-O-H-N."

"Haha," she laughed. "Trust me, the spelling is the only thing fancy about me. I epitomize the old saying – *plain Jane*."

A chill ran up his spine as he was reminded of the many times Kristen referred to herself as just that. As Jain continued up the sidewalk, John paused and gazed up into the night. The bright city lights prevented him from seeing the many stars dotting the sky, but this only reminded him of another one of Kristen's favorite sayings:

"It's all in the stars… It might be difficult to see sometimes, but you just have to look hard enough, that's all."

About The Author

Jody grew up in the Kittery/York area of southern Maine. He originally started out as a screenwriter. As of now, he has written nine feature-length screenplays ranging from dramas, to dramedies, to comedies. Not only did Jody grow up in Maine, but he makes it a point to utilize and represent his state as much as possible. From Maine's scenic rocky coast, to its remotely pristine backwoods, to its eclectic characters; all serve as backdrops and pay homage to his beloved state. His ultimate goal is not to just sell his scripts, but to have them filmed right here in the Great State of Maine.

Unfortunately, searching for the proper financing has been a long, tiring, and at times, disheartening process. Feeling helpless in the whole "funding" process, Jody decided to reverse the typical Hollywood blueprint. That blueprint being: It's almost ALWAYS a novel that gets turned into a screenplay and not a screenplay which gets turned into a novel. Jody's thought process was simple: It's much easier to self-publish a book rather than self-finance a movie, and who knows, maybe, just maybe, this will be a screenplay that gets turned into a book only to eventually get turned back into a movie! But even if this wild idea never comes to fruition, at least by turning it into a novel, the *stories* themselves will be able to be enjoyed by the public. Whether it's two or two million people who buy his books, Jody is just happy that they are no longer collecting dust in a desk drawer.

Other books by Jody Clark

"Livin' on a Prayer – The Untold Tommy & Gina Story"

"The Wild Irish Rose"

The Soundtrack to My Life Trilogy
Book one – *"The Empty Beach"*
Book two – *"Between Hello and Goodbye"*
Book three – *"The Ring on the Sill"*

Available at

www.vacationlandbooks.com

I do most of my posting & promoting via my Facebook profile

Feel free to *friend* me!

Jody Clark(vacationlandbooks)